Earthquake, Wind, and Fire

Rosemary Rowntree

Earthquake, Wind, and Fire

ISBN 978-1976593987

Cover photograph: WDG Photo/Shutterstock.com

Also by the same author

When Good Men Die

'Gripping stuff – a classic murder mystery set in a well evoked landscape. A complex and brilliant plot.' Dexter Petley

Chapter 1

Dawn had barely broken as he eased his old Series III Land Rover out of the yard. In the dense fog he had only the fence along the left-hand side of the track to guide him. He sighed as he turned onto the main road. Public highway it might be, but it was appalling. It had a surface like a roller coaster, crumbling edges, deep cracks and potholes. A typical fen road in fact.

After he made the turn he saw in his rear-view mirror the lights of an approaching vehicle. They remained on high beam, dancing and flickering and closing quickly. What kind of vehicle it was he couldn't tell.

It was now so close that the lights were blinding him. Involuntarily he increased his speed. The fog, still freezing in the early morning air, was almost impenetrable and he could see only a few yards in front of him. The vehicle behind fell back and he allowed his own speed to drop slightly, hoping the other driver had realised how dangerous the conditions were. Soon he would come to the first of the right-angled bends on his journey, but he no longer knew how far ahead it was. Suddenly the vehicle behind surged forward once more. He had no idea why. Did he want to over-take? If so, he risked crashing into an oncoming vehicle. If he didn't want to pass, what the hell was he playing at?

He could just make out the verge on the nearside. There were no fences or walls to provide visual boundaries, nor telegraph poles by which he could measure his distance. The heating system in his Land Rover was primitive to say the least; the windscreen was much scratched from years of misuse and still misting up on the inside. Visibility was dreadful. And there was black ice. The muscles in his neck and shoulders were rigid with tension and pain, his hands frozen inside his leather gloves as he gripped the steering wheel.

With every dip and pothole in the road he struggled to keep the Land Rover straight.

Suddenly the bend was upon him and he threw the wheel round hard to the left, taking the corner wide and skidding. He broke out in a cold sweat. Beyond the verge on either side, he knew, lay deep drainage ditches. He had just regained his side of the road when an oncoming tractor appeared and was quickly lost in the mist behind him. He hadn't even heard it: the fog seemed to deaden all sound, even muffling the noise of the Land Rover. For a moment, he forgot the vehicle that had been following him.

He had about a mile before the road took another sharp bend, this time to the right, following the bank of the lode that joined the Gt Ouse some miles ahead. The vehicle following him turned the first corner and speeded up. Now it was alternately accelerating and falling back, each time surging closer and closer. Fear gripped him and he lost his bearings completely. Briefly he thought of pulling over until he remembered that his cousin had done so once and had been viciously assaulted.

Before he knew where he was, the next corner was in front of him. He steered sharply, barely managing to keep the Land Rover steady, controlling the skid as best he could. The vehicle following was right behind him, but now fell back slightly. Then suddenly it pulled out, accelerated hard and slammed into him.

His Land Rover lurched across the narrow verge and plunged down the bank. It hit the water at an angle, breaking the surface ice and sinking to the bed of the lode. Immediately, water poured in from all directions. He struggled to free his seat belt, but his gloved fingers hampered his efforts. His right foot was already under water and stuck under the extended accelerator pedal. He tried to open the door, but with the vehicle canted on its side, the weight of water pinned it shut. Panic gripped him. His best chance was to equalise the water pressure. He tried to slide his side window open. It wouldn't shift. He pushed harder against the door, fighting to hold his breath as the freezing water filled the vehicle. Just as he felt the door give slightly, pain such as he had never felt before exploded in his chest and he could hold his breath no longer.

Silence fell and was broken only once as geese honked their way above the lode, their calls echoing in the gloom. Later, as the temperature rose, the fog burned off. Bubbles rose lazily to the surface of the inky black water and burst, bringing with them the unmistakeable stench of decay and rotting vegetation.

For DCI James Upwood it was a day off, rare enough given their case load. He had planned to go out to the Ouse Washes, bird-watching, a hobby that rarely failed to improve his mood. He preferred to go early in the morning but today the fog was too dense. He thought briefly about going over to Welney in the afternoon, if the weather cleared, to watch the swan feed, but decided he couldn't be bothered. Apathy, quickly followed by a sense of isolation and loneliness, set in. Reading his newspaper wasn't even an option first thing: he'd forgotten to put his iPad on charge overnight. No book could hold his attention and his mind flooded with memories of his late wife and child. He'd had hopes that a relationship might develop with a woman he'd met during a case a few years ago, but she was in Madrid and they'd not spent time together for more than two years. By the time he went to bed, after a completely wasted day, he'd drunk much more than usual and nightmares once again wrecked his sleep.

It would be more than a week before he even heard about the incident on Chilton Lode.

Chapter 2

DS Debra Graf and DC Tom Turner arrived at King's Mere Farm. They had spent much of the day outside and both were cold and grumpy. He was bad tempered because of his discomfort. She was cross because he wouldn't stop moaning. The late afternoon sun held no warmth and the prospect of the meeting ahead was not promising.

The farmhouse lay on the north side of the road that ran more or less parallel to the Ouse. Several large willow trees straggled along its bank on the far side of the field behind the house. Barns surrounded a yard on the east side. The door of one was open; two German Shepherds rushed out to inspect them as they got out of the car. Debra froze for a moment, heart racing. As the dogs came to an abrupt halt she realised they were on chains and gave a sigh of relief. Tom barely glanced at them.

The door was opened by a woman who looked to be in her early fifties. She introduced herself as Molly Shelford, the widow of Fred Shelford who had died in the lode. Her pale face was framed with short spiky hair; her eyes and nose were red. She let them pass into the hall without a word and pointed to the left. As they came in Debra noted the parquet floor was well-worn and lacked polish. There was a door to the right and a stair-case dog-legged up to the landing. A corridor led to the back where she imagined the kitchen would be. In Edwardian days, the room they entered might have been a parlour. Now it was just a den with a roll top desk, chairs, and shelves piled high with farming magazines and books. Weak rays of sun penetrated the two tall windows on the west wall, windows that had probably not been cleaned since the previous autumn. Motes of dust shimmered in the light.

Fred's father, Peter Shelford, sat in a worn leather wing-back chair nursing a glass of amber liquid, the only artificial light in the room a standard lamp behind him. Even slouched as he was in his chair it was clear that he was a fairly tall man, somewhat overweight. He bore a full head of white hair, brushed back from a high forehead. His face was florid. A long nose, while thread-veined, lent him a rather patrician air. A fire burned weakly in the cast iron hearth giving off a slightly acrid smell and creating faint shadows which flittered around the room. It was Peter Shelford who had called 999.

"Hello, Mr Shelford. I'm sorry we've been so long." Whatever she said to him when they arrived was likely to sound trite.

"Hello. Sit down, please." His voice was weary. "Will you have some tea? Molly will make some, won't you dear?"

She nodded, mutely.

"If it's not too much trouble? It's bitterly cold out there still. Let me help you, may I?", Debra asked. Molly nodded again, rising unsteadily to her feet from another arm chair beside him into which she had sunk only moments before.

Tom Turner sat on one of two leather club chairs on the other side of the hearth, uncomfortable that Debra had left him alone with Mr Shelford. Most aspects of his job he could tackle, but he was not good at dealing with the recently bereaved. "I'm sorry about Fred, sir. Is he your only son?"

"Yes. I don't know how I'm going to cope without him."

"Your wife must be very upset. Is she at home?"

There was a long pause. "She died ten years ago." He took a sip from his glass.

Tom paused. There was no reason why he should have anticipated the answer but he was momentarily thrown. "I'm sorry, sir." Tom knew he should find something more sensible to say but empathy was not his strong point, and he had no intention of starting to question the man before Debra returned. "Mr Shelford, I'm sorry to ask. But might I use your toilet?"

Shelford looked vaguely surprised but waved a hand. "Down the corridor. On the right."

When Molly and Debra returned from the kitchen, Tom was nowhere to be seen. Shelford realised that the sergeant was put out. "Went for a pee."

Debra tried to hide her annoyance, not entirely successfully, and passed round mugs of tea. As she did so, Tom came back into the room and sat down, evidently slightly embarrassed. Debra gave Tom a sour look and turned to the dead man's father. "Mr Shelford, I know you told us briefly this morning, but can you tell us again what happened please? We need to take one or two notes." She glared at Tom, who fumbled for his notebook.

Peter Shelford put his glass down and shuddered slightly. "Fred comes up here every day. Well he does unless he has to go to see suppliers or customers or something." He paused. Tom leaned forward as though he was about to ask a question, but Debra forestalled him by a slight movement of her hand. She wanted Peter to tell the story in his own time and in his own way.

"He and Molly live about five miles away, in Queen's Mere Farm. It doesn't have much land now, it was sold by my father. So Fred runs this farm for me now. I'm retired." He paused again. "He drives here of course. Usually here by eight or so at this time of year.

"By eleven he hadn't arrived. I called his mobile and there was no answer. So I called Molly." He looked across to his daughter-in-law. Both appeared grief-stricken.

She took a deep breath. "I was at work. Peter called me and said Fred hadn't arrived and had he gone somewhere else. I said I'd seen him off as usual before I left for school in Knapton. He was a bit later than usual because of the fog; he left about quarter past eight." She drew the last tissue from the box on her lap and blew her nose.

Peter resumed his account. "So I went out towards Queen's Mere Farm. I thought maybe he'd had some sort of problem with the Land Rover and gone home. Daft really. He'd still have answered his mobile, wouldn't he?

"Anyway, I was about half way there. Just gone past the riding school and the first of the right-angled bends came up. I could see tracks on the verge as though a vehicle had crossed it. I turned the corner and pulled off the road into a gateway and got out. I walked back to the bend and then I saw a corner of his Land Rover sticking up out of the lode.

"I knew he'd be dead." He paused. Debra did not respond and even Tom had the sense to keep quiet. Peter drained his glass. "You'd not last more than a few minutes in the water at this time of year. I called 999."

He lay back in his chair and shuddered again, his eyes closed. Tears squeezed out under his lids and glistened on his cheeks. Debra couldn't think when she'd last seen a man of his age cry. She paused briefly before turning to Fred's widow. "Molly, can you tell me a little about Fred please?"

Fred's widow had been staring blindly at the fire. She turned to face Debra. "What do you want to know?"

"I'd like to build up a picture of him, of you both really."

"He was fifty-one last month. A very fit man. He used to be a jump jockey – National Hunt – but he couldn't keep his weight down after a while. He's a good farmer. Peter taught him a lot, but Fred also went to Writtle – the first one in the family to go to agricultural college. He said farming was changing and so experience was no longer enough." Molly spoke almost randomly, twisting the tissue in her fingers. It was as though her brain could not compute properly and allow her to provide information that might actually be of some help.

"He was right", said Peter. "About farming changing. That's why we were looking into wind farms."

"Right. You say he was fit, Molly. Was he also healthy?"

"Healthy? Oh, I see what you mean. I suppose you can be one and not the other. Yes, he was healthy."

"So he didn't take any medications? Anything to help him sleep p'raps?"

"No, none. And if you're a farmer you sure as hell don't need anything to help you sleep. You're generally knackered by the end of the day, even in the middle of winter."

"How did you spend last evening?"

"The same way we always did." A note of impatience crept into Molly's voice. "Supper in the kitchen. I cleared up afterwards while Fred read the paper. I watched a bit of television. We went to bed."

"Did you drink with the meal?"

"Fred had a couple of beers, no more. I didn't have anything."

"And was supper much later than usual?"

"No. We ate about eight o'clock."

"How long have you been married?"

"What the hell difference does it make?" She blew her nose. "Oh, sod it – thirty years."

"Do you have children?"

"A son. He's twenty-nine."

"Does he live at home?" Debra was reluctant to put pressure on Molly, on whose cheeks there were now bright red patches. But she needed to cover all the ground.

"No. He lives with my brother and his family in Lincolnshire. Andy helps him with his farm. He's on his way back now. Excuse me." She got up and went back out to the kitchen.

Debra put down her mug and sat back in her chair and waited for her to return. She knew Molly would be furious with her next line of questioning.

Chapter 3

Molly came back, clutching a new box of tissues. She pushed the door closed behind her to keep the heat in the den, a habit so ingrained it required no thought on her part, even in her highly distressed state. With dusk deepening outside, and with the loss of the light from the hall, the room suddenly seemed much darker. Debra had a sudden vision of how it must have been in years gone by. She remembered an elderly neighbour telling her how, only thirty years before, her local fenland ironmongers had stocked twenty-seven different kinds of wick for oil lamps. She shivered and made an effort to pull herself together.

"Are you OK to carry on? Would you like a break for a bit?" Debra's tone was gentle but somehow conveyed the need to continue.

"No. Let's get it over with." She blew her nose again and threw a handful of tissues into the fire, creating a sudden small burst of light. The shadows danced with greater urgency for the briefest moment before subsiding again. Sparks shot out of the fire and died on the well-worn rug, no doubt adding additional complexity to its pattern. It was a trivial thing but for Debra, who lived in a modern flat with central heating, it was mildly unnerving.

"Did anything unusual happen this morning before you left? You and Fred didn't have a row for some reason?"

"What on earth are you suggesting?" Molly's hands were shredding another tissue; she looked at her father-in-law for support. He stared at her morosely, jaws clenched, and remained silent.

"The questions are just routine, Molly. We need to establish if there were any factors that might have contributed to his vehicle leaving the road."

"There was thick fog and ice. Isn't that a good enough reason for Christ's sake?" Molly's voice was a good half octave higher.

"I am sorry if these questions are upsetting you, but we need to know." Again Debra paused, not wanting to put too much pressure on the woman. It wouldn't take much for her to snap: she was as taught as a violin string. Debra's tone was once more gentle, but firm. "Was Fred more anxious than usual this morning?"

"No. No." Molly looked away.

Debra leaned forward a little and looked at her, trying to make eye contact, to regain her attention. "I have to ask: is there anyone who held a grudge of some kind against Fred?"

"Christ!" shouted Molly. "What kind of question is that? Are you asking if he had any enemies? This is too stupid for words."

No one spoke for a moment. Debra turned to Peter. "You wouldn't have seen it, Mr Shelford. But there is what looks like recent crash damage to the back of the Land Rover."

Molly looked ready to faint. Peter could hardly get his words out. "Are you saying he was rammed?"

"We have to consider every possibility, sir." This observation gave neither Peter nor Molly any comfort at all. A stunned silence fell.

Molly was gripping the arms of her chair, sobbing. "Fred didn't have any enemies, Sergeant Graf. Why would he have enemies for Christ's sake?"

Debra said nothing but looked at Molly's father-in-law. He shrugged and reached for his glass and grimaced when he realised it was empty. He reached for the bottle of Bells on the table on the other side of his chair and half-filled the tumbler. They waited as he raised it to his lips, Debra worried that if they didn't finish the interview quickly they might not learn what they needed to and would have to come back another time.

"I don't know about enemies, Sergeant. But there were one or two people he didn't get on with." He offered this information reluctantly.

Tom took over the questioning. "Tell us what you have in mind, sir. If it's not relevant, we'll discount it of course."

Peter took a sip of his whisky and leant forward. He put the glass down and picked up the poker, jabbing at the fire. Sparks flew and the flames gathered much more energy. The shadows danced frenetically around the small room, the effect more pronounced in the poor light, increasing Debra's discomfort. She and Tom both got the impression he was trying to decide how much to tell them.

Peter slumped back in his chair. "Well. There's David Brownlow for one. If you remember, I said that the land originally belonging to Queen's Mere Farm was sold some time ago. It was sold to David's father. Fred was always resentful. I think he would have wanted to manage both farms in time. David wouldn't countenance selling the land to him."

"It sounds as though Fred had more to be angry about than Mr Brownlow. What was he so upset about?"

"David was furious that we'd got our application in for a wind farm development before him. He wanted to go the same route but thought that permission wouldn't be granted for two sites so close together. He opposed our plans at the original consultation meeting in the summer last year." He paused, as though thinking back to the event. "His objections didn't carry much weight because he couldn't rely on the typical arguments about noise and flicker. If his application ever goes ahead he'll have to fight those arguments himself. It was jealousy pure and simple that drove him."

Molly sighed wearily, evidently deciding that having started down this track they had better continue. "There's more, isn't there Peter? Tell them about the row over last year's crops."

"Oh Lord." His eyes strayed round the room. Once more it seemed he needed time to gather his thoughts. "We farm organically here. Yields are lower but we can get better prices. David farms much more intensively. Last summer he sprayed his beet fields, like he usually does. His fields are alongside ours and they were sprayed when the wind conditions were wrong. Our customer refused our crop because it was contaminated. We lost a lot of money. Fred was angrier than I've ever seen him and had a blazing row with David. Fred accused him of sabotaging our crops. The local paper picked it up. Neither of them came out of it very well. David was livid and later accused Fred of trashing his reputation."

Debra intervened again. "As Tom said before, Mr Shelford, you could say that Fred had more to be angry about than Mr Brownlow."

"Maybe. But that lad's always had a fearsome temper. And like his dad, he holds grudges."

"Mr Shelford, you said there were one or two people with whom Fred didn't get on. Who were the others?"

"Well more than one or two. Any of the key campaigners against our wind farm proposal. Start with Kmag: the King's Mere Action Group. They've got their own website."

"And Facebook page", Molly interjected.

"It sounds well organised."

"It is. The Committee members are professional people. Bloody bigots about wind farms though. Bastards." He took another sip of whisky. "But at least they try to put forward their arguments rationally, I'll give them that. There are some real nutters out there though."

"Why do you say that, sir?" Debra asked.

"It's not bloody rocket science, is it? They were ranting at that public meeting, making all sorts of completely unsubstantiated claims. And then protesting outside the council chambers when the application was being discussed, waving placards. At least two of the councillors who supported us had their cars vandalised."

"Peter, this is mad! People always get angry over plans like these but they don't go round killing each other. Why would you even take the idea seriously?" If Molly was hoping for reassurance from him she didn't get it.

Peter turned towards her, a look of infinite sadness on his face. "Because there were more fresh tyre marks on the verge, Molly. Some the same side as Fred's, some on the other side. As if another vehicle had been swinging back and forth across the road. You saw them, didn't you Constable?"

"I did, sir. They were not from Fred's Land Rover."

Chapter 4

Brian Doughty carried his pint over to his two colleagues and sat down wearily. Their table was tucked away in a quiet corner close to the large open fire at the back of the Black Horse in Knapton. Light from the flames flickered on the brasses fixed to the beams overhead. A traditional pub, its décor had changed little over the years, although the ceiling no longer showed the ochre staining of nicotine. The present landlord had improved it in a number of ways, not least by pulling up the old, sticky, wildly patterned Axminster-style carpet and restoring the stone flags. He had had to bow to the inevitable however, and the bar snacks menu had been considerably improved and widened, although he had made no attempt to turn it into a gastro pub. He stocked real ale from a couple of local micro-breweries. He knew his market and while he didn't make a fortune, he worked hard and made a comfortable living.

A gentle hum from other customers further away was too quiet to distract the three men and their own conversation was unlikely to be heard. The older of the two already at the table, Geoff Grindlay, grinned, his high forehead glowing in the firelight. "Held up at the office again?"

"Yeah. I'm refusing to sign off the accounts for one of our corporate clients and the shit's really hit the fan. Their finance director is a golfing buddy of my boss. Between a rock and a hard place is where I am right now." He raised his glass and drank appreciatively.

Richard Gardiner, the eldest of the three, chuckled, although he was not without sympathy. "It's a good job you've got this to take your mind off it then." Richard Gardiner was the Chairman of their group: the King's Mere Action Group. Brian was Treasurer and Geoff the Secretary.

The three men were not, however, in a cheerful frame of mind despite the cosy setting.

The decision of the Knapton and Chilton District Council the previous week to turn down the application for the wind farm was, on the face of it, encouraging. They all knew, however, that the developer, Narbor Renewables, were nothing if not tenacious and certain to appeal the decision. Kmag therefore faced a great deal of extra work and were going to need substantially more funds to pay their legal bills.

"Do we have any idea what the timescale is likely to be?" Brian was probably the most concerned since he suspected that the burden of fund-raising would fall on his shoulders.

Richard responded. "If we look at other similar proposals I think we can expect Narbor to lodge an appeal within a couple of months. Their lawyers will crawl all over the council's decision and then have to prepare their response. Even with all their experience of similar cases it will be a lot of work. How's our bank balance at the moment, Brian?"

"It's fair. We've probably got some fifteen thousand in hand. But then we always knew we'd need a reserve. We're going to need a lot more, though. I'd guess at least 50k, but I could be way out. How much was our brief's hourly rate - four hundred pounds? Even 50k won't go far."

Geoff, too, was concerned about the finances. "We need to put some serious thought into how much work on the appeal we can do ourselves. Should we co-opt one or two people from the membership to research how appeals have been handled elsewhere in the district? Huntingdonshire district too, perhaps. There are plenty of precedents."

"Maybe", responded Richard, "but I doubt it will make much of a dent in our legal fees. At best it might help make sure we've got all the angles covered."

"But that's worth a lot in itself." Geoff swirled his gin and tonic and drank the little that remained in his glass. He stood up and reached out for Richard's, already empty.

Brian smiled. "Sorry, guys. I should have got you another round in when I got my beer."

"No problem. We were well ahead of you."

Geoff came back with the drinks and pushed a tumbler of Scotch across the table to Richard and a pint of beer for Brian. It clearly wasn't the same one he'd had before. "It's this week's guest beer – thought you might like to live dangerously for a change." They all laughed.

Brian looked at Richard. "You've had much more experience of managing the planning process than us. Will Fred Shelford's death have any impact, do you think?"

"God knows. I've never known anything like it. It's not his land that's subject to the application of course, it's his father's."

"But Fred was always the one making the running. Peter's getting on now, isn't he?"

Richard laughed. "Well he's probably ten years older than me, so yes, well over the hill!"

"Seriously, though, he doesn't look like a man with much stamina. Didn't I hear that he'd had a stroke a few years ago?" He looked at Geoff.

"No good looking at me, Brian. I may be a neurologist but I'm not going to tell you if he's ever been a patient, am I?"

Silence fell briefly and they tackled their drinks. They were vaguely aware of the conversations taking place around them: a few regulars, men on stools at the far end of the bar, a couple at one of the tables, and in the distance the sound of balls clacking on a pool table.

It was Brian who broke the silence. "What do you know about how Fred died? All I've heard is that they fished him out of Chilton Lode on Monday."

Geoff shook his head. "I know no more than you do. Richard?"

"I happened to bump into Ken Lloyd in town. Apparently, the police interviewed him yesterday. He got the impression that there might have been another vehicle involved."

"What, some sort of collision?"

"He didn't know. They weren't giving anything away. No doubt we'll find out in due course. There will have to be an inquest naturally."

"That won't be for weeks, probably. I don't like it." Geoff looked serious. "It's a minefield in PR terms. If we offer condolences to the family we'll be accused of hypocrisy. If we say nothing we'll be accused of insensitivity. And I have a nasty feeling it's going to bring out the conspiracy theory fruitcakes."

"Technical term, Geoff?" Brian laughed in spite of himself.

"I'm deadly serious, Brian. If some idiot doesn't accuse us of engineering his death I shall be very surprised indeed. I said at the beginning I didn't like the idea of the Facebook page. People can say what they like under assumed names and get away with it. Have you looked at our site today?" He pulled out his smartphone and fiddled for a moment. "I quote: '*RIP Fred Shelford. Kmag trying to derail the scheme?*' Posted by *Windwarrier.*"

Richard looked startled. "Christ Almighty. This could turn really nasty."

Chapter 5

A week later DS Graf was at her desk with DC Turner, armed with the morning's first cups of coffee. Her desk was piled with folders, leaning precariously against the monitor. At thirty-eight, Debra was much younger than the constable. Long, dark hair scraped back into a pony-tail, and good skin made her look younger than she was. Her body was still well toned. Although she had given up football some years ago, she now ran occasionally to keep fit.

In contrast, Tom, at fifty-six, looked older than his years. His skin was pallid and his short, sandy hair had gone grey and receded, leaving him looking a bit like an elderly mouse. He'd been with the police over twenty years following a career in the ambulance service and was generally well thought of. Recently, though, he'd come in for increasing criticism because of his erratic moods. Generally placid, he could now more often than not be bad tempered. No one could get to the bottom of it. He was unmarried and was not thought to be in any kind of relationship, and there was no obvious source of stress that his senior officers could identify. Debra had more time for him than most, although even her patience could wear thin at times. Today he was in one of his better moods.

They were no further forward in their investigation into Fred's death. Peter and Molly Shelford had both examined the damage to the back of the Land Rover. While they agreed it looked recent, neither could categorically say that it hadn't occurred before the day he died. It was an old working vehicle and suffered regular knocks around the farm. Debra and Tom remained open-minded on the issue. The dent to the rear offside side panel showed signs of paint that could have been transferred during a collision. If they were lucky, tests might determine the make and model involved.

As well as reporting on the paint traces, the vehicle examiner had confirmed that Fred's Land Rover had been in good mechanical condition. There was no evidence to suggest that any mechanical failure had played a part in the incident.

The tyre tracks they had seen on the verges near the crash site did not prove to be helpful. Peter had turned the corner before parking his Defender and had not obliterated these marks. The examiner's report showed that the tyres were a common make, probably used on a four by four. This didn't help much as there were so many in the area. In any event, the tracks could have been made earlier, or later, than the time at which Fred's vehicle left the road.

Certainly no one had come forward to acknowledge their part in an accident. Enquires at local body shops had not resulted in the discovery of a vehicle needing the kind of repairs that might have occurred in such a collision.

All the immediate neighbours had been interviewed. Nobody had seen anything relevant. And none of their vehicles showed any sign of damage.

The only member of the public to respond to their appeals for information was the driver of the tractor which had passed Fred. He had recognised Fred's Land Rover and noticed that another vehicle was following it. He did not recognise it, but thought it was also a four by four. There was a layby on the road out of Knapton just short of the lane to Queen's Mere Farm. With an uninterrupted view over flat arable land, even in poor light, it would have been easy to park and watch Fred leave the yard and start his journey with a view to following him. No one, however, reported seeing a vehicle parked there in the mornings before Fred died, so the idea was no more than speculation.

While toxicology results were not back yet, the post mortem report did not give any indication that Fred had any physical problem that might have played a part.

So was it an accident for which Fred alone was responsible? Or an accidental hit and run? Or a deliberate collision?

"What's your gut feel, Tom?"

"An accident. It may have been a hit and run, but I don't see it. In those conditions no one would drive so closely. They'd risk colliding. I certainly don't buy the idea that he was deliberately bumped off. I mean really. How likely is it?"

"I agree. It doesn't seem likely. Ken Lloyd at the riding school and Sheila Bennett at the care home are both on the Kmag Committee. But that doesn't give them a motive strong enough to kill Fred, surely. I grant you David Brownlow seems to have detested the man, but would he kill him? Maybe in the heat of the moment, but to plan an execution? Nah. Doesn't work for me. Anyway, his wife says he was home at the time."

"Joy rider?"

"Are you kidding? In those conditions? You'd be mental."

"What if he deliberately drove off the road?"

"What? Suicide? Shotgun is the method of choice for farmers, surely? You'd have to be seriously unhinged to choose to go the way he did."

"He might not have wanted Molly to know that things had got so bad."

"I don't know. I'm just not happy about it. Fred had driven those roads practically every day for more than twenty years. He'd know them like the back of his hand. It just doesn't feel right that it was an accident."

"But in fog you can get very disoriented. Did I ever tell you about that time a few years ago in Knapton? Very dense fog, like we had last week. I was driving out of West Street onto Chilton Road. Only I didn't. I turned too soon and ended up in the Co-op car park. There was a bus in there too. Done the same thing."

She laughed and reached for her coffee cup, managing to knock the top folder onto the floor. She reached down to retrieve it. "You're making it up! No way a bus would do that."

"Scout's honour, boss."

"OK, OK. But I think we should interview Peter and Molly again and see if the marriage was sound, see if there were any money problems. But let's also stick with the idea, just for a bit longer, that Fred was driven off the road. If he was, why can't we find the vehicle?"

"It's already three counties away. The owner's bunged it in a lock-up and chucked the key. It's been burnt out…"

"Have we had any reports of burnt out cars since the accident?"

"No. First thing I checked when I got back to the station."

"Did you check to see if any vehicle had been reported stolen recently?"

"I did. There have been three since the beginning of last month. One was a Porsche, almost certainly stolen to order. There was also an old banger. It was found a couple of days later, dumped in a field near Willingham. Neither are candidates for Fred's accident. There is one other. An old Mitsubishi Pajero. But it was reported stolen before Christmas."

"Has it been found yet? It sounds the right kind of vehicle for the job."

"No. But it doesn't seem very likely that it stayed in the area and was used three weeks or so later for a hit and run."

"Maybe there were reasons – circumstances not right. Maybe he wanted a foggy morning. Who knows? Anyway, let's arrange those interviews with Peter and Molly, shall we? Let's see them separately this time. We might get more out of them that way."

Chapter 6

DS Ramachandran and DC Starr had been called out to Chilton to make a preliminary assessment of a suspected case of arson. It was still dark and stars flashed occasionally between high scudding clouds. The Sergeant noticed them and vaguely wondered why it was windy high up when there was little wind at ground level.

The fire was now under control. Three appliances with their crews were on site and hoses were still available in case any smouldering material reignited. The roof of the barn had all but collapsed and the walls had been largely destroyed. Only the metal frame remained intact and that was bent and twisted. The air was dense, full of smoke and particles; the sour smell of burnt straw was pervasive.

The senior officer on site came over to meet them. "Hi. I'm Jack Forbes. And you are?"

"I'm DS Ramachandran. Mo Ramachandran. This is my colleague DC Margaret Starr. What can you tell us?"

"Not a lot yet. We got the call about midnight and were on site very quickly. I would think the fire had been going about an hour or so when we got here. There wasn't anything very complicated about it. We didn't see any signs of hazardous materials and no other property was at risk. Even so, it took a while to get it under control. You'll want to know why I think it's arson?"

"Please."

"Well, for a start, look around you. The plot's about three acres and completely overgrown. And the house is a shell. That was destroyed by fire more than two years ago. Ironically, I attended that incident – the householder died. The whole site is completely derelict. There won't have been any power in the barn, so no electrical fault. There is almost no chance at all of spontaneous combustion. Even if damp straw or hay had been piled in there by the householder, it would long since have gone up."

Mo Ramachandran looked sceptical. "Surely only dry stuff would spontaneously combust."

"You'd think so. But it's not the case. Put very simply, dampness promotes the growth of bacteria which produce heat. In certain conditions the temperature can rise high enough to allow the material to catch fire. But fires like that typically occur within six weeks of baling. I won't bore you with the reasons. So no spontaneous combustion from fodder or bedding material. There was no lightening last night, so we can rule that out. Peat and coal, and manure come to that, can spontaneously combust. But the circumstances here rule those out too. In certain circumstances rags soaked in linseed oil can combust. I could go on. But my point is that this plot is derelict and has been since the house fire. I go past here fairly frequently and there has been no sign of activity of any kind. No site clearance. No demolition of the shell of the house. Nada."

"Why would that be? Surely the land must be worth something to the owners?"

"Who are they though? My guess is that if you look into it you'll find that the householder died intestate and had no easily identifiable heirs."

"What happens then?" Margaret was interested although she had no idea if the issue was important.

"Not a fan of daytime TV then." Jack laughed. "My guess is that the estate is now 'bona vacantia' – ownerless property. Unless beneficiaries come forward, or heir hunters track them down, the estate will pass to the Crown. This site could remain like this for thirty years."

"That can't happen very often surely?"

"D'you want to guess how many entries there are on the government's Unclaimed Estates List? No? More than eleven thousand when I last looked." Margaret appeared suitably impressed.

Jack continued. "We need to start processing the site. We're not sure yet, because we haven't been able to get into the far corner, but we think there may be a body. One of my team has just told me."

"Can we talk to him?"

"Sure. Paul? Can you spare us a minute, please?"

A tall stocky firefighter clambered across the debris-strewn floor of the barn, his protective clothing grubby and his face sweaty and covered in soot. "How can I help?"

"I understand you think there's a body in there?"

"I know there is now. It's badly burned and half hidden under fallen roof materials. We've cleared some of it away – just enough to make sure of death. You'll get the pathologist in, of course. We won't touch anything else until your Scene of Crime Officers give us clearance."

"Is the body completely burned?" Mo asked.

"No. They rarely are in this type of fire because it doesn't get hot enough. Doesn't mean it doesn't do an awful lot of damage though. But the pathologist will have quite a lot to work on. Rather him than me is all I can say. The victim's in a hell of a state, and his car's not going anywhere."

"Car? What car?" Mo asked.

"Some old 4x4 by the look of it."

Chapter 7

By late afternoon an Incident Room had been set up and a briefing in an adjoining meeting room called for 5.00 pm. DCI James Upwood was Senior Investigating Officer and DI Herbert "Morton" Harrison his deputy. Morton had managed to pull together the relevant team members. Upwood thanked everyone for attending and spoke briefly at the start of the meeting before handing over to Morton.

Morton stood six foot two and was heavily built. His hair, once thick and curly, and a curious shade somewhere between blond and ginger, was now cut very short and was thin on top. His nose and one ear were misshapen. Had his neck not been so thick, some might have thought he'd been in too many brawls. In fact he'd been in too many scrums. He still retained a fairly youthful look despite his forty-one years.

Morton glanced briefly at his notes. "The call came into the control room at seven fifteen this morning from the senior fire officer, Jack Forbes. A resident of Chilton had phoned 999 at four minutes past midnight to report that a barn was on fire about half a mile away from his home on the edge of the village. The first appliance arrived twelve minutes later and two others arrived soon after. It took them nearly four hours before they had the fire properly under control. They then had to wait until the scene was safe enough to enter. He said that there had probably been a lot of flammable material in the barn. Mo, you and Margaret were first on site. Why don't you tell us what you found?"

Mo looked at Margaret, who nodded to him to go ahead. "The site is a three-acre former market garden on the south side of thc village. The whole plot is very overgrown. The house is set back from the road by about twenty feet but is screened by trees and tall shrubs. It had apparently burnt down some two years ago. Jack Forbes had attended that fire and told us that the householder had died in the incident. Margaret can give you an update on that in a minute.

"There is a cinder track down the southern boundary. The barn is at the end of this, about three hundred yards from the road. It had a metal frame and was clad partly with timber planking and partly with corrugated iron. It has been largely destroyed. We do know that there was a vehicle in the barn: a Mitsubishi Pajero. Completely destroyed of course. As Jack said, we'll be lucky to get more than a VIN from it.

"I can confirm that a body was found. It has been badly burned but not completely so. It was found in a concrete stall partly covered by a sheet of corrugated iron. We do not know at this stage whether the man – although we are fairly sure it is a man – died because of the fire or not. The pathologist should be able to tell us in due course.

"Finally I can also confirm that an accelerant was used. The fire investigation team detected petrol using their sniffer device – to be confirmed once they've done the full lab tests. They don't know yet whether the fuel came from the vehicle's tank. But there was apparently one of those old metal five-gallon fuel drums in the barn. That may have been the source, or the arsonist might have brought his own container.

"The fire investigators have begun collecting material that may provide us with evidence of how the arson was committed.

"House to house interviews have started but as yet we have nothing useful – no reports of any suspicious activity have been recorded so far. Margaret, will you tell us what you have found out?" He sat down.

Margaret had returned to the Parkside Station after an hour or so on site, leaving Mo to begin setting up the team necessary for the investigation. She relayed the information Jack Forbes had given them about the house fire and his theory of bona vacantia. She had looked up the Unclaimed Estates List and very quickly established that an Arthur Stanley Lamb had died in Chilton in November 2008. Notes against his name indicated that both his parents and a brother had pre-deceased him. There was no mention of a wife (his marital status was given as unknown) or children. Checks with the Land Registry confirmed that the property known as Orchard Farm had been owned by him for more than forty years with no mortgage outstanding. They were lucky to establish this. Only because Lamb had raised a modest, short-term loan secured against the property in 1999 had it been registered.

"Any questions or observations so far?" Upwood looked around the room.

"Are we sure it's arson, Sir? If petrol was the accelerant it's the sort of thing that might be stored in a barn. We've heard there was a fuel drum there. Perhaps it was accidental?"

"Jack Forbes says not. His people have identified three probable seats of fire."

"Might the victim be the arsonist, Sir?"

"Much too soon to say for sure, but unlikely we think. The seats of fire were between him and the door to the barn. If he'd set the fire himself he would have wanted a clear exit."

"Is it arson for the hell of it, Sir, or arson to conceal another crime – perhaps the murder of the dead man?"

"No idea. We'll have to look at every angle. But you know how we work. If there's any doubt, we tackle it as though it's a homicide case until the evidence proves otherwise. We are much less likely to overlook critical information that way."

"Was the house fire arson?"

Morton looked at Margaret. "Can you shed any light on that?"

"Yes. I checked the report. It looks as though it was an electrical fault. The householder was in his nineties and the house was in a bad state of repair."

"Have there been other similar cases of arson recently?"

"Not in Cambs. Mo, I think you were checking with other neighbouring counties?"

Mo looked at Morton. "Yes. Not in Lincolnshire, Norfolk or Suffolk, or Beds and Herts. There are plenty of smaller incidents – bin fires, fires in the open, and so on. But not arson on any scale in agricultural or industrial buildings. Except in Northants. The arsonist there was apprehended and convicted last October."

"Sir, the Mitsubishi. Might it be the one reported stolen last month?"

"Good question. No idea, but, Morton, make sure someone checks that out please. It may have belonged to the dead householder of course. But let's check.

"OK? Jan Murray has put out a press release asking people to come forward if they have any information. We're hoping someone late to bed or driving through might have seen activity on site. Let's meet again here at eight tomorrow. I've a feeling this is going to be a tricky one. If we don't keep on top of it, it'll come back and haunt us."

Chapter 8

DCI James Upwood arrived early the next morning and went straight to the Incident Room. The air was stale and the only radiator grumbled, unable to release an air bubble trapped inside. The room had hosted many such meetings over the years and seemed to have soaked up a whole range of emotions, from apathy to tension, despair to elation. Today the mood was definitely somewhere between apathy and tension.

He studied the white boards which showed separate details of the Fred Shelford event and the barn fire with an integrated time line. He also studied the briefing notes Morton had emailed him earlier. Team members straggled in, most clutching mugs of coffee, some with lidded cardboard mugs from one of the local coffee shops. Steam added to the general fug. When they were all assembled he opened proceedings and then handed over to DI Harrison. Morton was well used to giving such briefings and began a summary of recent events. Upwood watched the team as the meeting progressed and was interested to see their responses. Many, like Mo and Margaret, were paying close attention. Others looked a bit bleary-eyed; perhaps they were owls rather than larks. DS Graf and DC Turner were there, having been invited to join the briefing. Tom looked unhappy and was fidgeting. After half an hour Upwood gave his apologies to Morton and took his leave. His presence was required by the Assistant Chief Constable. Tom slipped out after him, to Debra's obvious annoyance.

After the previous evening's briefing Margaret had compared the VIN recovered from the burnt-out vehicle with that stolen in December. They matched. As a consequence, Debra Graf was asked to provide information about their case. A tall, self-confident woman, she delivered her report fluently.

"We are investigating an incident that happened on the morning of Monday 10th January. A vehicle had left the

Chilton Lode Road, that's the road running north out of Knapton, just short of the Mere Riding School. We estimate the time of the incident at approximately half past eight. DC Turner and I attended. We had patrol cars to stop traffic at road junctions either side of the scene. Fire and Rescue and an ambulance attended too. When the vehicle was recovered from the water the driver, local farmer Fred Shelford, was found still strapped in his seat. He was pronounced dead at the scene.

"The post mortem showed that the driver had not been under the influence of drink or drugs and there were no other physical or health problems that might have played a role in the incident. His mobile phone was not in use at the time of death.

"There were signs of recent damage to the rear off-side panel of the vehicle – a Land Rover Series III. The dead man's father and widow were unable to say how recent the damage was, but neither recalled having seen it before. The vehicle examiner subsequently recovered traces of paint from another vehicle at the site of the damage. The Land Rover was mechanically sound.

"No one has come forward to admit hitting the Land Rover. There are no witnesses to the incident. Those living locally have been interviewed and can account for their whereabouts at the time of the incident, and their vehicles show no sign of damage."

There was a clatter at the back of the room as Tom stumbled back into his chair. Debra shot him a filthy look as colour rose to her cheeks. She would give him a bollocking later.

"We investigated cases of recently reported vehicle theft and were able to eliminate two of the three from our enquiries. The third was a Mitsubishi Pajero reported stolen during the morning of 20th December in Knapton. It's an L reg short wheel base, 2.8 manual, diesel. DC Turner has interviewed the registered keeper and is satisfied that it was a case of theft. We have no suspect.

"We don't know the cause of the incident on the Chilton Lode Road but consider that it may have been a hit and run – whether accidental or intentional we don't know. We think that the Pajero may have been involved – it was dark grey, the same colour as the paint traces on the Land Rover. We are waiting for results from the lab on those. That's all we can tell you at present."

"Do you have any reason to suppose that the ramming might have been intentional?"

"It's hardly even an hypothesis, really. But we did ask the victim's father and widow if he had any enemies. The father identified one David Brownlow, another local farmer. We interviewed him and it's certainly the case that there was very bad blood between them and had been for years. And the father also mentioned Kmag – the King's Mere Action Group that is opposing the wind farm development proposed for the Shelford family farm. He said some of the opponents to the plans had been violent on previous occasions."

"And have you come to any conclusions on that line of enquiry?"

"No, we haven't. Unless we get some hard evidence it's no more than a theory."

"And do you have any other lines of enquiry?"

"We did wonder whether Fred Shelford might have driven off the road deliberately. Granted it's a bizarre way to commit suicide, but plausible if for some reason he didn't want his wife to know he'd killed himself. We interviewed her and her father-in-law again. The marriage seems to have been sound and there were no financial problems. I think we can rule it out."

"Thank you. Margaret, please tell us your findings."

"Simple. The VIN of the stolen Pajero matches that of the one burnt out in our barn fire. If it was a diesel, the accelerant can't have been siphoned out of its tank."

"Good thinking. So the circumstantial evidence does point to its involvement in the Chilton Lode incident. If it was an accident, the driver might still have wanted to dispose of the vehicle, but if we don't keep our minds open to the possibility that it was deliberate we may miss something important."

The briefing continued, reviewing actions completed and others outstanding. New actions were issued. The current priority was to establish the identity of the victim in the barn.

After the meeting ended Debra called Tom to the front, caring not at all that those leaving the room might notice. "What the hell d'you think you're doing walking out of a briefing?"

"I had something I needed to do."

"And what the fuck's that supposed to mean? We've just been invited to join this murder investigation and the first thing you do is behave like a complete prick and make me look stupid."

"I needed to take a call. It was important."

"But you didn't even look at your phone before you left the room. I was at the front remember? I could see you clearly."

"It was on vibrate. I was expecting it. Just not so soon."

"And what was so important that you needed to answer it then?"

"It's personal."

"It's not good enough. You could have rung back after the meeting. You shouldn't be taking personal calls at work and certainly not during a briefing." She was becoming more and more angry. He was becoming more and more stubborn and did not respond.

"I'm warning you, Tom. I used to have a lot of respect for you. But your behaviour recently has really pissed me off. If you continue to carry on like a complete prat I'll be recommending disciplinary action."

"Probably the least of my problems."

"What?"

"Pack it in. I've got better things to do." He got up and walked out, leaving Debra furious. Mainly because she knew that, once again, she had not handled the situation at all well.

Later that morning Morton went to DCI Upwood's office to bring him up to date on progress.

"It's a mess, frankly. We've got a crime scene in Chilton that looks like a war zone. Evidence collection is going to be a nightmare because the scene is so contaminated.

"We know the burnt-out vehicle was stolen last month in Knapton and it may or may not have been involved in an unexplained death in Chilton Lode. If it was involved, we have no idea why that incident's only recently occurred, or why the vehicle was left for a week before being torched. We've put out an appeal for information from anyone who may have seen it on the day of Fred's death.

"And needless to say, we don't know the identity of the victim in the fire."

"You're checking mispers of course?"

"Of course, yes. But identifying the victim is going to be very hard. Have you seen a body in circumstances like this?"

Upwood nodded. "No doubt shrunken and badly contorted? Fists up like a boxer?"

"Exactly. Virtually no flesh left on the face, or hair on the scalp. The only flesh that shows little sign of burning is between his thighs so we should get good DNA samples there. Visual recognition is out of the question. Dental records if we are lucky and he had a local dentist. But not a lot else, I bet. It's possible there may be some stomach contents fit to analyse."

"What about the idea that the farmer who drowned was deliberately pushed off the road?"

"It's a possibility, but we've no evidence. But after the briefing our bright new probationer looked at the Kmag Facebook page. Several green activists are posting comments all but accusing Kmag of causing his death."

"I thought the Kmag lot *were* green activists." Upwood looked decidedly confused.

"So they are, Sir. But it seems there's more than one shade of green, and they're not on the same side of this argument by any manner of means. So do we link the investigations?"

"I think we'll end up doing that. Let's get the results on the paint samples first."

Morton was just getting up to leave when there was a knock on the door. Mo Ramachandran put his head in. "Sorry to interrupt, gentlemen. But there is a significant new development. They've found candle wax in all three seats of fire."

Chapter 9

The discovery of candle wax at the seats of the fire forced changes in the investigation, not because they did not already know that it was a case of arson, but because it potentially confused the timings.

They would try to determine the type of candles used but they decided to work on the assumption that they were the typical white household type. If they were previously unused, or had not been shortened, they would burn for five hours. Jack Forbes had estimated that the fire had begun at about eleven o'clock on Monday night. If he was correct, they could have been lit as early as six o'clock before their flames ignited the accelerant. The arsonist would want to avoid early, accidental, ignition of the fuel. And he would want to get well away before the main fire began. Their conclusions, therefore, were that the candles would not have been shortened too much, if at all. On the other hand, the taller they remained the greater chance that they might perhaps fall over, and start the fire too quickly.

Nonetheless, they had to assume a worst-case scenario. Jack Forbes might not be right in his assumption that the fire had started at eleven; it might have been nearer the time at which the neighbour had seen it – ie midnight. Allowing for the fact that preparations inside the barn were necessary – spreading the accelerant, positioning and securing the candles – perhaps half an hour before the candles were lit might be required. So the window in which the arsonist might have been seen could be from as early as half past five to nearly midnight.

All those living within sight of the barn or the approaches to it, would need to be interviewed again.

Debra and Tom had been tasked with pursuing their investigations into Fred Shelford's death. They arranged to meet Richard Gardiner, Kmag's chairman. He lived on the northern side of Knapton so they stayed on the A10 until they reached the last exit. Just before they turned off Tom asked Debra if she would pull into the filling station. He'd not had breakfast and wanted a bar of chocolate. Reluctantly she did as he asked. It was several minutes before he came out. "What took you so long?" He dropped into his seat and rammed his seat belt on then started peeling the wrapper off his Kit Kat.

"I needed a pee. Is there a law against it?"

"No. I just wish you planned things better. It's such a waste of time."

"It's only five minutes for God's sake. Don't get into such a state about it. At least I did it before we got there."

She made no reply but was forced to acknowledge to herself that that at least made sense. She drove out of the forecourt and they started looking for Gardiner's home.

At five foot nine, with a slim build, Gardiner did not immediately strike them as having great presence. They soon learned, however, that he carried considerable personal authority. Sixty-one years old, until recently he had been a partner in one of the country's largest civil engineering companies, specialising in infrastructure projects of all types. He had taken early retirement when the possibility of a take-over by an American company began to look like a probability. His field had been in the construction of dams, flood defences and all manner of other projects involving water. Now he undertook the occasional project as a consultant, mainly to NGOs.

Dressed as usual in suit and tie, Gardiner made the two detectives look decidedly casual. Debra wore black trousers. A pale blue polo neck sweater under a grey fleece set off her Mediterranean complexion well. Those who did not know her background wondered how she came by those looks when her surname was Germanic. In fact her mother was Spanish. Tom wore somewhat crumpled cords, dark jumper and a leather jacket which had definitely seen better days.

He showed them into what he called his living room, although Debra would have been more inclined to describe it as a study, despite its having several easy chairs. The walls were lined with custom-built bookcases made from some fine-grained wood that she couldn't identify and which Tom didn't notice. Most of the shelves carried non-fiction, much of it presumably connected with his profession. On the top shelves were what she imagined must be souvenirs from his overseas travels – native carvings in ebony from Africa, in sandstone from India, in ivory from one continent or the other. She just hoped the ivory carvings pre-dated 1947, but given his age she doubted it.

"Thank you for seeing us, Mr Gardiner."

"My pleasure, although I don't know how I can possibly shed any light on Fred Shelford's death." He looked relaxed and untroubled by their wanting to talk to him.

"How well did you know Mr Shelford?"

"I didn't know him, Sergeant. I knew who he was, and I knew him by reputation."

"And what was his reputation?"

"If the evening paper is to be believed he was short-tempered. A small man with chips on both shoulders. He used to be a fairly good jump jockey by all accounts. Fearless over the fences. And notorious last autumn for his spat in the local pub with another farmer."

Tom, who was making a record of the interview, made a note to check the newspaper archive.

"Can you tell us about Kmag? Who set it up, for instance, when and why."

Gardiner stretched his legs and crossed one ankle over the other. "By all means. I suppose I was one of the driving forces. There was a report that Peter Shelford wanted to develop a wind farm on his land and that Narbor Renewables were to be involved. I was chatting with a friend, Geoff Grindlay, in the pub one night. Both of us are very opposed to wind farms. We decided to talk to other friends and associates to see if there was any appetite to oppose the plans. We found that there was and arranged a public meeting."

"When was that, sir?" asked Tom.

"That would be July last year. Narbor had undertaken what they called a consultation exercise the previous month." He snorted. "In reality it was an exhibition and a hard sell on their part, trying to convince the local community that there were real benefits for them. They were not soliciting views from the public, unless they were favourable. A lot of people were outraged. So Brian and I had that conversation, sounded out others, and called the public meeting. We invited Narbor to make a brief presentation. Geoff then spoke to explain his reasons for opposing the plans. Then we invited participation from the audience. To say the response was lively is an understatement. At the close of the meeting it had been agreed by a large majority vote that a committee should be formed to conduct a campaign against the development. We also asked for volunteers for the committee. People at the meeting were encouraged to give their names and email addresses so we could build up a list of supporters."

"And did many people sign up?"

"Yes. From memory I would think about a hundred and thirty. It's a lot more now though. Geoff could tell you."

Debra and Tom looked at each other. The longer the list, the longer this line of enquiry might take. And there might well be supporters of Kmag who preferred to keep their heads below the parapet and did not disclose their identities.

"Were there many volunteers for the committee?" Debra asked.

"Some. Not many. Geoff and I put our names down for it. So did a chap called Brian Doughty. And there were a few others. We held our first meeting a few days later. I was elected Chairman, Geoff was elected Secretary and Brian Treasurer."

"The others that joined: did you know any of them beforehand?"

"Geoff knew one of them: Veronica Mallon. Geoff is a consultant neurologist at Addenbrooke's. Veronica's husband is a doctor. Brian knew of another: Sheila Bennett. Apparently one of his colleagues audits her care home accounts.

"And now I think of it, I seem to remember Geoff saying that he'd also met Ken Lloyd. His daughter had taken riding lessons at his school for a while."

"Is it just the six of you?"

"Yes. There were two others at our first meeting. One decided the time commitment would be too great. The next day I persuaded another that he should withdraw his application. In my experience you can get a lot done if you have a small group of motivated people. You can always co-opt additional help if necessary."

"Presumably you are all highly motivated."

Gardiner nodded. "We are. For slightly different reasons."

"Motivated enough to take direct action?"

He raised an eyebrow. "I'm not sure I understand you, Sergeant."

"Motivated enough to vandalise cars belonging to the two council members who supported plans for the development?"

Gardiner stiffened and sat up straighter, uncrossing his feet. "Certainly not. The idea's preposterous. I have no idea who was responsible for that or even if they are members of Kmag. I gather the police were not able to identify the perpetrators."

"So I understand. But clearly there are people out there with very strong feelings on the issue. You said the public meeting was lively. Do you remember anyone in particular who was strongly opposed to the plans?"

"No. I can't say I do. We didn't ask people to identify themselves when they spoke – we thought it might put them off. But there were probably half a dozen or so who spoke more than once and were very angry about it."

"Would your committee colleagues know who they were?"

"Maybe. You'd have to ask them."

“Can you tell us where you were on the morning Mr Shelford died: Monday 10th January, say between eight and nine o’clock?”

“Good heavens. Probably.” He pulled his smartphone out of his pocket and tapped the screen a couple of times. “On my way to see a client in London.”

“And the morning of Tuesday 20th December last?”

“Good grief, Sergeant.” He tapped away at his phone. “At the garage having my car serviced.”

“All morning?”

“Yes. I was booked in for nine o’clock. I took a report with me which I needed to study and had coffee in their waiting area. I didn’t get home till lunch time.” He looked at them, his expression a mixture of annoyance and amusement. “Is there anything else?”

“Not at the moment, sir, thank you.”

As they drove off, Tom remarked: “Well, at least his alibis seem watertight.”

His behaviour earlier still rankled and she could not resist the bitchy response. “More than we can say for you, Tom.”

Chapter 10

The next day, DCI Upwood led the evening briefing, sitting casually on the table in front of his team. He'd taken his jacket off. The meeting room was even stuffier when the heating had been on all day. His eyes were clear, hazel, under slightly hooded lids and there were tiny wrinkles at the corners. His brown hair was flecked with grey, cut short and swept back without parting. A good-looking man in an unshowy sort of way. Generally even-tempered, his anger had all the more impact on those unfortunate enough to be on the receiving end. No one took liberties with him. Morton perched on the other end of the table.

Upwood started by relaying the results of the post mortem carried out on the victim in the barn. "We can confirm he was male, as we suspected. Caucasian. They estimate he was between five foot ten and six feet in height based on the length of the leg bones, but the extensive damage caused by the fire makes it impossible to be more precise. We have only a poor estimation of weight, for the same reason, but are told that he may have weighed seventy to eighty kilos. Based on bone development it is thought he was eighteen to twenty years old.

"There was no evidence of any damage to the skull such as might be associated with blunt force trauma, nor was there evidence of sharp force trauma elsewhere on the skeleton. Carbon particles found in his air passages and carbon monoxide levels in his blood indicate that he was alive when the fire started. The conclusion is that he died of asphyxiation and was burned post mortem." He took a sip of water from the glass on the table beside him.

"Why did he not escape the barn before the fire took hold?" This question came from Margaret Starr, for whom it was the first such death she had encountered.

"Most often if people die in fires it is because they are asleep, drunk or drugged."

"So it's likely he was out of it before the arsonist started his preparations and the arsonist didn't see him. Or somehow he got into the barn later and didn't see the candles. A bit strange."

"It is. We're still awaiting the results of the analysis of the stomach contents. We may have a better idea then. Mo, how are we doing with the house to house enquiries?"

"We've had to re-interview everyone we'd already seen, which didn't make us very popular I have to say. And we've widened our search parameters. The arsonist may have driven to and from the barn on the night of the fire, but he may have gone there on foot. If he was on foot, he may not have used the road. He could have parked in the cul-de-sac at the bottom of Duck Lane which leads from the centre of the village to the allotments on the south side. It is perfectly possible to walk through the allotments, across a field and enter the Orchard Farm plot at the back.

"We think it is most likely that if it was the arsonist who left the Mitsubishi in the barn he would have left on foot. If he was also the driver responsible for Fred Shelford's death then he is likely to have reached the barn between eight thirty and nine in the morning. So everyone who lives or works close to the routes that might have been taken on the day of Fred's death and the night of the fire is being interviewed. It's taking a heck of a long time and so far, we've got sod all out of it."

Morton turned to the Crime Scene Manager, Penny Fordham. At six feet tall, she was not heavy, but muscular. Her face had a classical look, handsome rather than conventionally beautiful. Her most remarkable feature was her hair, which was pure white, cut very short. Given that she was only thirty-six years of age, it gave her a striking appearance. She had long since given up rising to the bait 'Penny for 'em?'. "Penny, your team have been searching the plot and the possible cross-country route. Have you found anything that might help us?"

"We're still on it. There's a badger sett at the bottom of the orchard and there are what appear to be a couple of tracks that they use regularly. They are overgrown in places because of bramble and other scrub growth, but someone might move along them carefully. But there is another path which is a bit wider and more open. If someone had walked along it there might be very little evidence of flattened grass or twigs broken off the undergrowth."

"That sounds a bit too convenient for our arsonist surely. How would he even know of the existence of such tracks?"

"Actually it's not as far-fetched as you think. The bigger path is used by kids from the village to scrump fruit in the autumn. So far, though, we haven't found any trace evidence that looks very promising."

"What about forensics from the barn and the immediate area?"

"We've got masses of stuff we need to examine. Most of it will be of no use at all. We think kids have also been getting into the barn since the house burned down, judging by the empty alcopop cans. But two items are of interest. Firstly, we found a very dirty but evidently new padlock in the pile of burnt timbers which had formed the door."

"Which suggests that someone might have been locking the barn recently?"

"I'd say so, yes."

"And the other item of interest?"

"A ring, close to the body. A men's pinky ring. It has the symbol of a double-headed eagle. It looks like silver – certainly it's white metal – but it doesn't have a British hallmark. Almost certainly foreign."

"A trinket bought on holiday perhaps? Or might it tell us something about the origins of our victim?"

"The latter, for my money. That's what I'd look at. One fact may interest you. Although we found a few coins, a belt buckle and other odds and ends we did not find any key of any description in the immediate vicinity of the body."

Morton asked for questions and one came from the back of the room. "If the barn was locked, how did the victim get in?"

"You heard Penny say that they think children had been getting in. It's quite likely there was a gap in a wall somewhere."

"Where were the alcopop cans found in relation to the body?"

"In the other corner at the same end of the barn, at the back."

"Might they've been the victim's?"

"It's possible – Penny, any thoughts?"

"The lab may be able to shed some light when they've finished examining them. There's nothing we found to tell us either way."

The meeting broke up. The house to house teams would continue to work over the weekend, as would some of the support staff. Morton advised the remainder to get a good rest. As he slid off the table he felt his trousers snag on a splinter. No doubt Emma would give him hell when he got home.

Chapter 11

When Mo went into the office the next day he was surprised to see Margaret there. “Hi. What on earth are you doing here? You know there’s no overtime for you today?”

She looked up and laughed. Mo was tall with coffee coloured skin, thick, jet black hair and moustache, and a permanent six o’clock shadow which he sometimes allowed to develop into a well-trimmed beard. He also had arresting black eyes. In short, he was a very handsome man.

“I know. But I really am not in the mood for laundry. If I stayed in and didn’t do it I’d feel guilty. And I’d have been watching endless news reports looping round banging on about Andy Coulson’s resignation and phone hacking. Boooring! Anyway I wanted to do some internet research.”

“But you could do that at home surely?”

“Yeah, but it’s better here. If I find anything interesting I can bookmark it and read it again another time. Anyway, why are you in?” She leant back on her chair, accepting that she had been well and truly interrupted.

“Give you one guess.”

“Paperwork.”

He laughed, showing naturally pearly white teeth. She thanked the good Lord he didn’t actually whiten them – he’d look too much like a bandit on an American TV show.

“Bingo. I only ever manage to make inroads into it when the office is quiet. How are you for coffee? I’m just getting one.”

“Great. Black without please.” She passed him her mug.

“Mercy. Please tell me that’s not yours!”

“’Fraid so.”

“You’re a Taekwondo Black Belt?”

“Yep.”

"Bloody hell. Whatever got you into that?"

"It was at college. A lot of us got into it for self-protection."

"But you got all the way to black belt?"

"Yep. But don't worry, I haven't got to the top in black belt rankings. On the other hand, I could certainly take you down given half a chance." There was a slight smile on her face, as cryptic as Mona Lisa's, but her eyes conveyed a challenge.

He looked thoughtful. "You're too small."

"What d'you mean? Too small to get a black belt, or too small to take you down?"

"Both really."

"It's technique, not body mass." Her tone of voice conveyed conviction.

He thought about it. "I s'pose so. Do you still do it?"

"No. Not really. I still belong to the club, but you know what it's like. This job plays havoc with your social life." She looked at him. "Where are you from?"

"Well that's one way of changing the conversation. With my accent? You must be joking." It was his turn to laugh.

"Don't mess about. Where are your family from originally? Or am I not supposed to ask that these days?"

"Doesn't worry me in the slightest. They came from Madurai in southern India – a Tamil family."

"As in Tamil Tigers?"

"Not really. They were an insurgent group who wanted to create an independent state in Sri Lanka. Anyway, I'm third generation. My parents westernised very quickly. I'm Liverpool born and bred. Never been further east than Istanbul."

"Istanbul? I've never fancied it."

"My parents went, back in the late seventies. This time of year. It snowed. They loved it. Apparently, the city was full of old Ambassador cars. It's why I wanted to go. I've always loved the Amby. Such a daft looking car. It was practically a classic when they went, but it's still being made in India now." By this stage Mo was beginning to realise that he may have lost her. Her eyes had glazed and she had started doodling again.

"Is Mo your real name?"

"No. It's Aamodin. I got bullied something rotten at school. Half the time they were asking if I'd got the trots. Then some miserable little bugger found out what the name means."

"And?"

"Fragrant. You can imagine how that went down with a load of scouse kids."

"Oh shit."

"Precisely. And if you pass that along to any of the miserable buggers here you're in dead trouble. Why am I even telling you all this?"

"Because I'm a good listener?"

"Oh yeah. Right."

She giggled. "I'll keep mum. Promise." She giggled again.

"Anyway, go on, tell me what it is you're so interested in finding out?"

"The pinky ring." She shoved the photos of the ring found in the barn fire across the desk. "Low grade white metal, foreign silver probably. And look at the distinctive shoulders on the band. And the double-headed eagle."

"What d'you reckon then?"

"There's lots of countries associated with those eagles. Russia, Serbia, Montenegro and Albania. In fact they are associated with all kinds of stuff: Orthodox Christianity, some German, British and Spanish cities. But this example is very distinctive. And it is definitely Albanian. I'm positive.

"I reckon he was an illegal. Remember they picked up a few outside Bury St Edmunds before Christmas? They'd come into Orford Ness. Maybe this one got away."

"What, and was sleeping rough?"

"Why not? It's as good a theory as any."

"You're not just a pretty face, are you? Or am I not supposed to ask that these days?" They both laughed. Mo looked at her and wondered how it was he had not realised before what an attractive woman she was. Long, deep golden, almost bronze, hair, a little shapeless it was true, framed a heart-shaped face. Often when she was at work her hair was tied back but today it fell loose. It suited her much better. Dark eyes sparkled when she laughed and dimples appeared either side of plump lips. She wore no make-up and didn't really need to. "So what next?"

"Well I can't do much more before I report my findings at Monday morning's briefing. But I think we should see if we can interview the detainees. What Penny didn't say at the meeting is that there is an inscription inside the ring: PLD. It could be his initials. And I found a site on Google that says there is a recognised grade of silver in Albania called 'jewellery grade'. It's lower quality – I mean there is less silver in the alloy than you'd find in English silver, for example."

"Looks like the best lead we've got so far. Let's hope it pans out. Otherwise we'll be trying to track all the other illegals who've already run into the undergrowth. Complete waste of time probably."

Mo decided to try his luck. "Do you fancy a drink at lunchtime? I need something to look forward to after dealing with all the shit on my desk."

She thought about it for a moment. What the hell. "Put like that, how could I possibly refuse?"

Chapter 12

Sunday morning dawned with a hazy blue sky. Hoar frost shimmered in the reeds and grasses. Upwood was out early on the Ouse Washes in his warmest clothing. The land between the Old and New Bedford Rivers was, as was usual at this time of year, under water. In summer it drained and provided valuable grazing for cattle. Now it was Wigeon grazing the river banks. The males in breeding plumage were easily identified by their pink breast, chestnut head and yellow forehead. He delighted in seeing them year round – very occasionally a pair might breed – but January was just about the best month to see them in large numbers. Today he estimated that the flocks he was watching might number a couple of thousand, with the potential for ten times that number across the whole area.

Whooper Swans, winter migrants from Iceland, together with the smallest of the three species, Bewick's, from northern Europe, heavily outnumbered the native Mute Swan. Feeding in neighbouring fields by day, they returned to roost on the shallow waters of the washes. Dusk was one of the best times to see them. This was a sight Upwood would miss today. He had too much to do.

There were plenty of other ducks to be seen, Tufted, Mallard, Pintails, Shovelers, Gadwall. He had hoped to see raptors: Peregrines, Hen Harriers and Merlin were a possibility. Today they were not around, but he first heard the 'ping' of, and then saw, a fine Bearded Tit. The striking male, with its long tail, chestnut colour and grey head, actually has a long moustache, rather than a beard. And it isn't a member of the tit family. No matter, it was a pleasure to see it.

By the time he reached home he was in a much more relaxed frame of mind than he had been in the last few days. As the key turned in his front door he heard his landline ringing. Just as he'd put his bins down it stopped. Sod's law. He took off his gloves and dialled 1471. Tempting as it was to ignore, duty and habit kicked in. No sooner had he dialled it than his mobile rang. He put the cordless handset down and fished inside his jacket for his mobile. He was astonished to see that the caller was Katie Melhuish. He had not heard from her for more than two years. She had last called him before her employer, one of the big four, transferred her to Madrid. Before that, she had been instrumental in persuading him to investigate the suspicious death of her partner. After a very frustrating enquiry they had established that Mark had been murdered. Those responsible were now guests of Her Majesty, and likely to remain so for some considerable time.

"Katie. What a surprise. How lovely to hear from you. Where are you?" His surprise was tinged with nervousness. They had been close at one time, when she was still grieving Mark's death. Upwood had provided her with much needed comfort and they had briefly become lovers. In fact, he had come very close to falling in love with her.

"James. Hello again. I'm home. But I badly need your advice."

"What's the problem?"

"I'm getting threatening messages. On my mobile."

"What sort of messages?"

"Really nasty. And they refer to you too. Can we meet? It's beginning to frighten me."

"I think we'd better. When suits you?" Upwood tried to keep his tone as neutral as he could but had a nasty suspicion this might not end well.

"The sooner the better."

"Today?"

"Please, if you can. Can you come over? I don't want to talk about this in a pub."

"Give me an hour to sort some stuff out here. Say two?"

"That's fine. Thank you. See you then."

Upwood ended the call and wondered what the devil she would have to say to him.

Turning into the drive of Angelica House, Katie's home on the banks of the Gt Ouse in Oterham, brought memories flooding back for Upwood. It was here her partner, Mark Campion, had been found dead, strapped into the car in his garage, apparently killed by carbon monoxide fumes. After the trial was over, Katie could not decide what to do with the house, and had accepted a posting to Barcelona for a few months. And that was followed by her last posting, to Madrid. Now she was home again, but for how long?

She opened the door to him. Was it his imagination or had that lovely auburn hair lost a little of its lustre? Certainly she looked under strain, her skin dull with dark patches under her eyes. Those remarkable eyes, brown irises ringed with violet, looked apprehensive. She stood back to let him in, neither quite sure what the protocol was. In the end, he took the initiative and kissed her briefly on the cheek.

"What, no flowers James?" She attempted a smile but her eyes were moist.

"No. We can't have the ritual floods of tears", he replied as light-heartedly as he could. Flowers had taken her by surprise more than once in his experience.

"Tea?"

"I think so. It's way too early for anything stronger." They went into the kitchen and she switched the kettle on. He stood and watched her. She was wearing her trade-mark cashmere jumper in a very pale shade of lemon with navy trousers. She preferred classic, well cut clothes even when she dressed casually and they showed her figure off to perfection. His heart lurched for a moment.

"When did you get back?"

"Just before Christmas. A mistake. I should have stayed on. At least I have friends there I could have spent time with. Coming back here was grim."

"What about Melanie and George?" Mercifully Upwood managed to dredge up the names of practically the only friends she had locally.

"They were on a cruise."

"So. A quiet Christmas then."

"And New Year."

They went through to the drawing room. The blue sky was still clear and it was one of those rare days when the river took on its colour. Even though the level was high – the early part of the month had seen higher than average rainfall and the floodplain on the far side was under water – the flow was quite lazy. He did as he had almost invariably done when going into the room. He went straight to the patio doors and looked out. The view was spectacular.

After a while they sat down.

"Tell me about the messages. When did they start?"

"In the New Year when I went back to work."

"And what did they say?"

"Well some were calls, but nobody spoke. Then I started getting text messages. The first said I should be very careful using public transport. Accidents could so easily happen."

"I see." And he did. Katie could have lost her life during the investigation into Mark's death when someone pushed her towards an oncoming tube train.

"Then the next one said I should stop using open fires at home. Accidents could so easily happen, especially in a timber-framed house."

He nodded. "And were there more?"

"The last one was yesterday. It said I should be careful who I sleep with. Not all publicity is good publicity. Especially for high ranking police officers."

"Oh Christ." The implications could be catastrophic. "Did you delete the messages?"

"No. Well, I did the first one. Then I thought maybe I should leave them. Do you want to see?"

"Please." She handed over the phone.

"Number withheld. We should be able to get round that. Can you let me hang onto this? Get yourself a new one tomorrow. Don't let your firm put the new number in any internal directory. Don't have it on your business cards. Give it out only to people whom you absolutely trust."

"We know who's behind this, don't we?"

"It sounds like MacKay. Bastard. There is something deeply unpleasant about the man. Not least the fact he killed Mark of course."

"The tube attack was in the public domain. Anyone looking at the house would guess it's timber frame. But how does he know about us?" Anxiety was plain to see on her face.

"I know we went separately, but someone might have followed you to Southwold and seen us there. That was just after the attack. But I seriously doubt anyone followed us to Yorkshire. That was months later."

"But why would anyone follow me, or us?"

"Not sure. Maybe the idea was to have another go at you." Instantly he regretted the words he'd used.

"To kill me?" Katie's voice took on a higher pitch as colour flooded her cheeks.

"No, I don't think so." In fact, Upwood was by no means certain, but he didn't want Katie to become even more anxious than she already was. "No, I think maybe to frighten you. To make you stop looking for Mark's killer. Did you get any malicious calls or messages before these?"

"No. I didn't. I've been wondering about that."

"You've been out of the country virtually the whole time since the trial, of course. That would have made it difficult to reach you. You weren't likely to use your English phone. Can you think how he might know you're back?"

"Easy. I've been made up to partner. There was a brief report in the evening paper."

"Is this the same number you had before?"

"No."

"So how might he get your number? Would someone at the office have given it out?"

"I don't know. I suppose it's possible. Presumably someone has smuggled a phone into Whitemoor Prison?"

"It has been known to happen." His answer suggested that the incidence of ownership of mobiles by prison inmates was low. The cynical tone of voice indicated otherwise. And he knew for a fact that the previous year some 4 per cent of that prison's population were found to have mobiles and/or SIM cards, a percentage he felt sure would rise.

"Can you stop it, James?"

"The calls? Probably. I don't think you should worry about it. If he was planning anything more sinister he probably wouldn't mess about with threatening messages. He's probably just amusing himself at your expense."

"Sick. Sick. Really sick."

"Did you ever get a burglar alarm system installed?"

"No."

"Do, just to be on the safe side. Katie, I'm sorry. I'm going to have to go now. I promised Anne's parents I'd help them with something this evening. I don't want to let them down. Since her sister moved to South Africa I'm the closest thing they have to family in the area now."

"I was hoping you'd stay for supper."

"I can't. Really. But I'll come round tomorrow evening if you like and tell you if we've made any progress."

Upwood left feeling distinctly uneasy. He wasn't just nervous for Katie, but anxious that if details of their affair, brief as it had been, became known he could be in a shitload of trouble.

Chapter 13

Upwood drove into the city the next morning after a very poor night's sleep. He'd found it difficult to pay sufficient attention to his former in-laws' problems the night before and Katie's revelations had shaken him. He also had a shitty journey – unexpectedly low temperatures had caught those responsible on the back foot – the roads were icy and had not been gritted. In consequence there had been an accident on the A1303 west of the city, creating a large tailback. As usual the drivers who were stuck were not feeling generous enough to allow vehicles to feed in from his road out of Madingley.

It was little wonder he found it hard to concentrate on the morning's briefing. But concentrate he must, as the case they were working on had few promising lines of enquiry. Fortunately some progress was being made. The lab had reported that the paint samples so carefully removed from Fred's Land Rover did match the model of Mitsubishi burnt out in the barn.

In the end it was Margaret's contribution that engaged his attention fully.

She explained her theory that the victim in the barn was an Albanian illegal immigrant. She had copies of illustrations of double-headed eagles from a range of national and other flags. She had blown up a photo of the ring so that everyone could see the very distinctive shape of the bird, particularly its wings and tail. The likeness with the image of the bird on the Albanian flag was indisputable.

She went on to demonstrate her theory that the ring was indeed silver, albeit less pure than jewellery silver was in the UK.

Her proposition that the young man might have been an illegal immigrant was based partly on the fact that no key of any kind had been found close to his body. Why would someone be out of doors with no keys?

She reminded them of the arrest in Suffolk of the Albanian men just before Christmas and suggested they might be interviewed. She told them that the EU had relaxed their laws the previous month, giving Albanians freedom of movement through the Schengen area. This had apparently sparked a big increase in the numbers trying to cross mainland Europe to reach England.

Her final idea was that the various Anglo/Albanian networks might be asked to contact them if they knew of anyone who had worn a ring with the initials PLD engraved inside the band.

Upwood was not the only one impressed. She had transferred out of uniform a few years before and while she didn't make such a noise as some of her colleagues, showed tremendous enthusiasm and was more than happy to put the extra hours in. She'd been one of the first officers attending when the body of Katie's partner had been found. He expressed appreciation for her efforts and the fact that she had come in on Saturday to do her research. Her observation that she had never been any good at ironing met with general laughter.

Mo reported that the house to house team had come up with a couple of people whom they wanted to interview, generally referred to as TIEs, since the goal was to Trace, Interview and Eliminate people from a category that might include the offender, or fail to, as the case might be. One woman walking her golden retriever said she had had a brief exchange with a man on the path to the allotment. He was on his own and said his dog had run off and he was looking for it. She was sure it was the morning of Fred's death because it had been so cold and foggy. A resident in one of the neighbouring streets thought he had passed someone on a bicycle who was heading for Chilton just as he was leaving the village to his job on the industrial estate in Knapton. This incident took place on the same morning. So far, they had made no progress in identifying either of them. The fact that both were well wrapped, the dog walker with a beanie hat and scarf and the cyclist with a hood, made getting clear descriptions very difficult. The only potentially useful observation was that the man looking for his dog had protruding eyes.

Chapter 14

Upwood asked Morton to join him in his office. "Do you remember Katie Melhuish?"

Morton laughed. "How could I not, Sir? The delectable Katie. Why do you ask?"

"She recently returned from Spain and since she's got back she's had a series of particularly unpleasant and malicious text messages."

Morton laughed again. "And her first thought was to call you was it, Sir? Why am I not surprised?"

"Sod it, Morton. This is serious. The messages suggest that she is at personal risk."

"Oh, Christ." Morton sighed. He'd long thought Katie had the capacity to create trouble, even if unwittingly.

Upwood relayed Katie's story and handed Morton the mobile phone. When he had read the final message he looked at Upwood. "And did you, Sir? Sleep with her?"

"Yes."

"Shit. Fuck. You stupid bugger. What were you thinking of? I knew you fancied her but, honestly, I thought you had more sense." He slouched back in his chair, a look of incredulity on his face.

Upwood recognised that this criticism from his junior officer was entirely justified. He smiled ruefully. "A very difficult woman to resist, Morton."

They sat without speaking for a minute, looking at each other.

"And you're asking me to help sort this mess out, I suppose?"

"Yes."

"And no doubt discreetly."

"As far as that's possible."

"Jesus wept." Silence hung heavily in the room.

Upwood maintained a calm demeanour although he was by no means comfortable. His was a big ask of Morton. "I think we can be fairly certain that MacKay is behind it, even if he didn't send the messages himself. Get the number of the caller traced and track down the phone. And what was the name of the book-keeper? The one MacKay blackmailed into giving him an alibi? See if she's had any messages since he's been inside."

"But why would he target her for heaven's sake?"

"The man's bored. Too much time on his hands. He's angry. Maybe he just wants to make life miserable for those who helped put him away. Come on. Get a move on. The sooner we can clear this up the better. Not just for Katie's sake. We just don't need this kind of distraction. Not in the middle of a big case like this."

"This is going to be a bugger." Morton was thoroughly pissed off. Partly because his boss had behaved like an idiot. But more because he was now putting him in a very difficult position.

Upwood felt badly at having asked Morton to help. But he trusted him. He was sensible and discreet. He'd matured a lot in the last few years, shaken off the rugger bugger attitude he had sometimes shown when he was younger and still playing. His wife had been good for him, too. She was actually a couple of years older than him, extremely good-looking and a very accomplished artist. She specialised in animal portraits and made a good living from it while still managing to bring up their baby girl. He could scarcely bring himself to ask Morton how she was doing. The child was now the age at which Upwood's own daughter had died in mysterious and tragic circumstances.

That evening Upwood went back to Angelica House. They had supper in the kitchen as they had done on previous occasions. He told her that he had asked Morton to deal with the problem as quickly and discreetly as possible. Then he invited her to tell him what she'd been up to in Madrid.

She had enjoyed her assignment. He had not realised that she had grown up there nor that it was where she had met Melanie. They had both attended the same international school. Katie had studied there throughout her secondary education. Melanie had studied there for two terms on an exchange programme.

With her long association with the city, Katie probably felt as much at home there as she did anywhere. She certainly didn't feel rooted any more in her present home.

"I really didn't know whether to keep the house. Half the time I wanted to leave, because it was where Mark died. But then the other half I wanted to stay because we shared some good times here."

"So what's changed? Just the fact you have been away so much?"

"No. It's not that. It's having had tenants in. I can't say they were bad, because they weren't. I can't explain it. It's a kind of violation. It doesn't feel the same somehow. Anyway. It's too big."

"Where will you look? Have you given it any thought?"

"Probably in town, I think. I feel very exposed out here."

"Cambridge? Or d'you mean London?"

"Cambridge. It's where I'm based again and there's no reason why I can't maintain an office there in my new role."

Upwood was relieved. Now was hardly the time to rekindle the brief affair they'd had. But who knew? Maybe in time they could enjoy each other's company again.

He drove home thinking about the problem the text messages posed. Without question it would be deeply embarrassing if it became known. The Professional Standards Unit could become involved. The red tops would love it. To say that it could be damaging to his career was a massive understatement. He decided that he would do well to speak to his Superintendent before matters got out of hand. Her support might be crucial. He hoped to God she'd give it.

Chapter 15

Upwood woke from a short and fitful sleep to hear his mobile ringing. Cursing, he raised himself on one elbow and reached out to the bedside table. Inevitably all he managed to do was knock the wretched thing onto the floor. He sat up, reached out and grabbed it before it stopped ringing. There was a house fire on the outskirts of Chilton with the likelihood that the householder was trapped inside. It was just short of midnight.

Forty minutes later he was on site. The night was cold and overcast, with a breeze that seemed to penetrate even the warmest of clothes. It shivered through leafless branches giving Upwood a fleeting impression of countless small, unidentifiable creatures rustling through undergrowth. He was numb within minutes. Morton had arrived before him and was already beyond numb, although Emma had at least had the sense to tell him to take a flask of coffee with him. He offered some to his boss. Upwood thanked him but shook his head. "Later maybe."

Senior Fire Officer Jack Forbes was once again in charge. Upwood introduced himself and was somewhat embarrassed to be reminded that they had in fact met once before. He apologised. "What can you tell us?"

"Not a lot yet. Like the last one, we think this probably started about eleven pm. We're not sure it's arson but I didn't want to risk your losing valuable time if we called it in too late. We don't have big fires very often. Occasionally a workshop goes up on an industrial estate – often insurance cases – but we don't get many house fires that get such a good grip as this one. We haven't been able to get in to look for any casualties. Generally we can get the accidental ones out quite quickly. It's the fact that it comes so soon after the arson on the other side of the village that I don't like."

Upwood nodded. Like all experienced police officers, he didn't like coincidences. This might prove to be a coincidence only of location. Time would tell. They talked for a few more minutes and then Upwood left, leaving Morton to make sure that arrangements to secure and protect the site were adequate. He went home and managed to get off to sleep on his sofa just one hour before the alarm on his mobile went off at six o'clock.

Back in the office he left a message on his Superintendent's phone asking for an urgent meeting and got stuck into his paperwork until she responded.

Detective Superintendent Emily Adams had been in post longer than Upwood. He was grateful for it. She was one of only a small number of the most senior officers in the Cambridgeshire Constabulary who knew about the death of his infant daughter and the suicide of his wife. It was the second of those tragedies which had prompted his move to Cambridge.

She smiled at him as he entered her office. It was bright and benefited from windows on two sides. On the top floor, it was higher up than his own and gave her an even finer view over Parker's Piece. A little older than Upwood, she was of medium height and build but nonetheless commanded attention. Her clothes were understated but smart: navy blue jacket and skirt with a cream blouse. She wore no jewellery apart from a wedding band. "What can I do for you James? It had better be good – I am up to my eyes. Problems with one of your cases?"

"No. Something entirely different. And it gives me a personal problem."

She put down the pen she had been fiddling with and looked at him with interest. "Go on."

"Do you remember the murder case a few years ago? Mark Campion. Rigged up to look like suicide."

"Vaguely. I do recall that you secured convictions but that's about all. Why is it an issue now?"

"The victim's partner has just started getting malicious text messages from someone. I'm fairly sure the sender is Andrew MacKay, Campion's killer."

"So? It's hardly an MIT issue surely? And why does it give you a personal problem?"

Upwood told her about the last message.

"Christ Almighty, James. Are you telling me that you slept with her?"

"Yes. I'm sorry, Emily." He looked suitably chastened.

She got up and paced towards the side window. They could both hear the faint sound of sirens as fire engines shot out onto the street from the nearby station, evidently on yet another call. She watched them for a moment and then turned back to glare at him. "What on earth possessed you to do anything so fucking stupid?" Upwood tensed. It was rare for her to raise her voice, never mind swear. "She must have been a suspect at some stage surely?"

"I won't say we didn't consider it because we did. If the Policy File showed that we hadn't done we would certainly have come in for criticism. But we couldn't find a shred of evidence. No opportunity and no credible motive. We eliminated her at a very early stage."

"Even so. And this happened while the investigation was still in progress?"

"I slept with her once while it was still ongoing. And once more after MacKay and his accomplice were charged."

She strode back to her desk and sat down. "I despair. Your record and conduct here have been exemplary. Why would you jeopardise that?" She glared at him. He kept his counsel. "Don't tell me. She's attractive." She let out a long sigh.

He drew a deep breath. "She is. She was also deeply traumatised by the death of her partner and by what we considered at the time to be a deliberate attempt to kill her. She has very few friends in England and came to see me as someone who could offer her some protection. A shoulder to cry on."

"If she was deeply traumatised it's even more reason why you shouldn't have had a relationship with her", she shot back.

"I know. I know what you're thinking. But it really wasn't like that. We both knew that it wasn't a full-blown affair. In other circumstances I should have been happy for it to develop. But we talked about it and I was confident that I was not hurting her."

"The arrogance of you men is beyond me. Are you suggesting that she seduced you?" There was a definite challenge in the look on her face. His answer took her by surprise.

"She did as it happens." There was a sharp intake of breath from Emily. "But I am not blaming her. I created the opportunity when I arranged for her to spend a few days at Southwold after she was nearly pushed under the tube train. I went too. But I was in a hotel. She was in a cottage outside the town. I only slept with her once. But I have to say the attraction was mutual. She was alone." He paused. "And there are times when my own loneliness is almost more than I can bear." It took a great effort on his part to make such an admission. He had certainly not done so to her before. She looked at him, shocked to the core.

"I knew it was wrong from a professional point of view. In terms of personal ethics, I don't lose sleep over it and I'm perfectly sure Katie doesn't. But I made sure it didn't happen again…"

"Until it did", she snapped.

"Yes, until it did. But it was months later. By then there was absolutely no doubt in my mind that we had the right people in custody charged with her partner's murder."

"It's still not right." She stood up and paced backwards and forwards. Upwood kept quiet. She sat down again and stared at him intently. "What have you done about the malicious texts?"

Upwood breathed a mental sigh of relief that she had moved the conversation on. "I've asked DI Harrison to look into it."

“So he knows the full story?”

“The essential facts, yes.”

“And does anyone else? Here I mean.”

“No. Not to the best of my knowledge. If asked, Morton will say that we do not know the identity of the senior officer.” Upwood did not feel too guilty about admitting this. Certainly it would be no help to him if the news broke, but it would reflect badly on the force too, even if the allegations could not be proved.

“What happens now?”

She stood up. “Lord knows, James. Go away. Bugger off. I need to think about this.”

Chapter 16

When Upwood reached his office he was feeling anxious and depressed. News that a body had been found in the house fire at Chilton simply added to his woes. It was assumed to be Patrick Waldorf, who rented the cottage. Checks had quickly confirmed that the car on the drive outside the cottage belonged to Narbor Renewables. Waldorf had been their Project Manager for the proposed King's Mere Wind Farm development.

The Incident Room was already close to bursting point. Even more than usual it had that stale air of a room too often crowded with tired, sweaty bodies and fast food. Upwood could only be thankful that smoking was no longer allowed. His usual team members were there and DS Debra Graf and DC Tom Turner, along with others, had already been drafted in. If this new case was to be linked to the others, thc resourcing problems would be immense.

Debra was tackling her own pile of paperwork when Mo came in. "OK. I give in. What's the Weetabix League when it's at home?"

She laughed. "A youth league for football. I used to play in it until I moved up to the adult league. And then I carried on. I absolutely loved it."

"You're not still playing now, right?" The look on Mo's face was a picture.

"No. I played competitively for more than twenty years. I started getting too many injuries. Then a lot of my mates married and started having children and dropped out. So I gave up."

"I've never heard of it."

"Well it's not your patch is it? It's one of the Northants' leagues. Weetabix is a local company."

"Northants? It's a foreign country."

"It's not so far from here. Long way from the Mersey, I'll give you that."

"Is it serious, this women's league stuff then?"

"It is if you're involved. Trust me."

"So what's with the mug? Have you seen Margaret's? Black belt in Taekwondo. Why do you lot have to brag about this stuff?"

"Not bragging. Just saying don't mess with us." She smiled but the challenge was there with her too. Mo wandered back to his own desk, a chipped coffee mug bearing no message of any kind in his hand.

By late afternoon word came in that accelerant had been found in the cottage fire. And candle wax. Upwood asked for another urgent meeting with his Super.

"James, I told you to sod off this morning. What do you want now?" Emily was clearly in no better mood than when he had left her.

"Another aggravated arson. Another body. In the same village as the barn fire."

"Oh, Christ Almighty. What have we done to deserve this?" There was no answer to that question. "The cases are linked of course?"

"They have to be. Petrol used as an accelerant in both cases. Candles used as timing devices for multiple seats of fire."

"Serial pyromaniac?"

"Maybe. But there is one very disturbing feature. The latest victim was the project manager for the wind farm planned by the family of the man who drowned in what we believe was a hit and run. There's the possibility that someone is trying very hard to make sure that the project never gets off the ground."

Emily considered the idea. To her it seemed preposterous that someone should commit murder – two, if not three, murders – just because they disapproved of wind farms. The idea was absolutely extraordinary.

"So you are asking me formally to sanction the linking of this case with the other two?"

"We've got no option." They faced each other. "Where does that leave us with the matter we discussed this morning?"

"Oh, bloody hell James. You put me in an impossible position. I really don't like it. I still haven't made up my mind. You've told me what enquiries and checks are being made. Naturally it's far too early for any results. But it means more people are involved which makes me feel very uncomfortable. At least assure me there have been no leaks about the text messages."

"Not that we've picked up. I think it's containable. MacKay has to be behind it. It shouldn't take long to trace the connection between him and the phone. Once we have identified the sender we can consider charging him with malicious communications or harassment. Honestly, I don't think it will take too long."

"Have you considered that the sender might have proof of your affair with Katie?"

"Yes. But I think it's unlikely. If someone followed us to Southwold they should know that we were staying in different places. And the night we made love there was an almighty storm blowing. Even if they'd been watching the cottage there's no way they could have got photographs of us. If they took one of us leaving the next morning, we could argue that I stayed the night because the weather was so bad. It is a two bedroomed house. I don't believe for a minute we were followed to Yorkshire."

"But photos of you leaving the cottage could be pretty damaging."

"But not incriminating. In any case I think it's more likely that he saw us having a drink in a local pub and just made a guess." Upwood was trying to convince himself as much as her. "I hate to press you, Emily, but we do need a decision on the linking of these investigations. Urgently."

"And the announcement of who will lead them. Dammit. You're the strongest member of my team. You'll have to be OIOC."

"But what will you do about Standards?"

She sighed. "I won't pass it over to them. I hope to God they never get to hear of it. If they do I will have to support you and defend my position. I do understand how hard it must have been to lose your wife and child. I'm not inhuman. But the timing stinks."

"I know, Emily. Thank you. I'm sorry I've let you down."

"Tell Morton to deal directly with me over this phone business. He's to come to me if he needs authorisation for any action. I want daily reports. This has to be sorted as an urgency. You are to stay away from Katie. No phone calls. No emails. No meetings of any kind. For at least six months. Are we clear?"

"Yes. Crystal."

"Let's get on, then, shall we? After this latest fire we'll have to have a press conference. Ask Jan to put out the briefest report tonight will you, saying there'll be a conference at ten tomorrow? And for God's sake make sure you give me something sensible to say."

Chapter 17

The Incident Room was buzzing with activity. Sixteen days after Fred's death. Nine days after the barn fire and one day after the house fire. Some roles in the management team which had previously been combined had now been split because of the excessive workload. Tom and Debra were now trying to identify the victim of the barn fire. The detainees apprehended near Bury St Edmunds had been interviewed with the help of interpreters. One had applied for political asylum claiming that, as a result of a centuries-old feud, his life was at risk. Otherwise he had nothing to say. The other two would not speak at all. The authorities wanted to deport them, but without passports it would be difficult to persuade Albania to accept them, notwithstanding their fluent command of the language. Albanian was a significant minority language in the neighbouring countries of Montenegro, Kosovo and Macedonia, never mind in Romania, Italy and Serbia as well. Now however they had a new lead. Someone had called who might know the identity of PLD.

Debra picked up her jacket. "Let's go and interview her. If we can identify the body it may shed light on whether there was any intention to kill him."

Tom looked at her, a stubborn expression on his face. "Are you sure that's the best use of our time? I thought the post mortem showed that he died of asphyxiation? I doubt the arsonist even knew he was there."

"Don't start arguing again, Tom. It's annoying."

"But I've got too much to do already."

"Can it. We all do. Come on."

She was half way out of the room before he was on his feet. Once in the car, Debra driving, he was sullen. Fine. She didn't mind if he kept quiet during the journey. She was a good driver but preferred to drive in silence.

As usual traffic was heavy leaving the city and it took some time before they reached the northern suburbs. By then it was raining again, not hard, but enough to need wipers on intermittent. Just hard enough to be annoying. Hard enough to make all the other drivers bad tempered. And passengers, too, it seemed.

"Well at least tell me where we're going."

Debra gritted her teeth. "Farlingham."

"You're on the wrong road then. It's in Suffolk."

"No it's not. I think you're thinking of Framlingham. Farlingham is a village north of Chilton, on the other side of the Ouse."

Thirty minutes later they entered the village, sat nav having taken them to the right street. It was lined on either side by small yellow brick cottages, grey with age and pollution. Their slate roofs were embroidered with lichen. Each had a tiny patch in front, none tidy enough to qualify for the title of garden. Some still had walls. In most cases the walls had long since gone and wheelie bins and bikes stood there, the plots not big enough for even a small car. Bits of rubbish skittered along the edges of the road. Mean looking cats beat retreat. As Debra and Tom slammed their car doors, Jackdaws flew off a neighbouring roof, their harsh *chyak chyak* calls disappearing into the distance as they regrouped briefly in trees at the end of the road.

Number 22 definitely lacked kerb appeal. Paint on the front door and windows was flaking, bare wood showing through. Debra rang the bell. A woman in her forties opened the door. She must once have been very beautiful. Her hair was long and loose. Dark eyebrows added emphasis to her large grey eyes. Her lips were full. But life had perhaps treated her unkindly. Her face was prematurely lined and her skin lacked any kind of bloom. She used no make-up but her clothes, while not expensive, were well chosen and flattered her slightly over-weight body.

"Hello. Mrs Lauresha Broad? I'm Detective Sergeant Graf and this is DC Turner. May we come in?" She smiled reassuringly.

"Yes do."

The front room was small and cramped, with too much furniture, the pieces ill-matched and shabby. It was however clean and Debra was glad to realise that Mrs Broad was not one to use artificial fresheners as a substitute for fresh air.

"Mrs Broad. Thank you for telephoning us. I understand that you may know whose initials are PLD?"

Their host nodded. "I can't be sure. But my brother's initials were PLD. His name was Pjetër Lorenc Dushku."

Debra was alarmed. In the notices issued to the Anglo/Albanian networks they had not suggested that the owner was dead. She framed her next question carefully. "I'm sorry. You said 'was'. Has he died recently?"

"Yes. Earlier this month."

"Do you know how he died?" Debra was feeling very confused.

"Cancer. A brain tumour."

"Where did he live?"

"In Albania, our home country. In a village about one hundred kilometres from Tirana."

She had a sudden inspiration. "Did he have any sons?"

"Yes, one. Rajmond."

"How old would he be, do you know?"

Lauresha thought for a moment. "About twenty."

Debra breathed a sigh of relief. "Do you know if he has travelled to England lately?"

"No. Why are you asking me these questions?"

"As you know, we have found a ring with the initials PLD on it. We are trying to identify the person who was wearing it. Might that have been Rajmond?"

"It is possible. Is he in trouble?"

"No, I wouldn't say that Mrs Broad. But we'd like to find him. Does he have family at home who might be able to tell us where he is?"

"His mother, my sister, Agnesa."

"I thought you said Rajmond's father was your brother. Was Agnesa his wife?"

"Of course."

"Thank you. So, as we would say here, she is your sister-in-law?"

"Yes. I am sorry if I confuse you."

"No problem. We just like to get our facts right. Is it possible that we might telephone her? Does she speak English?

"She speaks a little, enough to get by."

"Your English is excellent Mrs Broad. How long have you lived here?"

"More than twenty years. I married an Englishman."

"Would you mind calling her to ask if she knows where Rajmond is?"

"She'll think it very odd. I didn't even go to my brother's funeral. We don't get on very well. She'll want to know why I'm calling."

Debra tried once more her best reassuring smile. "Why not say that a ring like Rajmond's father's has been found and we wonder whether he has lost it. There's no need to make her anxious. She might not like us to call her directly."

Lauresha nodded. "OK."

"Could we do it now? Would you mind?"

Somewhat unwillingly Lauresha went over to a table near the door and picked up the handset. She dialled. After forty or so seconds she put the handset down again. "There's no answer."

"Would you please try later and let us know if you manage to speak to her, please? It would be such a help."

"Alright. But I'm surprised you're going to such lengths over a ring. It can't be worth much."

Debra did not respond, other than to thank her. She gave her a card and Lauresha promised to call if she managed to speak to Agnesa.

Late in the afternoon Lauresha called. Agnesa confirmed that Rajmond was not at home. He had told his mother that he was going to take time out travelling after his father's death. She didn't know where he was.

Chapter 18

Detective Superintendent Adams and her team received a mauling at the morning press conference. She knew local TV crews and newspaper journalists would be there, but she was not prepared for the onslaught from national TV and press. Jan Murray, the press officer, suspected that someone supporting the wind farm may have started a more active campaign to counter Kmag. Whether Narbor itself would do so she rather doubted. But the stakes were high. She wouldn't rule it out.

The Superintendent had demanded that she be allowed to make her statement before questions were raised. Some attending would not grant that courtesy and bombarded her with questions from the outset, mostly demanding to know whether some kind of serial killer was on the loose. It was never going to be easy. All she could really report was that a second fire had occurred and the occupant of the house lost his life; that they were treating the two fires as linked crimes because of a common modus operandi and that several lines of enquiry were being actively pursued. Beyond that there was little she wanted to say except to appeal once more for the public's help by providing any information, however trivial it might seem. Many of the questions dealt with the issue of whether Fred's death was also being treated as linked to the other crimes, a question she was very reluctant at this stage to answer. But the more she tried to evade the issue the more the reporters challenged her to deny that there had now been three deaths, of which two concerned members of the pro wind farm faction, and two cases of arson in which one of those deaths had occurred. Were there not, therefore, at least three crimes relating to the wind farm? Were the lives of others who supported the wind farm at risk? Were members of the local community safe in their beds?

She held her ground as best she could and shielded Upwood and her other colleagues behind the table from answering questions. She was determined to demonstrate her intention to accept responsibility for the conduct of the investigation, which did her credit.

When the questions became increasingly acrimonious and repetitive, she called the meeting to a halt. She gave an assurance that regular press conferences would be held and that her team would do everything in their power to bring the perpetrators of these crimes to justice.

Upwood had anticipated that the press conference would be tough but he, too, was dismayed at the carnage. He had deliberately delayed the usual morning briefing until after the conference and was glad he had done so. It was important that the team understood the strength of attack they had come under from the press and also recognise how much more difficult it would make their investigation. Many of those whom they had yet to interview would be anxious and it was quite possible that some would be less willing to help the police than they might have been before, however illogical that might be. He needed to show the firmest leadership and somehow find it in himself to motivate and inspire them.

Since discovery of the house fire and Patrick Waldorf's death the day before, it had become inevitable that the focus of the investigation must be on activists opposed to the wind farm development, whether members of Kmag or not. Resources would be deployed appropriately.

While his meeting broke up in subdued fashion, Upwood thought he had been moderately successful: the vibes he picked up were, he believed, thoughtful rather than despondent. He returned to his office where piles of paperwork and dozens of phone and email messages threatened to swamp him. He was frustrated at how bogged down he was getting in the paperwork, despite the admirable efficiency of the Office Manager and all the document handlers, analysts and processors. Upwood decided that he simply had to escape from the office. If he didn't talk to some real people soon he would lose all sense of reality.

He decided that the following day he would interview Geoff Grindlay, Secretary of Kmag. He needed to understand what it was about wind farms that encouraged such strong reactions in people. Beyond thinking that turbines were an eyesore, almost certainly uneconomic, and capable of killing birds, he had not given the matter much thought. Now it was imperative he did so.

When he got home the first thing he did was pour himself a stiff drink, not something he did every evening (although he may have been deceiving himself on this point). He looked around the kitchen, which was less tidy than usual and realised that he hadn't taken out the rubbish or recycling for several days. The living room, too, was unusually untidy, newspapers and magazines scattered around most flat surfaces. Daffodils in a vase that no longer held water were as dry as parchment. He'd need to tidy up a bit before his cleaner came in. Though his cleaner told him it wasn't necessary, he still felt compelled to do it. It was a habit Anne had instilled into him, a reminder which only increased his depression.

He sat down in front of the TV. It was now after nine in the evening and while he knew he could watch national news round the clock, he had set his Sky box to record the early evening local news.

It was every bit as bad as he anticipated, if not worse. Questions were being asked about the competence of the Cambridgeshire Constabulary in general and of Upwood himself. Emily Adam's sterling effort to shoulder all responsibility proved an inadequate shield: the press knew he was Officer in Overall Command of these investigations and they were not about to let him keep a low profile.

It was unpleasant. But other than redeem themselves by solving the crimes there was little they could do. No charm offensive would deal with this crisis.

The final straw for Upwood later that night was watching the interview on Sky given by Peter Shelford outside his farmhouse, flanked by his grandson and daughter-in-law, a shotgun over his arm. He stared into the camera. "Molly and Andy have moved in here now with me. We've got good security and two German Shepherds. If anyone comes after us they will get both barrels."

By sheer chance, his mobile rang as the credits on the news programme faded. He could see that it was Emily, who had also picked up on the report. Naturally she wanted to know what he intended to do to limit the risk of a major catastrophe. He said that he would send out Morton and a Family Liaison Officer. Morton carried weight, not just in physical terms, although he had filled out since he'd stopped playing rugby, but also in terms of presence. His success in gaining promotion to his current rank had given him increased confidence and he had proved himself on a number of occasions when demanding situations needed to be contained. He was not hopeful that the family would respond well to the idea that an FLO might support them – they had previously refused this proposition.

Upwood knew that Morton would make it abundantly clear what the consequences of precipitate action might be. Morton's task was to make sure that Peter and his grandson Andy behaved responsibly if confronted by unwanted visitors. And Upwood wanted everyone in the control room to know that if a call came in from the farm concerning intruders, they were to treat it with the utmost seriousness and urgency.

He and Emily discussed the merits or otherwise of issuing some statement assuring the community that they were safe. Not only were they not confident that this was the case, but thought such a statement might make matters even worse.

Chapter 19

Geoff Grindlay lived in a large detached house on one of Knapton's better streets, with a good sized front garden and a fine lawn surrounded by a well-chosen selection of ornamental shrubs. On some, buds were beginning to swell. Snowdrops were nodding their delicate bell-like heads in sheltered corners. Starlings were strutting around the lawn, stabbing into the soft earth for any nourishment they could find. Upwood knew that most people thought Starlings dull birds. If they'd ever seen them as he did now, in even weak winter sunlight, he wondered how they could fail to be entranced by the iridescence and subtle variation in the colour of their plumage. As he walked up the path he was assailed by a wonderful sweet smell. He looked around but could not see the source.

Once inside, and having settled into a comfortable chintz-covered armchair, Upwood asked him what the fragrance was. "Sorry, if I don't ask now I'll forget. The perfume is beautiful."

Grindlay laughed. "And you didn't see the flowers?"

"No, I didn't."

"Sarcococca. I love it. It cheers me up on a winter's day. It's an evergreen shrub with tiny creamy white flowers. It's just inside the gate. Look for it when you leave."

Upwood made a mental note to track one down for his garden. Anything to cheer him up on a winter's day, other than watching birds of course, got his money.

"Can you please give me a brief overview of the proposed wind farm at King's Mere? I haven't seen much information on the actual proposals."

"Sure. It all started some years ago. The Shelfords entered into a preliminary agreement with Narbor who began researching whether a scheme would be viable.

“The first stage involved the erection of wind monitoring masts to collect data about wind speed and direction. That trial ran for the best part of three years. Presumably Narbor must have been happy with the results because work continued with background noise monitoring tests at a number of neighbouring properties.”

“Which were they, do you know?”

“Yes, King’s Mere Farm itself, King’s Mere Care Home, the riding school, Queen’s Mere Farm and a number of cottages which were probably once tied to the farms but are now privately owned or rented.

“Over a period of some years, too, a breeding birds survey was undertaken.”

“I’m slightly surprised at that. Given the habitat in the area there would be few other than ground nesters and I doubt they are plentiful there.”

“I bow to your greater wisdom. But it’s always done. I’m sure if you don’t follow proper procedures in an investigation you’re criticised, even if in the case in point it seems ridiculous. They carried out bat surveys too. Birds and bats are the creatures deemed most at risk by environmentalists when it comes to wind turbines”, a fact with which Upwood was indeed familiar.

“As part of the process they had to carry out an Environmental Impact Assessment. This didn’t just mean the stuff I’ve already mentioned, but consultation with utility companies, local government and just about every quango or charity that you can think of that has even the most tangential interest in wind power.

“Eventually, in April 2010 the local papers reported that plans were being developed. Narbor conducted their farce of a local consultation process – I think Richard told you about that?” Upwood nodded.

“Then in June of that year they submitted their plans together with the environmental impact statement to the district council. The planning committee turned down the application, although the decision was not unanimous. The main concern was the number and density.”

"What, of the turbines?"

"Yes. Although turbines are not the whole part of the built development. There would be transformers for every turbine, the foundations of course, a meteorological mast, tracks and access roads, sub-station and cabling. But you're right, it is the number and density of the turbines that determine how much other development there is."

"I suspect that the number of turbines raises issues which are different from those associated with density. Am I right?"

"Yes. Scale brings its own problems in terms of visual impact etcetera. But density can affect some of the impact issues quite differently. Can we come back to that? It gets quite technical."

Upwood nodded again. "So what numbers are we talking about?"

"The plans submitted were for seven turbines each about eighty metres high. Add on the blades themselves and you're looking at about a hundred and thirty metres high. The intention was to locate them in a plot of some two hundred and ten hectares."

"Help me here, please. I can't visualise that."

Grindlay chuckled. "About five hundred and twenty acres? Rather less than a square mile?"

Upwood smiled. "OK, a bit clearer."

"You're OK with a hundred and thirty metres?"

It was Upwood's turn to laugh. "I'm not a complete Luddite! I know a metre's a bit more than a yard and I can visualise straight lines. It's areas I have a bit more trouble with. Carry on."

"Well the objections raised focused on several issues, number and density as I've already mentioned. But also noise and amplitude modulation and something called flicker.

"Noise can be measured in decibels, and naturally high levels can cause discomfort and even health problems.

"Amplitude modulation is the term for the variation in noise levels by the passage of the blades through the air past the tower and through areas of differing wind speeds– it's often called the 'swish' or 'thump' effect. At least that's a very simple way of describing it. In reality it's more complicated because there are several ways in which modulation occurs but I won't bore you with the details. Because it's what's called an impulsive sound it causes more annoyance and distress than a constant noise.

"Flicker is the effect caused by the interruption of sunlight by rotating blades. It can be sufficient to pass through closed eyelids and moving shadows on windows can affect light inside."

"And on what grounds did you oppose the development?"

"All of the above and a few more. Kmag surveyed the community, not only its members. A very high proportion of respondents thought that the plan provided too many turbines overall and in particular in relation to the size of the site – in other words concerns about both number and density.

"Residents of the nearby cottages were particularly concerned about noise, AM and flicker."

"How on earth do they know enough about the technicalities of AM for example? Noise I get, and flicker. But AM sounds much more complicated."

"It is and it's a controversial subject. But it's been in the news a lot. And I guess if you live in an area where wind farms have been set up you take notice. There's a very high-profile case going on at the moment. A couple called Davis who had lived in Deeping St Nicholas have been through the courts fighting for compensation for five years. They say they were forced to move home and that their house in Deeping was worthless. That's been on national, not just local news."

"Do you know of anyone who has particularly serious concerns here?"

"I would say there are two people who are very worried indeed about the proposals. Both are on our committee. One is Sheila Bennett. She runs the care home. She believes noise, AM and flicker will all have damaging effects on her residents. Ken Lloyd runs the riding stable. He runs classes for young people with special needs whom he thinks will be especially vulnerable. Both think that their livelihoods are threatened.

"By the way, if you want to read up a bit about wind farms and the problems they cause, I can recommend a good book. It's *The Wind Farm Scam* by John Etherington. He deals very well with the issues of the lack of efficiency of turbines and the appallingly high costs of hidden government subsidies. They are some of the issues that most concern me. But they are very difficult to tackle in a case like ours. Since the Planning Policy Statement came out in 2005, councils are under pressure to support plans that purport to promote sustainable development, especially in relation to renewable energy sources. That's hard for us to fight. And most people believe that wind power is free. The way the industry is constructed that is a complete lie.

"I'm sorry, I shouldn't have started on my particular hobby horse. But it is such a difficult and emotive subject."

"Emotive enough to drive someone to kill?"

"Lord knows. That's for you to find out. It sounds lunatic to me. Were there any other questions you have for me? I need to go to a dental appointment soon."

"There are. I need to know your movements at the time of the three deaths."

Grindlay laughed. "What took you so long? I thought you'd never ask!"

"Right. The morning Fred Shelford drowned. Monday 10th January, between eight and nine o'clock."

Grindlay pulled out his smartphone. "Dentist, as it happens. I was on my way to the first of three appointments for a crown. Today's is the last. City Centre Dental Clinic, Cambridge. Next." There was a definite twinkle in his eye.

"Sunday 16th January, between five and eleven pm."

Grindlay glanced at his calendar again. "Playing bridge, with Richard Gardiner and our wives. My grandmother would not have approved. Cards on a Sunday! Whatever next?"

"Monday 24th January. Five to eleven pm again."

"At home with my wife by the look of it. That was last Monday. There's nothing in the calendar and I don't recall doing anything special."

"And where were you on the morning of Tuesday 20th December last year?"

Grindlay looked at him quizzically and then examined the calendar on his phone again. "A staff meeting at Addenbrooke's."

"All morning?"

"Yes. Boring as hell. Thank God we only have them once a month."

Having gained Grindlay's agreement to provide a formal statement in due course, Upwood left. He was thoughtful as he drove away. He was pretty confident that Grindlay was not involved and Debra and Tom seemed happy with Gardiner, but they should interview him again to establish whether he had alibis for the four events. It did seem, though, that two of the committee members might have solid motives for wanting to scupper the plans that Narbor and the Shelfords were pursuing. It would be very interesting to hear the views of Ken Lloyd and Sheila Bennett.

Chapter 20

That evening the Kmag leaders were again sitting in the same quiet corner of the Black Horse in Knapton. This early in the week it was quiet and only a few regulars sat on stools at the bar. The bar tender was polishing glasses and joined in half-heartedly with their conversation. The fire had only recently been lit and had not yet generated much heat. Damp logs hissed and spat. All in all, the atmosphere was less inviting than the landlord might have wished.

They had all watched the broadcast press conference with dismay. Several reporters had seemed determined to leave viewers with the impression that Kmag was behind the attacks.

Brian Doughty was the youngest of the three and had had little exposure to controversies of any kind. The scale of this issue worried him considerably. "We agreed after Fred Shelford's death not to put out any kind of public statement. Can we avoid it now?"

Richard Gardiner, the Chairman, responded. "It's tricky. What are your own views?"

"Instinct tells me we must. I don't see how we can ignore it. The three deaths must be linked and that means there has to be a wind farm connection."

"But the police haven't confirmed their view that Shelford's death was murder, have they? Or that they think it's connected. They've said only that the two fires are connected."

"But everyone knows they are."

"They don't. They think they are. It's different. Geoff, what do you think?"

"I'm sure the police believe the cases are connected. I had DCI Upwood come to see me today. Ostensibly it was to learn about the underlying issues, and why people's views become so polarised etc. But it didn't stop him asking me my movements on the days all three were killed. And for a day in December, the reasons for which he didn't explain."

Brian snorted with laughter. "I'm sorry. I don't mean to be rude about Fred Shelford. But the idea of Geoff driving round those lanes in thick fog like some sort of madman is a bit rich." Even Richard smiled. Geoff's pride and joy was a 1966 Morris Minor Traveller which got occasional outings when the weather was good. His usual motor was a rather sedate Volvo estate.

"So what did he want to know?"

"Well as I said, he wanted to know why we were opposed to the development so I gave him a brief overview. But he also wanted to know how the plans for the development had started. And of course, he wanted to know who was likely to be affected most badly."

"And you told him?"

"Of course. He'll find out soon enough. They'll be talking to all of us on the committee and to anyone else who has strong views on the subject."

"And what about the question as to whether we should make a statement of some sort?"

"I wasn't comfortable with the idea when we discussed it last time. Whatever we do it's a no win situation. The fire makes it worse somehow. If we put out a statement now we'll be asked why we didn't about Shelford. If we do nothing, they'll ask how many more crimes have to be committed before we respond. I just don't know, Richard, really I don't. What about you? You haven't said yet."

"I still think discretion is the better part of valour."

"We can't just keep quiet. We have to say something surely?" Brian's anxiety was clear, in fact there was a note of anger in his voice. "If we don't lots of people will assume we are behind it. We can't let that happen."

"Saying we are not responsible won't cut ice with anyone. Ideally there would be someone else, or another group, to focus on."

"Well there is no other group I know of opposed to the wind farm. And I certainly don't have a suspect in mind. Do you?"

"Of course not. Geoff, we've all met people with contrary views because of Kmag. Is there anyone you've met who strikes you as mad enough to carry out these crimes?"

"No. A few hot heads, certainly. But no one whom I recall as likely to be a credible suspect. Anyway, isn't that a job for the police?"

Before Richard could answer, his mobile rang. He looked at the screen and didn't recognise the caller. He apologised to his colleagues and accepted the call. Geoff could hear a faint voice talking to Richard. Brian got up to get in a fresh round of drinks. After a moment Richard said "Fine. Yes. Two pm" and ended the call. Geoff looked at him quizzically.

Brian returned to their table and put the drinks down. "Anything we should know about?"

"That was the BBC. They want to interview me for *Look East* tomorrow."

He presented himself at their studio in good time. Appearing on television per se did not worry him unduly. He had appeared before and sometimes this had meant defending developments which were opposed by environmentalists. But this interview was going to be one of the hardest because of the loss of life.

"Mr Gardiner, thank you for agreeing to talk to us. What is your response to the latest death?"

"I and my colleagues are shocked that someone should die as a result of arson."

"Are you not shocked about the death of Fred Shelford?

"Of course, yes."

"Why have you not said so until now?"

"Out of respect for the family."

"And just why do you think that not expressing any regret over Mr Shelford's death represents respect to the family?"

"When his death was announced we had every reason to believe that it was an accident, and therefore a private matter for the family."

The interviewer leaned forward. "We know that's not the case now, though don't we?"

"I don't believe we do know." Gardiner, who'd benefited from media training, maintained a comfortable position, upright, his arms on the arms of his chair. He knew if he leant back he'd look too complacent. If he matched the interviewer's stance, some would think him aggressive.

"And why is it that your action group has stirred up so much hatred over the proposed development?"

"I don't believe it has."

"But there have been two deaths now."

"There is no action that we have taken that I think any reasonable person could describe as stirring up hate. And there is no evidence that I know of which incontrovertibly links the deaths with the wind farm development."

"Don't you think it would be prudent to suspend your campaign now?"

"We are not actively campaigning at the moment."

"But you can't deny you are still fund-raising?"

And indeed he could not.

Upwood watched the late news as he often did and saw the interview. Gardiner had done as well as he could. He had avoided a trap many fall into, of extending his answers unnecessarily. He was measured and courteous. But in his view Kmag had suffered a broadside from that final question.

Chapter 21

Morton, accompanied by Family Liaison Officer Cheryl Brand, approached the farmhouse with caution. The weather had turned very cold again and an icy wind, throwing hailstones the size of peas, blasted them as they got out of the car. As it blew through the barns it whistled in the eaves and set the corrugated iron roofs clattering on their beams. They ran to the front door, Cheryl almost slipping on the slick surface of the path.

Cheryl had met Molly and Peter Shelford before and had been very disappointed with their response. Molly had been apathetic, bordering on catatonic, and said she couldn't bear to have anyone near her except family. Peter had simply been dismissive and challenged her to explain what possible benefit she could bring them. She wasn't looking forward to this meeting any more than Morton was.

Morton wasn't looking forward to this meeting for a number of reasons, not least the phobia of German Shepherds which he shared with Debra. His best friend had been badly injured by one – the family pet – when he was eight years old. Morton had been there at the time and watched in horror as the boy's father tried to wrestle the dog away from his son. Morton prayed that the dogs would be out of sight when they arrived.

Peter Shelford opened the door to them, a fierce glint in his eye. Morton introduced himself. Peter nodded curtly at Cheryl, acknowledging her presence. He led them into the den. His grandson Andy was there, but not Molly. "I hope you've come to explain how you intend to protect us, Inspector."

Morton, who had not expected this opening gambit from the farmer, took a deep breath. "We are here to discuss safety with you, sir. At this stage we have no plans to provide a police presence, if that's what you had in mind. But we do want to discuss what personal security measures you have."

"Let's start with that, shall we?" asked Andy of his grandfather, trying to defuse the tension before it got worse. "Why don't I show them what we have?"

Peter looked sullen and grunted. Andy took this as acceptance. "Come with me, Inspector, and you can have a look at the security systems. We had them put in a couple of years ago after a spate of thefts of farm machinery and red diesel." Morton fervently hoped that they would not be accompanied on their tour by the dogs. Knowing they were on site if needed was enough for him.

"How is your daughter-in-law Mr Shelford?" Cheryl had expected her to join the meeting.

"She's out in the kitchen."

"May I go and see her?"

"She won't want to talk to you. She is distraught about Fred's death. And she's been terrified since Waldorf was murdered. What else would you expect?" He shot her a furious look.

"I'd like to say hello, at least."

"Well don't blame me if she gives you an earful."

Cheryl found Molly sitting at the pine table with a mug of tea, a newspaper in front of her. The front page carried a report of the press conference. She was looking at it but gave no impression of absorbing the information it provided.

"Good morning, Molly. May I join you?"

"If you must."

"Would you mind if I make myself a cup of tea? It's another cold morning."

"I don't care."

Cheryl filled the kettle and put it on the hot plate of the Aga. Everything else she needed was on the Welsh dresser.

"Would you like a top up?"

"No. Thank you."

The first sign of normal courtesy from Molly encouraged Cheryl. "You must be pleased to have Andy back.

And your father-in-law must too, with all the work needed on the farm. Do you think he'd like a cup of tea?"

Molly nodded. Cheryl took a mug through for Peter and then rejoined Molly. "I imagine you have stopped working for the time being. Are the school being supportive?"

"Yes, so far."

"What about friends? Have you got people who can keep you company from time to time?"

"I don't want company! I just want to be left alone. I want my family to be safe. Don't you understand?"

Noise in the den suggested that Morton and Andy had returned from their inspections.

"Why don't we join them, Molly, and see what Morton has to say about your security systems?"

Reluctantly Molly got to her feet and Cheryl followed her through to the other room.

"Your systems seem very comprehensive. You've got good coverage of the yard and outbuildings as well as the house. And I'm sure Nimbus and Vulcan will be good deterrents." Morton had been relieved that Andy had shown him the dogs chained up in the barn, making it clear that once the gate to the yard was closed for the night, they would be let loose to deter unwelcome visitors. "There is one issue I need to discuss with you, though: your shotgun."

"What about it? A man's got the right to defend his family. And his home."

"You're right of course. But only if the circumstances warrant it and the force you use is reasonable."

"You're going to bring up that Tony Martin case again aren't you? Poor bugger. He didn't deserve what he got."

"Fred Barras d'you mean?"

"No I bloody well don't, you stupid bastard. Miserable young sod got everything he deserved all right. No, I mean Martin. I'd have shot the other one too, given half a chance, if I'd been in his shoes."

"Mr Shelford, I suggest you need to think carefully about this. Your family has suffered tragedy enough. If you were to wound or kill an intruder you could face the most serious of charges. You owe it to them to act responsibly."

Peter struggled to his feet. "How dare you tell me how to act responsibly? Get out of my house now. I've had enough."

Molly said nothing. Further efforts on Andy's part to defuse the situation were at best lukewarm. Morton and Cheryl left.

Back in the car she asked him about the Tony Martin case. She was twenty-seven years of age and the case had not come up on her radar.

"It was 1999. Tony Martin was a farmer. He was single and lived alone. He claimed there had been repeated burglaries and when Barras and Fearon broke in, Martin used his shotgun. He hit both of them, including a shot to Barras' back. Barras died at the scene. Martin was charged with murder and convicted. Later, on appeal, the conviction was reduced to manslaughter on the grounds of diminished responsibility. I'm surprised you don't know about it. The case is notorious."

"When did you say it was?"

"1999."

"Well I would have been nine at the time."

Morton laughed. "I'll let you off then. But read about it. It is an instructive case."

Morton was not laughing when later that evening he watched the news. Peter Shelford had had what was described as a massive stroke and was in intensive care at Addenbrooke's.

Chapter 22

Upwood was in Emily Adam's office, together with Morton and Cheryl by seven thirty the next morning. It was chilly. The insulation on the top floor was poor and the central heating had not quite kicked in. Or maybe it was just the vibes that Emily was giving off. There was no sign of coffee, much less biscuits. She nodded at them and indicated that they should take seats.

Morton recounted what had happened at the farm. Cheryl told them of her conversation with Molly. She also told them that Peter was shouting at Morton. Just before they left she had heard Molly say to her son: "I told you we should never have started this", which she took as disapproval of the wind farm plan.

Emily listened in stony-faced silence. When Morton had finished his account, she sighed deeply. "You know what the headlines will be tonight don't you? *'Deranged killer still at large – incompetent police trigger near fatal stroke in victim's father'*. I can just see it. It's going to be an absolute PR disaster."

Upwood responded. "Ma'am, I've worked with Morton for years now. The account he's given of the meeting sounds perfectly reasonable. I am quite confident he would not have said anything inflammatory. Mr Shelford Snr is nearly eighty. He's been under considerable stress since the death of his son and is now, after Patrick Waldorf's death, afraid for the rest of his family. Those circumstances alone are probably enough to bring on a stroke. And for all we know he may have high blood pressure anyway."

"I know all that, dammit, James. But being rational doesn't always help. The press will have a field day again and I don't know how to contain it. Do you?"

Upwood thought that if she was prepared to admit that in front of two junior officers, she must be more rattled than he had ever seen her before. In truth he couldn't see any ray of light either.

"It's not just the ACC. I've got the Chief Constable himself on my back."

Upwood and his team sat and waited. There was little enough they could say that would either calm or reassure her.

Eventually he said: "I suggest we get Cheryl to visit the hospital. If we send anyone other than an FLO we shall come in for more criticism. But for our own peace of minds I think it would be helpful to find out, if we can, if Peter Shelford had any history making him predisposed to a stroke.

"And I suggest we do not put out any statement about it. If asked, Jan can simply say that we are sorry to hear of his illness and that our thoughts are with his family. If – when – asked whether our visit precipitated the stroke I think she should decline to answer."

"Agreed." The Superintendent sighed again, the burdens of her office plain for all to see.

Upwood's team dispersed and after a few more words with Emily he returned to his office. Emily was to speak at the morning's briefing although he would run it as usual. But both knew her presence would be necessary if the team were not to be utterly demoralised and anxious.

The mountain of paperwork was even higher. His email system was like a snow storm. It showed one hundred and seventeen unread messages and there had been countless phone calls. He decided to call together the Office Manager and Action Manager. He needed a clear overview of where they stood in terms of the actions achieved, those outstanding and those not dealt with that might, in the light of current developments, be referred – filed. Their focus needed to be as sharp as possible.

He started on his admin once more, again frustrated by the amount of time it took. He would far rather be out in the field talking to people. He would have liked to interview Ken

Lloyd and Sheila Bennett himself, but as matters stood he would have to continue to delegate to his senior officers.

Later that day he was at last beginning to think that he was in control of the administration again when Morton came in.

"We've got the tox report on Patrick Waldorf, Sir. Special K."

"Ah. Ketamine. There was always the chance that a drug was used." All the signs were that Waldorf had admitted his visitor. Either he knew him or he had no reason to suspect him. "We have some TIEs for that evening, haven't we?"

"We have, but we haven't managed to eliminate them all yet. There are several we're still looking for. The most interesting lead at present – Margaret picked it up today – is an entry in his work diary. He logged into his office server remotely, so Narbor were able to tell us. There's an entry for that evening for a meeting with someone called Chris Bannister, a reporter for one of the Cambridge monthly glossies. Except he isn't. They've never heard of him. So we are concentrating our efforts on the local neighbourhood and revisiting potential witnesses. Having a possible time of arrival for the arsonist may make our life easier."

"Don't be too specific though. He might have anticipated that and deliberately arrived early or late, banking on Waldorf letting him in. Have you considered that he might be a woman?"

"What d'you mean?"

"Chris could be a woman."

"I suppose so. Either way, no one of that name works for the magazine."

"Let's hope to goodness we get some more leads. We really could do with a decent break for a change."

If Emily Adams ever decided to retire, a future in journalism might await her. The headlines in the evening paper were almost exactly as she had predicted. It was disastrous.

Chapter 23

For Upwood, Saturday's journey was scarcely better than it had been the previous Monday. This time it was not an accident creating long tailbacks, but the worsening of the weather from yesterday. There had been intermittent, heavy hailstorms by day. Overnight there had been sleet, turning to snow in the hours before dawn. Whether the gritters had been out he didn't know, but road conditions were treacherous. Visibility was poor. Wipers were of limited use as dirty spray thrown onto the windscreen froze on impact. By the time he got to Parkside he felt exhausted. And in a thoroughly bad mood. The whole team was on duty on Saturday and the meeting room for the morning briefing was full. Upwood opened by thanking them all for their hard work and dedication under extremely trying circumstances. He urged them to ignore the more lurid comments from the journalists. Their job was to sell newspapers; stretching the truth as much as they could to sell more copies was simply what they did. Even their sometimes outspoken comments about individual officers were rarely personal. They simply worked with the material they had.

He reported that there had been some improvement overnight in the condition of Peter Shelford and he had been moved out of ICU into a high dependency unit. There were grounds for optimism that he would survive, although it was far too early to judge what the long-term damage might be. Morton stared ahead, knowing that many in the room would be looking at him. He feared he would always be known as the man who drove Shelford to his stroke, if not his death.

Upwood continued. Working with the material they themselves had was their responsibility. Allowing themselves to be distracted by what the media might say, or what they overheard in the pub after work, was an indulgence they could not afford.

In his view, they had made considerable progress. They now knew that Fred Shelford's death and the two arsons were almost certainly linked.

This made it more likely that there was a connection with the wind farm project, which gave the investigation greater focus. There was a brief discussion about this theory. Several there found it hard to believe that someone would kill over plans for a wind farm. Upwood had to remind them that people had been known to kill with the flimsiest of motives. They could only follow the facts.

They were now fairly certain that the victim in the barn fire was 'collateral damage' and that the arsonist simply wanted to destroy the vehicle used to shunt Fred off the road.

They were also fairly sure that the person they were looking for had local knowledge and that he was an amateur rather than a professional hit man.

They were continuing to add to their list of TIEs and had already eliminated a number of them.

New leads were coming through.

He asked for questions.

"Why do you think the barn victim's death was accidental?"

"You heard Margaret lay out her theory that the young man was an illegal immigrant and that his presence in the barn may not have been known to the arsonist. Margaret, can you bring us up to date on that?"

"Well you know that Tom and Debra went to visit the woman who might know whose ring it was that was engraved PLD. She is Albanian although she has lived here for twenty years. They established that the ring might most recently have belonged to her nephew Rajmond. He left home in Albania earlier this month and his present whereabouts are unknown but he was thought to be somewhere in western Europe. His aunt, Lauresha Broad, agreed to provide a DNA sample. We've just had the results. There is a familial connection and we are now trying to obtain a DNA sample from his mother.

In addition, Mrs Broad gave us a recent photo Rajmond's mother had emailed her. Tom is going to the detention centre to re-interview the three men apprehended near Bury St Edmunds to see whether he can get a reaction from any of them. As I've reported before, we had no joy from them first time round. I have a hunch, though, that seeing the photo might help."

"Thank you. Next question?"

"Why do we think the arsonist has local knowledge?"

"Firstly, we think he targeted the Pajero because it's an old-fashioned vehicle and is one of the easier ones to steal. He might have cruised round the back streets of Knapton, it's true, but we think he may have seen the car around town and followed it to find out where it was usually parked."

"But wouldn't hot-wiring it in broad daylight be risky? We know it's a quiet street, but there might have been someone about."

"Sure. But if you were walking past along that narrow back street and saw someone in a vehicle in a private yard you might just assume they were on a fag break or wanted to use a mobile in private. Or having their elevenses.

"So, other reasons for thinking he has local knowledge? Secondly, the choice of the barn as a place to hide it after the collision with Fred's Land Rover.

"Thirdly the fact that we've so few sightings of people in the vicinity of the incidents suggests he knew which routes to take and how to conceal himself. We are almost certain that he did not drive to the barn on the night of the fire, and we know for a fact that he did not park outside Patrick Waldorf's house the night of that fire. Nor have we had reports of vehicles parked in peculiar places – the drives of empty houses for example. So we think he knows the area well and planned his missions accordingly."

"But you say he's an amateur."

"We think so. Fire and Rescue say that much more accelerant was used in both fires than was necessary, a common mistake made by people who are not career arsonists.

And the use of candles, as we've said before, is typical of someone inexperienced."

"What about the use of Special K? Isn't that a bit more sophisticated?"

"Hardly. Ketamine, and Rohypnol come to that, as we all know, are frequently cited in date rape incidents. And they're not difficult to get hold of. You could probably buy either of them easily enough outside several of the pubs in Cambridge."

"Is there a university connection then perhaps?"

"We don't know. It's possible but it's not a line we're pursuing at the moment although the analysts are trying to find potential sources of the drug locally."

"Isn't it more likely it was bought over the internet? If it was bought on the street there would be eye witnesses and possibly CCTV coverage."

"My own view is that you're probably right. But it's an avenue we have to explore."

Upwood closed the meeting, asking everyone to pull out all the stops. Only a skeleton staff would be required to work on Sunday. No one could work at the level of intensity they had shown without an occasional day off. "Go home at a reasonable time tonight. Go to the pub. Take your partner out for a meal. Binge on a boxed set. Don't look at the papers or the TV! Give yourselves a decent break. We'll meet again at seven o'clock on Monday."

Morton thought his boss had done well at the morning's briefing. Most people returned to their tasks with renewed energy. He still felt thoroughly depressed, especially as he was scheduled to see the Detective Superintendent early on Monday morning. It was rarely that he had a meeting with such a senior officer on his own and it made him nervous.

He was even more nervous when one of the techies analysing the mobile phone reported that there had been another text message.

Chapter 24

Mo had persuaded Margaret, with some difficulty, to have supper with him that night. But she had agreed and now they were sitting in an Italian restaurant near the centre of Cambridge. It was one he had suggested when she expressed concerns that they might be seen. It had been there for years, run the by a couple who were now probably in their sixties. The décor hadn't changed in years either – faux pillars against the walls to create alcoves, with murals depicting classical-style Italian scenery. Original it was not, but it was comfortable. The owner was a nice old boy, still with a strong Italian accent. His wife looked younger, but that may have been because she was fair-skinned, with a good complexion, and was blonde. She also spoke impeccable English with no accent.

"She must be English, surely?" Margaret whispered.

"No, she's not. Anna comes from Milan. Apparently her colouring's not so uncommon."

"Why do you think her English is so much better?"

"Had you not noticed Pino's hearing aids? He's very deaf. And I think Anna's one of those people who pick up languages quite easily."

They each had a glass of Pinot Grigio and a menu in front of them. Mo had been watching his partner discreetly. Her eyes kept scanning the room and she had paid little attention to the menu. "Come on, Mags, try to relax. There's no reason why we shouldn't go out if we want to, as long as it doesn't interfere with work."

"I know. It's just that the job takes up so much time and energy I don't have any left over to deal with all the barracking we'll get if the rest of them hear about it."

"Well let's just keep our heads down. Am I allowed to say that you are looking lovely this evening?"

She laughed and blushed. "I don't often get compliments."

She had, it was true, tried a little harder than usual. Her hair was sleek and not quite so much out of control; for once she had been to a hairdresser. She had accented her dark eyes with just a little brown eye shadow. Soft peach coloured her full lips. She almost didn't need the little blusher she had applied to her cheeks. For the first time she wore a skirt which showed off excellent legs. Like many women in the force she wore trousers habitually, as a form of protection, typically with rather loose tops, layered. For some it drew the inevitable jokes from the unreconstructed blokes that they were dykes. No one looking at Margaret was likely to think that of her, although he knew that it was by no means easy to guess someone's sexual orientation from their appearance.

The waiter hovered. They looked hastily at the menu and ordered: Spaghetti Aglio Olio for Margaret, a Pizza Quattro Stagione for Mo.

"What have you ordered?"

"The spaghetti? It's made with olive oil, garlic and chilli."

"Hell's teeth. Good job I like garlic then!"

"Why an Italian restaurant? I thought you might have chosen something Tamil."

"I wouldn't even recognise authentic Tamil cuisine – I know it is largely vegetarian and involves a lot of rice but there are regional variations in southern India and Sri Lanka. My grandmother used to try to recreate the family dishes when she first came over. Mum never really tried. Me? I'll eat anything. But I do like Italian."

"Me too. A pizza occasionally, especially thin ones, but pasta is my favourite."

"You did good work on the Albanian angle. Well done. It's about the only thing we look as though we might solve at the rate we're going."

"Thanks. I enjoy the research side of it. I feel sorry for Morton about Peter Shelford. I mean I'm sorry for Shelford, too. But Morton must feel really bad about it."

"Poor bugger. It will keep him awake at night for a bit. Until something worse happens to displace the memory."

The waiter returned with their food and topped up their glasses. They ate in silence for a minute or two.

"Do you think there will be more murders?"

"Christ knows. Hope not. We've got our work cut out as it is."

"Presumably it is the same person?"

"Has to be. Stands to reason. Sick bugger is all I say. I mean, really. Is a bunch of turbines worth killing over? The guy has to be seriously mental. Let's change the subject." He reached across the table and touched her ring finger lightly. "You've worn a ring there for a long time. But not now."

She drew her hand away, blushing. "No. The usual story, I'm afraid. Married too young. He had an admin job. Simply couldn't handle the long hours and broken schedules that we put up with. It's a miracle it lasted as long as it did." Oddly she didn't look at him when she said this.

"Divorced?"

"Yes. And now cautious. What about you?"

"Never married. Played the field hard when I was young and then found all the talent had been taken. And as you say, it's not easy in our line of work. Never stop hoping though!" He grinned at her.

He looked at her dish. "Can I try a bit?"

"Sure." She pushed her plate across.

He struggled to wrap some spaghetti round his fork to the point where she couldn't help but laugh. Eventually he managed it.

"Holy shit! You like this stuff?"

"Yep. Been known to have it as a starter and a main."

"What, at the same meal?"

"Yep."

"God Almighty."

"That's when I was still doing Taekwondo, mind."

"I was forgetting that. I'd better mind my Ps and Qs. Or better still, you can give me a lesson later."

"In your dreams, Mo."

"I love it when you laugh."

After their meal he drove her back to her apartment block on Fen Causeway.

"Going to invite me up for a coffee?"

"Nope." She looked slightly nervous but there was a twinkle in her eye that didn't entirely discourage him.

"But you enjoyed it, yeah? You'll come out again?"

"I did enjoy it. Thanks. It's been a long time since I've been out."

"So you'll come again?"

"Yes. But pace it, right?"

"Sure." He pecked her on the cheek and was rewarded with a blast of garlic. It would probably keep two vampires away.

Chapter 25

Morton was early for his meeting with Detective Superintendent Adams. And her prior meeting was running late, a fact that did nothing to increase Morton's comfort levels.

Twenty minutes later than scheduled another, somewhat harassed, officer came out of her office. After a further ten minutes Morton was instructed to go in.

Perhaps in an effort to make him feel a little less intimidated she was, unusually, sitting at a small meeting table in the corner between the two windows. Her intentions may have been good but unfortunately it meant she was sitting with her back to the light and in consequence looked more threatening than usual. Today she was in a black suit, pale grey silk blouse and grey tights. Morton's initial thought was that if she were given a top hat she could easily pass for an undertaker.

She gestured to him to sit down.

"What have you got for me, Morton? Do tell me you're bringing some useful intelligence."

Fortunately he was, and as he began to bring her up to date his normal confidence returned. "Well, we are making some progress, Ma'am. We know that the mobile being used is almost certainly a burner. We've run triangulations and the calls are not coming from Whitemoor."

"Which is where MacKay is held?"

"Correct. So I'm sure it must be an accomplice."

"And have you any ideas who this might be?"

"I don't think it's just some bent guy he's paying. When Katie Melhuish was pushed over on the underground platform we assumed that MacKay had just picked someone at arm's length and paid him to do it.

"I think MacKay has some sort of hold over the person making the calls and that it's probably the same person who was involved in the Charing Cross incident. It doesn't seem likely that MacKay could easily lay his hands on two people prepared to do his dirty work. So I've had one of the researchers look into his family tree. She's come up with a very interesting piece of intelligence. MacKay has a nephew, Bill Franklin, who was charged with rape following a New Year's Eve party while at Manchester Uni. Three days into the trial it collapsed because the victim withdrew her complaint. The boy had no parents, they died in a car crash a few months before, and MacKay is his closest relative. Leaning on the victim is just the sort of behaviour we would expect from MacKay – he's a bully by nature. If he thought getting the case dropped would protect his reputation, he might well try it."

The Superintendent had been listening carefully to what Morton had to say. The idea that the same person was involved in both the London incident and the text messages was perfectly sensible. Sometimes the simplest solution happens to be the right one. "It sounds promising. What are you planning to do about it?"

"I want to find out why the case was dropped. That will mean liaising with the Manchester force and maybe even interviewing the victim."

"By all means. But how will you find her? Most graduates spread their wings far away from uni."

"I know, but it's got to be worth a shot.

"And there is another update. Katie's mobile picked up another text message. 'Be careful who you let into your home. You never know what unpleasant gifts they might leave for you.'

"You'd authorised the use of a behavioural scientist. I consulted her. She thinks the person sending the messages is reasonably well-educated and that the intention is to intimidate Katie. She thinks it unlikely that the texter intends direct action."

"Which is pretty much what we thought. If MacKay is a bully as you suggest, he may get more satisfaction from terrorising Katie over time rather than from a single act of violence. What do you need from me now?"

"Only your agreement that I follow up on the rape lead. If that pans out I may want to bring MacKay's nephew in."

"Fine. How has Katie reacted?"

"She's glad she'd already moved out of the house. She's rented a flat in Cambridge and the house is for sale."

"The fact that the house is on the market is presumably what's prompted the latest text. I wonder if the texter knows she's not living there any longer."

"It's possible if he's watching her. Would he look on Rightmove for no reason?"

"He might have seen a sale board."

"There isn't one. For some reason Katie didn't think it was a good idea."

"Very sensible, I'd say. Are the agents giving viewings?"

"They've taken one couple round. They sold them their last house and knew they really wanted a riverside property. I've told them to suspend viewings for the time being."

"Good idea." She paused. "Has Upwood been in touch with her?"

The question made Morton feel very uncomfortable but he couldn't in all conscience criticise her for asking. "No. He respects the decision you took and knows how sensitive this is. And Katie understands too. She wouldn't want to cause embarrassment for the force. And I think she is fond enough of the Chief not to make matters difficult for him."

"Oh grief." She closed the folder in front of her with a snap, pursing her lips. "Get on with it then. It sounds as though you might be on the right lines. And keep me posted."

Later that day Upwood had some promising news.

Tom came back from the detention centre having interviewed all three men again. The man applying for asylum refused once more to answer questions and when shown the photograph of Rajmond, showed no signs of recognition.

One of the other two, probably younger than Rajmond, evidently did recognise the photo. Supported by the interpreter Tom managed to establish that Rajmond had been travelling with them. He had intended to find a relative, although he had not said who that was. He did say that his arrival would be unexpected.

It didn't help them with the main investigation but it would allow them to close down one line of enquiry, and importantly increase the likelihood that the barn victim's family could get some closure. Once they had the DNA results from Tirana they could be sure.

Chapter 26

For DS Ramachandran it was a relief to get out of the office and have the chance to interview someone. His role on the team had morphed once or twice as the scale of the investigation increased. Now his role with the house to house teams was more remote, for which he was thankful. He was happy to have Margaret along as observer and note-taker.

The subject of his interview this morning was Ken Lloyd, manager of the Riding School. Located on the road running alongside Chilton Lode, it was little more than half a mile from the site on which the nearest of the planned turbines would stand. The school stood on three acres of land and comprised an outdoor arena as well as stables and an indoor manège. His home was a large brick built, modern bungalow, unusual for the area where properties were normally two storeys. It was all carefully maintained although Margaret noted that no money had been spent on anything that might have improved its appearance. It was all grey and green, the green decidedly drab at the end of January. A few crocuses in the patches of lawn in front of the house would have brightened the scene nicely. She had the impression there would be no hanging baskets or tubs of flowers in the summer either. Shame. It didn't take that much time or money, surely?

Mo parked outside the bungalow and as he got out of the car, Lloyd came out to greet him. "Hi. I'm Ken Lloyd. You must be DS Ramachandran. And your colleague?"

"Good morning, sir. Yeah, that's me. And this is DC Margaret Starr. Thank you for seeing us."

"Come on through to the office."

Lloyd stood over six feet tall, and was slim with an athletic build with short, medium brown hair swept back over his head without parting. Together with rimless glasses over piercing blue eyes, it gave him a rather academic look at odds with his job. He strode ahead and opened the door into a very tidy, well-equipped and efficient-looking office. "Come and sit down." He gestured to the two chairs in front of his desk. "I'm sorry it's a bit formal, but my wife is in the sitting room with her manicurist. How can I help you?"

"Well, firstly we'd like to know how you came to be involved with Kmag."

He leaned back in his chair. It was a pose generally considered non-threatening, but somehow he managed to make it look confrontational. "I'd heard about the plans for the wind farm and I was horrified. There was a public meeting and I went along. When they asked for volunteers for the committee I offered like a shot." They'd only be talking a minute or two and already there was an intense look in his eyes.

"Did you know the organisers of the meeting before the event?"

"Geoff Grindlay, but only slightly. A couple of years ago one of his daughters decided she wanted to learn to ride. She fell off during her second lesson and was too frightened to get back on. So that was that. I probably only met him two or three times."

"What about any of the other volunteers?"

"What, for the committee?"

"Yes."

He leaned forward, resting his forearms on the desk, his hands loosely steepled. He stared at his blotter which was covered in doodles. "Funnily enough I did. Veronica Mallon. She works here two days a week as an instructor. She has an interest in the development of young people with special needs, which is one field in which we specialise. I knew of Sheila Bennett of the care home, but I hadn't met her before." He leaned back again.

Mo glanced at Margaret who offered a slight smile and nod, signifying she was keeping up with her notes. In fact he was trying to establish whether she was aware of Lloyd's body language.

“We know in general the grounds on which Kmag opposed the development of the King’s Mere Wind Farm. Are there particular issues you are concerned about?”

“I should say. He turned round and from the table behind him pulled a plan of the site superimposed over a large-scale map of the immediate area. “Look how close the nearest turbine will be. About half a mile. These three turbines here will all be highly visible and audible. It is likely that we will get noise from all of them when the wind is from the west.

“The problems Sheila and I both have are with noise, amplitude modulation and flicker. Are you familiar with those terms in the context of wind turbines?”

Mo nodded, making a mental note to borrow the book the chief had offered to lend him. He’d grasped the essentials but thought he would do well to gain a better understanding. However, what he wanted to know was how Lloyd thought his school would be affected.

“I’ve got a number of concerns. Take the ponies for example. We try to keep only the most placid of creatures. But they are on site the whole time. Their stables have typical doors – split – and are open at the top most of the time. Horses have far better hearing than humans. Some people believe that AM – that irregular whooshing sound turbines make – can cause stress and in extreme cases can spook them. So that is a major worry. Flicker worries me too. It can be a huge distraction and again can cause stress. Noise in an absolute sense can be a problem, especially when it is loud and sustained, which it will be on occasions if this scheme goes ahead.

“I worry about the young people. The classes that Veronica runs with me are designed for kids with a variety of problems: from some degree of physical disability to those on the autism spectrum or epilepsy. Noise, AM and flicker could have terrible consequences for some of them.

“Our problem is that some of these classes are funded by local councils and charities. I can’t see them sending their kids to us if the wind farm goes ahead. The income from these classes represents about a third of our revenue. Lose it, and the business won't survive."

Mo and Margaret could see the problem clearly. His potential problem was very real. Even if the actual problems caused by the turbines when built were less serious than he expected, the perceptions of those using his facility would be critical. Those responsible for vulnerable young people were likely to take a prudent course and move to another set of stables.

Lloyd watched Mo and Margaret digesting what he had to say. "And I haven't even started on the problems for my wife. She is paralysed from the waist down. A car accident", he said bitterly. "She has to use a wheelchair and doesn't leave the house very often. It may sound a bit melodramatic, but the thought of being trapped here unable to escape the aural onslaught and the flicker is causing her severe depression. What the reality would be like I dread to think." When he leant back this time the gesture was one of resignation.

"Thank you, Mr Lloyd. You've given us a very clear picture of your concerns.

"You will know, of course, that suggestions have been made that the person or persons responsible for the deaths of Fred Shelford and Patrick Waldorf, and the as yet unidentified young man in the barn fire, were trying to derail the wind farm development. We are therefore asking everyone with an interest in it to tell us their movements on the days in question."

"I knew that would be coming. Go on then."

"Can you please tell us where you were on the morning of Monday 10th January between eight o'clock and nine?"

Lloyd swivelled in his chair and tapped his keyboard, entered his log in password and unlocked the screen saver. His calendar was open – he was indeed expecting the question.

"There's nothing in the diary. At that time of day I would have finished morning stables and be in here preparing for the day's activities. The first session on Mondays usually starts about ten."

“Can anyone vouch for that?”

“Maybe my wife. You’ll have to ask her.”

“And the following Sunday, 16th January between five and eleven pm?”

“Again, nothing in the diary. So the usual routine, evening stables until about seven with Sally, my assistant, then prepare supper for me and my wife, probably catch the news on TV and then bed.”

“Last Monday, the twenty-fourth, between five and eleven pm?”

“I do remember that. I went into the village, to the Star Inn. There were several people there who know me.”

“What, for the whole period?”

“No. I did the stables first. I gave my wife supper on a tray. But I didn’t leave the pub until closing time.”

“What about the morning of Tuesday 20th December, last year?”

Lloyd seemed surprised. He turned to look at the monitor again and fiddled with the mouse. “Making a presentation to a school for children with special needs. In Ely.”

“All morning?”

“I got there for nine thirty for a pre-meet with the head. Then we showed a video to the staff and had a question and answer session. That went well so I showed the video to a group of the older children to get their reaction. So yes, all morning.”

Mo thanked him and chatted a little more about the kinds of young people they helped and the results they achieved. Margaret went through to the living room. Lloyd’s wife could not remember what she was doing on the morning of Fred’s death, nor whether Ken Lloyd had been in his office or not.

Mo and Margaret discussed their findings on the way back to the station. Mo had sensed that there was something Lloyd was uncomfortable about that he was not sharing with them. He definitely had a strong motive to derail the scheme and, from the sound of it, independent witnesses to vouch for his alibi only in the case of Waldorf's murder. Margaret was particularly interested in the answer his wife had given. She said she could not corroborate her husband's alibi although, it would have been the easiest thing in the world to do so. Was it the truth? If so, was it because she was so confident of his innocence that the idea an alibi might be necessary did not occur to her? Or was she unsure, and letting him take his chances?

Chapter 27

Late that afternoon they headed over to the care home. They took the road alongside Chilton Lode again. The weather was still changeable and had improved somewhat but there was now heavy cloud cover and the light was poor. Mo couldn't remember when last he had driven without the need for lights. Margaret stared out of the windows absently. Visibility was so poor she couldn't see the horizon. Sky and earth seemed to have merged into one. They might have been somewhere in Holland for all the landmarks she could see.

"Can you imagine what driving along here must have been like the morning Fred Shelford died?"

Mo grimaced. "I can't say I'm enjoying it now frankly. It's in a bloody awful state. Absolutely crap."

"The bloke that pushed him off took a hell of a risk. He could have gone straight in after him."

"Or sheered off the other side. He must have been out of his mind."

They passed the riding school and at the T junction turned left towards the care home. It looked as if it might once have been a farm although it did have a modern extension. Three storeys, the old part was brick, its front elevation almost completely covered by ivy. The ivy evidently hadn't been trimmed for some time: two of the windows on the top floor were partially obscured. Facing north as it did, the building did not look very inviting. Transplant it to the Yorkshire Moors, thought Margaret, and it would fit nicely into a Brontë novel. She rang the bell. It took quite some time for the door to open. A middle-aged woman of central European appearance greeted them. Margaret was astonished to see the name Lauresha Broad on her badge.

"Hello, Mrs Broad. I didn't expect to see you here."

"I've been working here for several years. Didn't I tell your colleagues?"

"No, but they probably didn't ask. May we come in? This is DS Mo Ramachandran. Mo, this is Lauresha Broad who has been so kindly helping us with our enquiry into the identity of the owner of the Albanian ring."

They followed her across a large parquet-floored hall into the Manager's office. The hall was well lit and decorated in an attractive shade of peach. The few easy chairs were upholstered in green with primrose yellow cushions. Perhaps the home was more appealing than it appeared from the outside. They sat down to wait for Sheila Bennett who had been called to attend to a problem with one of the residents a few minutes earlier.

"I hate these places", said Mo. "They always smell of stale pee and boiled cabbage."

"This one doesn't."

"I bet it does if you start off down the corridors."

At that moment, the manager opened the door and came in. A woman of medium height, she had a grey, shoulder length bob, a small pointed nose and rather prominent bags under her eyes. Margaret thought she looked a bit like the Home Secretary, whose name she could never remember. Sheila Bennett was dressed very functionally in what Margaret suspected was a machine-washable, non-iron trouser suit. She probably had several. It was that kind of job. She might be manager, but finances were almost certainly tight and she would need to be hands on. She would not be able to afford the luxury of sitting in her office all day.

"I'm so sorry to keep you waiting. One of our residents had just knocked someone over with his walking frame. I needed to deal with it. He's border-line dementia." She smiled ruefully. "Sorry, you don't need to know that. How can I help you?"

They explained what they wanted to know. She gave answers which in many ways were similar to those given by Ken Lloyd. The care home was close to the proposed wind farm and was likely to suffer from noise, AM and flicker. She was very concerned about her highly vulnerable residents. Many had mobility problems and were inactive, often spending a lot of time in the Day Room which had large windows overlooking the farmland that might soon feature seven turbines.

"I think it's going to be very stressful for them. Even if we turn a lot of chairs to face a different way the shadows will still flicker round the room. We can hardly keep the curtains closed all day.

"Did you know that the Home Office objected to plans for a turbine near Whitemoor prison because flicker could cause psychological damage and even physical injury to prisoners who had no means of moving to a different environment?"

Both shook their heads.

"There have even been suggestions that the high number of suicides there have been linked to the turbine. Our residents may not be prisoners, but in reality they won't be able to escape the flicker any more than Whitemoor's inmates.

"And their visitors aren't going to like it. The road we sit on runs east-west as you can see. The wind farm will be south of us, not much more than half a mile away. When the blades are turning, sun from the south will cause a strobe effect: very unpleasant for people driving along the road. I think some families will want to move their relatives elsewhere. That's not just a problem for us in terms of loss of revenue but potentially dangerous. However hard we try to keep people active, the reality is that most become institutionalised very quickly. They dislike change and can become very anxious and disoriented. It is not unknown for people to die when they are moved.

"And families of those looking for a care home for a relative will not want to bring them here. It could put us out of business within two to three years."

Margaret thought about it and suspected she was right. A lot of residents probably wouldn't last much more than three years anyway, so even if none was moved, an inability to replace those dying would ruin the business in very short order. Another depressing prospect.

Mo asked her about her movements on the relevant days.

She was working nights, finishing her shift at six in the morning Fred died. Her partner, a midwife in Knapton where they lived, could confirm that she got home at the usual time.

On the evening of the barn fire she had to work a double shift, from two o'clock in the afternoon until six the following morning.

On the night of Patrick Waldorf's death she was at home, alone until nine pm when her partner came in.

So, rather like Ken Lloyd, she had only one alibi out of the three that sounded solid – in her case, for the barn fire.

As far as the morning when the Pajero was stolen, she had been working.

Mo and Margaret were disheartened. While Sheila Bennett undoubtedly had strong reasons for wishing to see the wind farm plans abandoned, somehow they did not see her as a credible suspect. There didn't seem to be any credible suspect.

Chapter 28

Debra and Tom were charged with interviewing Veronica Mallon. This they were unable to do, but her husband Dr Jeremy Mallon agreed to spare them some time. It took them a while to find his home, which was in a smart modern estate on the outskirts of Knapton. Sat nav told them they had reached their destination before they even turned into the estate, leaving them to explore almost the whole of its maze-like complex of streets and cul-de-sacs before they found the right house. It was one of the larger houses in the development, set on a decent sized corner plot with a copse of silver birches behind it. There was an attached double garage and a Toyota was parked on the drive. The house faced south and Debra recognised the bare creeper on the front as Wisteria. In May it would be a picture. Now, like most others at this time of year, the garden looked neglected. The lawn had clearly not been cut since last autumn, and during the milder periods in early winter, the grass had continued to grow. Damp leaves lay singly and in patches, their number too great for earthworms to drag them all below the surface. Ornamental grasses stood in untidy clumps near the house, their seed heads now decidedly ragged. She hoped someone would get a grip with it all in the spring. In any event it was his problem.

Like Tom, Dr Mallon looked older than his years, but for very different reasons. Tall and slim, what little hair he had left was silver. His full, white beard was short and neatly trimmed but his moustache was dark and his bushy eyebrows were black. Altogether a dramatic appearance. For a man who was close to sixty in age, even a year or two older, he was handsome. His manner proved to be charismatic but somewhat arrogant. Debra saw him take in Tom's appearance, again only just the right side of scruffy. She made a mental note to have a word with him about it. Or maybe she'd get

Morton or another of the guys to do it. Somehow she did not imagine he'd take well to criticism from her, or indeed any woman, about his clothes.

Dr Mallon looked at Debra. "You are the police officer who phoned me?"

"Yes, Dr Mallon. I'm Detective Sergeant Graf and this is my colleague Detective Constable Turner."

"You have ID I take it?" They showed their warrant cards. Mallon looked as though he wasn't convinced that Tom was genuinely a policeman. "Come in then. I can't give you long as we have evening surgery on a Tuesday. And you're late." They were. Tom had made Debra pull into a garage forecourt. He was desperate for a pee. Again. She was annoyed. Again. She made up her mind to give him an earful when they got back to Parkside. Again. Why couldn't he have the sense to go before they left the station? It drove her mad.

Dr Mallon showed them into a living room with a pale cream carpet, white leather sofas and armchairs, and little by way of decoration other than some abstract oil paintings on the walls. The room lacked both character and warmth of atmosphere. Debra wished she had wiped her shoes more carefully as she entered the hall.

"What can I do for you? I thought it was my wife you wanted to see?"

"That's right", Debra replied. "You say she's away?"

"She's in Mexico. Her mother is dangerously ill. She left a couple of weeks ago. Saturday. The twenty second, I think."

"And do you know when she'll be back?"

"No idea. Depends whether her mother makes a dramatic improvement or snuffs it I suppose. Why do you want to know? You haven't told me why you want to see her even."

"You will know that we are investigating a number of deaths. There is a suggestion that opposition to the planned wind farm may be behind it. We are interviewing everyone known to oppose the plans. Your wife is a Committee

Member of Kmag. Do you know of any reason in particular why she should involve herself with that?"

"She's an eco-warrior. Believes wind farms are a complete scam and do untold environmental damage. She's wrong of course. Wind and solar are the future."

"It sounds as though you are an environmentalist yourself, sir."

"I am. It's one of the interests that brought us together. We met in Rio at the Summit. There are a lot of issues we agree on, like global warming. But our views on this are diametrically opposed."

Debra laughed politely despite the fact that she had picked up a mildly venomous tone in Mallon's voice. "So do you come to blows over it, or agree to differ?"

"That's a very impertinent question, Sergeant." Mallon smiled, but the smile most certainly didn't reach his eyes. "But mostly we agree to differ. When you meet Veronica you'll understand why that's the only sensible policy."

"Is that your wife in the photo, Dr Mallon?" Debra thought a change of tack might be prudent.

"It is." Mallon's eyes were on Debra; he did not turn towards the photograph, which she found somewhat disconcerting. It seemed to her as though it held no interest for him.

Debra looked at the photo again. It was obviously a studio shot and the photographer might have enhanced it somewhat, but Debra doubted it. Veronica had fabulous bone structure and caramel coloured skin. Her dark hair fell in thick waves onto her shoulders. She had strong arched eyebrows over black eyes and long lashes that Debra would have given her eye-teeth for. "She is a very beautiful woman."

Mallon smiled sardonically but said nothing.

"Is she perhaps Brazilian?"

"No, Mexican, as it happens. We met in Brazil. I told you. She was doing her masters in LA at the time and thought the conference in Rio would be educational. Which it was of course."

“Did you attend the public meeting last year, sir?” Having defused a little of the tension she was keen to get on with her questions.

“Which one?”

“The meeting at which it was decided to form Kmag.”

“Oh. Yes. I suppose it was inevitable that most of those attending would oppose the plans, but I wanted there to be at least one voice in favour.”

“Wasn’t that a bit awkward for you both?”

“We’ve made no secret of the fact that we disagree on this. We’d each written letters to the evening paper on the subject when the plans were first announced. Most of our friends think it’s a great joke.” The look on his face suggested that for him it was anything but.

“Do you know any of the other Committee Members, sir?”

“I’ve met Geoff Grindlay at the occasional medical conference. I don’t know the others.”

“What about your wife?”

“She’d met Geoff, too. There tends to be a cocktail party at the end of the conference.”

“Do you know a lot of other people who support the plans?”

“More than you might think. Some are just gullible. They believe Narbor is going to shower the local communities with goodies.”

“What? Bribes?”

“Oh nothing quite so crude. More like the kind of planning gain that housing developers provide when they put surgeries and schools into big new estates.”

“And did Narbor make any such suggestions?”

“If they did I don’t know. It all sounded a bit vague to me. Anyway, it’s not what interests me. Now I’m sorry, but I must ask you to go. I have to get to surgery.” He stood up abruptly.

Before leaving Debra handed him a card. “Let me know the minute your wife gets home please.”

Once in the car she exhaled slowly. "What on earth did you make of that Tom?"

"A bit touchy."

"Did you notice his response when I remarked how beautiful she is?"

"What response?"

"My point exactly. If you had a wife that beautiful, wouldn't you be proud of her?"

"Fat chance! I was more interested in the age gap. He must be what? Going on sixty. I don't know when the photo was taken, but if she was doing her masters while the Rio conference was on she must be fifteen or twenty years younger than him."

"When was it?"

"I can't remember exactly, but early nineties certainly."

She drove in silence for a few minutes. "Didn't even offer us a cuppa. Decent of him to condescend to see us, I suppose. We should be grateful for small mercies."

Chapter 29

Mo and Margaret drove out to see Brian Doughty. He lived in an apartment on the top floor of a converted mill on the north side of Chilton, overlooking the Ouse. The views were breath-taking and with a blue sky and full sun rare for late January, the swans on the river, and grazing on the banks, looked impossibly white. Margaret wondered how they managed to keep themselves so clean.

Doughty looked every bit the accountant that he was, with the possible exception of his hair. While not aggressively styled, and certainly not gelled, it managed a rather fashionable spiky look. The dark suit, white shirt and striped tie were almost an anachronism in the modern world. His firm was one of the big four, however, so Mo was prepared to make allowances for him. He wouldn't be seen dead wearing gear like that. Like Tom he tended to favour leather jackets, just not those which looked as though they'd come from a charity shop.

The room was furnished in a simple but modern style, with stripped wooden floors. One wall was of exposed brick. There were striking original prints on the other walls. Margaret hadn't had a close enough look but wondered if they were Pipers, or were by someone inspired by him. The chairs were black leather and they sat at a low glass coffee table. She hoped he had a cleaner. Even if she could afford it she wouldn't want something that would show every little mark so clearly. This one was spotless. So he probably did. She suppressed a giggle, though, as she imagined him in a pinny, mop in hand.

"Thank you for seeing us Mr Doughty." She was glad that Mo had started the interview, before her imagination got her into trouble. She got out her note-book.

"Brian, please."

“Fine, thank you, Brian. You know why we’re here?”

“Yes, of course. I’m happy to help in any way I can.”

“Firstly, can you tell us what your main objection is to the wind farm proposal?”

“Financial, mainly. I’m an accountant so I’m always interested in the business side of things. And when the government – any government – tells me that wind power is not subsidised, I smell a rat. Do you have any idea about wind power economics?”

Both Mo and Margaret shook their heads.

“I’m not surprised. And I’m not being rude. The way the wind power industry is subsidised is so complicated virtually no one who isn’t involved with it understands it. Let me try to explain. A wind power electricity generator has to report its output to Ofgem. Ofgem issues a Renewable Obligations Certificate for each megawatt hour of energy produced. The certificates are sold at face value together with the power to the electricity suppliers. Suppliers are legally required to buy a specified percentage of renewable power or be fined. But because ROCs can also be traded on the open market, suppliers who have not bought enough green energy can buy them to make up their shortfall – but then the price is inflated. The cost of the certificates is, of course, passed on to the consumer. Last year the face value of a certificate was thirty-seven pounds per megawatt hour in round numbers. But the value when traded could be double that. The wholesale price is very volatile. In any event you can see the additional cost passed onto the consumer is significant.

“That’s just the consumer subsidy. Would you like me to explain the Climate Change Levy exemption scheme? That’s a tax break the cost of which also gets factored into the price we all pay.”

Mo and Margaret looked at each other and in unison said: “No, thank you”.

Brian laughed. “Thought so. But it’s not just the hidden subsidies, it’s the fact that wind power is so bloody inefficient. There are days when there is no wind at all. And then on the days when it is too windy to allow the turbines to operate, the generators get compensation for loss of output. It's raving bonkers." He finally ground to a halt.

"Enough. I've over-simplified the issues a bit and they are still almost impenetrable. I think you get my general drift though."

"We do. Most illuminating, Brian."

"I like to shed a little light when I can, Sergeant."

Margaret wanted to say she'd like to lamp the pair of them.

Mo changed the topic.

"We have to ask. Routine questions, but we're putting them to everyone involved."

"Where was I when they all got bumped off?"

"Spot on. But there's another date we'd like your movements for, too. The morning of Tuesday 20th December 2010."

Brian pulled his smartphone out of his pocket. "Of course. My girlfriend and I went to Prague for a long weekend. We didn't get back until that evening."

"What about Monday 10th January between eight and nine am?"

"Nothing in the diary so I would have been on my way to my office in Cambridge."

"Sunday 16th January between five and eleven pm?"

"Crikey. About three weeks ago. Last Sunday we – my girlfriend and I – went out for a meal. The week before we had friends over. The week before that… Yes. Got it. We stayed in and watched a DVD."

"What was it?"

"You're joking, right?"

"No."

"What difference does it make?"

"Probably none, but I'd like to know."

"Not the faintest idea. I can't remember. Anyway, I seem to recall I didn't see much of it." He looked at Margaret and grinned. She felt goosebumps and it was not a pleasant sensation.

As usual Mo and Margaret exchanged views on their way back to the office. Neither saw Doughty as a very likely contender for the murders. As Mo said, using Special K might have come easily to him. But the idea of his stealing a manky old Pajero and driving it like a maniac in such treacherous conditions just didn't seem remotely likely.

Just as Mo was about to turn into the car park Margaret looked at him. "Have you seen Morton lately? He seems to have disappeared off the face of the earth."

"No."

"It's just that the chat in the canteen is that he's on some secret squirrel mission for Madam Adams."

"Don't know. If he's been seen going up to the top floor I'd keep well clear if I were you. I wouldn't want to cross her, even on a good day."

"It's odd though. It isn't as though we're short of anything to do. And he is Deputy SIO after all."

"I don't know. Don't go digging around is my advice. In my experience, the things that get dug up tend to be putrid and smell."

"Not a gardener, then."

"Do I look like a gardener?"

"No. I should think weed's more your style."

"What the hell do you mean by that?"

Margaret laughed. "Just winding you up. It's such good sport."

Chapter 30

Mo and Margaret didn't know what to expect from their meeting with David Brownlow. He opposed plans for the wind farm on the Shelford land but apparently wanted to build one himself. They knew he and Fred disliked each other, so Brownlow might not have shed tears over Fred's death. He seemed a more likely candidate for the theft of the Pajero, too. It was the kind of vehicle with which he would be familiar, and he could be expected to be able to deal with the technicalities of the theft.

Both of them were becoming heartily sick of their trips out to this stretch of country. If the land was so flat why in God's name were the roads so uneven? And why were so many of them straight with lethal right-angled bends? And why did so many have deep drainage ditches or canals alongside? And why was there so often an east wind so bitter you'd think it would shatter glass?

Brownlow was in his yard when they arrived, sitting in the cab of a tractor with the engine running. It was evidently a working farm, with various bits of machinery lying around, some obviously expensive, some looking as though they'd not been used in a decade. A stack of wooden potato crates stood against the wall of one of the barns. Sparrows hopped and scrabbled on the ground for whatever they could find. Rooks moved about restlessly in a nearby stand of trees, each clamouring for attention, the remnants of last year's nests awaiting renovation. An old tom cat woke and stretched before stalking into the nearest barn.

"Mr Brownlow?" The farmer nodded. "I'm Detective Sergeant Ramachandran. We spoke on the phone. This is DC Starr."

Brownlow turned off the engine, took out the ignition key and jumped down, looking decidedly bad-tempered.

"How can I help you? I'm behind schedule today. We've got a lorry coming any minute to collect sugar beet and we haven't opened up the clamp yet."

"I'm sorry to trouble you but we do need to talk to you. Is there somewhere we can go?"

Brownlow shrugged. "Oh, sod it. Follow me."

"Aren't you going to lock it?" Mo nodded towards the tractor.

"Hardly worth bothering. Ignition keys are standard on lots of tractors like this. They're always being stolen. Usually by continental organised criminal gangs. Nothing I do will stop them. Seems like you lot can't either."

At six foot two his strides quickly covered the distance across the yard to a modern barn. He led them into an office in one corner and slumped down into a rickety looking swivel chair. His hair was very fair, his eyes pale blue. He had a full beard trimmed short and could easily have passed for a character from one of the Scandi crime series on television.

There was one wooden chair and Mo told Margaret to have it – she was the one taking notes, after all.

Mo propped himself up, one arm on the top edge of a filing cabinet, managing to push a pile of catalogues perilously close to the edge. "We'll be as quick as we can, sir. Firstly, we'd be glad if you would explain to us why you opposed the plans for the King's Mere Wind Farm."

"I told the other two that came before. He was putting too many on the site, too close together."

"But you don't oppose wind farms in principle, do you?"

"No."

"So why so much concern about these plans?"

"They're greedy, the Shelfords. Always have been. Runs in the family. Ripped my father off over the price of the land they sold him. They'll make a fortune if they get the go-ahead."

Mo decided there was little point in pursuing this line much further. As Debra and Tom had found, there was a high level of animosity between the families. "Tell me about your altercation with Fred Shelford over the crop spraying."

"That was nonsense. He said his carrot crop had been contaminated."

"Can you explain that for us, please? We're not experts on farming."

"I have to spray my sugar beet in the summer, to control leaf disease. He claimed that some of the spray had drifted into a field of carrots and that their buyer refused the crop."

"Is that likely?"

"I think it's highly unlikely. It's not as though we use aerial sprayers. And there are fallow strips on the edge of both fields with a drainage channel between them. I don't think spray would drift that far even if the wind were in the right direction." Mo, who had seen crop sprayers many times on his trips through the fens and had often watched spray drifting, was not convinced. But there was little point in getting into an argument with him over it.

"But Peter Shelford says the customer tested his crop and found traces of fungicide."

"That's what he says. But if the customer refused the crop on straightforward quality grounds Shelford may have used that as an excuse. It didn't look like a healthy crop to me. But the daft buggers insist on farming organically. What is the point? The stuff costs more to the consumer and doesn't do you any more good."

"Where did the argument take place?"

"In the pub. I think Fred had had too much to drink. He was off his trolley. And sod's law. There was a stringer for the evening paper in there. So it was all over the news. But you think this is a motive for murder? Come off it. *You* must be off your trolleys. And why would I torch a derelict barn? And I've never met the chap from Narbor who died in the house fire. What possible reason could I have to want him dead?"

In truth, Mo couldn't think of one based on what they knew.

"Nonetheless I need to ask about your movements on the days in question. Where were you on the morning of 20th December?"

"December? No one got bumped off then did they?"

"Please answer the question."

Brownlow looked at the laptop in front of him and opened up the calendar.

"The twentieth did you say?"

Mo nodded.

"I had a meeting with my accountant." He gave them her name.

"Where was that, and at what time?"

"Knapton. Ten o'clock. Went on till midday and then we went to the pub for a bite to eat."

"Thank you. And where were you on the morning of Monday 10th January between eight and nine?"

"At home. No point even going out in those conditions. Had to wait for the fog to clear."

"Can your wife confirm it?"

"Of course, why wouldn't she?"

"The evening of Sunday 16th January, between five and eleven?"

"At home. I would have been out between about five and six, taking the dogs for a walk."

"And Monday 24th January, between five and eleven again?"

"We had a few people round. It was my mother-in-law's birthday and our turn to hold the party. Anyway, this is irrelevant. If you're trying to pin the death of that bloke in the house fire on me, you can't." Brownlow looked furious.

At that moment a large lorry drove into the yard. They heard the door of the cab open then slam shut.

Brownlow got to his feet. "Bugger off, will you? I can't tell you anything else. I've got work to do."

It was the cue for Mo and Margaret to leave. It hadn't been a very satisfactory meeting. On the way back into town, Margaret had refused the offer of a drink or a meal. He didn't know whether she hadn't enjoyed herself the first time, wasn't happy because they worked together, or just wasn't in the mood. Mo was beginning to feel bad-tempered himself. Maybe it's what the fens did to you. Those big skies hanging over you like thick grey woollen blankets. The endless mist. The horizon impossible to see or reach – like the solution to this case. As they drove away a flock of Pink-footed Geese rose up, wheeled round and landed in another nearby beet field. Neither would have been able to recognise them, or know the nickname birders gave them. Much less would they have known the bizarre and offensive definitions that the nickname threw up when Googled.

Chapter 31

Morton was again sitting outside Superintendent Adams' office at an ungodly hour in the morning. Some other poor sod was still in there, so heaven knows what time she got in. Rumour on the first floor had it that she slept there. Eventually her visitor emerged looking as though he had been savaged by a wild animal. Perhaps he wasn't used to encounters with such a senior officer. He indicated to Morton that she wanted him to go in.

This time she wore a dark green suit and cream shirt. She obviously rotated them. Perhaps she'd heard the rumours.

She looked up as he approached her desk. Her face was impassive.

"Good morning, Ma'am."

"I hope so Morton. What news?"

She gestured to the chair and he sat down. "Real progress, Ma'am. I talked to one of the officers involved with the case. The CPS told him they were very surprised when the victim dropped it. Her name's Jill Bryson by the way. Her brief was sure she'd honour her pledge to take the stand and was annoyed when she had a sudden change of heart.

"Her mother had been listed as a witness so her address was on file. I contacted her and she gave me her daughter's current address. She had moved of course. To Southampton."

"About as far as she could go in fact."

"I think that was the point. The case hadn't made national news but it was big in Manchester. And she agreed to see me. I wasn't expecting that frankly."

"Nor was I. How did you manage to persuade her?"

"I said we were investigating another crime, unconnected to her case, and we thought she might know something that would be helpful to us. I said that we did not expect our case to come to court and that there was no chance she would be called as a witness."

Emily stiffened. "That's a bit premature. We haven't even discussed whether we would prefer charges in the harassment case."

"But we won't, will we? Not based on what we've got at the moment. I don't think the CPS would touch it. And the force won't want the publicity." He looked at her pointedly.

She held his gaze. "I'm not sure you're right about the CPS if we get good evidence as to who is responsible. Whether a case would justify the cost is another matter. But you're right of course. I'd like to see the case sink without trace. Anyway, carry on."

"I went to see her yesterday. She has a good job now, with a regional TV station, and seems well settled. It was MacKay who paid her to drop the case. He paid her twenty thousand pounds."

Her smile was cynical. "More than enough to pay off her student loans no doubt."

"Exactly. But I think he was lucky because she said that she thought Bill Franklin had suffered enough after three days in court. She admitted that she was drunk at the time – the party got quite wild by all accounts. She still insisted that it was rape, though. But the money MacKay offered was enough to tip the scales."

"I'm surprised she agreed to see you. I'm even more surprised she admitted taking the money. Why do you think she did?"

"Not sure. She seems a decent enough young woman. She's married now and content with life. She may have taken MacKay's money but she certainly didn't warm to him. She says she's quite sure that he paid her off to protect his own reputation rather than that of his nephew."

"But he doesn't even have the same surname. Franklin must be his sister's son."

"But he is a complete control freak. We found that out during the investigation into Campion's death. It's how we got him in the end. If there was the slightest chance that the connection might become public knowledge, he'd want to stop it."

"If we charge Franklin, or even just stop him sending malicious texts, what happens if MacKay threatens retaliation against him by going public on his payment to Jill?"

"I've no idea how Franklin would react, I've not met him yet. But Jill said she would deny it."

"Why would she do that?"

"MacKay's in prison for murder. She isn't. She's hoping people would believe her rather than him and she wouldn't want to be thought of as someone who did business with a murderer. Anyway, how would he do it?"

"By phone. He must have a mobile, or access to one. I assume we'll be arranging to search his cell?"

He nodded.

"I suppose her response does make sense in a way. What now?"

"I need a warrant to search Franklin's home, office and car – anywhere that burner might be kept. If we do find it in his possession I'll arrest him and bring him in for questioning. But I'd also like the warrant to cover all his financial affairs going back to 2007. Maybe we can pick up the payment that MacKay made for the attack on Katie."

"I'll support the application for the warrants. Good work, Morton. Maybe we can wrap this one up fairly quickly after all. We need you back on the main investigation. Are you managing to keep up to date with it?"

"Yes, I go to the briefings most of the time. And the Chief throws as many actions my way as he can, some of which I have to offload. People are beginning to talk though. I can't keep this up for much longer."

"Let's hope you don't have to."

Morton closed the door after him as he left. Emily Adams swivelled so that she could look out of the window for a change. Thin clouds scurried across the sky, like flimsy banners tugged by someone out of sight. Only their movement caught the eye. Traffic moved slowly around Parker's Piece and a few hardy souls criss-crossed its paths. A day like any other.

She was greatly relieved that Morton was making progress. It's the first time she had dealt with him in other than the most cursory way and she was impressed. He might have the thick neck of a rugby player but he certainly wasn't thick. She admired his loyalty to Upwood, too. Upwood was one of her best officers and she wanted him out from under this particular cloud as quickly as possible for his sake, not only that of the force.

Chapter 32

Upwood opened the meeting and offered the good news that Peter Shelford was now out of the high dependency unit and on a general ward. It would still be some days before they could fully assess the damage, but at least he was out of danger.

"Let's just summarise where we are with the key people we've interviewed so far. Mo, will you start?"

"Fine. Margaret and I saw Ken Lloyd first. He's a member of Kmag but not an officer. He runs the riding stables and believes that the disturbance from the wind farm will seriously damage his business. He believes that to be the case even if the actual disturbance is less than he anticipates. He says it's all a question of perception on the part of his customers, who will be concerned about the vulnerable young people they send for riding lessons. His wife is in a wheelchair and dependent on him. He can't afford to lose his business. He has a motive.

"He was in Ely at a special needs school all morning the day the Pajero was stolen. We confirmed it.

"He has no witness to confirm his movements for Fred Shelford's death. His alibi for the barn fire was confirmed by the stable girl for the early part of the evening, and his wife for the latter part.

"Witnesses confirm that he spent the evening of Waldorf's death in the pub. It was quite busy because there was a big match showing.

"One interesting new piece of information emerged from the interview with the stable girl, Sally Brown. She thinks Ken Lloyd is having an affair with Veronica Mallon. I think she fancies him herself and is jealous of Mrs Mallon. It's not something we've followed up on yet.

"We saw Sheila Bennett who runs the care home. She has similar issues to Ken Lloyd. Margaret and I both think she is right and her business will be at just as great a risk from the wind farm as the riding stables. She has a motive.

"She was on shift all morning when the Pajero was stolen. Her partner backs up her alibi for Fred's death. Her alibi is solid for the barn fire, but she has only a partial alibi for Waldorf's death.

"We saw Brian Doughty, Treasurer of Kmag. He will not be affected directly by the wind farm but disagrees with the whole concept of wind power and its huge subsidies and its manifest inefficiencies. If anyone would like a personal tutorial on Renewables Obligation Certificates and Climate Change Levy exemptions, see me afterwards." Upwood wasn't sure whether the laughter out-weighed the groans. "Frankly we don't see it as a motive", Mo continued. "All four alibis have been checked and corroborated.

"Finally we went to see the farmer, David Brownlow. Debra and Tom had interviewed him after Fred's death. There does seem to be a long-standing feud between the two families. Even if it's sufficient to constitute a motive I don't see why Brownlow would kill Fred now. He says he doesn't know Waldorf and we've found no evidence to disprove that.

"He was with his accountant in Knapton from ten o'clock till about two on the day the Pajero was stolen. That's been confirmed. He was at home the morning Fred died. Interestingly, his wife had told Debra and Tom that she too was at home. When we talked to her she said she had been mistaken. She had a hospital appointment that morning at the Cambridge Lea."

"How could she make a mistake like that? It's a bit like everyone knows where they were when the twin towers came down. If there's a murder on your doorstep you know where you were when it happened."

"You'd think so. But she says she didn't hear about Fred's death till the next day when her husband told her. And she thought he meant the accident had happened that day, not the day before."

"Doesn't she watch the news or read the local paper?"

"Apparently not."

"OK. Carry on."

"He was at home the night of the barn fire apart from an early evening dog walk. His wife confirms that. His alibi for the night of Waldorf's death is solid: they were hosting a family party.

"I think that's about it."

Upwood thanked him. "Debra, what can you tell us?"

"Tom and I saw Richard Gardiner, Kmag Chairman. He won't be affected directly by the development. He disagrees with wind farms for a number of reasons but even taken together they hardly constitute a motive for murder.

"His alibis for all four events also check out.

"We also saw Dr Mallon. His wife Veronica is the one we really wanted to see, but she is in Mexico because her mother is dangerously ill. Veronica is Mexican by the way. What was interesting about the interview was the fact that he and she have diametrically opposing views on wind farms. He is for and she is against. We picked up some odd vibes at the meeting but we've no reason to think they are of any significance to the case."

"I wonder. Might he know about Veronica's affair? Why not go and see the stable girl and quiz her about it. She might shed a bit more light on it if she's interviewed by someone else. Then tackle Lloyd again."

Upwood then summarised his findings with Geoff Grindlay. "Like Gardiner and Doughty, he's well informed about a whole range of facts about wind farms but will not be directly affected by this development. All four alibis check out.

"Penny, anything more to report from Waldorf's home? We could do with some decent forensic evidence."

"Sorry, I can't give you much. I can confirm there were no signs of forced entry. The only solid piece of evidence is that gas chromatography tests show the petrol used as an accelerant is an exact match to that used in the barn fire. It's from the same source."

"We'll be lucky to find the source. But it's useful to be able to tie both crimes together so completely. Thank you."

Upwood asked for an update on the house to house enquiries.

The report was short. A number of TIEs had been tracked down and eliminated. Two were still being sought. But at least there was one nugget of information. A neighbour had seen a man wearing a blue and white scarf walking up the path to Waldorf's front door at about half past five. He was carrying some sort of bag over his shoulder, like a satchel or a laptop case. The same man was seen walking towards the Queen's Head, about a hundred yards away, by a shop-keeper who was locking up, at about six o'clock. He saw him enter the porch of the pub. Neither had a good view of his face but he was described as being on the short side and of average build. No one had seen him inside the pub and there were no other sightings. There was no CCTV footage.

Upwood could sense the mood improve in the room. This was the first promising lead they'd had since the case began. "Good. Thank you. Questions?"

Margaret was the first to catch his eye. "Sir, we've spent a lot of time working on the theory that these cases are all based around the wind farm. What if they're not? Maybe the motive's different. What about Fred Shelford's son? He stands to benefit from his father's death. Maybe he killed his father and Waldorf's death was just to confuse us. He'd know his father's routine. Like Brownlow, he'd know how to nick the Pajero. And he'd find it dead easy to get hold of Ketamine."

"Interesting. We've not interviewed him formally have we?"

"We talked about it if you remember, before his grandfather's stroke. But we never followed through."

"Perhaps it's time we did. But tracking down the man with the scarf has to be a key priority. Morton, can you organise a reconstruction? That might prompt a few memories from other witnesses."

Morton opened his mouth to speak but promptly shut it again. Instead he nodded. Something else he would have to try to delegate without making it look too obvious. And tomorrow he planned to execute his warrants.

Chapter 33

Franklin's cottage was in Elton Road in the centre of Wansford, west of Peterborough. They arrived before eight. Morton rang the bell. A moment or two later a young man opened it and appeared startled when he saw the number of people outside. Morton had the impression Franklin was not surprised to see them. When presented with the warrant he let the team in immediately. The fewer onlookers the better, especially as his door opened directly onto the street. Elton Road was busy. When the shop wasn't open, the pubs were, and there were always people going in and out of the Haycock.

Franklin was dressed, but looked as though he had not found time to brush his hair. He was fairly tall, close to six feet and his hair was fair. He was unshaven but the day's stubble could not cover a poor complexion. He watched as men took the stairs two at a time on their way to search the upper rooms. Two others went through to the kitchen.

When asked, he produced two mobile phones, an iPhone from his pocket and a cheap pay as you go mobile from a drawer in his desk. One of the search team produced his own phone and dialled. Franklin's cheap phone rang. It was promptly bagged as evidence, as was the iPhone.

Morton told him he faced charges under the Malicious Communications Act 1998, cautioned and arrested him. Franklin was driven to Parkside Station. Morton returned, too, leaving the team to continue their search of the cottage and car for any other evidence they might find of contact with MacKay.

Morton chose one of the probationers to join him at the interview. He was nervous about the whole business. If Franklin knew the name of the 'high ranking police officer' there would be hell to pay. Somehow he had to negotiate the interview without discussing the content of the messages.

Franklin refused the offer of a duty solicitor. A solicitor himself with one of the larger firms in Peterborough, it would have been easy for Franklin to call one up, even on a Saturday morning. He chose not to do so.

After the preliminaries were over and the camera was running, Morton put his first question. It threw Franklin completely.

"Do you know why Jill Bryson dropped her accusations of rape in 2007?"

Franklin gripped the arms of his chair. "What on earth is this about?"

"Please answer the question."

"No. I imagine she got cold feet." He looked around the bare room as if there might be someone behind him who could help.

"That's not true, is it? Your uncle, Andrew MacKay, paid her off."

Franklin now looked seriously worried as well he might.

"I don't know. If he did, he never told me."

"I don't believe that for a minute. Everything we've learned about that trial makes it very clear that Jill was determined to give evidence against you. Then suddenly she drops it. Why would she do that?"

"I don't know. You'd have to ask her." A sheen of perspiration was visible on his brow, certainly not a reflection of the ambient temperature which was only just bearable.

"We have done. She confirms your uncle paid her. He was your closest relative after your parents died, wasn't he?"

Franklin seemed physically diminished by this revelation. "Yes. But we weren't *close.*"

"But close enough for him to get you off a very nasty hook. You'd not have become a solicitor with a rape conviction. It cost him a good deal of money. Why would it be so important to him?"

"I've no idea. Not to help me. He's never helped anyone in his life so far as I know." Morton couldn't decide whether Franklin had known what had happened at the time, had only guessed, or was so relieved that he didn't want to think about it.

"What did you do after the trial collapsed?"

"I left Manchester and took a gap year."

"Immediately?"

"Yes."

"Where did you go?"

"What does it matter? Bangkok. Hong Kong. Sydney."

"How did you finance it?"

"I inherited some money from my parents."

Remembering the £5,000 MacKay was thought to have paid Katie's assailant, Morton had hoped the question might trouble him, but should have anticipated the answer. He changed tack. "Where did you spend the Easter holidays that year?"

Franklin took a sip of water from his plastic mug. "Easter? Christ knows. Probably went off somewhere with a friend."

"To London maybe?"

"I can't remember."

"But you remember pushing Katie Melhuish in front of a tube train at Charing Cross surely? Not easy to forget I should think."

Franklin shuddered but managed to look Morton straight in the eye. "I didn't do it."

"That's a lie isn't it? Your uncle paid you to, didn't he?"

"No he did not. And you can't prove it."

Unfortunately it was true, and Franklin seemed very confident of it.

"How did you end up in a firm in Peterborough?"

"I grew up there, I've got friends there."

"So not because your uncle introduced you to one of the partners in your firm?"

"Certainly not."

"Not to be closer to your uncle."

"No. I'd hardly ever seen him. He and my father didn't get on."

"Why would that be?"

"What on earth has that got to do with anything?"

Morton wasn't very sure either so reverted to his main line of questioning. "But your uncle did pay you to send Miss Melhuish those messages, didn't he?"

"No." Franklin practically spat his answer out.

"So you sent them for him out of sheer goodwill? Pull the other one. You've made it clear you don't think much of him."

"He did not pay me to send messages to anyone." To Morton, the observation was about as convincing as Clinton's statement to the effect that he 'did not have sex with that woman'.

"But you sent them nonetheless. It's no good denying it. We've traced the messages to your phone. No doubt a cheap one from Tesco. A tenner, that's all they cost now. Cheap enough to chuck away."

He nodded slowly.

"I need to hear your answer Mr Franklin. You sent the messages, right?"

"Yes." Franklin sighed.

"Do you know the sentence for a conviction under the 1998 Act?"

"No."

"You should do, you're a solicitor."

"I deal with probate."

"But you'd find out surely? You'd want to know what risk you were taking? Up to five years in prison?"

Franklin declined to comment.

"So if he didn't pay you, how did he persuade you?"

Franklin looked up wearily. "He threatened to tell my employers about the rape case."

Chapter 34

Upwood was up early the following morning. He'd decided to take the day off. He could ill afford the time but knew he faced burn out if he didn't, and that would help none of his team at all. Overtired, he was likely to make no decisions, or poor ones.

He headed over to Cley, after the Ouse Washes probably his favourite birding spot. One of the country's oldest reserves, Cley Marshes was established in the nineteen twenties and had been carefully managed from the outset. On the Norfolk coast, its northern boundary was the shingle beach of the North Sea. With reedbeds, marshland and saline lagoons it was a haven for a number of the species which he most enjoyed watching, including the Marsh Harriers that had so delighted Katie the day they'd first made love. At Cley, too, like Minsmere, there was the opportunity to watch sea birds. But at this time of year, especially with the wind in the right direction, there was a good chance of seeing something unusual.

The wind was light and visibility was good. Upwood spent a couple of hours in the reserve's hides. He saw twenty Black-tailed Godwit on Pope's Pool, which pleased him. One of the larger waders, they are winter visitors, but more usually found on inland lakes than those close to the shore. A Greenshank was another good sighting. Often seen at Cley on passage, it was unusual to see it here in the midwinter. Its wintering grounds in England were typically estuaries in the south west.

He spent some time watching the sea from the shingle bank and the shore and was rewarded with both Slavonian and Red-necked Grebe. He was focusing his bins on a single Smew when his mobile vibrated.

It was Emily Adams.

Scarcely two hours later he was in her office. Morton was already there.

"I'm sorry to drag you in on a Sunday, James, but we need to update you. And I gather that people are beginning to gossip about Morton not pulling his weight on our wind farm cases. Mo told him that one of his constables had asked him about Morton's secret squirrel job for me. So the sooner we can put this one to bed the better.

"Morton, why don't you tell DCI Upwood what you have found?"

"We have charged a man called William Franklin under the Malicious Communications Act."

Upwood looked startled. "Is that wise, Emily?"

"Listen, James."

"He's Andrew MacKay's nephew. Franklin was on trial for rape in Manchester after a New Year's Eve party got out of hand. Three days into the case the victim, Jill Bryson, withdrew her complaint and the case was dropped. Jill has confirmed to us that MacKay paid her twenty thousand pounds to pull out.

"During the interview I challenged him over the incident in the tube station. He denies it. I think he's lying but there's not a cat in hell's chance we'll prove it. And no large credits were paid into any of his accounts in 2007. If you remember we came to the conclusion that MacKay had paid money into an account set up with stolen ID. I've not managed to link Franklin to it. The only description we had of the guy that pushed Katie was vague if you remember. But it did say that the man responsible was fairly tall with fair hair and acne. Franklin matches that description. But so do a lot of other people. I think he pushed her. But I don't think he intended to kill her, even if that's what his uncle wanted. He hasn't got the balls.

"We do have him on the harassment though. It is one of his mobiles that was used to send the texts to Katie."

"Did MacKay pay him to do it?"

“He says not. He just says MacKay threatened to tell his employer about the rape charges.”

“He is a nasty piece of work. It’s like the way he bullied his book keeper.”

“Sheila Murray. I talked to her, too. She had a couple of unpleasant text messages after MacKay was sent down. Her husband made her get rid of her mobile and buy a new one. She had no problems after that.”

“So I was probably right. MacKay was simply taking his rage out on anyone who helped put him away.

“What about MacKay?”

Emily answered. “His cell’s been searched. No phone was found. So we’re not sure whether he borrowed one from a fellow felon or bribed a prison officer. He’s been told that his nephew has confessed to sending the texts and will not be helping him again. And the Governor has withdrawn all privileges.”

“And are you really going to refer the case to the CPS?”

“No. I don’t think it would be an altogether good idea, do you?”

Somehow Upwood didn’t think she expected an answer to that. “So do we think the situation is now under control?”

“Yes, we do.”

“I am very relieved to hear it. Morton, thank you for a job well done.” Morton nodded and got up to leave. Upwood remained seated. Once the door was closed he spoke. “Emily, thank you for your support. I very much appreciate it.”

“I’m glad we managed to keep the lid on it.”

“Is it OK if I contact Katie now it’s over?”

“James, I despair!”

“I can’t see the harm in it now. She needs all the friends she can get. She doesn’t have many.”

“Not yet. Let the dust settle for a few weeks. If MacKay’s as devious as you think, he might have other plans for us.”

“Can I at least tell her it’s finished?”

"No." Her tone was surprisingly sharp. "Morton will do that."

Upwood left her office feeling as though a weight had been lifted from his shoulders. But decidedly frustrated nonetheless.

Chapter 35

It was still dark when Jeremy Mallon stumbled out of bed, less hung-over than he might have been, but still decidedly the worse for wear. He cursed his wife again for buggering off to Mexico for such a long time. Her sister was there, wasn't she? Couldn't she do the dutiful daughter act? It was bad enough that he had to feed himself. Online deliveries were all very well, but studying the lists of ready meals made him suffer from what an elderly friend had called menu fatigue: the sense of ennui and lethargy induced by a range that no longer held any temptations. And as if that weren't enough to contend with, he'd got to walk the bloody dog. Why she ever got it he didn't know. Some daft idea that she'd meet other dog walkers and make new friends. Not that anyone in this God forsaken neighbourhood was likely to meet her exacting standards.

He dressed hurriedly and went down to the utility room where Button, the dog, slept. He was already awake and keen to get out. Mallon put the lead on and unlocked the side door and put Button into the back of the car. He reversed carefully out of the drive. He was unlikely to see any neighbours at this time of day, but it wouldn't do to knock down the paper-boy. Or was it girl? What the hell did it matter? He should be thankful, he supposed, that they still had paper deliveries.

It was cold, but not, thank God, wet or foggy. He made good time to the gravel pits on the edge of Knapton. He parked the car and changed into his boots. The ground looked damp and he wasn't keen to have his ordinary shoes mucked up. A slight breeze blew, making the branches of trees and shrubs shiver, shedding their moisture so that it might almost have been raining. He cursed Veronica again under his breath. Cursed the dog too. Button was straining hard at the leash and barking, as though keen to chase some rabbit or rodent in the undergrowth.

He walked for about ten minutes until he reached the first of the flimsy shelters some fisherman had put up years ago. He bent down to let the dog off its lead.

"Jeremy."

He stood up and wheeled round. The look of astonishment on his face as the first bullet hit him was profound. A flock of starlings shot off in alarm. A single Mute Swan pedalled furiously over the surface of the water before it became airborne and flew away to the neighbouring pit.

Button howled. And then, briefly, there was silence.

Chapter 36

By the time the briefing started on Monday evening most of the team were looking pretty jaded. Tom in particular looked very drawn, as though he'd been sleeping rough for a week. They had all worked long hours for a month and many had had little time off. Upwood was one of the fresher ones, having had the benefit of a morning at Cley and relief at the closure of the harassment case.

"We have a lot to cover this evening. Margaret, why don't you bring us up to date on the one part of the investigation we can close down?"

"Fine. We received the DNA results from Tirana. Our counterparts there were very helpful I must say. I wouldn't have wanted the young man's mother brought over and then denied the opportunity to see his body. It is, as we thought, Rajmond Dushku. We're sending a copy of the DNA report for him to Tirana. Once the police there are satisfied they will break the news to his mother. They understand that the body cannot be identified visually, and will advise the mother against travelling to the UK. We are suggesting that after the inquest, his aunt, Lauresha Broad, arrange his cremation. If the mother wishes, his ashes can be shipped to Albania."

"So our conclusion is that Rajmond was collateral damage. Asleep in the barn when the arsonist prepared the fire, out of sight behind the screen of the stall. Good work, Margaret. Jan, can you please draft a brief press announcement and run it past me? We should be ready to issue it as soon as we get clearance from Tirana.

"Remind me, who was interviewing Andy Shelford today?"

Mo answered. "I was, Sir. Morton and I agreed that it was better he didn't go because of the row with his father. Cheryl Brand, FLO, came with me. We tried to make the interview as low key as possible. Cheryl had learned the name of Andy's uncle when she was there before and that he farmed near Surfleet, the other side of Spalding. Our plan was to see him after our visit to Andy to make sure we could corroborate his alibi."

"And did you?"

"Andy wasn't best pleased to be asked where he was when his father died so we had to spin the usual routine procedures line. But his uncle did confirm what his mother had told us at the outset. Andy had indeed been on the farm at the time. He seemed a sensible chap and I think if Andy throws a wobbly about our going there, he will try to calm him down. He knows that Peter Shelford has had strokes before and that it will be vital in future to avoid upsetting him."

"So the theory that Andy killed his father for financial reasons and staged the house fire as a distraction falls at the first fence?"

"It does, Sir, but I'm glad. That family's suffered enough already."

"I agree. Thank you. Debra, I think you interviewed the stable girl and Ken Lloyd?"

"I did. She was very nervous about it. Thinks she'll lose her job. Says she wishes she hadn't mentioned it in the first place."

"Bit late for that. Go on."

"She sees Veronica Mallon often as she works there two days a week. She describes her behaviour with Mr Lloyd as flirty. Apparently she does a good line in fluttering eyelashes." A few muffled laughs greeted this observation. Upwood got the impression that Debra was likely to take a dislike to Mrs Mallon if ever they met.

"Once she saw them come out of an unoccupied stable. She says that Veronica was glowing." More laughter greeted this further observation, prompting Upwood to tell them to pack it in.

"Glowing?"

"As in just having had sex", she said bluntly. "Stable lads in my experience know more about sex than most of us.

She said Veronica was positively radiant. As in hot." The room erupted. Upwood made a half-hearted attempt to quieten them, but his heart wasn't really in it. They had little enough to laugh about with the cases they were dealing with.

"Mr Lloyd's hair was somewhat dishevelled", Debra added. Upwood thought this observation was probably superfluous.

"And did you ask Mr Lloyd about this incident?"

"I did, Sir." Her audience waited with baited breath. "He says they were having a heated argument about the best way to handle one of their more problematic youngsters. He denies that there was any impropriety and claimed that he loved his wife dearly."

"And did you believe him?"

"Yes and no. I think he probably does love his wife. I don't altogether believe his story about the argument. Why would they need to go into a stable for that? Would it really have mattered if Sally had overheard it? But his wife won't hear a word of criticism against him. He is caring, loving and attentive and she couldn't be more lucky to have him look after her."

"But no doubt he suffers a degree of frustration, and might be tempted by an exotic woman who seems to find him attractive."

"Yes, Sir. I reckon that sums it up. Mind you I can't see what possible relevance it has to the case."

"Nor I. But better we know than otherwise. How are we doing with our TIEs?"

This was another short report. The most promising, the man with the scarf seen approaching Waldorf's cottage, had not been found. They had still not traced the man who was searching for his lost dog on the morning of Fred Shelford's death. Their other two outstanding TIEs had been traced and eliminated.

"Morton, that brings us neatly to the question of the reconstruction. How are plans for that going?"

"Fine, Sir. We are going to do it on Tuesday next week, the same day as the fire. We've found someone who we think is about the right height and build and he will wear appropriate clothes together with a scarf like the one described. Jan's got all the arrangements in hand for the media" – she nodded – "so we are all systems go."

"Good. I wish it were a bit sooner, but these things do take time. And I think you're right to stage it on the same day of the week."

There was the usual question and answer session and then Upwood wound up the meeting having satisfied himself that everyone knew what they were doing.

Glass of whisky in hand after supper, Upwood tuned in to the local news. He was astonished to hear that Narbor had withdrawn their planning application for the King's Mere site.

He brooded for a while and realised he shouldn't be surprised. The media might be suggesting that Kmag supporters were behind these crimes, but Narbor would not want to risk that this campaign of terror could somehow be laid at their door. He slept badly that night. Unfortunately. The next day was to bring yet more bad news.

Chapter 37

A little after nine thirty in the morning a call was received from the practice manager at Dr Mallon's surgery. He had not appeared for work the day before and had again failed to appear today. The caller stressed that he was an active supporter of the King's Mere Wind Farm and that she was concerned for his safety. She was assured that the matter would be investigated. The call was rapidly reported to Morton who immediately went to see his boss.

"Sorry, Sir, but I think we have a problem: Dr Mallon's gone missing."

"Oh? Remind me, which side is he on?"

"He supports the development. It's his wife who is the Kmag member."

"Shit. What do we know?"

"He works full time and didn't show up yesterday or today. The receptionist tried to call him throughout the day yesterday, and one of his colleagues did during the evening. They've tried him again today. No response. They are afraid he may have had an accident. Or worse."

"His wife. Is she still away?"

"We don't know. But she can't be at home if no one is answering the landline."

"Get uniformed personnel over there. Force entry if necessary. Send a couple of people to talk to the neighbours. I'd better warn the Super."

Morton left and Upwood picked up the phone. "Emily. Have you got a minute? Just a minute on the phone then? Thank you. Dr Mallon, a supporter of the wind farm, has been missing for at least twenty-four hours. I know when an adult goes missing we don't normally rush into action. But if we don't find him alive and well at home I'm planning to start an immediate search for him. Thank you. I'll keep you posted."

An hour later Morton was told that there was no sign of Dr Mallon at his home and that there was a small car in the garage but none on the drive. There had been no sign of forced entry when they arrived but as they'd had to use the Enforcer, that situation no longer prevailed; there were no signs of disturbance inside the house. They were told to guard the house and, with whoever was available, to start canvassing the neighbours to see if they could reconstruct his movements. He also instructed Mo and Margaret to go to the house and search for any clues that might shed light on the doctor's disappearance. He sent Debra and Tom to the surgery to see what they could learn there.

He then convened the team who were involved in the reconstruction of 'Scarf Man's' movements that evening. They had already visited the scene and tried to imagine what might have happened. They had a number of scenarios in mind. One was that he had travelled the whole way from his starting point on foot and returned the same way. Another was that he had concealed a bicycle near Waldorf's cottage and covered the rest of the distance on foot. They had also considered the possibility that he had parked a vehicle in the car park at the Queen's Head. The way in which the film was directed would need to prompt eye witnesses to recall any such behaviour. When he was satisfied that everyone was well prepared he ended the meeting. They dispersed.

Debra was not thrilled at taking Tom with her to the surgery. He was in a particularly foul mood that morning and grumbled that he had too much to do, an increasingly common complaint from him. When he got into the car he slammed the door shut.

"Oh for God's sake, Tom, what is it with you? Get out of bed the wrong side again?"

"I didn't sleep well again. I've told you before I'm not sleeping well."

"Have you seen a doctor?"

"No."

"Well you should."

"That's my business, not yours."

"It's my business if it's affecting your performance and it is. This has been going on too long. Have you got problems at home you're not sharing?"

"No." He didn't attempt to face her.

"Is that the problem then?"

"Don't turn into a bloody counsellor on me, I can't stand it."

"Well go and talk to someone in HR then."

"I don't want to."

"I'm asking you to."

"I'm refusing."

"Then I'm instructing you to. Your behaviour is pissing me off. If you've got some sort of problem, let someone help you with it. You'll feel better about it and everyone will benefit. And if you don't agree I'm going to make the appointment for you. I'm sorry, Tom. You've not responded positively when I've raised this before and I can't let it go on. OK?"

"Oh, sod it. If I must."

They had reached this point in a difficult conversation just before arriving at Mallon's surgery. Debra had been meaning to talk to him about his appearance, too, but bottled it. Tackling him on his behaviour in the car wasn't the most professional way of dealing with it she knew, but they were so busy she decided to chance it. At least she had not had to look him in the eye. She was aware once more, though, that handling these matters was not one of her fortes.

At the surgery, the receptionist asked them to take a seat while she called the practice manager. Like so many waiting areas it was functionally furnished and thoroughly old-fashioned. Those waiting were either elderly, or young mothers with children. Many seemed to have coughs and colds. It was about as good a place to pick up an infection as a crowded tube train. A wooden crate stood in the corner. It was packed with plastic toys suitable for very young children. There were a few soft toys. Debra dreaded to think what germs they harboured. All in all, she thought you were likely to leave with more than you bargained for. A notice board advertised the services of homeopaths, hypnotherapists, practitioners of reflexology, reiki, shiatsu and heaven knows what else. Anything to keep the punters away from the surgery was her bet. Were general practices really in such a parlous state?

A woman appeared from one of the corridors leading off the waiting room. "Hello. I'm Pru Thompson. Come on through." She looked to be in her forties, rather over-weight but smartly dressed. She gave the impression of being very efficient. She led them into Dr Mallon's consulting room: pressure on space was severe in the surgery. It was built in the late eighties when the population of Knapton was around two thousand. Now it was double that, but surgery facilities had not expanded at the same rate.

"Thank you for coming so quickly. It's not like Dr Mallon to no show. In fact I've never known him do it. His diary was full for yesterday and today. And as you know we have been unable to reach him."

Debra responded with her first question. "Do you have next of kin registered for him?"

"We do. But it's his wife and she is in Mexico we believe."

"Do you have an address for her there?"

"No."

"Do you have a mobile number for her?"

"Yes. But it's a UK mobile. I've no idea whether she would use it over there."

"Do they have children or other close relatives that might know where he is?"

"They don't have children, that I do know. I've no idea about other relatives. He doesn't talk about his private life at all."

"So no idea about friends, then?"

"No, none at all."

"Is there some medical event on, perhaps, that he forgot to enter in your surgery calendar?"

"Not that I know of. There are meetings of the Primary Care Trust that he attends, but the last one was only ten days or so ago. There wouldn't have been another one."

"Are you aware of any problems he might have?"

"No. As I say, he doesn't discuss his private life at all."

"But did you sense perhaps that there might be something wrong?"

"No. He's a difficult man to read, if I'm honest. I've been working here nine years and he's never once asked me about my family. It doesn't bother me, but it's unusual. He can be moody, too." She looked as though she regretted it as soon as she had spoken.

"When he's moody, how does he behave?"

Pru hesitated, then realised that if the senior partner was honest with them they'd hear about it soon enough. "He sometimes has a vicious temper. He can fly off the handle for no obvious reason. It makes me nervous, frankly."

Chapter 38

When Mo and Margaret arrived at Mallon's house they found a uniformed officer at the front door, slapping his gloved hands, looking distinctly chilly. Not altogether surprising, since while the temperature was ten degrees, there was a brisk wind which made it feel much colder. It was strong enough to lift even damp leaves from the lawn and the ornamental grasses looked as though they wished they could lie down and die. The upper branches of the birches whipped as though in anger. The wind even seemed to stir up the smell of compost heaps. The officer confirmed that three of his colleagues were doing house to house interviews. He had called out the emergency building company. They had promised to send someone promptly to secure the property. The constable was not only cold, he was bored.

Mo and Margaret did a preliminary search of the house and satisfied themselves that there had been no prior forced entry. The fact that Mallon's car was not there suggested that he had left of his own accord. They had no reason to believe the house was a crime scene. While searching the kitchen they found a spare key for the back door. This could well be useful if they needed entry after the front door was secured.

Mallon did have a home office. So did his wife. Mo started on the former, Margaret the latter.

Mallon's computer was password protected so the techies would need to examine it. Mo concentrated on the filing cabinet, a four-drawer teak laminated one, unlike the battered grey metal one he had at home. It was extremely well ordered and looked as though the doctor was meticulous about keeping his files up to date. It seemed he was the one who took charge of the domestic finances and other arrangements. Unusually he appeared not to trust technology that much – all his bank statements and utility bills were held in paper form.

How long he would be able to keep that up was anyone's guess – most providers insisted that customers used online facilities.

Judging by the bank statements Mallon was not short of cash. And the year-end report from his investment manager showed that he held a very decent portfolio. So there were clearly no money worries.

Margaret was not having much joy in Veronica's study. There was a pretty mahogany knee-hole desk, possibly Victorian or Edwardian. There was no computer although there was a Wi-Fi printer. Margaret concluded that Veronica probably used a laptop or tablet and had taken it with her. There was no filing cabinet. Veronica stuffed papers she wanted to keep, or was too idle to dispose of, in the drawers of the desk. Clearly she was a keen shopper, judging by the number of receipts, many for clothes and shoes.

When the carpenter's drilling and banging had stopped the two of them went to the kitchen. It wasn't only the poor constable who'd held the fort who needed a caffeine fix.

"What have you found Margaret? Anything useful?"

"No not yet. What about you?"

"They're well off. His study's very organised."

Margaret laughed. "Hers looks it until you open the drawers and cupboards. Everything's stuffed in haphazardly. Just like my Mum. Looks as neat as a pin but actually it's a shambles."

"Chalk and cheese then. Just as well he runs the household admin."

They finished their coffees and got back to work. Margaret started searching through the contents of more drawers. Nothing of interest surfaced.

She decided to look at the photograph albums on the book shelf. On their spines were labels indicating that they covered a period from 1992 to the year 2000. There were no albums dated later than this. Probably, Margaret guessed, because the Mallons had started using digital photography. In the first were photos of Veronica and a much younger looking Jeremy Mallon, quite possibly at the Rio conference, Christ the Redeemer evident in the background to one. There were photos of their wedding, which looked to have been in the UK. Some were clearly holiday pictures taken in a variety of locations, mainly exotic. One trip looked as though it might have been made to Mexico. Margaret, who had studied the geography of Central and South America at A Level, thought she recognised Popocatépetl in a couple of photos.

If Veronica had maintained the albums she had not done so very methodically. Some photos were captioned, but by no means all. In one she found a dog-eared photo of a couple who looked to be in their fifties, accompanied by a woman who was probably in her late twenties. She looked not unlike Veronica. Maybe it was her parents and a sister? There was no caption so there was no way to tell.

Not having found anything of obvious significance she then opened a cupboard. In it she found a box labelled 'Christmas cards 2010'. Most were still in their envelopes. She opened each one. Finally she found one with a small label stuck on the back. The sender was a Sr F Padilla Martos with an address in Zihuatanejo. The card was signed by Mama and Papa. So now they knew where Veronica might be staying – good news.

Mo was still working his way through the filing cabinet. The most interesting find was a folder with a few pieces of correspondence between Mallon and David Brownlow. They had obviously had a major row.

He moved from the study to the main bedroom. It was clear whose side of the bed was which, not only by the oddments on the bedside tables, but by the state and contents of the drawers. Veronica's revealed nothing of consequence. The top drawer of his table held a variety of packs of pills.

Mo and Margaret crossed paths again. He searched the drawers of the console table in the hall but found nothing of interest. In the utility room off the kitchen she found bowls for food and water which, judging by their size, were intended for a dog. Of the dog there was no sign.

Chapter 39

Back at the surgery Debra and Tom had spoken briefly to the receptionist while waiting to see Dr Paxman, the senior partner. There was nothing she could tell them that they did not already know. She was however annoyed with Dr Mallon as well as worried about him. She'd had to phone countless patients to rearrange or cancel appointments. It had not been easy. She'd had tears and tantrums in equal measure. Altogether she was feeling very stressed.

They were directed down the corridor to Dr Paxman's room. "Sgt Graf and DC Turner, I understand?"

"That's right, sir. It's good of you to see us. I am sure you must be very busy."

"I am indeed. But I must, of course, do anything I can to help find out what's happened to Jeremy. Is there any news of him yet?"

"No, sir, not so far as I know. It's only been a few hours since we were notified he was missing."

Paxman was older than Mallon by some years. Debra thought he was probably past normal retiring age. He looked tired and anxious, his grey hair worn much longer on top than was commonly seen and combed close to his head. He peered at them over thick tortoiseshell glasses of the kind she thought no one wore any more. His tweed suit was vaguely shabby and in a style that had long since gone out of fashion. Debra immediately thought of Alec Guinness in the role of Smiley.

"Can you please tell me what you know of Dr Mallon? Anything at all about his work here from the time he joined you to his private life."

"Well he's been here quite a long time. I can't tell you exactly how long, but about ten years I think. Pru can tell you. He joined as a salaried GP and then after twelve months we made him a partner. He's a good clinician."

"How well do you get on with him?"

"Well enough. We don't socialise."

"Do the patients like him?"

"I don't really know. They can ask for an appointment with any of us here but some whose conditions are chronic like to see the same doctor even if it means waiting longer for an appointment. Some will ask for the earliest appointment they can get, never mind who it's with."

"Have you ever had any complaints from patients about him?"

Paxman removed his spectacles, wiped them with a silk handkerchief from the top pocket of his jacket and then settled them back on his nose.

"One or two." He stared at the files on his desk as though he would far rather be dealing with them.

"Can you remember any recently?"

"There was one last year from an elderly man who had a chronic chest complaint. He wanted Jeremy to prescribe penicillin for it. Jeremy refused, because in his view the condition was viral and therefore would not respond to antibiotics."

"Was it just Dr Mallon's refusal, or was there more to it?"

"The patient complained. He said Jeremy told him he was stupid. Jeremy denied it."

"Had there been similar incidents before?"

Paxman fiddled with his glasses again. "Yes."

"More so than with other members of your team?"

"Yes."

"Do you know why that might be?"

"Some would say that he doesn't suffer fools gladly. I'm afraid in a small town cum rural practice we have our fair share of fools."

"Like in 'normal for Norfolk' Dr Paxman?" This question from Tom came out of the blue and Debra was not best pleased.

Nor was Paxman. "If you are suggesting that our patients are inbred, Constable, I have to tell you that I find your question deeply offensive."

Tom shifted uncomfortably in his seat. "I'm sorry, sir."

Debra intervened to take back control of the interview.

"I'm still interested in Dr Mallon's behaviour, Dr Paxman. You say the two of you did not socialise. Was that his choice or yours?"

"His really. My wife and I did invite him and Veronica to a garden party the year he joined the practice. He refused subsequent invitations and after a while we stopped asking them."

"Do you have any idea why he refused?"

"If you want my honest opinion, he didn't like the way she was flirting with one of the other guests."

"Can you remember who it was?"

"No I can't. It's a long time ago and I had much more important things to worry about. It was their problem, not mine."

"Do you know how we might contact Mrs Mallon? Your Practice Manager could only give us her mobile number."

"No, I'm sorry I can't. I understand she's away at the moment but I've no idea where she is."

"Do you know of any clubs or societies he belongs to?"

"No. I haven't the least idea. I know he's interested in green issues. He wanted to put solar panels on the surgery roof. We took advice and were told it would not be a viable proposition. He was very annoyed about it at the time."

"Annoyance. Anger. Intolerance. I'm building a picture of a man whose character is volatile. Would that be a fair description, do you think?"

"It's not far off the mark."

"Can you think of any reason why that might be?"

Once again Paxman fiddled with his glasses. It was evidently a habit he had got into when he was uncomfortable about something. "I've wondered if he is addicted to prescription drugs."

Debra leaned forward. "Why do you say that?"

"Sometimes he's a bit hyper. The mood swings. Sometimes his co-ordination is a bit off. Occasionally he seems a bit drowsy."

"What kind of drugs does that suggest to you, Dr Paxman?"

"Opioid painkillers."

"Do you know of any reason why he should be taking them?"

"I understand he has a long history of back trouble."

"Is he a patient here?"

"No. He's with another practice I imagine."

"If he is addicted to painkillers is it possible he's overdosed?"

"It's possible. In fairness I can't say I've seen any clear evidence that he's addicted. It's just a feeling I have."

"Have you asked him about it?"

"That's not a question anyone but his own doctor would put to him. It's not been such an issue that I could deal with it as a performance problem. But it worries me nonetheless."

"Have you ever considered he might be a suicide risk?"

Paxman's eyebrows shot up and his spectacles slipped down his nose. "What an extraordinary idea. No. I haven't." But he looked as though he wouldn't rule the idea out.

Chapter 40

Reports are coming in that a leading member of the local community known to support the controversial King's Mere Wind Farm development has been missing for at least two days. Police were seen forcing an entry into a home in the upmarket estate of Birch Leys in Knapton yesterday morning. They have so far declined to comment but have indicated that a statement will be made shortly. The missing man was named locally as Dr Jeremy Mallon. Gary Deedes, Chairman of newly constituted 'Friends of King's Mere Wind Farm', spoke to our reporter: "It's outrageous. We've already had three people killed who were supporters of the scheme and two arson attacks. The police are doing nothing. It's an establishment conspiracy to stop the advance of green energy in its tracks. None of us is safe." We'll bring you more news as we receive it. Now, to other news...

Upwood had called the morning's briefing for eight o'clock. The room was packed and there was an air of nervous tension.

"Good morning everyone. Thank you all for being here on time, especially those of you involved in last night's reconstruction of the events on the night Patrick Waldorf died.

"How many of you heard the news on the radio this morning?"

Hands shot up, accounting for a third or more of those present.

"OK. Quite a lot, but not all. For those that didn't hear it let me play it to you."

His audience listened in stunned silence. But as soon as the recording had finished playing, voices rose in protest.

"Order. Order." Upwood did his best Bercow impression, detest the man as he did. Eventually the room quietened.

"You will understand that the atmosphere we have now is even more febrile –"

"Sir?"

"– that people are even more stressed and agitated. I am asking you to remain calm yourselves. We may need to take into account the potential impact of this new pressure group. We imagine it has been formed following Narbor's announcement that they have withdrawn their plans for King's Mere."

"Do you think there will be retaliation on their part, Sir?"

"It's a valid question. But let's look at it later. First I want us to review progress to date. There have been new developments which you won't all know about. Let's share them and then plan positive action to move this case forward."

"Notice he didn't say further forward" came a stage whisper from the back. Upwood couldn't hear what was said but could guess the general drift. He decided to ignore it.

"Debra, please tell us what you and Tom have learnt about Dr Mallon's disappearance."

"We went to Dr Mallon's surgery and interviewed three people. The first was the Practice Manager, Pru Thompson. She reported that Dr Mallon had a full appointment diary for Monday and Tuesday and that she had never known him no show. She told us his wife is in Mexico and gave us her UK mobile number. They have no children and she knows of no other relatives or friends. She describes him as moody and said he could fly off the handle for no reason.

"The receptionist couldn't tell us much. She was annoyed because she'd had to deal with a lot of angry patients.

"The senior partner, Dr Paxman, was interesting. He more or less said Mallon was anti-social. He had invited the couple to a garden party the year Mallon joined the practice in 1998. Apparently Veronica flirted with one of the other guests which made her husband angry. Mallon never accepted another invitation.

"Paxman describes him as a good clinician, but with a volatile nature. He's had more complaints from patients than the other doctors, at least that's the impression Paxman gave us. I asked him if he could offer any explanation for Mallon's behaviour and he said he suspected he had a problem with prescription drugs, specifically opioid painkillers."

"When you say 'problem', do you mean dependency or addiction?" asked Upwood.

"Addiction is what he said. I asked him if he thought Mallon might be suicidal. His answer was a bit equivocal."

"Interesting. Anything more of significance to report?"

"Only that we've tried calling her UK mobile several times asking her to call us and it keeps going to voicemail. Otherwise, no."

"Thank you, Debra. Mo, Margaret, what can you tell us?"

Mo went first. "Mallon is certainly not in the house, garage, shed or garden. He runs the household admin and is very well organised. Bordering on OCD, I'd say. They are certainly well off – no financial worries. There were no signs of his having prepared to leave home and his passport was in his desk and his wallet on his dressing table.

"The only thing of interest I found was a folder of letters between him and David Brownlow, the farmer. They'd had a row at the end of last year. Apparently Brownlow had ideas about converting old outhouses into holiday rental properties. Dr Mallon objected because he'd heard from a friend that there was a colony of bats there – Soprano Pipistrelles to be precise."

"You're kidding, right? Got form, have they?" A few sniggers broke out at the back of the room.

Upwood let this pass too. He recognised that the outbursts, much more common today than usual, reflected the high level of stress under which they were all working.

"They were roosting in the barn. They aren't rare, but they are, of course, protected like all bats. Anyway, they fell out over it big time. Brownlow put his plans on hold. I imagine he thought that after his row with Fred Shelford, discretion might be the better part of valour."

He moved on. "In the light of Dr Paxman's account, what I found in Mallon's bedside table is interesting. Packs of Paracetamol (OTC), Tramadol, prescribed by a private doctor in Cambridge, and Diazepam with no prescribing doctor's label on it. All were open.

"For those of you who don't know, Tramadol is an opioid painkiller and is often prescribed alongside Paracetamol to treat moderately severe pain.

"Diazepam may be better known to you as Valium, often used to treat anxiety disorders. It is, though, sometimes prescribed with the other two drugs in cases of severe pain. If I understand it correctly, the Diazepam helps reduce psychological tension and therefore also muscular tension, allowing the two pain-killers to work more effectively."

"Got another series of private tutorials coming up have you, Mo?" This question from the back generated more laughter.

He ploughed on. "Mallon apparently has had severe back pain problems. He was not a patient of his own surgery and Dr Paxman did not know what drugs Mallon might have been taking. I have established, though, that this combination of drugs can easily lead to dependency and addiction. Don't ask me to differentiate between the two, that *isn't* one of my specialist subjects. Margaret, do you want to say what you found?"

"Yes. I think you already know that there was no sign of forced entry to the premises and that although there was a Mini in the garage, the car that we believe Dr Mallon usually drove was not on site. Neither was there any sign of a dog in the house, although there was a bed and feeding bowls.

"The good news is that, just as we were packing up for the evening, I found an address for what I assume to be Veronica's parents in Zihuatanejo."

"Zee what?"

"*Zee – wah – tan – echo*. At least that's the best I can do. It's a small resort on Mexico's Pacific coast, about six hours by road from Mexico City. Less by air. There is an airport shared with Ixtapa – *Ees tapa* – a nearby coastal resort. And we think Veronica may have a sister living with them, or at least in the same town. That's about it, I think."

"Thank you. Simon, how are you doing with the house to house enquiries?"

Simon Hillyer had recently been drafted in to strengthen the team given the number of sites they were covering.

"Margaret's probably spot on about the dog, Sir. Several of Dr Mallon's neighbours report that recently he's been putting it – we think it's probably a Schnauzer – into the car, the Toyota that is, early in the morning and returning about an hour and a half later. We have two reports of him taking the dog out on Monday morning shortly after six o'clock."

"Thank you. More to do?"

"Yes. Once we learnt Dr Mallon had probably driven away from his home, we widened the enquiries to include properties facing roads approaching possible dog walking sites, like the park and the cemetery, as well as fuel stations and so on. There is still some way to go."

"Fine. Malcolm: the search for Dr Mallon?"

"Morning everyone." Malcolm Boyd had also been drafted in to beef up the team. An experienced Police Search Adviser, he was the obvious choice. "We were given intel about Mallon's car – a Toyota Prius hybrid – and others on the team are still going through CCTV footage, although there is precious little of that in Knapton as you know. They're even looking at footage from private cameras – some people use them for home protection. But they're not getting very far with that.

"We've been searching the most likely dog walking sites, like those Simon has mentioned. Nothing so far. The team is searching the Silver Birch Wood just south of Knapton, not far from Dr Mallon's house. After that it will be the land surrounding the nearby gravel pit."

After other reports had been delivered Upwood summed up.

"Right everyone. We are making progress on a number of fronts. As far as Fred Shelford's death and the barn arson are concerned, those of you with outstanding actions please complete them as soon as possible. We may need to divert resources.

"There are actions still outstanding in the case of Patrick Waldorf's death, and I am hopeful that we will get new leads from the reconstruction when it is broadcast tomorrow.

"Now, to summarise the case of Dr Mallon. We determined as soon as the report came in to treat him as High Risk, hence the scale and nature of our activities. We know he is not at home and he's not in hospital or custody. All the signs are that he left home voluntarily but failed to return.

"If we consider the possible reasons for that, we need to consider a number of issues.

"He may have had an accident and we have not yet found him. I don't think that's what happened. The chance of a wind farm supporter having an accident in the light of recent events is not one I give much credence to.

"There is no reason or evidence to support abduction.

"He may or may not be a suicide risk, and we can't rule it out. But again, in my view unlikely. Much easier to do it at home when his wife is away and anyway, why take the dog?

"Domestic violence? It doesn't look likely either. His only close relative is half a world away.

"So as we must in such situations, we think the worst. Murder. Our investigations will proceed along those lines.

"And I know it shouldn't need saying. But under no circumstances is anyone to make any comment of any description about the cases to the press or public. The situation we have is incendiary."

It occurred to Morton that, given there had already been two cases of arson, this was not perhaps the best choice of words.

Chapter 41

Later that morning Upwood was called to a meeting in the conference room on the top floor. The Chief Constable, Sir George Bland, the ACC, John Clarke, and Detective Superintendent Emily Adams were waiting for him. Judging by the empty coffee cups and jug, they had been there some time.

George Bland greeted him. "Come in and sit down, Upwood. You know everyone here? Of course you do." At six foot four and some sixteen stone in weight, his was an imposing figure. He was not far off retirement and while fit and ostensibly healthy he looked as though it could not come soon enough. Who could blame him with this series of cases likely to be his last? He was an old-school policeman and had found it increasingly difficult to keep up to date with modern culture, technology or even policing procedures. He relied heavily on his ACC as far as the paperwork was concerned. He was extremely well connected across the county and valued his reputation greatly. He had had some early successes and had risen quite quickly through the ranks. His current position was thought by many people, although not always the best informed, to have been gained on the basis of Buggin's turn. In the force he was known by the junior officers as 'Bland by name, bland by nature'. Their senior colleagues who had been on the receiving end of a lashing more than once did not refer to him in this way.

"I wanted us to get together so we could all keep on top of the latest developments. You will understand that there is a high level of concern here but also in the wider community."

"Of course, Sir." Upwood thought to himself that this was a statement of the bleeding obvious, but his face was impassive. Was he about to get a major bollocking? Or half-hearted support?

"Bring us up to date please."

Upwood did so, starting with Fred Shelford's death and ending with the latest measures to find Dr Mallon.

They listened, quietly in the main, occasionally throwing in a question for clarification.

After he had finished and they had exhausted their questions, Bland looked at his senior colleagues. Clarke looked calm enough. Emily's face and neck were lightly flushed. "You can leave now, Upwood. We need to discuss this and agree the best way forward."

Upwood went back to his office. He tried to tackle some of the urgent and important messages waiting for him. Not all fell into both categories but he was more skilled than most in recognising what he should deal with himself and what he should delegate. He found it difficult to concentrate.

It was nearly an hour later when Emily called him to her office. There was an empty coffee cup in front of her. Her face was still flushed. Perhaps it was just the caffeine. He sat down without being asked.

"James, you don't need me to tell you this is the biggest, most complex and controversial case we've had to deal with. We've got three bodies, arson and a misper, as well as two sets of green activists who have totally opposing views. The media are having a field day and the public are scared witless." She wound down, reached for her coffee cup and grimaced when she saw it was empty.

Upwood said nothing. Anything he said at this juncture was likely to sound defensive. He needed to know where they were coming from.

Eventually she spoke again. "You are to remain OIOC but I have been asked to review much more closely the kinds and quality of decisions you have taken and the effectiveness of the investigation to date. Am I going to find any glaring errors or omissions?"

"I honestly don't think you are, Emily. But I am happy that you take a closer look. The linking of all these cases has made management of them very difficult as you would expect.

It's entirely likely that we – I – have overlooked something. A fresh pair of eyes would be helpful."

Upwood knew that she had been carpeted too, in effect, and had no wish to make life more difficult for her. If she could make life any easier for him, all to the good.

She told him that the Chief Constable would chair the afternoon's press conference. She and he, Upwood, would also be there.

It was another mauling. Even the imposing figure of Sir George Bland, in full uniform, medal ribbons winking on his chest, did little to intimidate the media representatives. Not only were there reps from UK television but also from US and continental stations.

Much attention was devoted by the media to what they perceived as the rivalry between Kmag and Friends of the KMWF. Bland had been briefed to point out that the assertions made by the latter group were inaccurate and inflammatory and in the interests of community relations he urged them to tone down their announcements.

Confirmation that the misper was Dr Mallon gave rise to criticism. Why could the police not have announced his identity more quickly and gain public support in the search for him earlier? He stressed again that Dr Mallon's wife was thought to be overseas and while efforts were being made to contact her, there was understandable reluctance to make too much information public too soon. Upwood was seething about this. None of them liked having to confirm identity of someone who was known to be missing before the next of kin had been advised, but circumstances in this case were unusual, to say the least.

The TV, radio and newspaper coverage was predictably brutal. As he left the station, Upwood was besieged by reporters wielding their fluffy mikes and people toting impossibly heavy cameras. He made no comment but had a grim expression on his face.

By the time Upwood got home that evening he was shattered. The light was blinking on his landline. He played back the messages. One was from June, the mother of his late wife. One was from the boiler repair man, telling him it was time for his annual service.

The last message was from Katie.

Chapter 42

Upwood went out to the kitchen and poured himself a large Scotch with a little chilled water, took it back into his living room and sat down. It was not a large room but it was comfortable. A pale teal coloured carpet was set off by a paler teal sofa and a couple of arm chairs. He had a few pictures on the wall, most reflecting his interest in ornithology and wildlife. They included a limited edition print of a sketch of a group of *nettapus pulchellus* by Peter Scott, signed by him and which was given to Upwood when he was a young boy by his father when they visited Slimbridge. Upwood had no idea what the birds were until sometime later – they were the Green Pigmy Goose, natives of countries the boy imagined he would never visit. He was thrilled, though, to have a picture signed by one of his heroes.

His favourite picture was another limited edition print, this time of Wicken Fen, also signed by the artist, Phil Greenwood. This latter picture was one he could stare at for hours in the evening, glass in hand, as he thought over the day's events. The picture captured the landscape masterfully. Upwood could practically see the reeds swaying gently in a light breeze, water shimmering, reflecting the vast sky above. In his mind he might hear the call of the cuckoo, the drumming of snipe or the boom of the bittern, depending on the season.

Tonight he drained his first glass lost in that other world.

Then he phoned June. Like Upwood, she had never really come to terms with Anne's death, the circumstances had been too terrible. They both still had nightmares about it even after all this time. He saw her and her husband occasionally. He was fond of them. They had become fond of him too, although in the early days they had doubted whether she was wise to marry a policeman. Now June was just ringing to say that she and Jeff had been following the news and were concerned for him. If he wanted to come over for a proper Sunday lunch just to get away from it all, they'd love to see him. He thanked them warmly but explained that the likelihood of his getting any time off in the foreseeable future was remote.

He went out to pour himself another Scotch. Not such a strong one this time. As he sat down again the phone rang.

"Hi. It's me. How are you?"

"Hi. I'm not supposed to contact you, you know that." There was nothing at all accusatory in his tone. It was pure regret, which she could read without seeing him.

"I know, but I called you."

"It's the same thing."

"No it's not. Morton told me quite specifically that you were not to contact me. He said nothing about my not contacting you."

"It's still the same thing." He didn't sound convinced.

"No it's not. You guys do everything by the book. You've not contacted me since Madam Adams –"

"How on earth did you know they call her that? Did Morton tell you?"

"No. I made it up. It's obvious."

He laughed. "I s'pose so."

"Anyway. Since Morton did not specifically tell me not to call you I am taking what he did say literally and decided there was no reason why I couldn't phone you."

"I give up. It's lovely to hear from you by the way. The only bright spot in what has been an unmitigated disaster of a day."

"So I gather. I am so sorry, James. I can't begin to think how you manage a situation like this."

"I'm not sure we are managing it, but don't quote me. We are just about coping, but the volume of work is terrifying. And it doesn't help to have various unhinged members of the public sounding off to the media and the media blowing everything up into the sky. It's a nightmare."

"Is there anything I can do to help?"

Without thinking he responded: "Darling Katie. How could you?"

"By helping you re-charge your batteries. Didn't you once tell me that it was an SIO's duty to maintain resilience? Not to allow yourself to get over-tired?"

"Yes. But it's all hands to the pump now."

"When did you last have a day off?"

"You're sounding like June now. I had a half day off last Sunday. Before that I'm not sure."

"And how many hours have you been putting in each week? Too many, I bet. You'll burn out. Why don't we go out to lunch on Sunday?"

"I'd love to. But I honestly don't think I should. For starters we can't risk Emily catching wind of it."

"Easy. We go separately by different routes to a restaurant far from Cambridge."

"And I'm not sure what example it sets for the team if they know I've achieved nothing all day."

"For crying out loud – you are giving them some time off, aren't you?"

"Yes."

"Well then. There's nothing to stop you thinking during the drive there and back. Who knows? You might come up with some fresh ideas."

The idea was sounding more appealing, and sensible, by the minute. Or maybe he was just so damned tired that he couldn't resist the temptation.

"Where do you have in mind?"

"The Olive Branch, at Clipsham, on the A1."

The suggestion was just too good to pass up.

He was just dozing off to sleep feeling a shade more relaxed, with the idea of lunch with Katie to look forward to, when the phone rang. They had just found Mallon's body.

Chapter 43

Upwood called in for a car – he could not risk driving after his whisky intake.

The driver appeared after forty minutes, which earned him an earful. Upwood was getting very frustrated and unusually took it out on the poor chap. Fortunately there was an almost direct route over to Knapton, obviating the need to go through Cambridge. Despite that, it took some time to find their destination. The route might be direct but the roads were appalling. They were mainly B roads that threaded their way through dismal villages, the kind with brick cottages lining the main street, their features enlivened only by a disused Victorian Methodist chapel and a convenience store that had seen better days. Social housing would be hidden away in the back streets and there would be little sign of any modern, privately owned properties. How anyone could bear to live in them Upwood could not fathom. The roads were narrow, with frequent blind bends and the surface was as bumpy as a ridge and furrow field, if a little less regular in contour. By the time they had reached their destination, the journey, on top of Upwood's whisky, made him feel decidedly sea-sick.

Morton was already on site and had called for all the additional resources necessary.

Upwood did not recognise the place: a gravel pit east of Knapton. Favoured by coarse fishermen, it held little appeal for him as a bird watching site, except perhaps for its heronry, where in recent years a few Little Egrets had taken to sharing the roost. As a consequence of its use it did have a well-established car parking area. Malcolm Boyd's team had parked short of this to minimise contamination to the scene in case it proved to be where Mallon might be found. Later arrivals parked as best they could on the verges leading to the parking area which was already taped off.

Morton greeted his boss. "Evening, Sir. They've found his body about half a mile along the perimeter path. He's been dead for some time. Do you want to see?"

"Evening. Yes, lead on."

He donned protective clothing and footwear and followed Morton along the path of the stepping plates. The path was lined with scrub, and willows provided a high but not heavy canopy of branches. Before long the unmistakable stench of the early stages of putrefaction was apparent. The sniffer dogs would have picked it up as soon as they were released from the van. Lights had already been set up in a clearing beside the path. They stopped a few feet short of the body. Death had already been pronounced and photographers were hard at work. Despite the somewhat bloated face, protruding eyes and tongue, and the greenish colour to the skin, Mallon was still recognisable. That combination of white beard and black eyebrows was not common to say the least.

"Is there any indication yet as to how he died?"

"Yes. You can't see it from this angle but there are gunshot wounds to the chest."

"A complete change of modus operandi, then."

"Yes, but so there was from shunting Shelford into the lode and the arson which followed."

"True. I suppose that reinforces our idea that the guy is an opportunist, not a professional."

"I'd say so, certainly."

"Where's Mallon's car?"

"Good question. We're looking for it now. It must be fairly close by. If he was planning a circuit of the pit he'd not want a long walk before he got here. Schnauzer's are quite active dogs I believe, but I should have thought one circuit would be enough."

"And where is the dog? Not standing guard over his master's body?"

"No, clearly not. And it hadn't returned home either. Very odd."

"As you say, Morton. Is nothing about our cases straightforward?"

“Nope.”

“Everything else under control?”

“Yes. Go back to bed, Sir. I’ll stay on.” Upwood was glad to agree. As he made his way back to the car the white hair of Penny Fordham, Crime Scene Manager, shone under the lights as she approached him. She too had been beaten to the scene by her deputy.

When Upwood sat down at his desk the next morning he saw a message saying that Interpol had traced Veronica’s parents and confirmed that they believed her to be staying with them. He settled down to compose a suitable message to be relayed to her.

He then got stuck into his backlog of admin and began to prepare for the evening briefing. Only a few minutes had passed before a very tired Morton called to say that officers had discovered Mallon’s car in the car park of the adjacent gravel pit. Upwood steeled himself to avoid speculation and returned to his paperwork for an hour. After that he would relieve Morton on site.

When Upwood arrived back at the pits he told Morton to go home and to come back in for the evening briefing. The photographers were just packing up. Although they had arrived early at the scene they had wanted to take photos and video in daylight as well as by artificial light. Upwood began to gather information from the key specialists on site. It was going to be a long day.

The media had already arrived. No doubt their reports would be lurid and inflammatory as usual.

Chapter 44

The team attending the evening's briefing was smaller than usual – some had been sent home after working round the clock. Those who were there, almost without exception, looked exhausted. Even Morton, who had had the opportunity to rest during the day looked, in the words of Mo, like death warmed up. His child was teething. Morton had enjoyed the first few months in the girl's life – she had slept like an angel. Now she was screaming like the devil and there seemed to be nothing her mother could do to comfort her. So Morton's rest had been poor to say the least.

Upwood invited updates on the Waldorf case. There were none. It was hoped that the evening's broadcast of the reconstruction would generate more leads.

As far as Dr Mallon was concerned it was confirmed that he had suffered two shots to the chest, probably caused by a small calibre pistol. No weapon had yet been found at the site.

The police surgeon who pronounced death had volunteered the information that Mallon had been dead for more than two days but only after the post mortem could a better time of death be estimated. Bloating and skin discolouration together with the protruding eyes and tongue supported his estimate. Scavenger activity had been noted, probably foxes. It was thought that damage to the eyes had probably been caused by corvids. The body had been removed from the site during the afternoon and SOCOs still had much ground to search.

The question of Mallon's car was one which created a lot of interest. It had been discovered at a pit adjacent to that where the doctor's body had been found. Upwood hadn't realised there was a second pit there, but with very poor ambient light that night and with no close knowledge of the area, it was not surprising he had not seen it. The pit differed from the other in that it was fenced and gated. The gate was locked. The rather rough car parking area was outside the perimeter fence. A sign indicated that fishing was restricted to members of the Knapton and District Angling Club.

A very hungry Schnauzer was in the back of the car, which was unlocked and also smelt terrible for understandable reasons. Even the dog looked embarrassed. Keys were in the ignition. No car keys, mobile, wallet or ID had been found in Mallon's pockets.

The weather during the first week of February had been unseasonably mild (which accounted for the fact that some bluebottle activity had been noted on the body) and the ground was soft. The Toyota's tyre marks were clear to see on the approach to the gate. There were also tyre marks from another vehicle, which looked to be recent. This had approached the gate on the other side of the lane and there were signs that it had subsequently reversed, executed a three-point turn, and driven away.

It was agreed that members of the angling club be interviewed to determine whether any had seen anything happening at the pit since the previous Sunday.

Upwood reported that Veronica was said to be boarding the Air Canada flight from Zihuatanejo airport and was due to arrive at Heathrow at midday on Saturday. A driver and FLO had been arranged to meet her.

Upwood did not encourage a full Q&A session. Everyone was too tired. But the final question did lighten the mood somewhat.

"How is the dog, Sir?"

"He's fine and in protective custody." Laughter broke out. When it had died down he continued. "He's there for forensic examination. But he has been fed and watered."

He told them to go home and get a good night's sleep. They would meet again in the morning when they would also hope to hear early reports of feedback from the TV programme.

Upwood himself went home earlier than usual. He wanted to watch the programme as it was broadcast and then hope to get an early, uninterrupted and deep sleep.

For once he decided not to watch the news. He could anticipate what they would have to say and no doubt they would interview as many people as they could who held outspoken views on the conduct of the cases. Instead he made himself supper, checked his private emails (few) and his post (mostly bills and circulars). Thoroughly uninspiring, but at least he'd cleared it all in less than an hour. More than could be said for his correspondence in the office.

The producers of the TV programme had done well. They'd captured the rather run down atmosphere of the area in which Waldorf rented the cottage. The weather, too, had been kind. The last week of January had also been relatively mild so conditions for filming were similar. After the introduction the film opened with a shot of a man, relatively short and slight of build, approaching the cottage by the path that led through a scrappy front yard. This would no doubt once have been a garden but at some stage the wall had been demolished and gravel laid to allow off street parking. Waldorf's car, having previously been removed for forensic examination, had been returned for the purposes of the reconstruction. The man was wearing dark trousers and anorak and a blue and white striped scarf matching as closely as possible that described by the original witnesses. He had a satchel over his shoulder. He rang the bell and the door was opened by another actor playing Waldorf who could barely be seen in the doorway. 'Scarf Man' entered. The time on the screen changed to show 'Scarf Man' leave the house, pulling the door closed behind him. He then rejoined the pavement and turned right and walked the hundred yards or so towards the Queen's Head. As he did so another actor, playing the part of the shopkeeper, appeared to lock up, glancing at the pedestrian. 'Scarf Man' was seen entering the pub's porch and then the screen faded.

The programme returned to the studio. Viewers were asked to telephone with any information however irrelevant they thought it might be. Had they seen him go into, or out of the pub? Had they seen him in the pub? Had they seen him in the car park, getting into or out of a car? Had they seen him on foot further on from the pub? Had they seen any other vehicles or bicycles in the immediate area of Waldorf's cottage? All manner of questions were put, designed to prompt their recollections.

Upwood switched off when it had finished. He went out to the kitchen, finished clearing up after supper, poured himself a nightcap and went to bed. The drink was still on his bedside table, untouched, when he woke at six to the sound of his alarm. For once he had slept really deeply.

Chapter 45

Morton was tasked with running the morning's briefing with instructions to concentrate on the Waldorf case. Unusually Upwood had decided that Mallon's post mortem was one he should attend himself. Until the results were known and Penny's team had had a chance to examine the trace they had picked up at the site where the body was found, there was a limit to the progress that could be made on that case.

The briefing was short. After Morton had made a brief introduction the leader of the team manning the phones reported that a good number of calls was coming in following the televised reconstruction. Work was beginning to follow up those which sounded most promising. Those at the meeting had all watched the programme. Interestingly, one asked whether Waldorf's visitor might have been a woman, given the height and build. Morton reminded them about the entry in his diary suggesting a meeting planned with a man. One of the team argued, saying that visitor's name was Chris and it might have been a woman. Morton agreed they should keep an open mind. They dispersed shortly afterwards to their tasks.

Morton decided he needed to take a more active role in proceedings. Given the amount of time he had devoted to managing the various strands of the cases, and the time taken with the distraction of Katie's harassment case, he was feeling too disengaged. He asked Mo to go with him that afternoon to interview David Brownlow about his spat with Mallon.

When they arrived at the farm his wife told them he was out in the fields. She sent them to wait in his office while she called him in. Morton took the only seat leaving Mo to lean against the filing cabinet again.

"What did you make of him when you interviewed him before? Remind me."

"Stressed. A bit bad tempered. Maybe that's what farming does to you. It's not like some businesses where you can control most aspects. They've got the weather to contend with."

"And the EU. But the ill-feeling between him and the Shelfords was long-running. It will be interesting to hear what he has to say about his argument with Mallon."

At that moment Brownlow came through the barn into his office. He threw his cap on a hook on the back of the door. He nodded to Mo, then looked at Morton.

"And you are?"

"DI Morton Harrison, sir. Thank you for sparing us some time."

"Well, be as quick as you can. What's it about this time? I told your colleagues all I could about Fred Shelford last time."

"Thank you, we appreciate it. But we'd like to talk to you about Jeremy Mallon."

"Why in God's name would you want to do that? I don't know the man."

"But you have had correspondence with him I believe."

"You mean the bats." He threw his head back and laughed with not the slightest sign of humour. "Really. It seems as though everyone round here is as mad as a box of frogs. His wife opposes the King's Mere Wind Farm, along with a bunch of people with too much time on their hands. And he gets his knickers in a twist about bats. I ask you. They're not even scarce."

"Do you have them on the farm?"

"They're always about. The summer roost can be quite high, more than a hundred, hundred and fifty."

"Where do they roost?"

"We've got some old brick outhouses on the far side of the yard. Single storey. They go behind the boarding in the eaves. Why the hell is this of any interest to you lot?"

"Routine enquiries, Mr Brownlow. You know how it is."

"No I bloody don't. You come round here asking a lot of damn fool questions about Fred Shelford. And now you're asking about bats. It's mad. You must have much better things to do with your time given the crime wave we seem to be having round here."

"Tell me about your plans for the outhouses."

"You really think it's important. Words fail me."

"I gather you had plans to redevelop them into holiday cottages or something along those lines."

"I did think of it. But I never put any plans in."

"How did Dr Mallon get to hear of it?"

"Don't know. Maybe heard me chat to a mate in the pub."

"Do you remember the nature of his letters to you about it?"

"Pompous. That's what they were. Stupid arse. He's like all the rest of them. Think they know all about the countryside but they never go into it. The Soprano is one of our most common bats. It's not endangered. Its population is stable if not increasing. And they don't use the same roost year in year out, year after year. So he was sounding off completely half cock."

"How did you respond?"

"Told him to mind his own bloody business, what d'you expect?"

"And did he?"

"He wrote again threatening to get the bat conservation people involved and object to any plans that were submitted."

"Is that why you didn't go ahead with the scheme?"

"No. Don't be daft. Look at this place. Can you see converted outhouses here listed in some bijou holiday rental brochure? There's no market for it. If I was talking about it in the pub it was probably wishful thinking."

"You never met Dr Mallon?"

"No, why would I? My GP's in Chilton. We hardly move in the same social circles. I'd probably lamp him if I met him. Environmental do-gooders drive me mental.

Anyway, why the hell are you asking me all these questions about Mallon?"

"Routine questions, sir."

"Bollocks. Complete bollocks.

Morton and Mo thanked him for his time and left. The light was beginning to fade and as they crossed the yard they heard a blood-curdling scream. "Christ almighty, what was that?"

"You never heard a fox before, Mo? I bet there are loads roaming the streets of Liverpool."

"No, thank God. What's that all about?"

"It's the fag end of the mating season. It's the vixen that screams. The dog fox barks. You want to hear them when they're on the job. They can be locked together for an hour or more."

"You serious? Shit. Get me out of here."

Morton laughed.

It had been another unsatisfactory interview. Short-tempered Brownlow clearly was. Was he a murderer? Unlikely. He did, of course, also have an unbreakable alibi for Waldorf's death. And was six foot two in height.

Chapter 46

Upwood was already shaving when the radio alarm came on, just a moment before the news. International events took the lead with a report that President Mubarak of Egypt was likely to resign following widespread protests. Further coverage followed with reports of events in other countries in the region in what was now increasingly referred to as the Arab Spring. The final item on the national news was much closer to home.

Reports are coming in that a suspicious death is being linked to the disappearance of a Cambridgeshire doctor, Jeremy Mallon. Cambridgeshire Constabulary have confirmed that a body was found on the edge of a gravel pit north of the city of Cambridge but have not confirmed identity. A spokesman for a local action group, the Friends of King's Mere Wind Farm, said that Dr Mallon was a known supporter and it was therefore likely that his death was the fourth in a series linked to the proposed development. He said that they would be demanding police protection from what he described as a mass murderer, saying that nobody was safe.

Upwood was furious. Trying to solve these cases when there were so few tangible leads, and when activists were constantly fomenting the situation, was as difficult as it could be. He drove to the station in a thoroughly bad mood.

He entered the meeting room for the briefing to find it full and with an unhealthy buzz of conversation. It stopped as soon as he walked in. He noticed that Debra was not there and then remembered why. Debra had asked to be excused as she was taking part in a bridge tournament. None of her senior officers on the investigation had known she was a serious bridge player, but then she hadn't worked so closely with them before. Morton did recall once asking her about a mug she kept on her desk to hold pens and pencils. It bore the legend *'Old bridge players never die, they just lose their finesse'.*

When he admitted knowing nothing about the game she had told him, without patronising him, that she wouldn't explain as it was too complicated. She also told him, when asked, that she was a good player. When Upwood heard this from Morton later, it reminded him how Katie had once said of her elderly cleaner, whose hobby was military aircraft, that you should never take people for granted.

He opened the meeting, asking for updates in the Waldorf case.

Simon Hillyer spoke. "We have one neighbour who confirms she also saw a man wearing a blue and white scarf walking up his path. Unfortunately she can add nothing useful to the description.

"We have another person, a customer of the Queen's Head. He was coming out of the pub about six o'clock. He isn't a regular so we hadn't talked to him when we interviewed others known to be there at the time, although there weren't many as it was so early in the evening. Anyway, he says that he saw a shortish man wearing dark clothes get into a car. He pulled off a woollen hat as he got in. Our witness says he thinks the man had light or possibly grey hair, but he didn't get a very good look. He wasn't wearing a scarf but he was carrying a satchel. He didn't see which way the car went as he was on his mobile, but he thinks it was towards the town centre."

"Any information on the car?"

"Limited. He thinks it was a Golf. Dark coloured. He's fairly sure the reg starts FB69 – it's his wife's initials and his age. He didn't see the rest of it. We're trying to trace it now and checking CCTV and ANPR footage."

"Thank you. Anything else?"

"Not at the moment. We're still on it, but I'm not expecting anything better than what we've got now."

"Do we think it's the man who went to see Waldorf? If so why wasn't he wearing the scarf? It's distinctive enough?"

"It's a good question", said Upwood. "Any ideas anyone?" He had his own but it wouldn't do his team any harm to work it out for themselves. It didn't surprise him when Margaret answered.

"The scarf was chosen to be distinctive. He wore it going to and from Waldorf's house and as he entered the porch of the Queen's Head. No one in the pub admitted seeing him. I reckon he stuffed the scarf in his satchel, waited in the porch a minute or two, and then went back out into the car park as though he was just another customer."

"Sounds good to me. Well done. How are we doing investigating wider Kmag members and their supporters?"

It was Mo's turn to answer. "We've identified eight people who seem to hold unusually strong views on the subject of wind farms. Five of these are women so are unlikely to be of interest, though we are interviewing them. Although witnesses all talk of the person wearing the scarf as being male it's not impossible that it's a woman. One of the guys is interesting, though. He wrote several letters to the local paper after Kmag was formed complaining that they were not taking a robust enough line with the developers. Seems he's obsessed with the idea that the construction phase would involve irreparable damage to what he considers to be a potentially important Roman archaeological site. Used to be a fellow at one of the Cambridge colleges. We're hoping to interview him tomorrow."

"Morton, any info on who might benefit from Waldorf's death?"

"Yes. Principally his wife. Their home is near Norwich – he rented the cottage in Chilton. All to do with making the local community think he belonged. She has three young children and a friend confirms that she spent the evening with her the night her husband died. I think we can count her out."

"Penny, anything else you've managed to get by way of trace at Waldorf's cottage?"

"Only a bit of blue thread that snagged on the door post. We're thinking the scarf may have caught on it as he went out. It's being analysed now. We are fairly confident that Waldorf made a cup of tea or coffee for his visitor and there was also a glass near the remains of the chair we think he must have sat in. There were as I think you already know, the remains of a cup and saucer close to Waldorf's body."

"So Waldorf may have made a hot drink for both of them, the killer asks for a glass of water and while Waldorf is fetching that, he slips Ketamine in the hot drink. It seems entirely plausible. Ten to twenty minutes later Waldorf is dozing, the killer spreads the petrol and sets the candles and lets himself out. He could have brought the petrol in plastic bottles in the satchel. Dead simple. Anyone got any other theories?"

Silence reigned. It seemed likely that Upwood's theory was as likely as not how it had happened.

"Penny, surely there were prints? He can't have spent twenty or so minutes in Waldorf's company wearing gloves."

"Well there weren't many surfaces to lift prints from. And even if there were he would probably have wiped them before he left. Certainly there was nothing we could recover from the fragments of china and glass, other than Waldorf's."

"OK. Thank you. Let's see what we've got in Dr Mallon's case."

Simon spoke first. "We've talked to all the immediate neighbours. Several confirm that he has been taking the dog out in a car for a walk as you know. But one has told us that she knew he didn't walk in the park because he hated being accosted by patients when he was not in the surgery. She didn't know where they went except to say it was off the estate. No one in the surgery knows where he went. Most of them didn't even know he had a dog. I think Jan should put out an appeal for information from anyone who may have seen someone walking a Schnauzer near the gravel pit. It's difficult to be more specific until Mrs Mallon has formally identified him."

"Penny, what have you got for us from the gravel pits?"

"We've recovered one cartridge case and a bullet that presumably hadn't found its mark: it was embedded in a tree trunk just behind where we assume Dr Mallon was standing. They are 9 mm parabellum cartridges typically used in a semi-automatic pistol like the Glock 17. The shooter probably looked for the spent cartridge cases and missed one. Maybe he couldn't get the cartridge out of the tree trunk. We haven't found the pistol but we have divers searching the pit near where he died and a team searching the wooded area around the pit."

"Can you establish where the shooter stood when he fired?"

"No not really. It's a bit of a myth. I saw an abstract of an American forensic science paper on the subject that was published late last year. Provided the spent cartridge case hasn't been moved from where it fell, the best I can do is say the shooter was probably within twenty to thirty feet of Mallon. Probably just as likely to determine his position from damage to plant material or foot prints. We're still working on it."

"Anything else for us?"

"Like a cigarette butt with DNA on it?" She laughed. "That would be too easy."

Chapter 47

When Upwood reached the Olive Branch he found it difficult to park. Given that the next day was Valentine's day they had perhaps chosen a bad time to come. Always busy, it would no doubt be absolutely packed.

Katie was already there, sitting at a scrubbed wooden table near a window. She rose to greet him and he kissed her on the cheek. "You're looking good. Much better than last time I saw you."

"I guess I should take that as a compliment!"

"You were under a lot of stress then. We hadn't solved your little problem then had we?"

"Cheeky beggar! Little problem indeed. Makes me sound like a child."

"Teasing, Katie. Just teasing. Seriously, you've got some colour back in your cheeks and the gloss is back in your hair."

"I am sleeping better, that's for sure."

Someone came to bring menus and take their drinks order. Katie was still thinking about it when Upwood said he'd have a Virgin Mary. She nodded and said she'd have the same.

"I've seen you look better, James. How's it going?"

"Dreadful. You've seen some of the media coverage no doubt."

"Yes. It's brutal."

"I can't say I blame them though. Four deaths in as many weeks. It is a nightmare. We're all bushed."

"That's why I said you should take a break today. Just forget about it for a few hours."

"Well I'll have to. I can hardly discuss an ongoing investigation in a crowded pub, can I? Come on, let's look at the menu."

Their drinks arrived, suitably spicy, just the way he liked it. Katie was first to decide. "Devilled whitebait followed by roasted cauliflower risotto and parmesan crisp. Sounds delicious."

Upwood opted for the chestnut soup and the loin of venison with butternut squash and soused blackberries.

"So tell me how the new job is panning out. Are you enjoying it?"

"I'm not sure. It's a much more supervisory role and I do miss the investigative side of Mergers and Acquisitions work. There's a real buzz when you do the job well and you get feedback from clients who've acted on your advice and been pleased with the result. I should still get that to a degree, but it will be more because of the way I succeed in coaching and developing the team members."

"But that can give tremendous satisfaction, too, can't it? I found I enjoyed it much more than I expected."

"Maybe. I've not been doing it long enough. It will be quite a while before I can see much satisfaction like that."

"It'll come, I'm sure of it."

Their starters arrived and they each opted for a single glass of wine, she a South African Chardonnay, he a Pinotage, also from South Africa. He stuck his nose in his glass and drew in the plum and spicy aroma of the vibrantly coloured red wine. It smelt good. Each glass cost more than a bottle of the stuff he generally bought for himself at home, but if they were going to have only one glass, it might as well be a good one.

"How are Melanie and George?"

"I haven't seen them lately. I didn't dare tell them about the text messages. You know what George is like. He was furious when I pushed on with trying to find out who murdered Mark. He thought I was being thoroughly irresponsible and putting them at risk as well as myself. He'd never let me hear the end of it if he knew what MacKay had been up to."

"See them soon, do. You haven't got many friends as old as Melanie."

She pealed with laughter.

"You know what I mean."

"Yes, of course. I'll have to tell her that one though. She'll love it."

"Are you sure that's a good idea? Anyway, you haven't got a very wide circle of friends have you?"

"You're a fine one to talk. When did you last go out for a meal? With someone else I mean, not on your own?"

He thought for a long time and took a sip of his wine. "Probably with you."

"James, that's dreadful. That's more than two years ago."

"I get so wrapped up in what I do."

"Too wrapped up."

"You're no better. When did you last go out? With a friend."

"Just before Christmas I think. A guy from work. It was as much work as pleasure I suppose. We didn't do it again."

"We're a pretty hopeless pair, aren't we?"

They both laughed but neither of them felt very clever about it. Upwood also felt guilty because he had allowed Katie to persuade him to come out when he had declined the lunch invitation from June. June would have made a great fuss and mothered him, something he simply could not face at the moment.

"I know you can't talk about the case, James, but why does this wind farm proposal generate so much heat and light if you'll pardon the pun?"

"I'm not sure. The issues are no different from those relating to any other proposals. But there seem to be all sorts of underlying tensions in the community. A phrase has been going round and round in my mind since it started: *earthquake, wind, and fire.* It's as though the proposals have triggered a massive fracture in the community which have been followed by terrible aftershocks."

Katie thought for a moment. "It's a quote, isn't it? Or is it a play on words on the R&B band?"

"No, you were right the first time. It's a phrase from a hymn: *Dear Lord and Father of Mankind.* Do you know it?"

"It sounds vaguely familiar."

James hummed the first few bars of the Parry music.

"Got it."

"It's a lovely hymn but the story behind it is extraordinary."

"Go on."

"The words of the hymn are an extract from a long poem by an American Quaker in the nineteenth century. It deals with the ancient Vedic practice of taking hallucinogenic drinks to inspire religious fervour."

"What? Did he approve?"

James laughed. "No, far from it. He didn't even approve of singing in church."

She was silent again for a moment. "How do you know all this stuff?"

"Well I don't get out much as you know." He laughed. "No, actually my father was an Anglican minister."

"Do you still go to church?"

"Sometimes. Christmas usually. I'm afraid my faith took a serious bashing after Anne's death. I'm not sure it wasn't a bit flaky all along."

Katie decided to change the topic of conversation; it was getting too heavy. "What do you think about wind turbines?"

"I loathe them. Don't ask me to defend nuclear instead 'cos I can't. They may have a part to play in the overall energy mix, I don't know. I just hate them for the damage they do to birds, raptors in particular."

"I don't really understand why they do so much damage. The blades move slowly enough. Can't they get out of the way?"

"The birds are too slow. At their tips the blades can be travelling at more than a hundred miles an hour. I've spent several holidays near Tarifa, close to the migration route between Africa and southern Spain. There are several hundred turbines there. They reckon they kill more than fifty Griffon

Vultures a year. And before you say that isn't very many, it is when you take into account the fact that many of them could well be young birds – it's the young ones that tend to migrate to Africa rather than the adults. So over time the numbers decline and the population ages.

"And it's not just the Griffons. They are relatively numerous. But there are a lot of rare species that cross the Straits, like the Egyptian Vultures. I could go on."

"And on. And on." They both laughed.

They looked up to see the waitress hovering, waiting to take their dessert orders. Katie declined a pud but Upwood decided he couldn't resist the white chocolate and mint mousse with blood orange sorbet. Katie half regretted her decision when she saw how much he enjoyed it.

What they hadn't noticed was that someone on the next table had been watching them. The man picked up his mobile. "Smile, darling." His wife looked at him in surprise. Only after James and Katie had left their table did he explain. "It is him, I swear it is. He's the senior copper on those wind farm murders. The one that looks a bit like Daniel Craig. You'd think he'd have better things to do."

Upwood and Katie went out to the car park. He took her hand and squeezed it. "Thank you for suggesting it. It's been wonderful to see you again. Perhaps we can do it again one day?" On occasion he had an unfortunate habit of sounding more formal than he should.

"Oh James. You are such a muppet sometimes. The day is young, as they say. Come home with me."

"I can't, Katie."

"There's no such word as can't." She gazed up at him, her eyes, tinged with violet, were captivating. "I want you to, James." She lowered her voice, conscious that there were people at the car alongside hers. "I want you."

As usual he was powerless to resist. He nodded.

She left before he did. By the time he had his car out onto the road, a farm tractor towing a fully laden trailer was ahead of him. It only turned off just short of the A1. Katie was long gone.

When he arrived at Angelica House, Katie greeted him with a kiss that held considerable promise. "What kept you? I was beginning to think you'd got cold feet."

"Bloody farm tractor. Must have added at least ten minutes to my journey."

She laughed. "Well, you're here now, that's all that matters. I'm going on up. Will you fix us some drinks? We didn't have much at lunch."

He looked in the fridge. There was a bottle of white wine, but not much more than a glass was left. He decided on whisky.

When he reached the bedroom, she was nowhere to be seen. He put one glass down on her side of the bed and one on the other.

"There you are." She came out of the bathroom naked, but still wearing calf-length black leather boots.

He looked at them apprehensively. "Are you planning to keep those on?"

"No. I thought you'd like to help me take them off."

Several hours later he woke. Katie was already awake and smiling at him provocatively, her eyes sparkling with mischief.

He raised himself on one elbow and looked down at her. "What got into you? I've never seen you in such an erotic mood."

She pursed her lips. "Madam Adams."

He snorted. "What?"

"I got really pissed off when she tried to keep us apart. The harder she tried, the more I wanted to see you." He bent down and kissed her.

"And I enjoyed lunch so much; it made me realise how much I'd missed you." He kissed her again.

"And then I remembered you were a half-decent lover." She giggled.

He looked anxious. "Only half decent?"

"Last time you seemed to be holding back."

"You were going away again."

"That's no excuse."

"I can't explain." He didn't know how to. He just knew at the time that the better their love-making, the more he would miss her.

"You've got no idea how attractive a man you are, do you? You're incredibly naive in some ways. And that increases the attraction."

"It's not something I think about." He began rubbing his palm lightly over her nipples. As they hardened, his hand strayed down to her navel and stomach.

He still looked troubled. "Did I pass muster this time?"

Her laugh was husky. "Oh yes." She grinned at him. "I've decided you have hidden talents, Chief Inspector."

He smiled ruefully, his hand caressing her. He thought for a moment. "And your lips, Miss Melhuish, are simply luscious."

Katie thought for a moment, too, and then laughed. "Wicked." Desire flooded through her as she remembered how he had kissed her.

They made love again, slowly and sensuously.

Chapter 48

Upwood woke to find that Katie was shaking him. "Wake up! It's six thirty. What time did you say you had to be in?"

"Oh shit. Seven thirty. I won't get home in time."

"You can shower here. I can find a razor. You can just do it."

She could even find him a clean shirt – she'd kept a few of Mark's and had worn them at the weekends after he died to keep him close. They were a size smaller than he normally wore but they were clean and pressed.

He managed to get to the office just in time.

After the Monday morning briefing the team dispersed. Morton and Debra headed out to Knapton. "How was your weekend, Deb?"

"Fine thanks."

"Anything special?"

"Just personal stuff."

Morton knew he'd get nowhere if he pushed it but was pissed off that she was getting more time off than the rest of them. If she'd got a good reason they'd be more sympathetic. As it was she ran the risk of making herself seriously unpopular, which would be a shame for someone who was as good at her job as she was.

This time they managed to find the house without too much difficulty. The front doorway was still boarded up following the forced entry, so she phoned Veronica to announce their arrival. They were directed round to the back.

In the flesh Veronica was every bit as striking as her photo, although her face looked drawn and there were dark shadows under her eyes. Her hair was loosely tied back and she was casually dressed in a black polo neck jumper and black slacks. She took them through the house to the sitting room. She had already put a pot of coffee and cups and saucers on a tray on a side table. When she had passed them drinks she sat down in a deep armchair. It seemed to swallow her.

Morton began by offering their condolences. She nodded.

"What can you tell me, Officer?"

"Not a great deal, I am afraid Mrs Mallon. We received a call from Pru Thompson, the Practice Manager at your husband's surgery, on Tuesday last week saying that he had not appeared for work that day or the previous day. Are you aware of the crimes which have been committed recently that seem to be related to a wind farm development?"

She nodded. "I keep up with the news on my iPad if I'm away."

"Well, because your husband was known to be a supporter of the development we decided to treat his disappearance as high risk. That's why we forced entry. I am sorry we had to damage the door to do so but if there was a chance he might be inside and injured we had to get in."

"I see."

"As you know, we didn't find him here. But we did find his body at a nearby gravel pit. On Wednesday evening. He had been shot, probably by a semi-automatic pistol. We think he died on Monday morning when he went out to exercise the dog. The post mortem was conducted on Friday and we are waiting for the results. We'll know then with some certainty."

She shuddered. A few tears rolled down her cheek. She brushed them away with her hand and looked away briefly, then turned back to him. "Do you have any idea who is responsible?"

"We are pursuing several lines of enquiry but it's early days, Mrs Mallon."

"Hardly. The first man died, what, a month ago? It's obviously the same man. Why haven't you put a stop to all this?" There was a brittle tone to her voice. There were more tears. This time she pulled out a tissue from the bag on the table beside her.

"The cases are very complex. We have a very large team working on it. May I ask you a few questions?"

"Of course."

"When did you last speak to your husband?"

"A couple of weeks ago probably."

"That's a long time ago, Ma'am." Debra couldn't help intervening.

Veronica shrugged. "Not really. We text more than we speak if I'm in Mexico. There is a six-hour time difference. He's very busy with his work and my mother is dangerously ill. So I've been busy."

"When did you last hear from him?" Morton took control again.

"A few days ago." She took her mobile out of her handbag. The bag was a Mulberry, Debra noticed. Expensive. Veronica opened the phone. "The sixth of February. Sunday. He wanted to know how my mother was and if I knew when I would be coming home. I told him I didn't think she would last much longer but I didn't know when I'd be back."

"Do you know of anyone who would have wished him harm?"

She gave a rather nervous laugh. "No. Not really. He could piss people off royally if he was in one of his moods. But I doubt he had any real enemies."

"How would you describe his character?"

"He could be charming. He was very charismatic. He was very intelligent. He didn't suffer fools gladly."

"You mentioned his moods. Was there anything in particular that sparked them off?"

"No. Might be anything. I just ignored it. I was used to it. He was often in pain with his back. He didn't sleep well. It's enough to make anyone moody. Never mind working in a third-rate rural practice. He deserved better than that."

"So why did he?"

"He was a difficult man to please, Officer. He didn't like all the back-biting and politics in his last practice. He wanted to concentrate on the medicine."

"You support the wind farm development, don't you?"

"You must know that. I am a member of the Kmag committee. Richard will have told you, I'm sure."

"Indeed. Did it cause any friction between you and your husband?"

"No. We had one blazing row about it early on and then agreed to differ. It was the only way to deal with it. Neither of us was going to change our minds." She cast him a desolate look. "When can I arrange his funeral?"

"Not yet I'm afraid. There will have to be an inquest. Because this is a criminal case your husband's body may be retained to allow another independent post mortem after a period of time if we have not charged someone with his murder. Or if we have charged someone, the defence team may demand that a post mortem be carried out on their behalf."

"So it could be a long time." It was not the answer she wanted, clearly.

"I'm sorry, yes. Do you have any other questions for us?"

She shook her head. "Oh. Yes. Can I have a new door fitted? And who will pay for it?"

"By all means have a new door fitted. I can't give you any hope about compensation. There were very good reasons for us to enter the property. And we did no more damage than was necessary. I'm sorry. Do you have any plans to return to Mexico?"

"My mother's condition seems to have stabilised, so no, not at the moment. There will be a lot to do here."

"Good. Please don't think of leaving without consulting us. We shall need to speak to you again, I'm sure."

She nodded.

"Thank you, and thank you for giving us your time."

She showed them out via the back door.

"Well what did you make of that, Debra?"

"You know what I think was most peculiar? She didn't even ask about the dog."

"Perhaps it was his rather than hers."

"I don't think it was his. From what we've heard of him he wouldn't waste his energy on a pet. Anyway I'm fairly sure Simon's team reported neighbours saying he'd only been walking the dog since she'd been away. She didn't ask about the car either."

"She does have a lot on her mind, Deb. And she does have her own car."

"Even so. She just seemed very detached from it all. She didn't even seem that upset, just a few tears."

"She's probably still jet lagged. Maybe with his moods she's learnt how to keep her counsel."

"You're being very defensive of her. Fancy her, do you? She's a looker I'll give her that. And not too upset to put her lippy on either. Scarlet lips. Scarlet woman."

"That's a bit bitchy." Morton was becoming exasperated and trying desperately hard not to show it. Even before she'd met Veronica, Debra seemed to have taken a dislike to the poor woman.

"Well what about her affair with Lloyd?"

"OK. OK. I give in. Come on. Who've we got next?"

"Ken Lloyd as it happens."

"Fine. By the way, where's Tom today?"

"He's got three day's leave."

"Why the hell's he taking it now?"

"No idea. He told me HR had OK'd it."

"Why HR?"

"Dunno. Except I did make him go to see them because I was getting thoroughly hacked off with his behaviour. Said he wasn't sleeping well. Told him to see his doctor and he got bolshie. So I told him he had to see HR. No idea what's going on."

Why was everyone taking so much time off all of a sudden? Now Morton really was seriously pissed off. "Maybe it's time we found out."

Chapter 49

Mo and Margaret were going to interview David Brownlow for the second time.

When they arrived he was waiting in the yard for them, clearly in a foul temper, kicking aimlessly at the weeds forcing their way through the concrete. If anything, there were even more rooks in the stand of trees than there were the last time they were there and nest renovation was now underway. They were also noisier. The dominant call was the *'caw'* but there were also harsher, flatter *'kaahs'*. Margaret was heartily glad she had no rookery close to her home, it would drive her mad.

"What the hell do you lot want this time? There were two of you here on Friday, for God's sake."

"I'm sorry for troubling you again, sir. Routine enquiries have a habit of taking us in a number of different directions."

"Precisely. Don't know whether you're coming or going."

"Might we go through to the office, Mr Brownlow?"

"Come on then if you must. You're lucky my wife made the appointment. If I'd answered I'd probably have told you to go to hell. I've got a farm to run. Do you have any idea how hard that is? Of course you don't." He stamped off towards the barn.

Once in the office he threw himself into his rickety chair and let them sort themselves out. Margaret took the only other chair as before.

"You will be aware by now that Dr Mallon is dead. He was murdered."

"If the papers are right he was killed at the beginning of last week. Why didn't you mention it when you came last time?"

"It's customary to notify the next of kin first, sir. Can you please tell me where you were between eight am on Monday 7th February and eight am the following day?"

"Are you absolutely raving bonkers? You are, aren't you? You must be. Am I supposed to think that is when Mallon was killed?"

"If you'd just answer the question, sir."

"And you honestly think I might be responsible?"

"We'd like to eliminate you from our enquiries."

"I'd like you to as well. What a bloody waste of time this all is. I was in Norwich for a two-day conference on developments in GM science and practice if you must know."

"When did you arrive?"

"The night before. We had to register and decide which of the various workshops we wanted to attend the next day."

"And when did you leave?"

"Late afternoon on Tuesday."

"Which workshops did you attend on the Monday?"

"The first was about the extent to which modified crops have been given regulatory approval around the world."

"What time did it start, and end?"

"It started at nine thirty and finished at eleven."

"Can anyone vouch for your attendance?"

"I haven't the least idea. You can't seriously think I'd drive back here, kill Mallon and then go back to Norwich?"

"As I said, we'd like to eliminate you from our enquiries."

"I bet you'd rather bang somebody – anybody – up as soon as you can. The media are giving you a hard time that's for sure. Don't blame 'em."

"We are concerned only to bring the person responsible to justice."

"You're talking bollocks again. As soon as you revert to platitudes I know you have nothing useful to say. Bugger off. I've had enough of this nonsense. And don't come back. I'm not answering any more of your damn fool questions."

Later that day, Mo and Margaret interviewed two members of the Kmag committee. Both were polite and seemed mildly amused that they might be considered suspects.

Richard Gardiner said that he had been on his way to London to a meeting at the Institution of Civil Engineers. During the interview Mo had asked him whether they planned to disband Kmag.

"No, not yet."

"Even though Narbor have withdrawn their plans?"

"They didn't have much choice, did they? They'd lost their project manager and the PR has been terrible."

"But what will your members think, the ones who contributed funds for your campaign?"

"We shan't refund any contributions. We were very careful when we set this up to say that any funds held in Kmag's accounts would remain there unless and until the outcome was decided beyond any reasonable doubt. Narbor will resubmit plans after a decent interval, provided you can convict someone for these crimes. They have invested too heavily to walk away from it entirely."

His answer didn't take them any further forward but Mo did wonder if Gardiner was too sanguine about the attitude of contributors who might want a share of their funds back. Yet another opportunity for tension in a community already split wide open.

Geoff Grindlay had been at Addenbrooke's discussing surgery with a neurosurgeon on one of his patients.

Both alibis checked out. It would take longer to check out Brownlow's but it was possible that he had driven back on the Sunday evening, or early on the Monday morning, and got back to Norwich in time for the coffee break. All in all, not a very productive day. Mo was even more pissed off when Margaret refused to have supper with him, saying she wasn't in the mood.

The same day, Morton and Debra had interviewed three others for the second time.

Ken Lloyd offered as an alibi the fact that he had been in the stables. Sally Brown, his assistant, confirmed it.

Sheila Bennett had no alibi. She had been at home as her shift did not start until later in the day. Her partner had left home just before eight.

Brian Doughty was on his way to work in Cambridge. This was later confirmed.

They were still in the situation that they had no more potential suspects. All of those whom they had interviewed had unshakeable alibis for at least one of the crimes. The team was becoming demoralised again.

They would be even more disheartened – and shocked – when they saw the evening paper's headline.

Chapter 50

Bland leading the blind

It is becoming increasingly obvious to the public that Cambridgeshire Constabulary are completely out of their depth with the Wind Farm Murders. It is more than a month now since Fred Shelford lost his life. Since then there have been three more deaths. We have seen no sign of any progress in their investigation and some members of the local community are complaining of police harassment. One local farmer, who did not want to be named, has complained that the police have interviewed him three times when they can have absolutely no good reason to suspect him. Gary Deedes, Chairman of Friends of King's Mere Wind Farm told us: "They are completely incompetent. The Chief Constable should resign – it's a case of the Bland leading the blind."

The usual spokesperson for Sir George Bland did not return our calls.

Meanwhile criticism is being levelled at Detective Chief Inspector James Upwood, Senior Investigating Officer, who apparently had time to enjoy a leisurely lunch at one of Rutland's finest gastro pubs. As a member of the public asked: "Didn't he have better things to do with his time?" DCI Upwood declined to comment.

The article was accompanied by a photograph of Upwood and Katie at the Olive Branch.

When Upwood entered the Chief Constable's office the following morning at seven thirty, the ACC, John Clarke, and Emily were already there. Bland looked thunderous; his face was red and the veins stood out on his neck. He looked as though he was in the early stages of a seismic eruption. Any minute, now, thought Upwood, and he would be giving off steam.

Clarke looked as though he would rather be anywhere else on earth.

Emily looked close to tears, a state in which Upwood had never seen her before. He hoped she could hold it together.

"What in God's name is going on, Upwood? The reputation of the entire force is in tatters. What have you got to say for yourself?"

"We are making progress in our investigation, Sir. Since the reconstruction in the Waldorf case we've received two more reports which are of interest. As a result, we now have reason to believe that his attacker was driving a VW Golf and that he was heading out of Chilton north up the A10. We're checking out those sightings now.

"We have also identified three others whom we wish to interview. Unfortunately efforts to contact them over the weekend were unsuccessful, but we will try again today.

"And we have recovered cartridges from the site of Dr Mallon's death. We are waiting for the forensic report. We also have some useful trace evidence from the site."

"Is that it? After more than a month that's all you've got?"

"I've only given you the headlines, Sir. We have a good deal of useful information which may help us confirm the identity of the perpetrator." Upwood was winging it slightly.

Bland grabbed a glass of water on his desk and took a large gulp.

"Emily, I asked you to review Upwood's management of the case. What have you got to say?"

"I've been through the Policy File very carefully, Sir George. I can see no obvious errors or omissions in the investigation except that there has been no sign of exploring the possibility of domestic violence in the case of Dr Mallon's death."

"But I did record my reasons for that, Emily. His only family member is his wife Veronica who was in Mexico at the time of his death."

"So I understand, but there is no evidence that you checked that for a fact."

"I accept that criticism."

"What I really want to know Upwood is why you thought it remotely suitable to swan off on Sunday and have lunch in a very crowded pub."

"It's a question of resilience, Sir. I was getting over tired. We are required to show resilience."

The lid that Bland had been keeping on finally blew, with the full force of volcanic rage. "Don't you dare start quoting the bloody manual at me, Upwood. You know damn well that when we have a murder no one gets time off. And when we have four murders –"

"We think one was manslaughter, Sir."

He slammed his fist onto the desk. "Are you deliberately trying to wind me up? When we have four murders you work round the clock. And if you feel the need for a little resilience you don't bloody well let yourself be photographed at some poncey Michelin-starred eatery. Get out. Now." He banged his fist again. "Do something useful for a change and see if you can redeem yourself."

Upwood went out and waited for Emily. He had a feeling that the meeting in Bland's office would not last long. He was right.

She looked thoroughly uncomfortable as she led him into her office.

"I'm sorry about that, James."

"Why should you be sorry, Emily?"

"Because he wasn't being fair on you. You know he's due to retire soon?"

Upwood nodded.

"Well you can imagine how he feels retiring with this as his last major investigation. That headline was brutal. He's furious beyond all reason and he's taking it out on you."

"I can see that the photo is unfortunate. We tried very hard to be discreet. We went separately, and the Olive Branch is well outside our patch."

"But your picture has been in the news recently. People recognise you."

"I understand that. But everyone has to have some time off otherwise they burn out."

She sighed. "I know. I suppose I don't need to ask who your companion was?"

"Katie Melhuish."

"I thought so. I warned you off her. You had no business getting in touch with her."

"I didn't. She called me. Twice. She persuaded me that I should recharge my batteries. I've been putting in seventy or more hours a week, you must know that."

"But what if someone recognises her and stirs the pot even further?"

"Emily. Be reasonable, please. Her partner was murdered four years ago. She has a right to have lunch with anyone she chooses. His murderer is behind bars. What business is it of anyone else?"

"You're always so damned rational, James. Do you know that? It drives me up the wall half the time."

"Better than being irrational. And by the way. I did not 'decline to comment' to the newspaper. When I was called to say the reporter was on the line I told them to put it through to Press Relations. The report infers that I refused to comment on the news that I had been seen at lunch. It's simply not true."

"Oh, spare me the righteous indignation, James. We've all been the victim of that kind of reporting. Get over it." She leaned back in her chair and stretched her neck muscles.

"Are you going to see her again?"

"Katie? I hope so. Whether she'll want to go on seeing me now the harassment issue's been sorted remains to be seen. She suggested lunch because she wanted to thank me."

"She should have taken Morton out then", she said sharply. "Are you sleeping with her again? Judging by the clothes you were wearing yesterday you didn't get home on

Sunday night." She pointed to the photograph. "Your jumper reeked of Chanel No 5 yesterday."

"Emily, pack it in will you? It's none of your business! You go on and on about it. Anyone would think you're jea –"

"How dare you!" She shot to her feet. The chair behind her crashed into the wall and then ricocheted into a display cabinet. The sound of shattering glass was followed by a deafening silence.

He rose to his feet. He had no idea what made him say what he did, but he could tell by the flush on her face and neck, and her body language, that he was right. He was deeply shocked.

"Oh Christ. I'm sorry, Emily. I'm so sorry."

"Get out. GET OUT!"

He left the room, pulling the door closed behind him and leant against the wall. What a fucking mess. He was still there a minute later when a junior officer approached her door with a bundle of files.

"I should leave it for a bit if I were you."

"But she said she wanted these files."

"Leave it!" He yelled at the poor guy, who finally took the hint and turned back the way he had come.

Chapter 51

Later that morning, Emily led the briefing again in a vain attempt to re-motivate the team. She had recovered her composure following her argument with Upwood but could not look him in the eye. They were all tired and most were fed up that they seemed to be getting nowhere. Upwood remained impassive throughout and barely acknowledged her firmly iterated statement that she and Sir George had every faith in Upwood and the team.

A brief report was given as to interviews conducted with members of the angling club. None had anything useful to say.

There were few new pieces of information to be reported at the meeting. Mallon's PM results did suggest habitual opioid use, and based on the state of decomposition it was likely that he had died on the Monday morning. It was also reported that a minute trace of glossy red paint had been recovered from the gate to the angling club pit.

Their one potentially promising lead in the Waldorf case had fizzled out. The only Golf with a reg starting FB69 was owned by a tall young lady of Indian origin who boasted a very full head of glossy black hair. She also had a cast iron alibi for the night Waldorf died. Results had come back from the analysis of the blue fibre recovered from his door frame. DNA had been isolated but no match had been found on their databases. It would only be useful if they could identify a suspect and make a comparison.

As the meeting broke up Morton again paired with Debra.

"Did you get any sense out of HR about Tom?"

She nodded, her black ponytail shaking on her shoulders. "Eventually. They kept muttering about confidentiality. I wasn't having it. I told them he shouldn't be taking time off, we're too busy. They said he went to hospital yesterday. Suspected prostate cancer. When he saw HR the first time they did manage to persuade him to see a GP urgently. His PSA was very high and there's a family history. The GP arranged for an urgent biopsy. Tom told HR but said he didn't want his colleagues to know in case it's a false alarm. He told HR he'll get the results in a day or two."

"Poor bugger. Has he got family?"

"No. Long since divorced I think."

They didn't speak again till they got to the pool car.

"Want to drive?"

Debra laughed. "OK. Trying to set me up for something I bet. I hope you are a good navigator. Men aren't on the whole."

"Cheeky. We're better drivers and navigators."

"Not. So where're we going? Where does this chap live?"

"Chilton. Sick to death of the place. Miserable little village. Hugh Maskell-Grant. An archaeologist. Sounds a right prick with a name like that."

"He sounded a bit obsessed in the letters he wrote to the paper, too. Should be a real bundle of fun."

They found his cottage on the western edge of the village. On a good day it would probably offer a view across the meadows to the Ouse. Today was not a good day. It was dark and overcast. There was almost one hundred per cent humidity. Even a slight drop in temperature and there would be rain. Debra needed her lights all the way there. She parked on the verge outside his cottage and turned to Morton. "So?"

"What d'you mean, 'so'?"

"How did I do? Drive well enough for you?"

He grinned. "Not bad for a woman."

She punched him on the arm. "Arse. I passed advanced driver training with flying colours."

She raced up the short path as rain began to fall and knocked on the door. By the time Morton had got there Maskell-Grant had opened the door and demanded to see her ID. Morton got his out too.

"Come in. Don't just stand there, you'll let all the heat out. He shut the door behind them. Debra strongly doubted that it was much warmer in than out and opted to keep her Puffa jacket on. Morton zipped up his fleece which nearly sent her off into paroxysms of laughter. She didn't dare look at him. It wasn't just his zipping up his fleece. It was Maskell-Grant's appearance. He was of medium height, wearing a black polo neck sweater under a heavy cable-knit cardigan. His trousers were corduroy and he wore woollen socks under his sandals. He was clean-shaven with dark bushy eyebrows. He had a high forehead and his hair was grey and wispy, worn over his collar, perhaps to try to disguise how thin it was. A comb-over completed the look.

Maskell-Grant led them into a small sitting room and indicated that they should sit down. The furniture was old and worn and not very comfortable. Debra perched on the edge of her seat, notebook on her lap. Morton leaned back in his chair, found himself practically looking at the ceiling, and then sat upright again.

"Thank you for seeing us, sir. You know why we're here?"

"Something to do with the wind farm murders I gather. Although what it's got to do with me I've no idea."

"Just routine enquiries, sir. Good old-fashioned policing."

Debra shot him a look of astonishment and hurriedly scribbled something on her pad so she had a reason to hide the expression on her face.

"We're talking to anyone who opposes the wind farm development at King's Mere. You oppose the plans I understand."

"I do. It's a disgrace. Narbor should never have been allowed to carry out their feasibility studies. The development could do untold damage."

"Why do you think that is?"

"Fragments of pottery and coins – Roman remains – have been found in the vicinity. I'm convinced there's a settlement there waiting to be excavated."

"Is there widespread support for that view do you know?"

"I know others who would like to see the site excavated properly, yes." There was a touch of defiance in his voice.

"But you've had no real support for the idea have you?" Morton was winging it.

"I've not been allowed the opportunity to do the research necessary to start a campaign."

"Why not?"

"The Shelfords were not willing to let me onto the land. I've tried, but last time they said it was the wrong time of year, it would spoil their crops."

"When was this?"

"Last summer. Just about the time news of the wind farm plans came out."

"When did you start writing to the newspapers about the plans?"

"As soon as I heard about them. Why? It's not a criminal offence so far as I know."

"Just wondered, sir. What about the public meeting that was held in July last year? Did you attend?"

"Of course I did."

"Do you use email at all?"

"Yes. Why?"

"It's just that we didn't see your name on the list of supporters they collected after the meeting."

"I don't like every Tom, Dick and Harry knowing my email address. I get quite enough junk as it is, thank you very much."

"What about the committee? Did you volunteer for that?"

"Yes. Gardiner said they didn't want me. Arrogant bastard."

"Did he give you a reason?"

"Said they had enough already."

"What about the demonstrations when the council met? Were you involved with that?"

"No. I wrote to the planning people setting out my objections. I don't go around waving placards."

"Did you take any direct action to discourage Narbor from pursuing their plans?"

"Such as?"

"Well, cars were vandalised."

"That's a disgraceful suggestion, young man. I'm a respected academic."

"A retired academic, I believe?"

"Now you are being impertinent."

"But you no longer hold a fellowship at Cambridge, am I right?"

Maskell-Grant's colour rose and his fingers drummed on the arm of his chair.

"That is correct."

"Mr Grant –"

"Maskell-Grant"

"My apologies, Mr Maskell-Grant. Would you mind telling us why you are no longer a fellow? You are rather young to retire, aren't you?"

"It is absolutely none of your business. And it can have no conceivable relevance to the reason you're here."

Morton decided not to pursue it. There was no real reason to, in truth.

"Fine, sir. I am now going to ask you questions that we have put to other opponents of the wind farm. They are designed to help us eliminate you from our enquiries."

Maskell-Grant stuck his chin up, although given that his chin was not altogether impressive, this did not achieve a very intimidating pose.

"Well?"

"Did you know Fred Shelford well?"

"I didn't know him at all."

"What about Patrick Waldorf?"

"No. I might have seen him at the public exhibition that they held last year. I imagine he would have been there."

"What about Dr Jeremy Mallon."

"I'd never heard of him until I read about him in the paper recently."

"Where were you on the morning of Tuesday 20th December last?"

"This is outrageous. I shall complain to the Chief Constable."

"Nevertheless, sir, I ask that you answer the question."

"I've no idea. What day did you say again?"

"Tuesday 20th December 2010. Perhaps you have a diary you can consult?"

Maskell-Grant shrugged, as a fairly small man it was not an easy manoeuvre in an armchair, but somehow he managed it. He got up and went over to an old-fashioned bureau and dropped the front flap. He reached into one of the cubby holes and pulled out a small, scruffy, pocket diary.

He returned to his seat. "There's no entry. I would have been here."

"Can anyone vouch for that?"

"No. Unless a neighbour can confirm that they didn't see me leave the house. Difficult to prove a negative, young man."

What about the morning of Monday 10th January, between eight and nine o'clock?"

Maskell-Grant got up and went to his bureau to fetch his current diary.

"Nothing in the diary. I would have been here."

"What about Sunday 16th January, between five and eleven pm?"

He looked at his diary again, his growing impatience evident from the way he flicked the pages over.

"No entry. Home alone again."

"Can you tell me where you were on Monday 24th January between five and eleven pm?"

Maskell-Grant consulted his diary again. "In Ely, meeting one of my academic colleagues." He shot them a triumphant look.

"For the whole of that period, sir?"

"I would have left here about five. I probably got home at about half past ten."

"Could you please give us a name and contact number for your colleague?"

"His name is Matthew Ferry. Professor Matthew Ferry."

"And his number please?"

Maskell-Grant got up again and went back to his bureau, muttering grumbles. He came back with a hard-back address and phone number book of the kind Debra had not seen since she cleared out her granny's house. She wrote down the number he read out.

"Thank you, sir. And finally. Can you account for your movements between eight am on Monday 7th February and eight am on the following day?"

Pages flicked over in the diary. "I went to Bath on the Sunday morning and returned on Tuesday morning. I went to see an exhibition of Roman mosaics."

"Did you drive?"

"No, much too far. I went by train via London."

"Do you still have the train tickets, or a hotel bill perhaps?"

"This is harassment. It's scandalous." He got up for the fourth time and rummaged around in one of the bureau drawers. He returned with a receipted bill from a B&B in Bath. "Satisfied? You think I don't know what you're doing? Trying to see if I murdered all those people. You must be completely out of your mind." He threw himself back down into his chair which creaked in protest. Debra stifled a laugh and tried to hide it by coughing.

"As I say, sir. It's a matter of routine." He didn't dare look at his partner.

"Have you finished yet? I really have to get on."

"Just a couple more questions, then we're done. What car do you drive?"

"A Škoda Fabia."

"Could you give me the registration number please?"

Maskell-Grant did so.

"Finally, which football club do you support?"

"Have you taken leave of your senses? Do I look like someone who would watch football?" His eyes nearly popped out of his head.

"Thank you, sir. I think we've taken up enough of your time." Morton stood up and nodded to Debra. She rose and put her note book back in her pocket and smiled thinly at Maskell-Grant. They managed to get back into their car and shut the door before she exploded with laughter. "He's an absolute arsehole!"

Chapter 52

Upwood invited Morton to have a drink with him that evening, something he rarely did. When he did, Morton liked to accept, although he knew Emma would prefer it if he went home, given that Minda was teething. Nonetheless, he phoned to say he'd be another hour or so.

They settled down in a quiet corner of one of the local pubs, each with a pint of the week's guest ale.

"How is she?"

"Emma?"

"Well, both of them, really."

"Em's fine. Just tired all the time. Not very often, but sometimes she gets a bit ratty. You know how it is."

It was just a turn of phrase but Morton had no idea how much grief that last observation caused him.

"And your daughter? Teething, I think you said."

"Isn't she just? Why did God give the little blighters such good lungs?"

"She'll grow out of it soon enough. You gave her an unusual name. I've never heard of it before."

"It was Emma's choice. She had a favourite great auntie called Araminda. We shorten it. I just hope she doesn't get teased rotten when she goes to school."

"Emma sounds very patient."

"She is. I am very, very, lucky. I think she gets it from her mum. She's just the same."

"And she's still managing to get some painting done?"

"Yes. She finds it engrossing. Hard work, but relaxing as well."

"How did she come to paint animal portraits?"

"Apparently when she was at art college, they did a trip to Holland. Went to several of the museums in Amsterdam. The Rijksmuseum of course. The Van Gogh Museum. But also one I had never heard of in The Hague: the Mauritshuis. There's a painting there by a pupil of Rembrandt. Chap called Carel Fabritus. Very famous, she tells me. She's shown me a reproduction. It's called The Goldfinch. She was captivated by it. Said she had never known that such a tiny creature could convey such character and emotion. She was hooked. And of course it's quite a good market. People have always liked having portraits of their favourite pets."

"And horses. Prize bulls come to that."

"Yeah, but she's not into that. Strictly small animals and birds. But they sell well. She displays paintings in the waiting room of a local vet. A lot of it is word of mouth of course. She's good. Works mainly from photos but insists that she's got to meet the subject and spend a bit of time with it before she'll take the commission on. She's being very disciplined. Everything she earns goes into a special account to help Minda through uni. We rely on my income. It's why we hardly ever go abroad for a holiday."

"Admirable. If anyone had ever said you'd settle down with an artist, I'd have been astonished."

"Chalk and cheese. What is it they say? Opposites attract? I think the fact that she gets so absorbed in what she does that she loses all sense of time is why she's so tolerant of me."

"You are indeed a lucky man."

They finished off their pints. Upwood opted for a whisky chaser and Morton for a half of ale.

"So are we getting anywhere do you think?"

"Christ knows. We keep saying this bugger is an amateur but he's not giving us much to go on is he?"

"No. How did your interview go today with the archaeologist?"

"OK. Apart from the fact Debra was practically having hysterics. The man's a complete plonker. But like all the rest, he seems to have good alibis for some of the events and none at all for others. But he is short and has grey hair. Certainly an odd bloke. Threatened to complain to the Chief Constable."

"Does he know him?"

"He didn't say. But from the way he said it, it might be an idea to check it out. Forewarned is forearmed."

"I think you're right. I'll have a word with Emily and get her to sus it out. We need another PR disaster like a hole in the head."

Driving home, Upwood wrestled with the tricky question of whether he should apologise to Emily again, or leave it be. In the end, he decided to ignore it. If she was jealous of Katie, it would probably be better to say nothing which might encourage her to think that he knew. The apology he'd offered at the time, after all, was ambiguous. It might have meant that he was sorry to realise that she might have feelings for him which he was unable to reciprocate. Or it might simply have meant that he was sorry to have offended her. Discretion was the better part of valour. If she raised the question he'd have to think on his feet. But somehow he thought she'd probably not want to raise the issue again.

He also decided he would not tell Katie about the row. It might be embarrassing for her if she was to meet Emily.

When he got home he called Emily before he forgot. He was glad that it went to voicemail and left a brief message asking if she could check out Maskell-Grant's relationship with the Chief Constable. He sat at the desk in his study. His eye lighted on the watercolour of a sparrow on the wall in front of him. He'd bought it at the Bird Fair some years ago from the artist, Steve Palin. It was the original artwork for a book and was inspired by an old Afghan tale told in it. The sparrow was shown trapped by one leg in a snare. The wily bird tricked the hunter into releasing it. He feared Emma's goldfinch had not been as lucky.

Half an hour later Emily rang back. She sounded brisk and formal.

"He does know him. Lady Mary is the sister of Maskell-Grant's late wife. The women didn't get on very well. Lady Mary thought her sister had married beneath her. Mrs Maskell-Grant thought the same about her sister. Sir George hasn't seen Maskell-Grant since the funeral and has no wish ever to see him again. He did learn how it was that Maskell-Grant came to lose his fellowship. Something disreputable apparently, although he was not keen to go into details."

"Is it something we should explore?"

"No, probably not. If what he says is true, Maskell-Grant was probably bluffing."

They bid each other good night. Upwood gave himself a last whisky and turned in for bed. He didn't sleep well. He had a nagging feeling that there were a couple of loose ends which needed to be tied up. But the answer did not come to him in his dreams that night. He also worried that June would have seen his picture with Katie when he had turned down her invitation. He would somehow have to apologise to her. He eventually dropped off with the last verse of *Dear Lord and Father of Mankind* churning round and round in his head, over and over again.

Chapter 53

The mood at the briefing meeting the following morning was subdued. Upwood was leading and the senior members of the team attended.

There were no new developments in the Fred Shelford case and no new leads.

There were no new leads in connection with the barn fire.

They were not being very successful with the leads, such as they were, in relation to Patrick Waldorf's death.

So far, so bad.

A diver on Malcolm Boyd's team had, however, recovered a Glock 17 from the gravel pit used by the angling club. Since ownership of handguns had been outlawed following the Dunblane massacre in 1996, it was entirely likely that this one was not licensed. Checks were underway to see whether the cartridge case found close to the other pit had been fired from it. The checks had to be carried out but no one seriously doubted that confirmation would follow. The chances of there having been two Glock 17s at the pits were non-existent.

There was some discussion as to why the pistol had been thrown in the angling pit rather than the one at which Dr Mallon had been found. The consensus was that the killer was simply trying to impede the investigation and that climbing over a padlocked gate was a small enough deterrent to that end.

Questions were raised about the whereabouts of his mobile. It was agreed to be unlikely that he hadn't taken it with him. After a discussion that became more and more circular they parked it: the most likely explanation was that the killer had either stolen it, or chucked it far out into the gravel pit and it had sunk without trace in the mud.

The report that the flake of red paint found on the underside of one of the bars to the gate was in fact nail polish generated some amusement. Most there pictured a young couple scrambling over for an illicit tryst. Frankly, Upwood couldn't see the attraction. By all accounts the polish was fresh and was unlikely to have been there long. But surely at this time of the year, lovers would just stay in their car?

Morton reported on the interview he and Debra had conducted with Maskell-Grant.

"A bit of an oddball frankly. His cottage was colder inside than out. We had to keep our jackets on."

This observation generated the only laughter of the morning.

"He was very touchy. Very defensive, we thought, about the fact that he was no longer a fellow at Cambridge.

"He was very defensive, too, about the fact that Gardiner didn't want him on the Kmag committee. He was told they had enough members.

"He claims to have been home alone on the morning the Pajero was stolen, the morning Fred Shelford died, and on the evening of the barn fire.

"He has given us an alibi for Waldorf's death which Debra and I are checking out after this meeting. Deb, do you want to say a quick word on that?"

"Yep. I called Professor Ferry after we'd finished with Maskell-Grant yesterday. He confirms they met but, his timings don't agree with Maskell-Grant's. We want to talk to him face to face about it." She handed back to Morton.

"He does seem to have a firm alibi for Dr Mallon's death. He showed us a receipt for accommodation in Bath. He went to an exhibition.

"The only other thing of interest is the fact that he threatened to complain to the Chief Constable about our behaviour. Sir, I think you were going to see if there was any connection?"

"Yes, there is. Or rather, was. I don't think it's anything we need worry about. He doesn't seem to be very popular with Sir George." Upwood thought he heard a mutter to the effect that he was in good company then, but he couldn't work out where it came from.

After the meeting, Debra and Morton headed out to the car park. Their meeting with Ferry was at his home in Ely, a journey that shouldn't take them much more than half an hour, provided traffic wasn't too bad.

As they left the station, the sky was brighter than it had been and there were actually some blue patches. The temperature had now risen a little above freezing, but when Debra had left her flat earlier that morning she had not been sure whether her breath had condensed into vapour or ice crystals. There was still a bitterly cold wind from the east, as was so often the case. She'd often heard it said that there was nothing between Cambridge and the Urals to block its path. Quite where they were, or even what they were, she'd never troubled to discover.

Traffic for once was on their side and they quickly cleared the suburbs and headed out north up the A10. They found Ferry's house in Brewery Close without too much difficulty. Morton was a bit surprised. He'd always imagined senior academic types to live in large Victorian properties with three floors and a library. He mentioned this to Debra as they were parking. "You read too many novels. You shouldn't stereotype people, especially not in our job."

"I know, you're right. But it certainly isn't what I expected." They stood on the doorstep of a decent sized modern brick house, detached and with a very small garden at the front.

Professor Ferry opened the door himself and invited them in. He looked younger than Maskell-Grant, although that may have been deceptive given that the other man not only looked older than he was, but behaved like someone from a previous generation. Ferry did, nonetheless, conform visually to Morton's stereotype of the mad professor. He wore baggy mustard coloured cords with a Tattersall check shirt complete with frayed collar. And he wore a very loose, beige, ribbed cardigan with leather-covered buttons, and pockets that sagged from years of misuse. "Come in, come in. It's still nippy, even with the sun." He smiled at them. "Tea, coffee?"

"Coffee please", they said in unison. "Just black, please, and neither of us takes sugar", added Morton.

Ferry laughed. "Every police officer I've read about takes coffee like that. Why is it?"

"In the smaller stations there's no canteen. The milk gets left out and it goes off. The sugar bowl gets brown lumps cos people use wet spoons..."

"Put like that it makes good sense." He went off to the kitchen and returned a few minutes later with two mugs of coffee and a cup of tea for himself. They were both still standing. Debra had been looking at his bookshelves. Morton had been looking at his pictures. They looked good to him, but Emma would have learned a great deal more from them than he did.

"For heaven's sake sit down. Don't stand on ceremony. Now how can I help you?"

"Firstly, thank you for seeing us. I know you spoke to DS Graf on the phone briefly but we thought it would be very helpful if we could meet you. We should be very grateful if you would tell us how you spent the evening of Monday 24th January."

"Well, as I told Sgt Graf yesterday, I had a meeting with Hugh Maskell-Grant. He and I used to be colleagues many years ago when we were both at Bristol University. We've kept in touch over the years and meet from time to time. This time we were discussing a proposal from him that we should collaborate on a new book about early settlements in and around the Nene Valley, including the Roman settlements."

"Is that your area of specialisation, too, Professor?"

"Frankly, no, it's not. I'm a bronze age man. In a manner of speaking." They laughed politely. "The early bronze age specifically. Have you heard of Flag Fen?" They nodded as though in assent, though neither was any the wiser. "I thought not." He had read the look on their faces correctly.

"When did he approach you about the idea?"

"Just before Christmas, from memory. I think he may have sent me an email."

"How did you respond?"

"Probably said I was not very interested, reminded him I study settlements much older than those which interest him. I do remember telling him that I had a big project on at the moment."

"But he persisted?"

"Yes. He emailed me an outline of the book he thought could be done. Examining the many layers of civilisation in and around the Nene Valley up to the Anglo Saxons, and allowing each of us to demonstrate mastery of our specialist subjects. He thought we could use PhD students to do a bit of leg work on the other periods in history."

"So you agreed to see him. Wasn't that going to make it even more difficult to disengage from the project?" Ferry glanced at him appraisingly, fiddling with a loose button on his cardigan.

"You're right. Clever of you. I shouldn't have agreed to let him come over. It made him think I could be persuaded."

"So he came here on the night of the 24th January. At what time?"

"Just after seven if I remember correctly."

"Might it have been half past six?"

"I suppose it's possible, but I really don't think so."

"Six o'clock?"

"No, certainly not. Seven is when he was due. I've got a pretty good sense of time. You need it when you're teaching."

"And how did the meeting go?"

"Difficult, frankly. I told him I didn't think he'd researched the idea well enough. Neither of us is an expert on the Iron Age, and certainly not on any of the civilisations that followed the Romans, especially the Saxons. So we might have been tackling a book with sections written by masters of two periods and relying on what might well have been some pretty half-baked research by students in relation to the others."

"How long did he stay?"

"Until about ten o'clock, I suppose."

"So he was here about three hours discussing a project that did not really interest you. Why did you allow it to go on so long?"

Ferry fidgeted with the loose button on his cardigan again. "I suppose I feel sorry for him in a way. His career rather went off the rails at Cambridge, and I never really understood why. He would never discuss it with me.

"I tried to work out why he would come up with such a half-baked idea as this one. After a day or two I came to the conclusion that he wanted to hang on to my coat-tails: my reputation is pretty good, if I say it myself. Maybe he thought that if we could produce a book that achieved some critical success, if not profit, it might buff up his own reputation again. I take it you're not going to tell me why you're asking all these questions?"

"Sorry, Professor. Routine enquiries. That's all I can say."

"No more than I expected. Still, I'm a law-abiding citizen. I must do my duty when asked." Debra groaned inwardly. Now he was beginning to sound almost as much a prick as Maskell-Grant.

When they got back to the station they went to see Upwood. "Ferry says Maskell-Grant didn't arrive until seven on the 24th. Maskell-Grant said he'd left home for the meeting at about five. That's at least an hour unaccounted for. We want to talk to him again."

"I think you should. If that alibi doesn't hold it means he's only in the clear for Dr Mallon's death."

"And we've not checked the Bath alibi yet. There's no name on the B&B receipt, just a room number.

"But what I'd like to do is find out why he got chucked out of his fellowship. Everyone keeps alluding to it and no-one knows what happened. Or if they do, they're not telling us."

Upwood pondered for a moment. “Go for it. We’ve got bugger all else to go on.”

Chapter 54

Morton phoned Richard Gardiner, who agreed to see them later that afternoon. They were lucky that he worked from home; it made it easier to see him.

He showed them into the sitting room, a comfortable room which had a lived-in appearance. Gardiner offered them drinks but they thanked him and declined.

"So, you're DI Harrison. And DS Graf, have I got that right?"

"Yes, sir. And thank you for seeing us. I know we've called on you three times already."

"And you, DI Harrison, are the third officer I've met."

"It's a very complex case", offered Morton. "Four suspicious deaths."

"All apparently linked to the wind farm project. It's a very bad business. I've never been involved in anything like this before, I can tell you. And I've worked in some pretty lawless places over the years. How can I help you this time?"

Debra opened. "You mentioned to me when we first met, Mr Gardiner, that two volunteers for the Kmag committee did not in fact join. Can you tell us who they were?"

"Yes, there were two. One was a woman. I can't immediately recall her name but Geoff Grindlay will be able to tell you. Or I suppose it will be in the minutes. Hang on." He left the room, returning a short time later with a ring binder and sat down. "Tricia Marsh. I'd not met her before. She'd no real experience of campaigning, or committee work either. I didn't think she was altogether suitable, nor did Geoff. We had agreed before the meeting that we wanted the committee to be small with effective members who'd have something useful to contribute. If we weren't satisfied with any of the volunteers, we'd find appropriate ways of discouraging them. In her case we laboured hard on the question of the amount of time membership would take up. She took the hint and stood down."

"And the other volunteer?"

"Was one Hugh Maskell-Grant."

"It sounds as though you knew him."

"I knew of him."

"And you persuaded him to stand down."

"In fact I told him I was not prepared to have him on the committee."

"Why was that?"

"I thought he might be disruptive."

"Why?"

"Because of an incident that occurred some years ago."

Morton intervened. "Can you please be more specific? We've been hearing that his career at Cambridge derailed and he lost his fellowship. Does the incident you refer to relate to that?"

"Yes."

"We need to know, Mr Gardiner."

He sighed heavily. "I can't see the relevance. But if you insist. A friend of mine was also at Cambridge. He had published a paper on the excavation of a Roman settlement at Castor, west of Peterborough. Maskell-Grant accused him of plagiarising his work. It was complete nonsense. There was ample evidence to show that my friend had been on site earlier than Maskell-Grant and had been much more actively involved. But Maskell-Grant wouldn't let it go. The Master of his college advised him to withdraw his accusations. He wouldn't. Eventually there was a stand-up row in the Senior Common Room. Fortunately there were very few people there at the time. Maskell-Grant lost it completely, I'm told. He threw more than one punch at his colleague. Laughable. The man was several inches taller than him and probably several stone heavier. He complained to the Master. After that Maskell-Grant's position became untenable."

There wasn't much more Gardiner could tell them. But what they had learnt intrigued them. They decided to call it a day.

Mo and Margaret were still at the station. They had been studying some of the witness statements again.

They were not happy that they had failed to identify the car driven away from the Queen's Head the night Waldorf died. The witness had clearly not remembered even the partial reg number accurately. They were inclined to think that he may not even have been right about the make and model of car. What they could not decide was whether he was an attention seeker, who had seen nothing at all – always a risk following televised reconstructions – or whether he had bad eyesight.

Working on the assumption that he was honest but wrong, they worked out several more possibilities – trying to identify similar cars. They considered other VWs, a size up and a size down from the Golf. They also looked at combinations of letters and numbers which might most easily be mistaken for those he gave them. Eventually they came up with a list which they could check out the following day.

"I don't know about you, Margaret, but I'm shattered. Can't even be arsed to bung anything in the microwave. Come out for a meal with me?"

It was tempting although she wished they worked on different teams if this budding relationship was going to go anywhere. And that included if it went pear-shaped. In the end, she decided she was so knackered she couldn't be arsed to argue.

Chapter 55

The following morning Mo and Margaret were heading out to Chilton to interview themselves the witness who had reported seeing someone looking for a lost dog on the morning that Fred Shelford died.

Mo was feeling rather ratty. He wasn't sure whether it was because he was so tired or because the meal with Margaret had not been a resounding success. Neither had been very good company and they found themselves arguing over trivial things. They'd gone to a Greek restaurant in Regent Street on the other side of Parker's Piece from the station. It suited Margaret because she could walk home. It didn't suit Mo as well since it gave her an excuse not to ask him back for coffee again; he would have to re-cross the park to get his car. And on top of that, despite having told her when they first went out that he'd eat anything, he wasn't very keen on Greek food. Especially when the rice served with his moussaka was topped with something vaguely resembling the worst English-style Bolognese sauce.

Margaret wasn't feeling much more cheerful either. The retsina had definitely been a mistake. Particularly since she had drunk most of it because Mo was driving.

The woman they were to see, a Mrs Foster, lived in a small terraced house in a side street off Duck Lane. When they rang the bell a dog instantly began barking. They could hear the owner trying to quieten it. When she opened the door she was leaning over with one hand on the dog's collar. "Come in my dears before she gets away from me!"

They squeezed past and found themselves in the front room. With the three of them and a retriever there wasn't much space for anything else, given how crowded the room was with furniture. It was all what was called brown furniture these days. The kind of stuff you could hardly give away, never mind sell. Both of them found the atmosphere distinctly depressing.

Mrs Foster, though, proved to be a cheery lady, obviously only too willing to help. "I told that nice young man who came round before all I could dearies. But do ask me anything you like."

"What we'd really like to do is to take a walk with you to the spot where you saw the man looking for his dog on 10th January, the day Mr Shelford died. Could we do that?"

"Why not? Shall I bring Dolly too? She's had her walk but she's always ready for another."

"No reason why not."

"Right, I'll just get my coat on." She went out through a door which appeared to lead into the kitchen. She came back moments later wearing a bright red woollen coat and clutching a dog lead.

It took no more than a few minutes to reach the path to the allotment where she had seen the dog walker. From that spot a network of paths spread out through the plots of land, most of which were looking predictably scruffy at that time of year.

"So were you on your way out or your way back, Mrs Foster?"

"My way out. I normally turn right here and follow a path down to the gravel pit."

"And the dog walker. Which way was he going?"

"He was coming towards me through the allotments."

"Can you please try to describe him again for us?"

"I didn't look very closely my dear. It was so cold and foggy I wanted Dolly to do her business and get home as fast as I could."

"If you could try."

"Well he was wearing dark clothes, that I do know. Some sort of warm jacket. He had a scarf on too, so I could hardly see his face. A dark one. And a beanie hat all pulled down over his ears."

"You say he wasn't very tall. Was he taller than you?"

"I'm not sure."

"Did you have to look up to see his face or could you look him straight in the eye?"

Mrs Foster was obviously struggling a bit.

"Was he as tall as Margaret here?"

"Yes, I think so. Maybe a bit more."

"But not as tall as me?"

"No, I'm fairly sure about that."

"Good, that's very helpful. Now, did he speak first, or did you?"

"Oh, he did. I'm not a great one for talking to strange men."

"He was strange?"

"No. I didn't mean that, exactly. But I didn't recognise him and I know most folks round here. I've lived here since I was born. I'm ninety-two, you know."

"We'd never have guessed, Mrs Foster. You're remarkable for your age."

"It's Dolly. She keeps me fit. You should get a dog. Everyone should have a dog."

Margaret wanted to say that there was more than enough dog poo in the world without more dogs. People were better about bagging it up than they used to be, but it really annoyed her the way some of them would then leave the bags hanging in bushes and trees like so many shrivelled party balloons.

"So you didn't know him. What did he say, do you remember?"

"Well, he looked a bit anxious I can tell you that, even though I could only see his eyes. You can, can't you? And you would be if you'd just lost your dog. I'd be beside myself." She ruffled Dolly's head. "But you wouldn't run off, would you my pet? You're a good girl." Dolly's tail thumped in acquiescence.

"And what did he say?"

"He asked me if I'd seen his terrier. Said he'd lost it."

"And how did you reply?"

"I said I hadn't, but there were rabbits about, so if he'd let it off the lead it would probably have been off in a flash."

"Was he carrying a lead?"

She thought long and hard. "I don't remember seeing one. I suppose he might have had it in his pocket."

"It's a possibility I suppose. Shall we go back home now. We can't have you catching pneumonia now can we?"

She cackled. "More likely you'll catch it, dearie. I bet you've always had central heating. When I was a kiddie we had ice on the inside of the bedroom windows all through the winter. The inside."

They laughed. Nonetheless they turned and made their way back to Duck Lane. As they reached her front door, Mo had a couple of final questions. "You've mentioned his eyes. Can you describe them?"

"I think I told the nice young man in uniform that they stuck out. I did wonder afterwards whether I might have been mistaken. It might be I got that impression because of the way he was muffled up. D'you see? But the more I think about it, the more sure I am. I've always been quite observant."

"Do you remember the colour? Or the colour of his eyebrows?"

"No, not really. But they were pale. Definitely not dark. His eyebrows were dark, I think. I think I remember seeing tiny drops of water on them. From the fog. Like you see on those polar explorers. Only then, it's ice, isn't it? Still, my first impressions are usually very reliable."

"Mrs Foster, you have been very helpful. Thank you for your time."

They saw her into her house and walked back to Duck Lane where they'd parked the car.

"What do you think, Mo? Are we any further forward?"

"I thought she was pretty credible. She's very much on the ball. So yes, I do think we gained a bit. We have a better idea of his height. You're what, five foot six or so? I'm five foot ten. So our man might be five foot eight or thereabouts. And I bet good money his eyes are exophthalmic."

She laughed. "Ex what?"

"Gotcha. It means they stick out. That was her first impression. I think she was being cautious today and not wanting to sound more certain than she was. If I'm right about that, then I bet he has dark eyebrows too. His eyes were the only feature she could really see so she'd likely notice his brows as well. And that was quite a vivid image she gave us."

"What about the dog lead? Would you put one in your pocket?"

"No, but I don't have a dog."

"Don't be an ass. I wouldn't. They can trail on the ground and get muddy for one thing. And get clarted up with dog hair. And other unmentionable stuff no doubt. No thank you."

"But a bloke might not worry about something like that."

"Especially if he's a Neanderthal like you."

They both laughed, sense of humour restored.

Chapter 56

The team that met for the evening briefing was much smaller than usual. There was little more that some of the specialists could contribute as this stage.

Upwood was able to relay some new information, though.

"The first piece of news is that forensics confirm the Glock 17 was the weapon that fired the cartridges which killed Mallon, not that we had any doubts. They weren't able to get any other information from it."

"Didn't I read somewhere that you can get latents even when a firearm's been underwater?" Morton asked.

"You might well have done. Forensics said they'd looked but the polymer frame of the Glock takes prints less well than metal, and prints last less well in fresh water than in salt. But they had no joy with this one. However, we have tracked the Glock to the US. It was first licensed to a James Arlington in Los Angeles in 1989, making it a second generation model. It has never been relicensed."

"I'm surprised it was still working", offered Debra.

"Glock are famous for their longevity, I'm told."

"So somebody smuggled it in", Morton volunteered with a weary tone in his voice.

"Must have done. It can't be licensed here as we know. When it was brought in we don't know."

"Do we know anything about the original owner?"

"He was apparently an undergraduate at one of the universities there. Twenty-two years of age. He gave his university hall of residence as his address. We have asked whether he can be traced but I'm not feeling very optimistic about it."

"So we don't know whether he smuggled it in, or whether he sold it to someone else, perhaps illegally."

"No. He might even have given it to someone without any paperwork involved.

"The only other piece of fresh information is that we now know the make of nail polish of which we found a trace at the gravel pit."

That brought hoots of laughter, even though those there knew it might turn out to be a crucial piece of intelligence.

"Chanel. Quite an expensive brand."

"So why on earth would a classy woman be clambering over a locked gate to get to a gravel pit? In the middle of winter."

"If she'd been there with a boyfriend they'd have stayed in the car surely?"

"We've had this conversation before. And we must remember Malcolm did stress that it could have been chipped by someone who was just leaning on the gate and looking over.

"Margaret, Mo. Have you got anything for us?"

Mo looked at Margaret to kick off.

"We've passed over a list of cars similar to the VW Golf and with similar partial reg numbers to see if it throws up any new lead on the system. And we had a fascinating talk with the woman who spoke briefly with the dog walker on Chilton allotments the day Fred Shelford died. She confirmed everything she'd said the first time but we managed to get a bit more detail from her."

"And you think it's credible? She's not just stringing you along?"

"No. She may be ninety-two but she's a cracker. We are now fairly confident that the man she was talking to was about five feet eight tall, with pale, exophthalmic eyes", Margaret rolled hers theatrically, "and dark eyebrows. The estimation of height, the paleness of the eyes and the colour of the eyebrows are all new bits of info."

"Good. Ought you to see the witness who came forward about the sightings near Waldorf's house? Maybe some careful questioning might elicit a few more nuggets there too. I know what it's like when you're on door to doors. Your brain numbs after a while. Have a go, will you?

"Morton, you and Debra were going to chase up Maskell-Grant about the time discrepancy. Any progress?"

"No. Couldn't get hold of him. He wasn't answering his phone all day."

"What about his mobile?"

"Claims he hasn't got one."

"Must be the only one left in the whole world, then. What are you going to do?"

"If we can't get an answer tonight or tomorrow morning, we'll go and see if he's at home. Maybe he's just lying low."

"What about his alibi for Dr Mallon's death?"

"We had a uniform stationed at Bath interview his landlady. It looks solid. She's really scatty. Whoever had the room hadn't booked in advance. Like a lot of others she has a sign in the window to show whether she has vacancies or not. He was a walk in. Paid cash and she never bothered to ask his name. She obviously doesn't pay much attention to the rules requiring her to maintain a register of guests. But she did describe someone looking like Maskell-Grant. Grey hair. Dark eyebrows. Not very tall."

"A bit like the dog walker? What about the eyes. Did they stick out?"

"We had prompted the local lot to probe, if she didn't volunteer it. When they asked if there was anything unusual about them she said she didn't remember."

"Did he have a dog with him?"

"Didn't think to ask them to check. But she didn't say that he had, and it didn't sound like the kind of place where she'd let a dog stay. She might be scatty but apparently the place was squeaky clean. Usually places like that run by old biddies smell. Too much over-cooked vegetables. Or too much aerosol polish. This one didn't, we're told."

"Does Maskell-Grant have a dog? Anyone?"

Debra answered. "No, not that we know of. He might have had one out the back somewhere that we didn't see, I suppose. But he doesn't look to me like someone who could be bothered to look after an animal. Or a human being, come to that."

"Well, check it out. By the way. Where's Tom? Debra?"

"I don't know, Sir. Can I speak to you privately about it?"

They waited till everyone else had left. "What d'you mean, you don't know?"

Debra was embarrassed. "HR told me he was off for three days having a biopsy for possible prostate cancer."

"From when?"

"Monday."

"It's Thursday, Deb. Have you not followed up?"

She shook her head. "I should have done, Sir. He's got no family that I know of. I'll check with HR."

"Do that. We may be rushed off our feet, but we've got to keep an eye out for each other. Right?"

"Right, Sir." She felt suitably chastened. She ought to have followed it up when he didn't come in yesterday. She resolved to do so the next day. She was more ashamed that she hadn't put two and two together. She knew men with prostate problems were likely to need to pee more frequently, but she'd thought Tom was just disorganised. If she'd pushed him months ago, might his cancer have been diagnosed sooner? It was a question that would torment her for a long time.

That evening at home, Upwood was restless. They were covering all the same ground over and over, only occasionally turning up anything of interest. He hoped to goodness they'd get a break soon.

His mobile rang. Katie.

"Hi. How are you?"

"I'm fine James. What about you? I've been waiting to hear about your bollocking. You did get one, I assume?"

"Oh yes. A right royal one. I'm afraid the Chief Constable was a distinctly unhappy bunny."

“I’m not surprised. Clever headline, though.”

“Clever. But vicious. You think of the countless people we have working their butts off on these cases, and all the others involved. To describe them as blind is downright mean.”

“But what d’you expect? It’s the clever headlines that sell the papers.”

“That and the photos.”

“Ah yes. And what did Madam Adams have to say about that?”

“Right royally pissed off about that too.”

“What has she said?”

“You don’t want to know.” This was more true than she could have guessed. “I told her it was none of her business who you had lunch with.”

“Did she ban us from meeting again?”

“She tried and I told her in no uncertain terms that I was not going to have her interfering. It’s your decision whether we meet again or not.”

“Does that mean you would like to meet again?” He could imagine a look of faux innocence on her face.

“Do you really not know the answer to that one, Katie?” he said softly.

She chuckled. “So when’s it to be?”

“In fairness, I think we should give lunch out a miss. I don’t want you to get media attention.”

“You’d better come over to me then. But let’s make it dinner, not lunch, shall we? Saturday?”

That to Upwood sounded like the best idea he’d heard in a long time.

Chapter 57

Morton and Debra headed out to Chilton early the following morning. They had been unable to raise Maskell-Grant on the phone.

"Do you think he's trying to avoid us?"

"No idea, Deb, but we're going to find out."

It was a miserable day. Heavy skies and steady rain. Traffic was bad and it took all Morton's concentration to get them there in one piece. Debra sensed this and kept quiet.

They ran for the small porch at his front door although it gave them little enough shelter. Morton knocked loudly. He waited. He knocked again. Finally they heard footsteps and the door opened, but only as far as the chain would allow.

"Who are you? I don't buy at the door."

"We're police, Mr Maskell-Grant. DI Harrison and Detective Sergeant Graf. We'd like to speak to you again. May we come in please?"

"Not unless you show me some ID."

They thought this was a bit rich given that they'd interviewed him once already, but produced their warrant cards. Grudgingly he pushed the door shut, released the chain and let them in.

"What do you want? I've already told you everything I can."

"We'd just like to clarify one or two points in your statement, please. Perhaps you'd be kind enough to let us sit down. We shan't take too much of your time."

"Take your jackets off then. I don't want water dripping all over the floor."

They did as he asked and looked around hoping to see somewhere to put them. He offered no help. Morton threw his over the newel post and Debra hung hers on the back of a Windsor chair.

He indicated that they should go through to the same sitting room they had used on the previous occasion. Each sat in the same seat as before, trying to sit carefully to avoid ending up in unnecessary discomfort.

Morton plunged straight in. “Mr Maskell-Grant, when we saw you last, you said that you had visited Professor Matthew Ferry on the evening of 24th January.”

“That is correct.”

“Can you please remind us at what time you left for your meeting?”

“I left about five o’clock.”

“The Professor tells us you did not arrive until about seven o’clock. Your journey shouldn’t have taken anything like that long. Did you go anywhere else before you got to Professor Ferry’s house?”

“No, I don’t think so.”

“Did you stop for petrol, perhaps?”

“I really can’t remember. This is ridiculous. It’s nearly a month ago.”

“But why would you set off at five in the afternoon to travel the short distance to Ely when your appointment wasn’t until seven?”

Maskell-Grant looked at them. “Sainsbury’s. I remember now. I didn’t have any food in the house, so I went to Sainsbury’s and did a bit of shopping. Then I went to their café for a sandwich and a cup of tea.”

“Would you have a receipt from the store?”

“No, I shred everything like that.”

“What, your credit card receipts, you mean?”

“I don’t have a credit card. I have a debit card to draw cash but I don’t make payments by card. Don’t believe in it.”

“Isn’t that rather inconvenient?”

“Not to me it’s not.”

“Why do you shred receipts for cash payments?”

“I just do.”

Bonkers. Morton saw no purpose in pursuing the point. “Which Sainsbury’s did you go to?”

“There is only one in Ely, I believe.”

"Just one more question, sir, before we leave. Have you had a problem with your telephone the last day or two?"

"No. Why?"

"Because you haven't been answering it."

"That will be because I haven't heard it."

"I'm not sure I understand."

"I work in a timber chalet in the garden. There is no telephone. I hate to be disturbed when I'm working."

Morton resisted the temptation to ask him why he didn't have an answerphone system. The man was unreal.

"Mr Maskell-Grant. Sorry, there is another question I'd like to ask. Do you have a dog?"

"What on earth would I want a dog for? Dirty, smelly creatures. Can't abide them."

There was little point in remaining any longer.

They decided to head off immediately to Sainsbury's in the hope that there might be CCTV footage available. Their visit was unproductive. Usually the store kept records for four weeks but they had had a problem with the system. As a result they no longer had recordings for that day. The store's HR supervisor checked the rosters and none of the staff working in the café that evening was on duty then. They left feeling they had wasted their time. Before they left the car park Debra put in a call back to the station and asked that ANPR footage of the A10 for that evening be checked for Maskell-Grant's car.

"What a pillock that man is."

"What is it with you, Deb? Gardiner was stuffy. Doughty was full of himself. Mrs Mallon was a scarlet woman. Ken Lloyd was weak. I'm not sure you had a good word to say about Sheila Bennett, come to that."

She laughed. "Don't take it too seriously, Morton. But you have to admit Maskell-Grant really is something else. He's getting on for being seriously weird. It's those eyes and the comb-over that get me."

"Perhaps being an academic in a rarefied atmosphere like Cambridge does that to you."

"Or being thrown out of it. One or the other."

When she got back to the station Debra suddenly remembered she had not checked with HR about Tom. When they said only that to the best of their knowledge he had been sent home after his biopsy on Monday with instructions to stay off work for a further couple of days, she became anxious. If he was at home but unwell, why had he not phoned in? She called Upwood who agreed a home visit might be a good idea and suggested she take someone from HR with her. When she called them, she was told that if the visit was to be made the following day, Saturday, the only person available was Amanda Reacher and she would not be free until midday. Debra was not at all happy about this, but there was nothing she could do.

Chapter 58

The following morning most of the team were in early again for a briefing before pursuing the tasks assigned them.

At the briefing Debra and Morton relayed the results of their latest interview with Maskell-Grant and their fruitless visit to Sainsbury's. However the results of the ANPR checks had come through for the evening of his visit to Professor Ferry. His car was recorded twice on the A10, once at six thirty-five, just north of Chilton, and again at six forty-five, on the outskirts of Ely. If he had left home at about five he had not spent the missing time at Ely's Sainsbury's branch, nor anywhere far from Chilton, come to that.

Upwood spoke. "I think we are seeing a number of pieces of circumstantial evidence to suggest that Maskell-Grant is a person of interest. His height and build are similar to those described by the lady who saw someone walking towards her on the morning of Fred Shelford's death. It may have been him walking across the field and allotment back to Chilton. Morton, Debra – is the distance between the barn and his home, cross country, feasible?

Morton was nearest to the map stuck up on the whiteboard. He studied it. "Yes, Sir. No problem."

"And he claims to have been looking for a lost dog but according to our witness carried no dog lead. Not conclusive, but perhaps suggestive, if the witness is as reliable as we think. And she described him as having pale, protruding eyes, and dark eyebrows, which Maskell-Grant does.

"And the 'Scarf Man' was of a similar height and build. A witness calling in after the reconstruction says the man whom he saw carrying a satchel and getting into a car at the Queen's Head had light or grey hair. Maskell-Grant has grey hair.

"His visit to Ferry could easily be interpreted as an attempt to create an alibi and his accounts of the timings are inconsistent.

"So he has no alibi for the first three incidents and a questionable one for the fourth – Waldorf's death."

"But", said Morton, "he does seem to have a solid alibi for Mallon's death." He paused. "Is it remotely possible we have two murderers?"

A stunned silence greeted this question. Chasing one murderer was hard enough. The idea of chasing two of them was more than most of them could contemplate.

Upwood replied in measured terms. "It's a question we can't ignore, however unlikely it sounds, especially since the modus operandi for Mallon is completely different. Let's for the moment focus on Maskell-Grant. Let's question his neighbours to see if any can tell us about his movements on the days in question, going back to December.

"And I think we do these interviews ourselves – given the passage of time the interviews need a degree of interrogation skill a little above routine door to door enquiries. I'm not being rude about our colleagues in uniform but we need real investigative talent at this stage.

"So, Morton, you partner Debra again, Mo, you and Margaret stick together. Work out the logistics between you."

"Sir, I do have an appointment at twelve." Debra looked at him. Morton glanced at her, a look of confusion on his face. There were mutterings from the back of the room.

"Is that what we discussed yesterday?"

"It is, Sir."

"OK, Morton, can you find one of the junior officers to go with you? It could be useful experience for someone." Morton wondered what was going on, but sensed that questions would not be welcomed. He nodded.

There were few other issues of any import to discuss so the meeting broke up. The four officers went back to their office to develop a strategy.

Upwood wiped down the whiteboard in the office; most of the notes on it were now redundant, either of sufficient import to be featured on the boards in the Incident Room, or deemed irrelevant. He drew up a time line down the left hand side with the critical dates. They then talked through, and he recorded, the potential sighting points they needed to explore, such as the times of departure from, and arrival at, all key locations. Three of these, which were not single points, but stretches of road on which the Pajero might have been seen, had already been investigated and they accorded them low priority for now.

This left them with the following list:

- His departure from home on the morning of 20th December to go to Knapton to steal the Pajero by car, or foot and bus
- His approach to the barn in the Pajero
- His return home having parked the Pajero in the barn, probably on foot
- Leaving home, probably on foot, cross-country to the barn early morning on 10th January prior to Fred Shelford's death
- His trip from the barn to the lode in the Pajero and then back to the barn
- Returning home from the barn, on foot, after Fred Shelford's death, which journey may have been witnessed at one point by Mrs Foster, on the allotment
- Leaving home early evening on the night of the barn fire, 17th January, by car or foot
- Returning home from the barn, by car or foot
- Leaving home early evening on the night of Waldorf's death, by car
- Returning home on the night of Waldorf's death, via Ely, by car.
- Leaving home by car in the early morning of 7th February, by car, for Knapton Gravel Pits
- Returning home by car later on.

Upwood then left them to it. They knew that getting people to remember events that happened as much as five or more weeks ago would not be easy. So they decided to research facts relevant to those days which might perhaps trigger memories: news and sports events and weather conditions in particular. Having developed their game plan and agreed which team would tackle which households and other establishments from which he might have been seen, they dispersed. There was not the slightest chance they would finish their tasks today – they'd be lucky to complete them by close of play on the following day.

At eleven thirty Debra met the HR representative, Amanda Reacher. She looked scarcely old enough to be out of uni. In fact she was twenty seven but her clothes did not help. In Debra's view, they were too informal, even allowing for the fact that it was a Saturday.

They spoke little during the drive to Tom's house. It was a fairly short distance since he lived in a terraced cottage in a narrow street off Mill Road which ran down in the direction of the station. They parked with considerable difficulty and had to walk a couple of hundred yards before they reached his home. There was no front garden. All the houses opened onto the pavement. Debra knocked on the door. There was no answer. She saw a bell push and tried that. There was no response to that either. Amanda was fidgeting, clearly uncomfortable with the situation. Debra peered through the letter box, then called. There was no sign of Tom. She straightened up and looked around. Along the terrace there were narrow openings, presumably to provide rear access. She strode along to the nearest, Amanda in her wake, and ducked into it. Once past the end of the cottages on either side they saw miserable back yards overflowing with bins, neglected toys, derelict garden equipment and other rubbish. Debra suspected that in some there would be used syringes, condoms, empty cans and soiled nappies. She shuddered and turned left back towards Tom's house and when she had reached what she expected to be his, opened the decaying wooden gate and went up the short path to the back door. She peered through a mildly grubby kitchen window but could see nothing. She tried the door handle and for some reason she could not later explain, was not surprised to find that it opened. She went in first, with Amanda close on her heels. The kitchen was old-fashioned but reasonably tidy and clean. A few plates, a mug and some cutlery were on the draining board. A small shrivelled Christmas cactus sat on the window sill; the soil had shrunk away from the side of the pot. A bowl on the floor by the fridge was crusted with food, whether for a cat or small dog was not obvious. They opened a door and moved through to the hall. The stench of piss and shit and something even worse hit them immediately. Amanda screamed. There, hanging from the top banister was Tom's body, turning very slightly in the movement of air their entry had caused, his face hideously distorted, eyes popping and his tongue, black and bloated, sticking out grotesquely. Amanda ran out to the garden and threw up.

Chapter 59

After the two teams had agreed their strategy for checking out Maskell-Grant's movements they broke up. Mo and Margaret were going to concentrate on the properties nearest his home. Morton and a young PC would concentrate on those people living closest to the approaches by foot to the barn. Mrs Foster, whom they had already interviewed, was one of these. They would also concentrate on those whose properties he would pass elsewhere in the village if travelling by car from or to his home.

By the time Mo and Margaret had left the station, weak sun had melted the early morning hoar frost and the temperature had risen to a respectable eight degrees Celsius. She at least was grateful for this, being a fair weather girl at heart. Even the wind was playing ball – just a gentle breeze. They left Parkside in good humour and headed out towards Chilton.

Maskell-Grant's cottage was in River Lane, a small cul-de-sac running more or less parallel to the Gt Ouse close to the point at which Chilton Lode emptied into it. It was separated from the river by a field which normally carried livestock. There were a few other cottages, some detached, a few terraced, and the odd bungalow, scattered along the length of the lane which led off a larger street. Most were brick built or pebble-dashed some generations ago and most had slate roofs. The whole effect was grey and oddly artificial. It could have been built in a film studio. Margaret shuddered at the thought of living in such a place. From her flat she could easily walk into the city centre to decent shops, bars and restaurants. Chilton was behind God's back as far as she was concerned.

They started at the side of River Lane on which Maskell-Grant lived. They assumed that the fact that it was

Saturday might give them some advantage, since few of the residents would be at work. They soon found out that very few of the residents were of working age – but at least in the main they were at home.

It was slow and tedious work. Few of those whom they questioned had any recall of the days in question; certainly they drew a complete blank as far as December 20th was concerned.

They were just about to call it a day when the householder living opposite Maskell-Grant offered them some interesting intelligence. She lived in a thirties bungalow the kitchen of which faced the lane. Her name was Mrs Bulleid. She had welcomed them in quite happily. Margaret got the distinct impression she was glad of anyone to talk to. She probably wasn't as old as Mrs Foster but she was not far off it. A short, dumpy woman, she wore a tweed skirt, jumper and pinafore and had over-processed, tightly curled, thin grey hair. Her blue eyes twinkled merrily, though, which counteracted the dowdy appearance.

"Come along in then and sit yourselves down. A nice cup of tea? Of course you will. I've seen you working your way down the street. You must be chilled to the bone." They were happy to accept and not at all surprised to see that she came back with cups and saucers on a tray, rather than mugs. She also had chocolate biscuits, which cheered them up even more.

"Mrs Bulleid, thank you for letting us ask you a few questions. We are asking lots of people, all over the village and in the surrounding hamlets." This of course was not true but it was part of the strategy they had agreed to try to avoid making it too obvious that the subject of their interest was Maskell-Grant.

"That's all right, my dears. I know you've got your jobs to do and I know it's not easy. I've got a nephew in the police, in Norfolk. I know how hard he works. What do you want to know?"

"Well, we are interested in anything you may have seen in the Lane, particularly anything that might be a little out of the ordinary on a number of days in recent weeks.

"Could we start with the morning of Monday 20th December? I know it's a little while ago, but is there anything unusual you can remember about that morning?"

She chortled. "Oh yes", she said. "I was staying with Charlie – that's my nephew – and his family. I always have a day or two with them before Christmas. I take the kiddies' presents over. It's easier for them than having me there on Christmas Day. And I prefer it, if I'm honest. Children shrieking and screaming long before dawn is not my idea of fun any longer."

"Fine, that rules that one out. What about Monday 10th January?"

She looked troubled for a minute. "That's the day my Mick died. Not this year, you understand, last year." She thought for a moment and neither Mo nor Margaret pressed her. "Yes. There was something out of the ordinary. It would have been early in the morning. I make myself a cup of tea and go into the sun lounge and listen to Today on the radio. I can't afford a paper any more. Mind you I don't miss it. Too full of celebs – is that what they call them? Not real news at all. Radio 4. That'll do for me."

"You were saying something unusual happened, Mrs Bulleid?" Margaret leant forward, putting her question in as neutral a tone as she could manage.

"Where was I? Yes. In the kitchen. I was looking out the window waiting for the kettle to boil. It gave me such a fright. It was very foggy. I could hardly see across the street. But I saw my Mick outside the front door opposite. Nearly had a heart attack."

"But I thought you said your husband died the year before."

"He did. But I was thinking of him, you see. And then I saw someone who looked very much like him. But in swirling mist. It was like seeing a ghost. Came over all queer, as I said."

"Do you know who it was, Mrs Bulleid?"

"Well, I assume it was the chap who lives opposite. I don't know him as such. He keeps himself to himself. Won't even pass the time of day. But he's about the same height as my Mick. And wearing a dark jacket and scarf like Mick always did. Well, in winter anyway."

"Can you remember what time it was?"

"Well it was after six of course, because Today had already started. I'm not sure I can be much more precise than that. It was certainly well before sunrise, I know that. I remember the way the fog swirled around the street lamp at the top of the lane. It made it go yellow. The fog I mean."

"Was he wearing anything on his head – a hat or hood perhaps?"

"Maybe. I don't remember. It was just the impression he gave me of Mick, more than anything."

"Did you see which direction he walked in?"

"Well this is a cul-de-sac so he'd have walked towards the town centre."

"But did you see him do that?"

She thought long and hard. "I think he must have done. Otherwise it's not likely I'd have noticed the street lamp at the top of the lane where it joins Cross Street."

There was little more she could tell them but they thanked her warmly. They were calling it a day. But they felt excited for the first time: the circumstantial evidence against Maskell-Grant seemed to be growing.

Chapter 60

Debra stumbled out into the garden after Amanda and leaned against the wall of the cottage, her heart racing. Why in God's name had she not checked up on him sooner? Why hadn't she at least telephoned? Why hadn't she realised long ago that there was something wrong with him? She rummaged in her handbag and found her mobile to call Upwood.

He was deeply shocked, but asked Debra to stay there until he arrived. After the call ended he made arrangements for all the resources they would need, before heading over to Chilton himself. He found Debra and Amanda still in the back garden sitting in old and very dirty white plastic chairs that they'd found inside a practically derelict garden shed. The light had faded and the temperature was dropping again quite quickly after cloud had covered the skies. When he handed them a large Thermos of coffee and a couple of bars of chocolate, they were pathetically grateful. Both were frozen, never mind in shock. Upwood had arrived twenty minutes after Penny Fordham and her team. He took one of the spare protective suits together with head and shoe coverings and entered the kitchen.

Penny looked uncharacteristically upset. "Did you know there were two bodies here?"

Upwood looked at her in astonishment. "Christ Almighty. Where? Who?"

"We don't know who. But it's an old lady. We'll have to see what the pathologist says in due course but I'm told it looks as though either she was suffocated in her bed or had a heart attack. They've both been dead some time."

With her permission Upwood went through to the hall where two people were taking video and still shots. He edged his way upstairs following noise and light from one of the bedrooms. Two more photographers were at work. Upwood glanced round the room. It could have been a stage-set for a mid-fifties boarding house. A motheaten rug covered much of the badly scratched, varnished, floor. The bed was iron and could even have been a post-war utility model. Upwood had seen nothing like it except in photographs of his grandparents' home. Floral paper was peeling away from the wall underneath a picture rail, from which hung a couple of reproductions of Victorian Scottish landscapes. The limewashed ceiling, probably lath and plaster, dipped here and there as though it was waiting for an excuse to collapse on anyone rash enough to be underneath, ready to dump dust, dead mice and heaven knows what other detritus on them. Maroon and cream striped brocade curtains hung limply at the window. On the dressing table there were crocheted mats, a hair brush and a hand mirror. A glass, ringed with limescale deposits, stood empty on the bedside table. The only other piece of furniture was a single mahogany wardrobe, probably Edwardian. Other than in the houses of the truly destitute, Upwood could scarcely think when he'd seen a more depressing room.

The old lady was shrunken and looked as though she would have been very weak. Pale staring eyes showing petechiae may well, in the absence of any marks on her neck indicating strangulation, have prompted the suggestion of suffocation or heart attack. Claw-like hands with translucent skin blemished by a mosaic of liver spots, gripped the edge of the bedspread, but there was no obvious sign of a struggle.

Upwood went back outside. He was pleased to see that they had polished off the coffee and biscuits and hoped that higher blood sugar levels would give them some strength. Even in their distressed state Debra and Amanda could see that he was upset. "There's another body. An old woman." He looked at them, allowing the news to sink in for a moment. "Do you have any idea who it might be, Debra?"

She began to shake. "No. Before I sent him to HR I asked him if he had problems at home. He said not. I know he was divorced and had no partner. It didn't occur to me that he had anyone else living with him." Tears now fell freely and

Upwood did something he rarely did to a fellow officer, male or female. He put his arm round her shoulder. When she flinched he knew he shouldn't have done so.

"You and Amanda go home. Amanda, take the rest of the weekend off. I know it's hard, Debra, but we do need a meeting this evening. I'll set it up for five. Can you manage that?"

When they met, the news that Upwood gave them before they started shocked them all. "I'm sorry to say that Tom has died. Debra called on his home this afternoon with Amanda Reacher from HR. It was not natural causes. He was hanging in the hall and he had obviously been dead for some time. I'm also sorry to say that we also found another body in one of the bedrooms, an old woman. We don't know yet whether she died of natural causes or not."

They were stunned. None could think of any questions that it was appropriate to ask, given he was a colleague.

"I know you will wonder, but at the moment we don't know whether he took his own life or whether there was foul play. Nor do we know who the old woman was or how she died. Naturally we've had Scenes of Crime in and I'm awaiting their report. So let's try to put the matter out of our minds until we know more. Anyone want to get themselves a coffee before we start?"

Most had brought coffee or tea with them to the Incident Room but the break he offered gave them a few minutes to digest what he had said and settle down before they started the meeting proper.

"Good. Now, Mo and Margaret, tell us how far you've got please."

Mo tried to lighten the mood. "All down one side of River Lane and part way back up the other."

Nervous laughter broke out.

"Very good, Mo. Details please."

"Most of the residents we spoke to are elderly and I think I'm right in saying there was only one house we've tried so far where we got no response?" He looked at Margaret, who nodded. "Most saw nothing at all. However the last house we tried belongs to a Mrs Bulleid. She lives almost opposite Maskell-Grant. She believes she saw him outside his cottage on the morning of 10th January, sometime soon after six."

"Does she sound a credible witness?"

"Yes. A bit like Mrs Foster. Perhaps not quite so observant but quite sure what she'd seen. She remembers it because it was exactly one year to the day since her husband had died, and he looked a bit like Maskell-Grant in his outdoor clothes – you'd say similar jizz, I think, Sir, wouldn't you?"

Upwood smiled. "For those of you not familiar with bird-watching terminology, that means 'general impression of size and shape'. Well done, Mo."

"And that's what it was. It was foggy as we all know that morning, and it was well before dawn. But she says that the man she saw was wearing a dark jacket and scarf, which is what Mrs Foster said the man she saw was wearing a bit later that morning."

"Good work. Anything else?"

"No, as I said we called it a day after her. We've got a lot more to see tomorrow."

"OK. Morton, what have you got for us?"

"We had a pretty thankless time of the interviews, Sir. We were talking to people a little further away from his home, like those at the key junctions he might have negotiated in Chilton if he was travelling by car. We know there's no CCTV in the village, apart from the petrol station but he wouldn't pass that on his way to the barn, the lode or Knapton Gravel Pit – it's at the northern end of the village. He would have passed it to and from Ely but we have ANPR records for that trip. We had previously checked those records for his trip to Ely and established that he had left later than he had first claimed. Interestingly, the checks on his return journey show him approaching Chilton much later than he claims. He and Ferry both say he left Ferry's house at about ten. Maskell-Grant says he got home about ten thirty. But the cameras have him coming down the A10 just north of Chilton at eleven thirty."

"What does that tell us? Apart from the fact he either has a lousy sense of time or has lied again?"

"I don't know. If someone had seen him arrive home at eleven thirty that might be one thing. In theory he could have gone to Waldorf's house and lit short candles then. But why would he? If he is the man who visited Waldorf earlier in the evening, why go back again? Too risky. It's bonkers. But we'll have to follow it up."

"Yes, I agree. But not yet. Let's see whether we can gather any more bits of info before we hit him again. I don't want him getting too nervous at this stage."

Margaret had a light-bulb moment. "Sir? What if Maskell-Grant stopped somewhere to kill time so that he could drive past Waldorf's house to see if it had caught fire?"

"Margaret, you're a star!" Not a very original joke from Upwood but it helped lighten the mood again. "It's certainly plausible. Morton, do you want to check that out if you've finished your list?"

"Fine, good idea. We've exhausted all our current lines of enquiry. For the record we learnt nothing of interest in relation to the morning that Mallon was killed."

"OK, all done? Who's up for a drink? My shout." If it was unusual for Upwood to ask Morton to join him in a drink, it was even more unusual for him to ask the others. They all trooped round to The Stag, one of the local pubs. It was early so they had the place almost to themselves. They were there only about an hour but they felt a little more relaxed by the end of it. Upwood made sure that conversation did not drift onto the subject of Tom's death. Debra hung back until the others had gone and Upwood rightly sensed that she wanted a word.

"Is there anything else you can tell me about Tom, Sir?" It was clear she was anxious.

"I can't, Debra. I don't have the information. But if you want my opinion I think he probably took his own life. If you're beating yourself up over him, don't. Just put it to the back of your mind until we have more facts. When we do, if there are lessons we need to learn, we'll learn them, OK?"

She thanked him and left. Not so much reassured about Tom, but reassured at least that Upwood showed no signs of criticising her for her actions. Or lack of them. Nonetheless, when she walked through her front door she felt as depressed as ever she'd been in her life.

Chapter 61

It was just after seven when they left The Stag. With the prospect of a drive home, quick shower and change and drive back into town to Katie's apartment, Upwood had restricted himself to an alcohol-free beer. He'd called her to apologise for the fact that he would be half an hour late.

By eight thirty he was approaching the apartment complex in which Katie now lived. It was modern and as unlike Upwood's home as it was possible to be. Her apartment came with two parking spaces in the undercroft garage and she had given him the entry code and directions to find her flat.

He parked, took the lift to the top floor and quickly found her door. He hesitated for the briefest of moments and then rang the bell.

She opened the door with a dazzling smile. For once she looked relaxed and was immaculately turned out in wide, black silk, finely pleated slacks and a peach coloured shirt cinched at the waist with a narrow patent leather belt. Unusually her hair was loosely caught up at the back of her head, held in place with a large clip. Her skin shone. Upwood, who was sporting dark green cords, a cream coloured shirt and a jade coloured cashmere sweater, felt his age.

"Come in. No flowers again, James?"

"No. Didn't want to ruin your make-up at the first pass."

She laughed, a deep, rich laugh. He handed her a carrier. "Not for tonight, necessarily, although the claret is fit to drink: it's been out of the cave for a couple of days and standing."

As she removed the 2005 Chateau Beaumont from the carrier, she looked at him. "I didn't know you had one."

"I do now. I was so impressed with the one Mark had. Mine's a lot smaller of course, but it does allow me to keep a few bottles of better wine in good nick."

She pealed with laughter again. "Locked up?"

"Not quite."

They moved through to the open plan kitchen and dining area. Upwood could see a large covered terrace closed in at both sides. Much as he always went to look at the river when visiting her former home, he went over to the sliding doors. "May I?"

"Of course."

They went out and looked over the communal gardens, more imaginatively planted than most, colourful even at this time of year. They were clearly well maintained and discreetly lit.

"What will you have to drink, James?"

"What d'you suggest? You know what's on the menu."

"How about a glass of Sauvignon Blanc? That should see us through our starter, and main course too."

"Sounds good to me."

She got a bottle from the fridge and started to open it.

"Here, let me."

"I'm quite capable, you know, James. It's within my competence." She wasn't cross, just teasing him.

"I know. But I'm restless. I'd like something to do." She moved over.

"Bad day at the office?"

"You could say that. We had to do a house visit to one of our team. We found him hanging from the banister." The minute he'd said it, he regretted it. As an opening gambit for their first dinner date in her home, it was hardly a winner.

"Christ, James. Murder?"

"I don't think so, but we'll have to wait and see. I'm sorry, Katie, I shouldn't have dumped that on you. I'm not really thinking straight. None of us is. The wind farm murders are beginning to get us all down."

"I'm not surprised. I shouldn't even have mentioned work. You're here to relax."

He handed her a glass and they moved over to the other end of the open plan area where she had sofas and comfortable chairs.

"How do you like it here?"

"It's fine. I like the space. Angelica House had big rooms and an open feel, if you remember. And this has got views, even if they are urban."

"Space to sit out on the terrace in summer."

"Yep. Walking distance to the station if I have to go to town. And it's not a bad drive to the office."

"Don't you miss the countryside? I know I would."

"I do some of the time. In the winter not so much. You know how it is. It's dark when you go to work and it's dark when you get home."

"But what about the weekend?"

"I'm usually catching up on chores and shopping."

"The apartment is lovely. Very modern. Did you furnish it yourself?"

"I cheated. I knew more or less what I wanted but I did get an interior designer to help. Just to save time. It was nice to be able to choose my own things. As you know practically everything in Angelica House had belonged to Mark's parents. He didn't have the time or inclination to change much, and it wasn't my place to do so."

They fell silent for a moment, enjoying their wine.

"I ought to make a start on the first course. Why don't you bring your glass and sit while I get on with it?"

He perched on a stool at the breakfast bar.

The starter took very little time since she had done all the preparation. She grilled one side of each of two circles of toast, put rounds of goat's cheese on top and put them back under the grill. She stirred some finely diced bacon in a pan on the stove until it was crisp. The smell was tantalising. When she'd put the cheese on plates, already garnished with a little green salad, and sprinkled it with the crisp bacon and a few pine nuts, they were done.

When their plates were ready, she turned off the main kitchen light, leaving weak task lighting on above the granite work-surfaces, and lit candles on the table. It was a clear night, and even with the candles it was still possible to see the city lights winking in the distance.

She was right. The soft gooseberry flavours of the Sauvignon Blanc, from Marlborough, went beautifully with the tang of the goat's cheese. The contrast in textures of the dish worked really well.

"That was delicious. I can't wait to see what's next."

"You like scallops, don't you?"

"Love them."

"Black pudding?"

"Great combination. If you can cook, how is it you've only ever given me frozen pasta before?"

"Didn't want to spoil you too soon…but it is morcilla de Burgos."

"Sorry to show my ignorance, but what is?"

"The black pudding. It comes from the Castile y León region. It's drier than most because it has rice grains in it, and it has a subtle hint of cumin. A friend sends it over to me."

It took her little time to cook the main course which she served simply with petit pois. The dessert was chocolate mousse which she served with Muscat de Beaume de Venise.

When they'd finished he leant back in his chair. "Katie, this is an absolute treat. I can't tell you how much I'm enjoying this. A beautiful woman who is an accomplished cook and an intelligent conversationalist. A lovely environment away from prying eyes. What more could a man want?"

"Music? Dancing?"

"No. Music, maybe. Although as you know, if I play music at home it is to listen to, not as background. Dancing? You must be joking. Not in your worst nightmares."

She laughed as she cleared the table. "What d'you think? Too cold for a spell on the terrace? We could take a brandy out there. Or perhaps an Armagnac?"

"Armagnac, please. I love the nuttiness of it. But a small one, please. I have to drive, remember."

"Really?" She giggled. She had drunk a little more than he had, but while they'd finished the Sauvignon they had made only a tiny dent in the dessert wine.

She got up and went to one of the kitchen cupboards and reached for the bottle. Before she knew it, he was right behind her and she felt a kiss below her ear. She shivered with pleasure and turned towards him, putting her arms round his neck. He removed her hair slide, allowing her hair to tumble to her shoulders and slid his hand down her back, pulling her close. She could be in no doubt about the extent of his desire for her and her body brushed his briefly in acknowledgement.

She extricated herself gently. "There's something I should tell you", she murmured.

He frowned and anxiety clouded his eyes. "You're going away again…"

Katie stroked his cheek softly. "Poor darling. Do you always fear the worst?"

He nodded. "Usually. That way I occasionally get a pleasant surprise."

"Like now perhaps: I'm on the pill."

He laughed with relief and pulled her into another tight embrace.

"Later." She giggled again. "I want to unwind a bit and enjoy the anticipation." She filled the glasses and led him outside. It should have been bitterly cold, but it was an unseasonal fourteen degrees Celsius. That side of the building was sheltered and with the door open some warmth flooded out from the kitchen. They sat in chairs at the end of the terrace. He was suddenly aware of a delicate fragrance and struggled to remember when he had noticed it before. It came to him: sarcococca, and he reminded himself he'd still not found time to track one down. After a moment or two, Katie slipped off a shoe and lifted her foot onto his lap. She began to knead him gently. Upwood moved her foot off. "You can't do that here. People might see."

"Don't care, frankly." She lifted her foot and began kneading him again. He stroked her ankle, conscious that he was again becoming more and more aroused. She watched him in amusement.

"Can we go in? Please? I'm getting quite uncomfortable here."

"Chair not to your liking?"

"Damn it, you know perfectly well what I mean."

They were both laughing as she led him to the bedroom. For Upwood, whose whole life, it seemed, was bound by rules and regulations, policies and procedures, their love-making was an unfettered joy. For once he felt emotionally and physically liberated.

Chapter 62

Early the following morning, Morton and Debra headed out up the A10 again. It was a thoroughly gloomy morning with just enough rain to justify the intermittent wipers, but not enough to keep the windscreen clean. Morton constantly had to use the screen wash, especially when passing traffic threw up muddy spray. Not a pleasant journey. And not improved by the fact that Debra was clearly still very upset about the events over the weekend. He tried to broach the subject, but she wouldn't discuss it.

Once they were past the camera which had recorded Maskell-Grant approaching Chilton at about eleven thirty on the night of Waldorf's death, they began to look for places where he could have killed time. There were lay-bys on the southbound carriageway but it was quite common for truckers to park up overnight, so they thought he would be more likely to stop at what he might consider the comparative safety of a proper service area. There was only one realistic contender, as they had thought the previous day, at the roundabout on the A10 for the main road into Ely from the south.

It took them time to find the centre manager but when they did they were pleased to hear that the CCTV footage of customers entering and leaving the main building was held for twenty-eight days. This time they were in luck. It was fortunate, too, that he had a healthy respect for law and order, having had to call on various of the emergency services in his time. As a consequence, he was prepared to give them access without the need for a warrant.

They asked to see footage for the time in the earlier part of the evening for which Maskell-Grant had been unable to produce a convincing explanation, in case he had killed time there rather than at Sainsbury's. It seemed he had not. Or if he had, he had not entered the building. And they could see no reason why he would leave home early and then sit in his car rather than go in.

Then they checked the footage for the period in which he might have killed time after leaving Ferry. Sure enough, he was recorded entering the building at ten fourteen and leaving about an hour later. Result.

At the evening briefing they were able to report their findings. It was agreed that Waldorf's neighbours should be canvassed to establish if any had seen Maskell-Grant cruise past at or about eleven thirty.

Mo and Margaret reported on their remaining interviews. They too had achieved a result.

"We spoke to one of the residents in Middle Street. It runs parallel to River Lane. His name is Stuart Laing. He was walking down the street, having got off the bus from town in the village centre. He described a fairly short man of normal build, wearing a dark jacket and headgear of some sort, walking ahead of him. Laing lives close to the end of the street – it's a cul-de-sac like River Lane. At the bottom there is a hedge on the other side of which is the bridle path that skirts the village and ends up at Chilton Gravel Pit. He thought it odd because although some people do take their dogs out onto the bridle path that way – over time they've established a gap in the hedge – this man didn't have a dog. And he couldn't think why someone should walk down there otherwise. He said that he didn't recognise him as an immediate neighbour, although given that it was dark he couldn't be sure. But when he was watching the early evening local news on TV and heard the report of the big jewellery robbery in Cambridge that day, it occurred to him that the man's behaviour was a bit suspicious. Not that he thought the guy had anything to do with the robbery. It just reinforced his idea that his behaviour was odd."

"So it was before six thirty, clearly. Could he give you any closer time than that?"

"He thinks it was probably about six, as that's when he normally gets in when he catches that bus."

“So if Maskell-Grant was going back to the barn to set the fire for the Pajero, it would fit.”

“I think so. And he might have thought it smart to take a different route. If you remember, if it was him that Mrs Foster saw coming back after having dumped the Pajero following Fred Shelford’s death, then he was heading home via Duck Lane.”

“So what do we think, team? Enough circumstantial evidence to justify a warrant?”

Most seemed to think there was, but Upwood didn’t immediately commit himself. He wanted a little more time to think it through. He was concerned that Maskell-Grant’s motive for killing Shelford and Waldorf was flimsy. Would somebody take such risks to try to protect a site whose archaeological importance was unproven? Certainly, based on the circumstantial evidence, he had opportunity in both cases, and the discrepancies in the alibi for the night of Waldorf’s death were interesting. But there seemed to be no link to Mallon’s death.

In the end he decided to talk it through with Emily. He had to wait until the following morning, Monday, before he would have the opportunity to do so. He drove home unsettled about the case. He had another sleepless night.

Chapter 63

It was eleven before Upwood could see Emily. It was the first time they'd been alone since their argument. She looked stressed and given what he had heard about the progress of the other two major investigations she was responsible for – the cannabis farming and illegal immigrant cases – he was not altogether surprised. He didn't discount, though, the fact that she might be nervous he'd raise again the subject he was determined to avoid. He sat down and she offered him coffee. He was happy to accept. Her coffee was a lot better than the stuff they could get on their floor. He gazed out of the window while she poured. For once it was a cloudless day and he could see several contrails. At that altitude the air must be saturated because the ice crystals forming the trails were not dissipating quickly; he knew they only did that in dry air. He was miles away when she spoke to him.

"So what can I do for you, James?" Her voice was somewhat brittle, its tone conveying impatience.

"I need your advice, Emily." He hoped this opening gambit would restore in her mind his recognition of her higher status and his respect for her. "We are making progress but I wouldn't call it straightforward by any means. We have no clues as to the identity of the person who stole the Pajero.

"We have a witness who says she saw Maskell-Grant leave his house on foot shortly after six am on 10th January walking towards the town centre. He would have no reason to do that. The village shop doesn't open until seven thirty and the first bus doesn't run until seven forty-five."

"But how does that help us?"

"He lives in a cul-de-sac. To walk across the allotments to Orchard Farm he'd either have to turn east along Cross Street and then right into Middle Street, or go a bit further along and turn into Duck Lane."

"OK, so we think he may have been going to retrieve the Pajero before driving over towards Shelford's farm?"

"Yes. We think he would have got over there a bit early and parked up in a layby on the nearside of the road. Even in thick fog he would have been able to see Fred's headlights as he drove out of their yard. He would have had plenty of time to start up and rejoin the road ready to follow him.

"Then we have another witness who saw someone of a similar height and build walking across the allotments, as though coming from Orchard Farm, the same morning at about eight-thirty. So he might have bumped off Fred and driven back to secure the Pajero in the barn and then walked home. This witness says he has pale, protruding eyes and dark eye-brows, which Maskell-Grant has."

"Did she describe any other useful features?"

"No. He was wearing a beanie hat and was wrapped up in a scarf."

"Not a blue and white one I take it?"

He laughed. "No. That would be too easy. But not many men wear woollen scarves do they? Apart from football supporters. Then we have another sighting of a man, again of the same general height and build, walking down Middle Lane towards the gap in the hedge that gives access to the allotments. The witness says he did not recognise him as an immediate neighbour and thought it odd that anyone should walk in that direction at that time of night unless exercising a dog, and he had no dog.

"We have witnesses who saw a man, again of the same general height and build, this time wearing the infamous scarf, approaching Waldorf's front door on the night he died, walking away about half an hour later and entering the porch of the Queen's Head. No one in the pub reports seeing such a man actually enter the pub itself. Then we have a man of broadly similar description, sans scarf, coming out of the porch of the pub and getting into a car in the car park. He is described as having light or grey hair. His is grey.

"We have CCTV footage of Maskell-Grant's car driving north up the A10 when he went to see a friend one evening. CCTV puts him on the A10 twice, once at six thirty-five, just north of Chilton and again at six forty-five, on the outskirts of Ely. Professor Ferry says he arrived about seven. Maskell-Grant claims he left home for Ely at about five and killed time at Sainsbury's in Ely. We cannot verify that – nor can we refute it: the store's own CCTV system was on the blink.

"He claims he left about ten (Ferry confirms that) but CCTV footage shows him southbound on the A10 just north of Chilton at eleven thirty. We found CCTV footage showing he spent an hour at the service area on the edge of Ely between ten fifteen and eleven fifteen."

"Why would he do that? Hungry?"

"Maybe, but the fact that he lied about the journey suggests to us that he may have killed time in order to cruise past Waldorf's house to make sure it had gone up.

"The other interesting thing though is that Maskell-Grant's reason for wanting to see Ferry is suspect. Ferry thought it odd himself. We think he was trying to create an alibi for himself with someone of good reputation.

"And that's it. We have nothing to connect him to Dr Mallon's murder. He has a cast iron alibi – he was in Bath at an exhibition."

"Any forensic evidence?"

"None, yet. He would have had no physical contact with Fred Shelford. Any trace in the Pajero would have been destroyed by the fire. Ditto in the fire at Waldorf's home, although we did get DNA from a blue fibre from Waldorf's doorpost. So we would like to get his DNA checked."

"It's all very circumstantial. If it's him, has he been clever or lucky?"

"A bit of both maybe. But if it is him, he's not been very bright allowing witnesses to see him."

"But from what you've said they'd not be able to identify him."

"Maybe Mrs Foster. She's the one who said he'd got pale, protruding eyes. She also said that his eyebrows were dark. His are, even though he's got grey hair."

"So if he is responsible for the first two deaths –"

"Three, Emily. Don't forget the Albanian."

"– someone else is responsible for Mallon's death."

"Yes."

"It's not very likely, is it?"

"No. But not impossible. And it's a completely different modus operandi. Someone may have taken the opportunity that the idea of a wind farm serial killer provided to kill him for some other reason."

"And who might that be?"

"We always look closest to home, don't we? We have to consider seriously the idea that his wife may have been involved, indirectly, if not directly. There is a bit of an age gap – she's about nineteen years younger than him. They have a volatile relationship and have opposing ideas about the benefits of wind energy. It is said she is having an affair with Ken Lloyd, at the riding school, although he disputes it."

"Is that it?"

"Pretty much."

She sighed. "It's a bit thin. It's all circumstantial. And his motive doesn't seem very strong."

"Our impression is that he's obsessed about what he thinks is an important Roman site. He hasn't managed to produce any compelling evidence to support his theory apart from a few artefacts – and we only have his word for it that they came from a field near the proposed wind farm site. But he is passionate about it."

"I still think it's a bit thin."

"I agree. But it's all we've got. I want to get a team into his house and his home office – a shed at the bottom of his garden. We know he's a bit of a Luddite. If he's researched arson, or bought Ketamine online there's no question we'll find evidence on his computer. He won't be smart enough to know how to cover those trails.

"Remember, we have DNA evidence from the blue fibres from Waldorf's doorpost. If we can match that to Maskell-Grant then we can surely charge him with Waldorf's murder.

"And I'd like to see if we can find a satchel or laptop bag. Waldorf's visitor probably carried petrol and candles in that bag. There might be forensic trace there. And we know that the petrol used as an accelerant for the barn fire and Waldorf's home came from the same source. If we can find trace of the same fuel at Maskell-Grant's home we've got him for the Albanian's death as well as Waldorf's. And probably Shelford's."

She poured them both another cup of coffee. The fact that it was cold seemed to pass them by. She drank half of hers before putting her cup down. Upwood said no more. She would not take kindly to his trying to put pressure on her. She sighed and then looked at him.

"On the face of it it's flimsy, James. But I think you're right. You have to go for it. Let's hope to God you come up with some concrete evidence."

Chapter 64

Later that morning, after steps had been taken to secure a warrant to search Maskell-Grant's property, car and phone and financial records, Penny Fordham came in with news on Tom Turner's death.

"Sit down, do. What can you tell me, Penny?"

She slouched in the chair in front of his desk looking uncharacteristically uncomfortable. "It's suicide, James. There's absolutely no trace evidence to suggest otherwise. And we found a letter from his oncologist and a note he'd written for us. The letter from the hospital confirmed he had prostate cancer. Specifically it said it was graded as T4, N1, M0, and Gleason score 6."

"In English?"

"The cancer had spread outside the prostate gland itself, into the lymph glands but had not yet metastasised into other parts of the body, such as the bones. Fairly aggressive. 6 out of 10."

"So what would his prognosis have been?"

"No idea. You'd have to ask his oncologist. But the important thing is what he thought it meant." She passed him an evidence bag in which his note could be seen. Upwood read it.

"So his father and uncle both died from it and he didn't want to go the same way."

"In a nutshell, yes."

"But the science has moved on fantastically in a decade. Why was he so pessimistic?"

"No idea again. Maybe his oncologist said something to him that made him fear the worst."

"Poor sod. No wife. No friends that we ever heard about. And the sword of Damocles hanging over him."

"And in the letter he left us he admits smothering his mother whom he says was senile. He was worried about who would care for her if he went. Did you read the post-script?" She handed back a photocopy of his letter. *'Please can someone give a home to my cat? He's with the next-door neighbour.'*

"Oh Tom. Tom. You kill your mother but you want someone to look after your cat." He sighed deeply. "Poor bastard." He paused for a moment. "Are you a cat lover, Penny?"

"No way. Marginally cleaner than dogs but I wouldn't have any animal in the house. You never know what they're carrying."

Neither spoke for a moment; neither really knew what to say. Eventually Upwood broke the silence, returning to the practical. "Did you find anything else of interest?"

"No, not really. A couple of thousand outstanding on a credit card. No other signs of financial difficulty. His house was utterly normal. Apart from being in a time-warp, of course."

"His ex-wife must really have taken him to the cleaners. How infinitely depressing."

"Just what we thought."

"Thanks, Penny. We should get the PM report soon but I'm not expecting any surprises. Look, I know it's not your job. But do me a favour? Get someone to take a photo of the cat and a description. Put them up on the notice board saying he needs a good home. Don't say he was Tom's."

He was right, it wasn't her job. But she agreed.

Late afternoon, Upwood got together with his senior officers working on the wind farm investigation.

"Detective Superintendent Adams supports the plan to get a warrant to search Maskell-Grant's home and finances so we've applied for that. Now we need to consider what we have on Mallon's death. Who's good at mind mapping? Let's see if we can arrive at some new lines of enquiry. Morton? No? Who then?"

"I've done a bit, Sir. We used the technique when I was at uni."

"Good, Margaret. Thank you. You be scribe please. Let's start by throwing out random facts we have in relation to Dr and Mrs Mallon on one white board and then let's see if we can develop a couple of coherent maps. Margaret, have you got enough coloured pens?"

They spent the next hour and a half working on it.

They explored Veronica's life history line: born in Mexico, going to school and university in Los Angeles, travelling to Rio for the Summit where she met Jeremy, and ending up in England.

On the family branch she had father, mother and sister, all still alive.

Her career branch was empty apart from riding instructor.

On her interests branch there were the environment, wind energy and Kmag, as well as clothes, make-up and her dog.

On her relationships branch there were her family, Jeremy, Ken Lloyd.

On her skills branch there were languages and riding, and query shooting.

"So what does this tell us? What strikes you?"

Morton was the first to answer. "She's well-travelled and good at languages, well Spanish and English at least."

"She's spent time in Los Angeles, through uni. The Glock 17 was first registered in LA. Did she learn to shoot there? Is there any connection between her and the man to whom it was registered?" Debra's questions were noted.

Mo asked "How serious is her relationship with Lloyd? We've assumed so far that she may well have seduced him because of the frustration of his wife's circumstances. But we've seen nothing to suggest that he'd ditch her for Veronica."

"Do we know what religion she is? And Jeremy, come to that? She's almost certain to be Catholic. What if he is and he wouldn't divorce her?" This idea from Debra was novel to the rest of them.

"But if she wanted a divorce he couldn't stop her, could he?"

"He might be able to. Some divorces aren't allowed by the courts, although it is a tiny number. I still think it's very odd that she didn't ask about the dog or the whereabouts of the car when we first interviewed her. We know that Jeremy's car was driven to the other gravel pit at Knapton. How did the murderer persuade the dog to get in the car and go with them? Was the person familiar to him – like Veronica?"

"He may have been bribed with some treat or other", volunteered Morton.

They tossed around a few more ideas. It was agreed that they would ask Interpol for help again to check out her university time, including whether she had belonged to any gun clubs.

It was also agreed that they would have to examine the logistics of her having returned to the UK, murdered her husband and then returned to Mexico in time to respond to the news that her husband had been killed. Morton was charged with responsibility for following through on that. It reminded him that he'd once been through a similar exercise when they were establishing whether Katie could be eliminated from their enquiries into Mark Campion's death. She had been in Spain at the time. In that case it was demonstrated that she could not have been responsible. Would that prove to be the case with Veronica?

Next they brainstormed Jeremy. They looked at motive. They had already considered his support of the wind farm and eliminated those who might oppose him on that ground. Was financial gain an issue and who benefited from his death? Was there someone who blamed him for perceived negligence in relation to a patient? Was there another doctor in the practice who saw the opportunity for a partnership if he were eliminated? Was there someone in another practice who thought there might be an opportunity for take-over if he was out of the way?

They didn't have the answers to these questions. But at least they had some hypotheses they could examine. Upwood left in a slightly more hopeful frame of mind.

Chapter 65

It was Debra and Tom who had first interviewed Dr Paxman, Senior Partner at Mallon's surgery. This time she was partnered by Morton.

"Dr Paxman, it's good of you to spare us some more time. This is my colleague DI Harrison."

"Not at all. Anything I can do to help."

Morton took the lead. "Doctor, when DS Graf was talking to you before we were interested in whatever you could tell us about Jeremy Mallon. But our assumption at the time was that his death might be linked to the wind farm plans. We want to explore a bit more widely now."

"You mean it wasn't linked?"

"We don't know as yet. But we think there is a real possibility that there is no connection at all. I've read the record of your first interview. I understand that Dr Mallon upset a number of patients. Can you give us more details on any of those incidents?"

"There was one last year that I told you about before, my dear", he said, looking at Debra. "An elderly man had a chronic chest complaint. He wanted Jeremy to prescribe antibiotics for it. Jeremy refused to because in his view the complaint was viral and therefore would not respond to them. And I think I also told you that the patient complained that Jeremy had said he was stupid. Jeremy denied he'd said that."

"Are there others that you can tell us about?"

"Not from memory. Pru Thompson may be able to. She's the Practice Manager. It's her job to record any complaints that we get and how we deal with them."

"What about complaints from relatives about the way he treated them?"

Dr Paxman took off his glasses and rubbed them with the silk handkerchief from his top pocket, behaviour Debra recognised from before as indicating that he was uncomfortable with the line of questioning.

"We've had no such complaints so far as I'm aware."

Debra sensed his unease was deeper than before. "Are you aware of any such complaint about him at another practice before he joined you?"

He put his glasses back on his nose and peered over them at her. "You're very perspicacious my dear, aren't you?"

They waited.

"I was so much hoping you wouldn't raise this issue."

"Please tell us what happened, Dr Paxman", she urged.

"It was before he joined us. We didn't know about it at the time. He had been in practice near Oxford. He'd trained at the JR."

"The JR?"

"Sorry, the John Radcliffe Hospital in Oxford, it's a teaching hospital. Anyway as I say, he was working as a GP in one of the market towns between Oxford and Swindon. A little girl died." He paused again.

"Go on, please."

"I gather she suffered from severe asthma, had been hospitalised several times. Her mother had taken her to the surgery but was a few minutes late for the appointment. Apparently Jeremy refused to see her. Told her to come back the next day. She died at home that night." He was fidgeting and clearly upset.

"And you didn't know about it at the time?"

"No."

"So how did you find out about it?"

"The girl's father moved to Cambridge last year and saw Jeremy's photo in the newspaper. I can't remember why his picture was in, but it was. The girl's father tracked him down to this surgery. He wrote me a letter saying that Jeremy wasn't fit to practise. I talked to Jeremy about it. It seems that the GMC, sorry, the General Medical Council, warned him but did not strike him off."

"Did you ask him why he hadn't disclosed it when you hired him?"

"He said it was old history."

"How did you feel about that?"

"Not at all happy."

"But you kept him on."

"I don't suppose you have any idea how difficult it is to recruit doctors to a rural practice like this. We couldn't afford to let him go."

"Why did he move here from Oxfordshire?"

"I imagine he needed to leave the area. And I think he may have said he had parents living in East Anglia."

"How did you deal with the letter?"

"I took legal advice and our solicitor sent off a bland letter that deflected any criticism of the practice and alluded to the consequences of any defamatory action on his part."

"Did you hear any more from him?"

"No, thank God."

"Presumably Pru will have copies of the correspondence on file? May we see them please?"

Dr Paxman thought for a moment, mindlessly polishing his spectacles again. "I don't see why not. The man isn't a patient of ours. And Jeremy's dead, God bless his soul. Yes, ask Pru by all means for any help you want. She'll know if there are any confidentiality issues."

They thanked him for his time and went to find her. She furnished them with a copy of the letter from the dead girl's father, Winston Brown. It was short and badly written, saying little more than that Mallon should be struck off. With it was a photocopy of an article about his daughter's death from one of the Oxford papers. She also gave them a copy of the letter from Paxman's solicitor. There was nothing else she could tell them that was of interest. But they did seem to have one promising lead.

The evening briefing was again limited to the core group of officers.

Upwood invited Morton to tell them what enquiries he had put in place in relation to Veronica.

"I'm prioritising the enquiries we can manage in the UK before involving Interpol again. I've asked the Border Agency to give us what information they have on her leaving the UK – her husband told us he thinks she flew out on 22nd January. I've also asked them to tell us if they have any record of her returning to the UK since then, and of leaving after 5th February.

"I've also got someone checking with airlines. It's going to take a while, several airlines fly from London to Ixtapa-Zihuatanejo, so we are concentrating to begin with on those which involve only one stop. Even when she first went out she would probably have wanted the shortest journey time if her mother was dangerously ill.

"I'm inclined to leave the US enquiries for the moment. We'd need to know her maiden name which we don't have."

"Don't we? I thought you'd found her family name, Margaret?"

"I found her father's name. But her maiden name will be different. It's complicated, Debra told me."

Upwood shook his head and decided not to pursue it for the time being.

Morton continued. "I assume we don't want to approach her yet, Sir?"

"Correct. Let's see how the first round of enquiries pans out. Mo, you were looking at other surgeries which might have had an interest in Mallon's?"

"Yes, Sir. Not much progress yet. We've identified those close to Knapton. That gives us Waterbeach, Histon, Oakington, Longstanton, Willingham and one or two others. We've interviewed the senior partners in Waterbeach and Histon and haven't come up with anything to suggest that they would have the slightest interest in taking over, or merging with, Knapton. We'll carry on tomorrow.

"We did also interview the two other salaried GPs at Knapton to see if disposing of Mallon would benefit them. Both are female. One is close to retiring. The other is part-time with a young family. Neither would see themselves as partnership material, nor aspire to it. So if we draw a blank with the other surgeries we can probably write off a killer from within the profession."

"Fine, thank you, Mo. Morton, what have you got for us?"

"I'm going to hand over to Debra, Sir. She can tell you more than I can."

"Fine. Debra?"

"Well we both went to see Dr Paxman. We drew a blank effectively on patients with serious complaints about him at Knapton. Then we asked him whether a relative might have complained about negligence towards a family member. I thought he was being economical with the truth. On a hunch I asked him whether he was aware of any such incident before Mallon joined the practice. We hit pay dirt!"

"Not normal police terminology, Debra, but it sounds promising. Come on, tell us all."

"He trained at the John Radcliffe in Oxford and then joined a small town practice a few miles from the city. A mother brought her five-year old daughter to an appointment for severe asthma but was a few minutes late arriving. Not only did Mallon refuse to see her, he told her so in the waiting area in full view of several other patients and the reception staff. He told her to come back the following day. The mother took the child home. The poor little kid died that night."

"Good God. What happened?"

"It was all over the local papers. There was coverage for some weeks. Mallon was suspended pending a GMC hearing. In the end they gave him a warning but they didn't strike him off. He moved over to Cambridgeshire soon afterwards. He didn't disclose the incident when he applied to Knapton."

"Why did he choose Knapton I wonder?"

"Paxman told us Mallon had said he had elderly parents in East Anglia. I suspect he wanted to move somewhere where his past wasn't known, and maybe Paxman was so desperate to recruit him he didn't make any very thorough checks. But the best is yet to come, Sir."

Debra's warm skin tones blushed with her excitement. "The father, Winston Brown, the son of Jamaican immigrants, blamed his partner, a white British woman, of being too weak, saying she should have insisted that their daughter be seen by a doctor, any doctor, even if not Mallon. He assaulted her repeatedly, the last time so badly that she ended up in the JR with a broken jaw, a broken arm and heaven knows what else. He got eighteen months in Bullingdon for his sins.

"When he came out, he moved to Cambridge and saw Mallon's picture in one of the local rags and tracked him down."

"So we have someone with a real grudge against Mallon."

"Twice over, I'd say", said Morton. "First his daughter dies because of Mallon's callous treatment. Secondly he probably blames Mallon for the fact that he was angry enough with his wife to keep beating her up, landing him in prison. And he clearly has anger management problems."

"Would he have access to small fire-arms? Jamaica maybe?"

"Who knows? Anything's possible."

"Good. Morton, are you and Debra going to track him down and interview him?"

"You bet. We're on it."

The meeting broke up. Upwood managed to waylay Debra before she left.

"I hear you have Tom's cat. Penny told me. I hope it wasn't because it was Tom's."

"I didn't know when I agreed to take him. And when Penny told me it seemed like some kind of poetic justice."

He decided to let it pass. "I'm glad to see you are tackling the case with such enthusiasm. I can imagine how hard it's been, coming to terms with Tom's death."

"And his mother's. Not that I knew her. It's just that I feel if I'd done things differently they might both still be alive."

"You mustn't think like that, Debra. Tom was quite capable of making up his own mind. If you'd phoned him or gone round there as soon as he came out of hospital he wouldn't have told you much, knowing him. Even if he'd had the biopsy results I can't see him disclosing them to you. He was stubborn, we all know that."

She looked at him, wanting to believe him. But guilt is corrosive and it was eating away at her.

Chapter 66

As they were all clearing up to go home Mo went over to Margaret's desk. "D'you fancy a quick bite?"

She looked round the room hurriedly, conscious that the others might hear their conversation. "A quick drink if you like." She gave him a pointed look and he decided not to challenge her.

"OK. I've got stuff to do tonight anyway. See you downstairs in ten?"

She smiled at him and turned back to her PC to close it down.

Ten minutes later she was downstairs. Mo was waiting for her. "Where do you fancy?"

"How about that pub in Dover Street, near the Grafton Centre."

"What, the Tram Depot?"

"Yes, I think that's what it's called."

They set off at a brisk pace through the streets behind the station and before long reached the pub. Margaret secured a table in a secluded corner and Mo brought drinks over: a dry white for her and a pint for him. She'd not been inside before. Brick walls, wooden floors and tables and a décor evidently aimed at a young crowd. Posters advertised live entertainment. A pub you'd need to be in the right mood for, perhaps.

"Have you really got stuff to do tonight then?" She smiled at him, a slightly arch smile.

"Nope. I just picked up the vibe that's how you wanted to play it."

"Well done. We'll make a detective of you yet. You know I don't like others in the station to know we go out occasionally."

"We've been round this house before, Margaret. It's OK as long as we don't let it get in the way of work. Anyway, I am free tonight. So we can have a meal, right?"

"Sure. We can eat here." She waved at a blackboard with the day's specials. Other than that, it was mainly pizzas and burgers. But there were good spicy smells coming from the kitchen. It would be fine for a casual meal.

"Method in your madness then. Cheers."

Over supper he told her how it had been growing up in Liverpool with a brother and three sisters. She talked about her childhood in rural Hertfordshire – their backgrounds could not have been more different.

After they'd finished their meal they went out of the restaurant trying to decide whether to walk or take a cab. It was not much more than a mile to Margaret's flat in Fen Causeway and less to the car park in Queen Anne Terrace where Mo had left his car. They decided to walk. They'd only gone a few yards when one of her heels caught in the gap between some paving stones.

"Hell and damnation. I can't get it out." He laughed. "It's not funny. It's stuck."

Mo dropped down to one knee and once she'd slipped her foot out of the shoe he tugged gently trying to free it. It didn't budge. He pulled a little harder. The shoe came free. But the heel remained stuck in the pavement.

"Christ I'm sorry Margaret."

"Bugger. Bugger. Bugger. They're the only heels I can wear all day."

"Not now you can't. I'm really sorry. Look I'll have to get this out somehow otherwise some poor sod's going to trip over it." After waggling it about for a bit he managed to get it out. Even if a cobbler could stick it back on it probably wouldn't last very long, and the leather had been torn off the heel.

After that they had little option but to hail a taxi. She protested that she'd manage on her own. He wouldn't have it and insisted that the least he could do was to see her home.

When they got back to her apartment block she knew she'd got no good reason not to invite him in for coffee.

The building was old fashioned. Her flat was on the top floor and from her living room she could see over to Sheep's Green, a very pleasant outlook for such a central location.

She kicked off her other shoe and padded through to the kitchen to put the kettle on. "I've only got instant. Sorry."

"It's OK. Just make it good and strong please." He was browsing her bookshelf when she came back in and put both mugs down on the coffee table. "These all yours?"

"Yep. Why? Have me down as a Mills and Boon type, did you?"

"God, no. But I would have thought fiction. These are nearly all history and biography."

"And travel."

"And travel. These places you've been to?"

"I wish. On my salary?"

"This flat must have cost you a bit."

"I don't own it. Don't be daft. I rent. Even that's a struggle. But at least I don't need a car."

"How long have you been here?"

"In this flat?"

"Yeah."

"A couple of years. Before that I shared a terraced house with a couple of other girls on the Huntingdon Road."

"Near the centre, or out towards Girton?"

"Close to the centre. Noisy. And dirty. Inside and out." She laughed ruefully at the memory. "Ill-fitting sash windows. Grime from the constant traffic. And flat-mates who were not remotely house-trained. Drove me up the wall. I'm much happier on my own."

Mo looked at her, trying to interpret the remark. It could be she meant it literally. Maybe it meant it gave her the freedom to entertain friends if she chose…

"Where do you live?"

"I've got a maisonette in King's Hedges. It's grim, frankly, but it does have off street parking and it's all I can afford."

"You don't share?"

"Nah. Growing up in a big family I wanted my own space. And I'm quite a tidy person. I had to be when I was growing up. Mam insisted on it. And I've got used to it. Makes life easier really. So how do you spend your free time?"

"You're joking, right? It's about as much as I can do to keep the flat straight and do the laundry. And shopping's a pain."

"Do you not use online shopping?"

"I do. But if you've tried it you know you have to be incredibly organised. It's OK if there isn't a big case on cos you can book a mid-evening slot and stand a chance of being at home. But it's when there is a big case on you most need it and it's impossible to organise. Thank God for home delivery meals!"

"I know. But how would you spend your time if you had more of it?"

"Cinema. Theatre even. And I do read. You?"

"I s'pose it's the pub mainly. Typical bloke. Meet a few mates and argue about the football."

"Which team do you support?"

"Liverpool."

"Not Everton?"

"No. Why?"

"Just wondered. My dad supports them."

"I went to a C of E school."

"What on earth has that got to do with it?"

"Remember this. Could come in handy in a pub quiz. Everton was founded by a Methodist. Liverpool by a Protestant."

"Hell's teeth. I know football's like a religion for most blokes, but I didn't know it went that deep."

"Surely even you know about the rivalry between Celtic and Rangers?"

"I've read about it but I can never remember which is which. Not that it matters."

"Except to their members and supporters! Celtic are Catholic and Rangers Protestant. C for Catholic. Easy."

She laughed. "If you say so."

"I'd better be going. Another early start."

Margaret rose to her feet immediately, which gave Mo no encouragement at all. He had hoped she might have offered him another cup of coffee. She followed him to the door. Before he opened it he turned to her. "I'm really sorry about your shoe, Mags. But it's been a nice evening, thank you."

She smiled at him and nodded. He put his arm lightly around her back and pulled her gently towards him, kissing her briefly on the cheek. She stiffened. Colour shot to her face as she pulled away.

"Good night, Mo."

He went outside and began to walk back to the car park, wondering what on earth had got into her. Did she really not enjoy his company after all? Or was there a deeper problem?

Chapter 67

With a copy of Brown's letter to Dr Paxman, Morton and Debra had no trouble finding his house in Bermuda Road near the Histon Road Cemetery. They arrived just after seven in the morning hoping to catch him before he went to work, if indeed he did work. They were in luck. Lights were on. He was at home.

Morton knocked on the door. A short while later it opened as far as the chain would let it. There was a spy hole so they knew he could see them. "Who are you? What do you want?"

"We're police officers, Mr Brown. We'd like a word, please."

"What about? I ain't done nothin'."

"If we could just come in please? Don't want your neighbours involved do we?"

"I ain't got nothing to say to ya."

With long years of practice, Morton jammed his foot in the gap between the door and the frame, just as Brown tried to push it shut.

"Winston Brown, I am arresting you on suspicion of perverting the course..."

"Oh bollocks. Shift yer foot." Morton did so. Brown pushed the door to and released the chain. He pulled the door open and they found themselves in a small front room from which stairs led to the first floor. They could see a tiny kitchen through an open door at the back. The room was sparsely furnished with what looked like mis-matched second-hand furniture. The only new item in the room was the ubiquitous large flat screen television on the wall. There was a smell of stale beer and weed. An over-flowing ashtray sat on a table beside what was evidently his chair, empty beer cans in a basket beside it. There were no books, no magazines and no newspaper. A pile of DVDs under the TV screen gave some clue as to how he spent his time. It didn't create a scene of the most exciting life in the world. Although that might depend on the content of the DVDs, Morton thought.

Brown was a tall well-built man, dressed in dirty trousers and a very grubby vest. He was unshaven, not so much designer stubble as several days' ragged growth. His hair was in short dreads. When he sat down he seemed to overflow his chair. Debra found his manspreading both repulsive and offensive.

"Waddya want?"

"We are making enquiries into the death of Dr Jeremy Mallon."

Brown uttered a harsh laugh. "An' you wanna fit me up for that, man? Bollocks."

"Where were you on the morning of Monday 7th February between six and ten?"

"New York."

"What?"

"No friggin' idea, man. Here probably, before goin' to work."

"Where do you work?"

"All over the place, man. I'm a brickie."

"Who do you work for?"

"DED Builders, mostly"

"Not all the time?"

"Have to go where the work is don' I?"

"Were you working for DED then?"

"Think so."

"So they'd have records?"

"No idea. Ask 'em."

"You wrote to the senior partner at Dr Mallon's surgery."

"Yeah."

"Why?"

"Bleeding obvious. He ain't fit to be a doctor. Killed my little girl."

"You were very angry about that."

"Course I were bleeding angry. I loved that kid. Five. That's all she were. Shouldn't have died. He sent her home to die."

"But you blamed your partner, too."

"Stupid cow. Should've stood up to him. Made him see her. Made someone else see her. Shouldn't 'ave given in and gone home."

"You were angry enough to assault her, more than once."

"Yeah, yeah. And I've done my time for it. Didn't think she'd have the balls to go to the police about it."

"Where is she now?"

"Dunno. Don' care."

"Why did you move to Cambridge?"

"Why not? Plenty of building goin' on."

"And you didn't have trouble getting work?"

"No. I'm a good brickie. Can earn decent money."

"What did you hope to achieve with your letter to the surgery?"

"Wanted 'im exposed. Wanted 'im struck off."

"And what response did you get?"

"Letter from a bleeding lawyer. Threatening, it were."

"So you thought you'd take the law into your own hands. Again."

"No I bleedin' didn't. He were shot weren't he? Where am I gonna get a bleedin' gun?"

"Not difficult is it?"

"Wouldn't know. Never tried."

"Do you drive?"

"Yeah. Ain't got no car though."

"How d'you get about?"

"Bike. Bus. Depends."

Morton had few other questions he could usefully put to Brown. Their next port of call was the building company he claimed to have been working for.

They found the firm on an industrial estate on the northern fringe of the city. The office was single storey and scruffy. There were bars across the window and a steel door was clearly padlocked across the entrance out of hours. Hardly a good image for a builder. The main door opened into a small unmanned reception area. If anything, the interior was even less prepossessing. Coarse carpet tiles, ingrained with mud, cement dust and heaven knows what else, covered the floor. A plywood counter ran across the back of the room. The varnish had long since given up what was evidently an unequal struggle. A small old-fashioned monitor sat on the counter. The place had not been painted in years. There was a bell, which Morton rang. A rather harassed looking man came out to greet them. He took one look at them and recognised them for what they were.

"What can I do for you?"

"I'm DI Harrison and this is DS Graf."

"Well I knew you were the police."

"And your name is?"

"Dugdale. Danny Dugdale."

"And you own the company?"

"Such as it is, yes. What do you want?"

"We'd like to ask you about one of your employees. Winston Brown."

"What do you want to know?"

"How long has he worked for you?"

"On and off about four years, I suppose."

"So he's not permanent?"

"No, I've only got a few who are. It depends what jobs we've got on."

"How do you rate him?"

"He's a good worker. Bit lippy. But they mostly are so I don't pay no heed to that."

"Have you had any trouble since he's been with you?"

"No. Only a bit of a slanging match with one of the Irish lads who told him to get back to the jungle one day. Might've come to blows but I stepped in pretty sharpish. Mick had been in the pub at lunch time. Told him to mind his tongue or I'd kick him out."

"Anything else?"

"No. He keeps to himself."

“Can you tell us where he was working on the morning of 7th February?”

“I’ll have to check. He went back into the room behind reception and came out a minute or two later with a large diary, already looking tattered, all the pages for the first few weeks turned in at the corners where they’d been thumbed so often they’d no longer lie flat. He opened it and flicked through until he came to the right page. “He would have been in Knapton. He and Stan together. They were rebuilding a wall that had been knocked down. A couple of days’ work, that’s all.”

“And you can confirm he was there?”

“I can’t. Stan could tell you. But if he’d not been working Stan would’ve told me.”

“Is Stan here today?”

“No. He’s on a job in Milton.”

“Can you give us the address please, and the address where they were working in Knapton?”

Dugdale rummaged around for a bit of paper and copied out the addresses from the work diary. He pushed it over to them.

“What’s he supposed to have done?”

“I can’t answer that, Mr Dugdale. Just routine enquiries.”

“Might have guessed. That’s what you lot always say.”

They thanked him and headed off to Milton.

They found Stan easily enough. He remembered the job in Knapton. Usually they’d go in the van together after they’d loaded the gear they needed. That day Brown had said he’d meet Stan on site, which was unusual, especially as he knew that Brown didn’t have a car. Stan had got there for eight. Brown had turned up, on foot, about twenty minutes late. Said he’d missed the bus.

Chapter 68

While Morton and Debra were following the Winston Brown lead, the warrants were being served on Maskell-Grant. He answered the door with a look of intense displeasure on his face.

Mo showed him his ID.

"Whatever time of day do you call this, Officer?"

As it was only just gone eight o'clock, Mo assumed that Maskell-Grant did not start his day very early. At least he was dressed.

"Mr Maskell-Grant, we have a warrant to search your property." He handed him a copy. Maskell-Grant studied it.

"This is quite outrageous. Outrageous." He stood back and allowed Mo and the team in.

"Constable Griffin will supervise the search, sir. I suggest you take a seat." Maskell-Grant watched as three pairs of police came into the house.

"Perhaps you will give us keys to your home office in the garden, your garage and any cupboards or drawers in the house which are locked. We don't like to damage property unnecessarily."

Maskell-Grant fished a bunch of keys from his trouser pocket and handed them to Mo. "I've no idea what you think you'll find. I'm a reputable and respected academic." He sat down gingerly on the Windsor chair in the hall.

"I think you'll be more comfortable in your living room, sir. This might take some time." The man rose again and walked stiffly into the sitting room. He sat in his usual chair but rather than settle into it he sat on the edge, points of colour prominent on his cheeks. His knees were together with his heels tucked back, giving an effeminate impression. Mo passed the keys to the search supervisor and left.

The search lasted all day. Maskell-Grant remained impassive throughout. When he was shown the list of items they had seized, he became extremely angry. "How am I supposed to work without my computer? I'm writing a book. You can't take that away."

"We can, sir, and we will.

At the evening briefing they were all rather subdued again. While it wasn't on the front page of the evening paper, there was a short article inside asking whether their enquiry had not stalled. After more than seven weeks the police appeared to have no clue who was behind the murders. It was time to call in reinforcements, according to the editor whose byline, unusually, was on the article.

"Evening everyone. Have we made some progress today?"

Morton was the first to respond. "We went to see Winston Brown, whose daughter died because of Mallon's neglect. A scruffy bloke, even allowing for the nature of his work, and a dodgy Jamaican accent. He's not first generation, but perhaps he likes hamming it up a bit. He's managed to keep busy most of the time since he came out of Bullingdon. He's said to be a good brickie and they can usually find work. He's not been in trouble since.

"He told us he couldn't remember what he was doing the morning Mallon was killed. He denied having anything to do with it.

"We talked to the guy who runs a building company he works for. He told us he was on a job in Knapton that day and the next with another of his men. That guy confirms that. Interestingly, he says that although they normally go out together in the firm's van, that morning Brown said he'd meet him on site. He did so but was twenty or more minutes late. He turned up on foot, which given he lives in Cambridge is a bit odd. We haven't had the chance to ask him about that yet, but we will obviously."

"So. We know he had motive. It sounds as though he had the opportunity."

"Maybe. But the fact he doesn't have a car complicates it."

"He might have borrowed one."

"Maybe. But he's not the sort to have a lot of mates, I wouldn't think. Would you, Debra?"

She shook her head.

"Well, follow it through."

"Sir."

"Mo. How did the search go at Maskell-Grant's home?"

"They found a laptop case with a shoulder strap which might have been used on the night Waldorf died. And we've seized his computer of course, and a few memory sticks. There wasn't very much more of interest to be honest, apart from a dark woollen hat. We should get DNA from that, and I'm hopeful we'll get something from the IT guys."

"What about the airlines, Morton? Any sign of Mrs Mallon's movements?"

"No. None at all. I've come to the conclusion she must have retained her maiden name. I've been racking my brain trying to think how to discover it without asking her or going through Interpol again."

"But we tracked her family down through Interpol. Surely we've got access to that information?"

"Only partially. We know her father's name. But her name won't be exactly the same. They have a funny system for names, like the Spanish, I think."

"How does that work?"

Debra answered. "Everyone has two surnames. The first part is their father's first surname. The second part is their mother's first surname. Both surnames have to be used on all formal documents like passports. But in conversation someone is likely to be referred to by their forename, or title, and their first surname. Unless that name is very common, in which case the second surname might be used." Upwood thought it all sounded about as clear as mud. He vaguely remembered that Debra had told him once that her mother was Spanish.

"What was her father's name?"

Margaret thumbed through her notepad. "Francisco Padilla Martos."

"And her mother?"

"Don't know."

"So all we know is that she may still be using Veronica Padilla something."

"Yep."

"Morton, you'll have to get the airlines to search their databases again."

"Bet they'll be really pleased about that."

"Get them to give us any names which include either Veronica or Padilla as well as both."

"Might be a good idea. I'll do that."

"Mo, did you check out the other surgeries to see if any had designs on the Knapton surgery?"

"I did. Drew a complete blank. I think we can shut down that line of enquiry."

Upwood summarised.

"So we still have Maskell-Grant in the frame for the first three incidents. And Brown and Mrs Mallon for the doctor's death. Let's try to chase down the Brown angle tomorrow. That shouldn't be too difficult. No doubt it will be a day or two before we get any forensic feedback on the stuff seized from Maskell-Grant or information from the airlines."

It was frustrating. The parameters of their investigation seemed to get narrower week by week.

Chapter 69

Morton and Debra headed out to Bermuda Road again.

"Do you suppose it makes him feel at home?"

"What d'you mean?"

"The street name."

"Daft pillock. Have you any idea how far it is from Jamaica? Bermuda's way off the coast of South Carolina. Jamaica's nearer Central America by far."

"It's all the same to me. They're both warmer than here is all I know."

They parked and got out of the car. It was just after seven again. Now they knew that he typically started work at eight they wanted to be sure to catch him at home.

He opened the door to them.

"What the hell d'you lot want now for Chrissake?"

"Just a few more questions, Mr Brown. We won't keep you long."

He held the door open and they stepped inside. The room was stuffy and they could see the kitchen window was steamed up. They could smell coffee but he certainly wasn't feeling inclined to offer them any. As it smelt sour and metallic, like cheap instant stuff, they weren't unduly bothered.

"Mr Brown. The morning of 7th February you were working with Stan in Knapton. Rebuilding a wall that had collapsed, we understand."

"OK. Yeah. What of it?"

"Stan says you arrived on foot, late. Why was that?"

"Man, that's a while ago."

"But you must remember. Stan says you always travel together on jobs in the firm's van. Why not that day?"

A large smile spread slowly across his face.

"Got lucky, man. Stayed over with a woman in Histon."

"Can you tell us her name?"

"Just said she was Sandy. Didn't give a shit what her name was."

"Can you tell us where she lives?"

"It was a bungalow, I remember that."

"What else can you remember about it?"

"Not a lot. It were dark."

"Where did you meet her?"

"In the supermarket."

"Which one?"

"Aldi. The one near here. Works there part time."

"How did you end up going to her home?"

"I don't have no trouble with women." He smirked.

Debra could see it. She didn't fancy him, far from it, but there was a certain animal magnetism that some women would find attractive.

"So you stayed the night?"

"Yeah. Got the bus up to Knapton the next morning."

"And she'll confirm this?"

"You'll have to ask 'er, won't ya?"

"We'll have to find her first", Debra said as they walked back to the car. "Aldi. Let's go there. At least we can get her full name."

Ten minutes later they parked in the store's car park and headed in to the Service Desk. A few minutes later the Deputy Store Manager came over to meet them.

"Is there somewhere quiet we can go for a quick word sir?" The man looked at their IDs and nodded.

"Is this about the shoplifting?"

"No, something entirely different."

He took them into a minutely small office overflowing with paperwork, samples, packs of damaged goods and heaven knows what else.

"What is it then? Trouble?"

"No, not at all. And nothing that concerns your store. We're just trying to trace a lady called Sandy who works here part-time. And before you ask, no, she's not in any trouble either. It's just we think she may be able to help us with something. Can you confirm you have someone here called Sandy?"

"Aren't you s'posed to have a warrant or something before I give you any information?"

"All we need are her surname and address. It's nothing to do with your store, as I say."

"But I'm not supposed to give out stuff like that about staff. Data protection and all that. HR wouldn't like it."

"We'll get a warrant if we have to. But there's no harm in giving us the information and she need not know how we obtained it."

He looked back and forth between them. In the end he decided that the sooner he gave them what they wanted, the sooner they'd be off the premises. He also confirmed that she would not be on shift again until two that afternoon.

They set off for Histon. They found her bungalow in Knapton Road on the northern side of the village. She was in, if the car in her drive was anything to go by.

She opened the door to them warily. "What is it? I don't buy nothing at the door. And don't start spouting off about Watchtower or whatever it is. Can't be doing with God botherers."

"We're police officers, Ma'am. May we come in for a couple of minutes? I promise you we won't be long. We just have a couple of questions for you." They showed their warrant cards.

She stepped back into the hall and led them through the kitchen at the back which had been extended by a garden room. Well, it certainly didn't qualify for the name conservatory. But garden room was pushing it a bit. It looked out onto a scruffy overgrown lawn so small you could probably stand in the middle and cut it with a Flymo without moving. A few shrubs that offered no aesthetic charms by way of colour or form stood against a rickety fence. Other than providing space for a clothes airer, the garden had no redeeming features. The only bright spot was a male blackbird, singing its heart out at the top of the tallest shrub.

She gestured for them to sit down, looking at them warily. "What's this about then?"

"We understand you know someone by the name of Winston Brown."

She now looked alarmed. "What if I do?"

"Can you confirm that he spent the night here on Sunday 6th February and left the following morning?"

She considered the question, trying to work out what she'd let herself in for. Couldn't. "It were a Sunday. It might have been the 6th."

"Not much more than two weeks ago. Can you think back?"

"Well it weren't last week. I went to me Mam's after I finished work. So yes it probably was the 6th. Why? What's this all about? Can't I entertain a friend without the police being involved?"

"Of course you can Ms Ferguson. Can you just please tell us what time he arrived and what time he left?"

"Well he came back with me, in the car. I finish at five on a Sunday. We went for a drink at the Fox and Duck near the store. Then we went back to the car and came here. I dunno exactly what time he left here in the morning, but he said he didn't need to be very early cos he was on a job in Knapton. Half past seven maybe? He'd looked up the bus times on his phone. Said he could get a bus. Why're you asking me all this? Is he in some sort of bother?"

"Just routine enquiries Ms Ferguson. We don't need to trouble you anymore."

They left, not knowing whether to be pleased or not. It looked as though Brown was out of the frame and that Veronica was the only one left in.

Chapter 70

Morton and Debra broke the news that Brown was almost certainly out of the running for Mallon's murder at the following morning's meeting. On the one hand it gave them a sharper focus. On the other, they'd have an awful lot of work to do to make a solid case against Veronica.

"So you're confident about Brown?" asked Upwood.

"We are, Sir. We know he had a motive but we are sure he didn't have the opportunity to kill Mallon. We don't think he had the means either.

"When we interviewed him he told us he'd picked up a female member of staff at his local Aldi as the store was closing. They went to a nearby pub for a drink and he must have charmed her sufficiently that she invited him to go home with her. They travelled in her car to Histon. He stayed the night. Ms Ferguson says he left her house at about half-past seven on the Monday morning."

"Charmed the pants off her then." Whoever muttered this at the back of the room must have thought himself funnier than he was. No one could be bothered to snigger.

Morton carried on. "Brown was at Knapton that morning, but his colleague says he didn't get to the site where they were working till twenty past eight. Brown told his mate he'd missed the bus and that could well be true. He'd likely be on the one after the one he was aiming for. We don't see how he could have got to the gravel pits and back in time."

"And I don't see him with a hand-gun, either", said Debra. "We know he used physical violence against his former partner. I would say that's more his style than a gun. Anyway, to have shot Mallon he had to know his routine. That means surveillance, maybe for a number of days. He'd have stuck out like a sore thumb in that street Mallon lives in and he's got no transport. No, I really don't think it's him. I think he wanted to cause trouble with Mallon with his letter to Paxman. But he's not smart enough to take on the surgery's law firm. He probably reckoned he'd done as much damage as he could."

"Is Ms Ferguson's statement credible?"

"No reason to think otherwise. They both made it clear they were up for a bit of casual sex – he was very crude about it. We can't see any reason she'd give him a false alibi. He was no more important to her than she was to him."

"You made a good point about surveillance. I don't think it's something we've considered, and we should have done. Whoever shot Mallon had to know he was going to be at the gravel pit. It's not a random killing. Veronica would know where he'd walk the dog, and when. Unless a neighbour was watching and following him, anyone else would have needed to carry out surveillance."

Margaret looked sceptical. "How easy would that be on that street, though? From what I remember all the gardens at the front are open plan – no walls or hedges. And whoever wanted to see where he was going would need a vehicle of some sort. That wouldn't be easy to hide."

Mo disagreed. "But you wouldn't have to hide it, would you? Just park it on the street. In fact you could stay in the vehicle. The street is a cul-de-sac. You could park round the corner from the junction with the other road and follow him as he drove out." His logic was irrefutable.

"Any other ideas? No? OK, so we need to consider the proposition that someone might have been watching on foot with a vehicle nearby, or was watching from a vehicle. Morton, can you organise a team to look for possible observation posts, and to interview neighbours to see if any of them had seen anyone acting suspiciously in the days before the murder or noticed any unusual vehicles in the vicinity?"

They were digesting the significance of this new line of thinking when someone knocked on the door and came in. "Thought you'd want to see this, Sir. It's the reports back from the airlines." He handed a paper to Upwood and then left. Upwood looked at it.

"At last. Aeromexico have her on their flight out of Heathrow on 22nd January. But not coming back here and then returning to Mexico." He looked at it more closely. "But Air Canada have an Encarnación Padilla Pérez flying from Zihuatanejo via Toronto to Heathrow on the 4th February, arriving eleven twenty am and back again on the 7th leaving at four pm. Does that help us?"

"Encarna, Sir. Her sister. Must be. I looked at some photo albums when we first got into their house. If you remember I said I thought I'd seen one of her parents and what looked like a sister. There was another photo of the girl and the name underneath it was Encarna. Short for Encarnación. My gran had a cleaner once, called Encarna. That's how I know." Margaret beamed at the rest of the team. "Veronica could have borrowed her sister's passport."

The idea galvanised them. Body language changed. They were more alert. Upwood sensed adrenaline beginning to pump once more. Could you smell adrenaline? He doubted it. But the atmosphere definitely seemed more charged. Upwood detailed Mo to arrange the checking of all car hire movements into and out of Heathrow on the days in question within appropriate time parameters. For the time being they ruled out her having travelled by public transport to Cambridge because there would have been too many places where she'd be caught on CCTV. It was an idea they might have to revisit if they made no progress with the hire companies.

Debra was tasked with checking CCTV footage from Heathrow airport for her presumed arrival and departure as, apart from Morton, she was the only team member to have met her. It was agreed that she had a better chance of recognising her.

Now they had a renewed sense of purpose.

Chapter 71

It was Friday and Mo and Debra were at Heathrow again. Debra had spent several deeply frustrating hours the previous day in the Security Control Centre examining CCTV footage of arrivals on 4th February and departures on 7th February. Today she'd asked Mo to come and see for himself.

"There must be something I'm missing. I've been through this lot twice allowing much wider time parameters than are realistic. I just can't see her. But we know she has to be here."

"So is she disguising herself somehow?"

"That's the conclusion I've come to. I thought maybe together we could spot something I didn't see on my own. I know you've not met her but you did see some good photos of her when you searched the house you said – full length as well as portrait."

"OK, fine. I've made enquiries at all the car hire firms represented here and won't get any answers for a while, so let's have a look at the footage. Start with arrivals? What time was the plane due in? Or rather what time did it actually get in?"

"It was due in at eleven twenty but was twenty-eight minutes late. Let's call it eleven fifty in round numbers."

"And how long before she'd get to the Arrivals Hall?"

"Well on an aircraft that big and unless you're in First Class, which she wasn't, you might be twenty minutes getting off the plane. Then immigration – she'd have to go through the non-EU lines and baggage reclaim."

"Did she have hold luggage?"

"Yes. One suitcase. So she'd have to collect it before reaching arrivals. My guess is it could take an hour, but I've been looking at everyone coming through from half an hour after she landed to two hours later."

"And can you tell which flights are coming through at any one time?"

"In theory yes, but in practice, no. Passengers're coming through at a rate of up to a couple of thousand an hour. And of course there is more than one camera filming the hall. I was completely bug-eyed by the time I finished last night."

"So how are we gonna do this?"

"Can you start on this one and I'll look at another? We know she can't be on a buggy or wheel-chair because that would have been arranged through the airline before landing. And it wasn't. So she's on foot. But she might be using a walking stick, or even a frame as disguise. Never mind wig and stuff."

"Heck, Deb. Needles and haystacks come to mind."

"Now you know why I needed help. I think even having met her this is difficult. For someone working just from a photograph it would be nearly impossible."

"So we are looking for jizz as much as anything else."

"What did that mean again?"

"General impression of size and shape. But I'm told it also means behaviour and mannerisms. So the way she walks and stands and so on."

"Oh, crikey."

Every now and then one would pause the film and ask the other to look at an image. Each in turn was ruled out. This went on all morning as they moved from the footage from one camera to another.

"Do a deal with you?"

"Yeah, OK."

"I'll pay for them if you get them?"

"Sarnies? Coffee?"

"Sarnies and a Red Bull please." She handed over a twenty pound note and he slipped out of the room.

Debra carried on scrutinising her film. Then eventually someone caught her eye. She was wearing a light coloured hijab over dark trousers and coat or tunic top. She was also wearing reflective sunglasses, an affectation she found really annoying. Even if she'd been outside, the weather would hardly have justified the glasses. There was no need at all for them indoors. There was something about this woman that caught her attention and she couldn't work out why. She was still looking at the image when Mo got back.

He dumped the bag of sandwiches, crisps and drinks on a table. "What you got, Deb?"

She ran the footage back until the woman had disappeared from sight. Then she ran it forward at normal speed. Then she reversed it and replayed it at slow speed. "What d'you reckon?"

"She's only got a carry on case."

"Doesn't mean she didn't check it in."

"Not convinced. Scarf and glasses are effective disguises for sure and her hair, eyes and eyebrows are distinctive features. But what else are you seeing? It's clearly not the rest of her clothes. Size and shape?"

"About right I'd say."

"Gait?"

"What?"

"The way she's walking. Length of stride and so on."

"Not sure I could tell. Although she does have good posture. A straight back. Probably all the riding she does."

"OK. So that fits. What about shoes, handbag?"

"Don't know about shoes. Handbag? She had a Mulberry when we interviewed her. Expensive job. Black patent croc effect with a brass catch on the front. Handles and a shoulder strap."

"Let's zoom in a bit." They did but it was fuzzy. "OK, let's follow her and see if we get a better image."

But sod's law came into play. In no time at all she was out of range of that camera. Mo said he didn't recall seeing anyone quite like her on the footage he'd seen, so he went back to work on his while Debra tried to work out which camera might have picked her up. She munched on her sandwich without much enthusiasm. By the time she'd finished it she had no idea what it was. Even the packet didn't tell as, like Pret, the packaging did not describe the contents. It was fuel. She wished she'd gone for a burger, like Mo. The beef smelt really spicy – jalapeños probably – and judging by the look on his face he was enjoying it. He wolfed it down. She'd finished her Red Bull and decided against crisps. They would just make her thirsty again. The Red Bull hadn't really satisfied her thirst come to that, but at least it was cold and a caffeine shot.

She stared at her screen again and caught sight of the woman whom she now thought of as Veronica walking towards a man with a clip board. Someone was meeting her. She paused the film and called Mo back again. They watched as they walked towards the car park. Damn. She was out of range again. It took them another twenty minutes to find the right one and another ten to spot her and her driver.

Would they be able to trace the car to her home in Knapton? Somehow she thought Veronica was not going to make it too easy for them.

Chapter 72

They left Heathrow at just after five and it would be nearly eight when they got back to Cambridge. Both were very tired, with sore eyes and aching backs and neck muscles. Just after they left King's Cross, Mo sent Margaret a text. *"fancy a chinese? i can b with u about 8. m xxx"*

"rather have an indian if thats ok. cu. m xxx"

Mo nearly laughed out loud. She obviously hadn't thought very hard about what she'd written. He must remember to tease her when the opportunity presented itself. They hadn't spoken since he left her flat on Monday evening. He'd suggested a meal at the end of the week and she seemed willing. He'd been worrying the whole time about what had happened when he kissed her cheek. But then she had put three kisses on the end of her text. It must be a good sign. Or was she just being polite because that's what he'd done? Shit. His mind was in turmoil. He was feeling like a hormonal teenager. He took his phone out again and started playing around, picking up the news headlines and generally trying to while away the journey. Debra seemed engrossed in hers, too. Probably Facebook; he could vaguely see lots of photos flashing up and down.

Once off the train he made some excuse for hanging back, leaving Debra to go off alone. He found his car and headed off to the nearest takeaway and picked up some dishes he hoped she'd like. As he'd left a couple of bottles of wine in the boot of his car that morning he was pretty well laden by the time he got to her front door.

She opened it to be assailed by spicy aromas. "Hi. Smells good."

She closed the door behind him as he took the food straight through to the kitchen. "Hot plates are in the oven. I'm famished."

They enjoyed the food. Chicken Tikka, Prawn Dhansak, rice and Naan bread, washed down with glasses of white and red wine. Neither spoke very much, they were too hungry.

When they'd finished, Margaret threw all the rubbish away and put the plates and cutlery into the sink.

"Ought I to wash them for you now, Mags? They'll smell terrible in the morning."

"The rubbish will smell anyway, so I don't think it will make a lot of difference. But thanks. That's a first for me."

"What?"

"Having the bloke offer to do the washing up."

"Mam was good, but we were a big family. We were expected to help. I think she did us a favour. The transition to living away from home wasn't so hard."

He settled down on the sofa, she in the arm chair. "Look at me, Mags. Tell me the truth. Did I upset you when I left last time?"

"What do you mean?" The fact that she coloured again made it perfectly clear to him that she knew.

"When I kissed your cheek. You froze on me. I didn't mean to upset you."

She stared at her lap. "You didn't upset me."

"You do like me, don't you?"

She turned to look out of the window. "Yes."

"So what's the problem?" Only when he saw that her shoulders were shaking did he realise he was on dangerous ground. He kept quiet. She didn't. In no time she was in floods of tears. Soon she was hyperventilating. Mo was stunned. He went out to the kitchen and came back with a handful of tissues and a glass of water, which he put down beside her. He sat down again, knowing that it would be wrong to touch her, much as he wanted to take her in his arms and hug her. Eventually she calmed down.

"Do you want to talk about it?"

"Not really."

"Have you ever talked about it?"

"Not really."

"It might help." Silence descended for several minutes. Mo couldn't decide whether he should just go and never mention it again. But he was becoming fond of her. He didn't like to think that she was bottling up some terrible trauma.

"Can you get me a brandy, please? There's some in the kitchen."

He found it. Not so much Dutch courage, as French courage he thought. It wasn't a brand he recognised. Perhaps it was cooking brandy. What the hell. He poured a glass for each of them.

She gulped about half of hers in one go. He sipped his.

"I'm damaged goods, Mo."

Whatever he'd been expecting, it wasn't this. What in heaven's name did she mean? HIV? STI? It didn't bear thinking about. He kept quiet.

"He raped me. My husband. The first time was bad enough. The second time was vicious. I was in hospital for nearly three weeks. And only when I was well enough to come out did they tell me I'd been pregnant. Eight weeks pregnant. I lost the baby, and I can't have any more children." She stared bleakly at him and then drank the rest of her brandy. She held out her glass to him.

Mo's mind was working overtime as he went back to the kitchen. To say he was shocked was an understatement. He was also humbled that she'd felt able to confide in him. He handed her the glass, topped up again, and sat down once more. He was still sipping his first, instinct telling him it would be wise to stay sober.

"How long ago was it?"

"Six years. I was still at Hertford."

"Was he charged?"

"No. I was too much a coward. I kicked him out after the first time."

"But you divorced him."

"After he raped me the second time."

"And you didn't have him charged then?"

"No. I was a basket case. I realised that I must have become pregnant when he raped me the first time."

"Were you not taking precautions?"

"No. It's a long story. I'm too upset to say much more tonight." Tears began to roll down her face again.

"Saying I'm sorry is hardly adequate. Is there anything I can do?"

"Just be a friend to me? I can't offer you more than that. I don't know whether I'll ever be able to." She looked at him, her eyes red-rimmed, her face blotchy. "Do you mind going now? I feel absolutely exhausted."

He stood up, but she remained seated. He moved over to her and put his hand under her chin and gently raised her face to him. "If there's anything I can do, or if you just want to talk, call me?" She gave the briefest of nods. His lips barely brushed her forehead. "Sleep tight, sweetheart." He left behind him a very troubled woman. He was a troubled man.

Chapter 73

There was a buzz in the room even before Upwood came in, almost as though people could sense they might finally be making a breakthrough. A cheer went up when they saw him carrying bags. There was a scramble for bacon butties and doughnuts. Upwood never knew whether none of them ate before they came out in the morning or whether they were all gannets. Sometimes he thought it was a bit like a loo break. If the opportunity came you took it, because you never knew how long you might have to wait for the next.

"OK everyone. Listen up. We've got really good news back from the search of Maskell-Grant's place. Morton, do you want to run us through it?"

"Sure." It wasn't as though he'd found the results himself, but Morton was pleased Upwood had given him the chance to present them. "Firstly, the inside of the laptop case that we found in his garden shed cum office had traces of petrol. Gas chromatography demonstrates that it came from exactly the same source as the accelerant at both fires. We think he must have carried it to Waldorf's house in plastic bottles and taken them away to dispose of them. There were also small specks of wax from candles that have been identified as being made by Price, the kind we think were used in both fires.

"If you remember we also removed a black beanie hat. The lab have confirmed that they have DNA samples and are analysing them.

"The other really good bit of news is that our techie friends uncovered some good gen on his computer. Maskell-Grant had tried to delete it but it was still there. He'd bought Ketamine online from a Canadian company called Candy Pharm and paid using PayPal. It took a bit of digging but they tracked it down.

"We think we have him for both fires and Waldorf's death for certain, and of course the illegal immigrant. And logically he must have killed Fred Shelford too – one of the fires destroyed the car that rammed his Land Rover."

"And do you want to tell everyone about your brain-wave?"

"Ah, yes. I kept thinking about the Pajero and hot-wiring. Maskell-Grant is definitely a bit odd, but somehow I couldn't see him doing it. I got someone to check. He used to own the vehicle. He sold it some years ago and it was then sold again to its most recent owner. I think he still had a key."

Cheers broke out once more.

When they died down Upwood spoke again. "So we're confident we can nail him for Dushku and Waldorf. And probably Shelford. But not Mallon. There's no doubt that was someone else. At the moment our prime suspect remains his wife. Mo, Debra, how did you get on at Heathrow?"

Upwood wasn't sure whether Morton looked embarrassed or just annoyed. "Debra's not here, Sir. She told me she had cleared it with you." There were rumblings around the room. This was the second Saturday she'd had off in as many weeks. She had pleaded that she and her bridge partner had won their local regional heat at the last tournament and were now into the final. She'd persuaded him there was no question of her asking for time off again until the case was over. It was obvious that Upwood would need to hold her to this.

"Yes, of course, so she did. I'm sure you can bring us up to date."

Mo nodded. "It's hard going, Sir. But we think we might finally have found her coming out of arrivals.

"She was disguised. Her most distinctive features are her hair, her eyes and her eyebrows. She is a very striking looking woman – a bit like Bianca Jagger in her prime."

"Who?" This from one of the younger team members.

"God, I must be older than I thought." More laughter. "Look her up. Anyway, she'd covered those distinctive features with a hijab and large reflective sunglasses. She was wearing dark trousers and tunic or coat. She could easily have passed for a Muslim with her colouring.

"One thing that confused us was the fact that we knew she'd checked a bag into the hold but she was wheeling a case that could have gone in the cabin. When we watched the driver lift it into the boot we figured it out. It was clearly much heavier than he expected."

"I'm not following you."

"We think she'd deliberately weighted it so that it had to go in the hold."

"Because the Glock couldn't go in hand baggage?"

"That's what we think, Sir."

"Very good thinking. It was a risk of course. But we know that weapons do get smuggled in. She may well have disassembled it of course, if she's familiar with handguns. We still haven't checked out gun club memberships in LA have we?"

"No, we didn't have her maiden name when the question came up. But we do now, her surnames will be the same as her sister."

"Not if her sister married, surely?"

"She'd keep the same name even if she married, Debra told me."

"Veronica didn't."

"No, but she came to England to marry an Englishman. If she was going to make her life here it would have been easier to take his name."

"In that case, let's get those enquiries into gun club memberships going – there is still the open question of whether there's a connection between her and the man to whom the gun was first registered. Morton, those were your actions, I think?"

Morton nodded. "I'm on it, Sir."

"Good. So how far have you managed to track her?"

"That's it so far. We ran out of time. We're going back after the meeting."

"How did your investigations go in relation to surveillance of the Mallon property?"

"A complete blank. I don't think there was any. I'm convinced it was Veronica."

Chapter 74

Maskell-Grant was taken to the station the following day. There he was cautioned and told his rights, including that of his right to have a solicitor. Given the nature of the potential charges, and despite his rather arrogant attitude, he elected to call his usual law firm. It was a high street firm, taking all kinds of work, but the cases he was being interviewed about were not the kind they dealt with. Finally he agreed that they should invite someone from another firm to represent him. When the man arrived he was told that Maskell-Grant was to be interviewed in relation to a number of specified incidents and allowed to see his new client. It was more than an hour later that the solicitor, Colin Parker, signified that they were ready for the interview to begin.

Upwood decided to conduct the interview himself, with another officer attending. Maskell-Grant and Parker were waiting for them in the interview room. The former looked apprehensive. Parker had no expression on his face. Considerably taller than his client he was well-dressed, well-groomed and wearing a much stronger aftershave than Upwood would have liked, given the size of the room.

Once the introductions had been made and all the necessary formalities completed, Upwood began his questions.

"What is your profession Mr Maskell-Grant?"

"I am an archaeologist and a writer."

"Do you undertake archaeological investigations yourself?"

"Sometimes."

"Do you write books or articles?"

"Both. On Roman archaeology. That's my speciality."

"What are you writing at the moment?"

"I'm not. Not at the moment."

"Why is that? You described yourself as a writer."

"I am researching my next book."

"What is the subject matter? Specifically?"

"Roman settlements in Cambridgeshire."

"And you can do that from home?"

"Yes. There's a lot of material online."

"But you would be depending on other people's field work?"

Parker intervened. "Chief Inspector, I don't think this line of questioning is going to get us very far. Can we move on?"

"Very well. How did you spend the morning of Monday 10th January?"

"That's weeks ago. How do you expect me to remember what I was doing then?"

"You might consult your diary, sir. I understand that's what you did last time you were interviewed. And you were asked to bring it to this interview, weren't you?" Upwood's tone was conversational but Maskell-Grant was clearly uncomfortable. He fidgeted in his jacket and reluctantly brought out his diary.

"There's no entry for that day. I must have been at home."

"All morning?"

"All day. There's no entry there at all."

"What were you doing?"

"I would have been researching."

"How?"

"Online. Seeing if there had been any new finds, or even new sites."

Parker was beginning to fidget.

"One of your neighbours says she saw you leave by the front door and walk towards the top of the road, towards the town centre."

Colour shot into Maskell-Grant's cheeks. "Then she's mistaken. I did not go out."

"She said she saw you go out between six and seven in the morning."

"I tell you she's mistaken. Who is it? That silly old biddy across the road? Always gossiping in the village shop. Most of it she makes up. Completely unreliable. Can't believe a word she says."

"If you say you can't remember what you were doing that morning, how can you remember if you went out or not?"

"I'd never be out at that time of day. Why would I?"

"We also have a statement from someone who saw you walking across the allotments towards the village at about eight thirty that morning."

"It wasn't me. I was indoors."

"Either you remember or you don't. You can't have it both ways. We've actually got quite a good description. Did you ever find your terrier?"

"Terrier? What terrier? I haven't got a dog."

"So that was just an excuse for being out there when nobody in their right minds would be there otherwise?"

"I have no idea what you're talking about, Inspector."

"Let's talk about the following week. Monday 17th January. What were you doing that day?"

"At home. Working."

"You don't need to check your diary for that?"

Maskell-Grant looked at his pocket book ostentatiously. "At home. Working."

"All day?"

"Yes."

"Including the evening?"

"Yes."

"So our witness who saw you walking down Middle Street towards the gap in the hedge that gives access to the path is also mistaken?"

"Clearly. The people who live in this village aren't very educated or very bright you know. You can't believe everything they tell you."

"But cameras never lie, do they Mr Maskell-Grant? You told us that you left home at about five the night you went to see Professor Ferry. But we have CCTV footage showing that you drove north up the A10 much later than that."

"Then I must have been mistaken."

"Then you've been mistaken twice in relation to that trip, haven't you? We know you didn't get to Professor Ferry until seven. First you said you had killed time in Sainsbury's, having left home at five. But we know for a fact that you were not in Sainsbury's. And you had no time to kill because you left later than you said."

"I don't recall." Maskell-Grant looked furious.

"And then your account of your journey home that night is also false. We know you left the professor at ten. You claimed that you got home about half past. We have you on CCTV footage that proves you could not have got home much before midnight. Why are you deliberately trying to mislead us about the events of that night?"

"I'm not. I must have been confused."

"Why did you stop for an hour on your way home?"

"I can't remember."

"I don't believe you. You're telling us a pack of lies."

"I am not. I am a respected academic."

Upwood leaned forward and placed both forearms on the table between them, looking him straight in the eye. "But you aren't, are you? You keep telling us that." He tapped his hand lightly on the table in front of him.

"It's more than seven years since you were asked to leave your university college. You were lucky to avoid being charged with assault then." He tapped the table again, more firmly. Maskell-Grant looked at Upwood's hand, clearly unnerved.

"You haven't had a paper published in a peer-reviewed journal for ten." Tap.

"Your first two books are out of print." Tap, tap.

"Your last book was published privately because presumably no commercial publisher would touch it." Tap.

"Chief Inspector, I protest." Even Parker was becoming distinctly uncomfortable.

"I haven't finished, Mr Parker.

"You've done no speaking engagements in years." Tap. Tap.

"You have never been interviewed by local TV companies about Roman settlements or finds." Tap

"You are no longer an academic and frankly, I don't think you are much respected either." Tap. Tap. Tap.

"Mr Upwood, I protest. There is no reason to conduct a character assassination on my client. I insist that you focus your questions on the allegations you make."

"Mr Parker, the point I am making is that your client's alibi for the night Mr Waldorf was murdered is deeply flawed. We know that for an absolute fact. And we already have testimony from the professor saying that the collaboration your client suggested to him was for a book that would never find a publisher."

Upwood turned his attention once more to the archaeologist. "You were trying to give yourself an alibi, Mr Maskell-Grant. Unfortunately you have failed."

The man said nothing, the fingers of one hand plucking his trousers.

"Where did you learn how to hot-wire a car?"

Maskell-Grant looked thoroughly put out. "Do what?"

"Hot-wire a car."

He looked genuinely startled. "I have not the least idea what you're talking about."

"Did you retain a key to the Mitsubishi Pajero when you sold it? Did you use that to steal the car from its then owner on 20th December last?"

He didn't answer the questions. Upwood repeated them.

"No comment."

"Why were you carrying petrol in the laptop case when you called on Mr Waldorf on the evening of Monday 24th January?"

"I didn't call on him. I didn't carry petrol anywhere."

"Traces of petrol were found in the laptop case that exactly match the petrol used to start the fire in his home."

Maskell-Grant looked desperately at his solicitor. There was no response. "It's nothing to do with me. I've not had it more than a couple of weeks. I got it in a charity shop."

"Which shop was that?"

"British Heart Foundation. In Peterborough. In one of those pedestrianised streets near the Cathedral. There are lots of them there. I go there on the lookout for books."

"When exactly was this?"

"I can't remember."

"Do you go to Peterborough often?"

"No."

"So, you'll have made a note in your diary, won't you?"

"Maybe."

"May I look?"

Maskell-Grant looked at his solicitor, who nodded. Upwood looked backwards and forwards over a three-week period. There was no mention of Peterborough.

"There is no entry for Peterborough. But if you don't go very often it shouldn't be too difficult to remember. When was it?"

"I think it was the week before last. Monday or Tuesday."

"How much did you pay for it?"

"I can't remember."

"Why did you buy it?"

"I thought it would be useful."

"But you don't have a laptop – your PC is a tower."

"I had other things I could put in there."

"Do you remember buying something online from a Canadian pharmacy?"

"No. This is preposterous. Why would I do that?"

"We have records of your searching online for date rape drugs."

"Certainly not. I have no reason at all to do that."

"But the records are on your computer."

"They can't be."

"They are. So is the record of the transaction being paid for via PayPal."

"I don't even have a PayPal account."

"You don't now, because you cancelled it the day after DI Harrison and DS Graf first interviewed you."

"None of this is true. Someone must be hacking into my computer." The look on his face was one of passable righteous indignation. He was almost smug, as though congratulating himself for thinking up such a plausible reason for the evidence they had found.

"We have a witness who saw you enter Mr Waldorf's house." Tap.

"We have another who saw you walking towards the Queen's Head later on." Tap. Tap

"Will you stop *doing* that?"

"And another who saw you getting into a car in their car park." Tap. Tap. Tap.

"No. It was not me. It wasn't." Maskell-Grant's eyes were now wide, giving him a decidedly wild appearance. He was also sweating profusely. No longer smug.

"Why are you so opposed to the King's Mere Wind Farm development?"

"There is a Roman settlement there. They'll destroy it."

"What evidence do you have?"

"I've found coins and bits of pottery when I've been walking there."

"Where exactly were you walking?"

"In the fields on the other side of the lode from my house. They'd just been ploughed."

"In the fields between King's Mere Farm and the Great Ouse?"

"Yes."

"Fields owned by Mr Peter Shelford?"

"I believe so."

"They are some distance from the site of the proposed windfarm are they not?" He produced an Ordnance Survey map. He pointed to it. "More than a kilometre. How many coins did you find?"

"Several."

"How many?"

"Five."

"Tell us about the pottery fragments."

"They're definitely Roman. From domestic vessels."

"When did you find them?"

"Three years ago."

"Can you prove you found them on the Shelford farm?"

"You have my word for it, Mr Upwood."

"Why does that not give me any confidence?"

Maskell-Grant glared at him. Parker intervened once more. "Chief Inspector, please refrain from making personal comments. They are unhelpful. If you have further, new, questions, please put them."

"How did you find these artefacts?"

"I found the coins with a metal detector."

"Did you have Mr Shelford's permission to use it in his fields?"

"I didn't ask. Lots of people walk along the river bank."

"Did he know you were doing it?"

"Yes."

"What was his response."

"I don't know."

"Did you carry on searching his fields?"

He looked uncomfortable again. "No."

"Why not?"

"His son said they'd set the dogs on me."

Parker rolled his eyes, but it was too late, the damage was done.

"How did you respond?"

"I told him I thought there was an important settlement there that might stretch back some distance from the river. I've seen aerial photos which support that view."

"Do other respected academics share your view, Mr Maskell-Grant?"

"Some."

"Can you give us their names?"

Maskell-Grant looked at his solicitor, but no support came from that direction.

"Does *anyone* support your view?"

"They would if Shelford had allowed us to carry out geophysical surveys, ground penetrating radar and so on. We needed to do a full excavation. If we'd found treasure they might have gained financially."

"If a coroner had determined that any finds you made were treasure, you'd have shared the reward?"

"Yes."

"So you had a financial motive, not just an historical one, for wanting to excavate the site. So why didn't you?"

"Why didn't I what?"

"Continue searching the site."

"I told you. He wouldn't allow it. He was downright obstructive."

"You say 'we needed…'. Who else was involved?"

Maskell-Grant did not answer.

"Was there anyone else involved?"

"I could have found people who'd be willing to join in. I could have got funding. It's not right that sites like that aren't properly excavated. And now they are going to destroy it. It can't be allowed to happen. It's too important. They have to be stopped."

Parker turned to his client. "Just answer the question."

"But they have to be stopped. Why does no-one see it? This is probably the last chance I'll get at a major excavation…"

"Chief Inspector, might I have a few moments with my client?"

"If you wish." Upwood suspended the interview.

He returned to his office to see if he could clear some admin while they waited to hear that the interview could resume. On his way there, Morton caught him. "How's it going?"

"Well, either his solicitor hasn't briefed him very well or he's not following the advice. And his solicitor isn't doing much to help him, frankly. Maskell-Grant's made some fairly incriminating admissions. Have you got anything useful for us?"

"I'm told we'll have the DNA results from the beanie hat later today. We asked them to fast track them and for once they have done."

"Good."

Half an hour later Upwood and his colleague were back in the interview room. He explained that the interview was suspended until further notice and that Maskell-Grant and his solicitor were required to wait until they reconvened.

Shortly after four, the DNA results came through. Upwood asked that Maskell-Grant be returned to the interview room and that Parker be recalled.

Both men were already there when Upwood, this time accompanied by Morton, joined them.

Upwood did not remind Maskell-Grant that he was still under caution: he cautioned him again and insisted that he confirm his understanding of it.

"Mr Maskell-Grant, I am arresting you on the suspicion of the manslaughter of Rajmond Dushku on Monday 17th January 2011, aggravated arson at Orchard Farm barn, also on 17th January 2011, aggravated arson at Church Cottage, Back Lane, Chilton and the murder of Patrick Waldorf, both on Monday 24th January 2011. DI Harrison, please arrange for two officers to take him down for processing. Interview terminated at four thirty-eight."

When they were back in Upwood's office, Morton asked him why they hadn't included Shelford's murder and the theft of the Pajero.

"We will, Morton, we will. We just need to make sure with the CPS that we frame the charges in the best possible way. I want that nasty little man to go down for a long time."

"Daft isn't it, Sir? He's presumably intelligent otherwise he'd never have been a Fellow at Cambridge. But a bit short on common sense."

"Why, because he left some elementary clues behind?"

"Yes."

"Maybe. I think he just doesn't live in the real world. Can't see him watching CSI can you?"

"CSI is hardly the real world, Sir."
"No. But watching it is."

Chapter 75

Upwood brought bacon sandwiches and doughnuts to the briefing on Monday morning to celebrate Maskell-Grant's arrest. Never before had he provided goodies twice in such quick succession. Once they had been briefed he released all those not actively concerned in Mallon's case. That left Morton, Mo, Debra and Margaret.

Morton had nothing to report from his US enquiries: insufficient time had elapsed. Mo and Debra were square eyed from staring at screens all day long. Veronica had certainly made life hard for them. For a start, the private hire car had not driven up either the M11 or the A10. It had gone up the A1. It dropped her at the entrance to the Great Northern Hotel in Peterborough, opposite the railway station. By this time she had removed the hijab but retained the sunglasses. Enquires to the hotel had elicited the information that no room had been taken by a single woman answering her description and arriving at the time she had got out of the car. That was as far as they'd got. It was a very short meeting.

Mo and Debra chatted as they left the meeting room, speculating on what Veronica had done after she'd gone into the Great Northern.

On a hunch they phoned the hotel again and the receptionist did, when asked, confirm that there was another entrance which gave access to the car park. On the basis that she may have walked straight in one side and out the other, they looked for another hotel at which she might have stayed. It would not be until Monday morning that she killed her husband so she would need to stay somewhere and she might feel safer, less likely to be recognised, in Peterborough. Sure enough, they found that a woman of her description, albeit under a different name, had checked into the Bull in Westgate for two nights some twenty minutes after she had entered the Great Northern.

"Why d'you think she only booked for two nights?", Mo asked Debra.

"She must have hired a car on the Saturday. She could hardly ask a taxi to take her to the gravel pits and wait while she bumped off her hubby. She might have wanted to get to the one where we found his car parked and stay there overnight."

"Or she might have stayed somewhere closer overnight."

"Too risky I think. She's probably quite well known by sight. She's very recognisable and her picture's been in the papers a fair bit because of Kmag."

"OK, so we hit all the car hire companies in Peterborough. How many d'you s'pose there are?"

They found eight and started phoning. They were looking for pick up sometime on the Saturday and drop off in Heathrow on the Monday, or possibly back to Peterborough again if she took public transport to the airport.

Four of the rental companies were local and didn't provide an airport drop off facility.

Of the other four none had a booking with a drop off at Heathrow on the Monday.

Only one had rented a car to a lady driver for the three days in question: PeeBo Car Rental. They decided to call on them.

They found the office, a run-down establishment in Lonsdale Road. A long straight road, it had a jumble of mainly two storey buildings, many formerly homes but now with a variety of small traders operating on the ground floor. PeeBo was one such.

There were only two desks in the office which was scarcely larger than the waiting area in any of the kebab, pizza and other takeaways along the street. A young man sat behind one of them. He smiled cheerfully. "What can I do for ya then?"

Mo and Debra showed him their ID. He didn't bat an eyelid, he'd clocked them as soon as they'd got out of the car.

Mo explained that they were trying to trace a lady who might have rented a car for three days, and gave the dates. He showed the man, whose badge proclaimed him to be Gavin, a photo of Veronica.

"Don't recognise her, mate."

The telephone on his desk rang. "Sorry." He picked it up and, much to the amusement of Mo and Debra, answered in an entirely different manner of speaking. "PeeBo Car Rental. How may I help you?" He was on the phone only a minute or two.

"Sorry about that. Customer wanted to return a car early. We're only a small business. Can't afford to lose any punters. Now what were you saying? Oh yeah. Bint in the picture. Never saw her."

"But you did make a booking for a woman. Did she not come here to collect the car?"

"You joking, mate? We wouldn't let the punters within a million miles of this place. Would you?"

They smiled but let the question pass. He was right: it was a dump.

"So how did you get the paperwork done? You'd need to see her driving licence and collect her payment."

"We have a couple of blokes who work freelance, just when we need them. One of them will have delivered the car to her place and then picked it up at the end of the rental. Whoever picks it up then valets it."

"And how did she pay?"

"Credit card by phone when she booked."

"You have a record of that payment on the computer?"

"Sure."

"You keep copies of licences of course."

"Course we do. Insurance isn't valid otherwise."

"Can we see the paperwork for this customer please?"

"Sure." He turned to the filing cabinet behind him. "Pete would have filed it after he got back from the drop off."

He passed a large envelope to Debra.

"And no doubt you'll have a record of all the details of the rental on your computer?"

"Should do."

"Mo – look inside the envelope." There was a note of urgency in Debra's voice.

He looked. There was a top copy of a multi-part set giving details of the hire, but no copy of passport or driving licence. From the form it appeared that the woman was a Mexican national. Her name was given as Maria Pérez Rodrígues. Her address was given as Manzanillo, Mexico.

"May we have a copy of this please, Gavin?"

"Sure. Be my guest." He got up and took the form, went over to the printer and returned with a copy a minute later.

"Where can we find Pete?"

"Not a clue. Probably in the pub."

"One of your drivers. In the pub?"

"We got two. They're on call. Not often we need to call out two at once. Jim's on call today. But Pete was rostered those days."

"Who would have entered the details on the computer?"

"Me."

"May we see them, please?"

"I ain't done them yet."

"From three weeks ago. That's extraordinary."

"We don't man the office every day. No need. If we're out, the phone switches through to the office mobile."

"Can you give us Pete's mobile number?"

"Sure." Gavin looked at the phone book on his handset and read out the number.

Gavin was right. Pete was in the pub. But he was working behind the bar, not boozing. It was a large double-fronted establishment close to the city centre, with full-length windows. Immediately inside was a sitting area with leather covered sofas and armchairs. The walls were wood-panelled and the overall effect was art deco. Faux art deco. But it was comfortable enough and the range of ales and wine, food and snacks, on offer catered to most tastes.

Mo persuaded him to ask a colleague to cover for him. Pete looked to be about thirty and wore the pub uniform of black polo shirt, complete with logo, and jeans. His hair was buzz cut, flattop in style, but getting a bit ragged around the edges. Debra hoped for PeeBo's sake he tidied himself up a bit for their customers.

He sat down with them in the seating area near the front and looked as though he'd rather be outside having a fag.

Debra took the lead. "We're interested in a lady to whom you delivered a car on Saturday 5th February, just over three weeks ago. Do you remember her?"

"Yeah."

"Can you describe her?"

"Not very well. She were all wrapped up. Big coat with a fur collar and a big black fur hat. Very Dr Zhivago."

Debra laughed. "Bit before your time, Pete, that one?"

"I like old films. Not a crime is it?"

"Of course not. What else can you tell us?"

"She had dark glasses on."

"Reflective?"

He thought for a moment. "No. Don't remember seeing my ugly mug staring back at me. I tell you what, though. She had the most lovely set of lips I've ever seen. Bright red."

"Did she have an accent?"

"Yeah. American, like. The passport she showed me was Mexican."

"And she gave you a copy of that and her driving licence?"

"She wrote her details onto the form. Said it would be easier because some of the spellings were difficult."

"But you checked her documents?"

"Yes. She hadn't got copies to give me. They don't always. Some folks we deliver to don't have printers. And she was in a hotel."

"When did you collect the car?"

"It was fairly early in the morning on the Monday. I think I got to the Bull about eight and she was already waiting for me."

"What's your interest in PeeBo?"

"What?"

"You seem interested in the business yourself, not just the jobs you do for them."

"It's run by my uncle."

"Gavin?"

"No. He's a cousin. Frank Silver is the boss."

"Did you valet the car after you collected it again?"

"Had to. Don't get paid otherwise."

"Is that something you enjoy doing?"

"Are you kidding? It stinks. There's no heating in that barn of a place where they store the cars. Bleeding cold at this time of the year."

They left. If Pete was unenthusiastic about valeting, maybe he wasn't very thorough. But did they even have the right woman? They had expected the car rental customer to be Encarna. The name on the rental agreement was altogether different. Debra began to wish they had stayed at Heathrow to check the Monday departures before assuming that the woman with the hijab was Veronica.

That evening's paper had a short story on its front page. It said unconfirmed reports had come in that a man had been arrested on suspicion of the murder of Patrick Waldorf and an Albanian national, and of arson. It went on to say that more information was expected shortly.

Chapter 76

The core team met early the following morning. Upwood used a smaller office this time which created a more relaxed atmosphere. He was a great believer in the idea that people can think and behave differently in different environments. He himself, though, was not as relaxed as he would have liked. He had been annoyed at the report in the previous evening's paper. In fact the CPS had agreed that Maskell-Grant should be charged with the offences that were specified when he was arrested. But they were still deliberating on how best to frame the charges in relation to Fred Shelford. Maskell-Grant had been charged and was in custody with no possibility of bail. Upwood wanted the other charges preferred as quickly as possible so they could put out a full press release.

He greeted the team and launched straight into business. "Morton, what have you got for us?"

Morton looked distinctly bleary and dishevelled, no doubt his daughter was still teething. "Some good news. Veronica was a very active gun club member and shot competitively. She was said to be competent. She would certainly know how to break down the Glock – it is one of the models she shot with.

"The bad news is that we cannot positively connect the original owner of our Glock with her. He wasn't at her university. They weren't members of the same shooting club. That's not to say they might not have met at one of the competitions they both entered. We just don't know."

"Helpful, but it still doesn't give us anything very concrete does it?"

"No. Sorry. It doesn't."

"Mo, what have you and Debra got for us?"

"We think we have traced Veronica to Peterborough, as you know. We found out yesterday that a supposedly Mexican woman by the name of Maria Pérez Rodrígues arrived at about the right time on the Friday afternoon and booked a room at the Bull for two nights."

"Three, surely?"

"No, two. We think she slept in the car the night before she shot her husband, parked at the other gravel pit where we later found his car. That's why we think there might still be trace inside.

"The same woman did book a hire car from a small local company. But their admin is lousy. The copy of her passport and driving licence aren't on file and her details have not been entered into the computer. She filled out details of her passport and driving licence onto the car hire agreement. She told the agent that the spellings were difficult so it would be easier for her to do it. He says he didn't collect copies of her licence and passport because she didn't have them available. The guy in the office said they always collect them: the insurance isn't valid without them."

"And where was the agreement completed?"

"In the Bull."

"Who would have made copies of her documents if she'd asked."

"Without doubt. Although she had checked out the day before, so she probably wouldn't have been keen to ask them."

"Why are the copies not on file?"

"We've come to the conclusion that if anyone looked at them closely they'd see there was a problem with them."

"What, forged?"

"No. We reckon it's because they just don't belong to the person carrying them."

"Why didn't she use Encarna's?"

"No idea. Maybe she just wanted to muddy the waters a bit."

"More likely Encarna didn't want her credit card used. She may not even have realised that Veronica had borrowed her passport", suggested Morton.

"Good point. But then who is this Maria woman?"

Debra answered. "Remember when I explained how Spanish names work? Her mother's name will not be the same as her father's. When we asked Interpol to help originally we were only given his name. I've been thinking about it overnight. I reckon Maria is her mother. And that she didn't give Pete a copy of the passport because of the age difference. Or it might have expired."

"But surely the photo wouldn't look like Veronica."

"It could do. She might not even be sixty. Some women of that age look years younger. And the photo might be years out of date anyway. Her mother's passport wouldn't get her through airport security, although her sister's probably would."

"So you're convinced it is Veronica?"

"It has to be. What are the chances of another Mexican woman arriving at Heathrow at the right time and hiring a car in Peterborough just long enough to allow her to get back to the airport in time for her flight?"

"It's a bit thin. But you'd better stay with it. Get back to Interpol and check her mother's name."

"We've already put the call in, Sir. But what we'd really like to do is get forensics onto the car she rented. The guy who valeted it probably isn't very thorough. Can we get a warrant?"

"Why don't we try asking? If they're not involved in any way they might be prepared to let us have a look. I don't suppose the business is fully stretched at this time of the year."

They agreed to give it a go.

"Margaret. I gather you were looking to trace Veronica by public transport back to Heathrow?"

"Yes. I spent most of yesterday on that. I looked at footage from eight o'clock to eleven o'clock. If she was on the four o'clock flight out of Heathrow she'd need to be there for one. It would take about an hour and a half from King's Cross to the check in desk, and maybe an hour or an hour and a quarter on the train, depending whether she used the fast or the slow service. I'm guessing she'd use the fast service.

Anyway, I reckon she'd have to be on a train by eleven at the absolute latest.

"I looked for women with the right jizz wheeling a carry-on bag and carrying a Mulberry." Upwood smiled. They had all caught on to the expression. It had become a useful piece of shorthand for them.

"Plenty of women leaving Peterborough Station with wheelie cases. If the Bull's right, hers was grey, but that's no real help at all. I saw no one wearing a light coloured hijab, or a large furry hat. But there were several wearing jackets with hoods. I'm not sure why. It wasn't particularly cold that morning."

"When did you last travel by train?"

"Don't follow you, Sir."

"Most station platforms act like wind tunnels."

"Oh. See what you mean."

"What about the famous Mulberry handbag?"

"No sign of it. The women I saw had all sorts of bags with them, including carrier bags as well as the wheelie case."

"So it could have been inside the case or another bag."

"That's what I assumed."

"Did you get a clear look at their faces?"

"Not good. The CCTV quality was poor, and most of them seemed to be looking at the ground the whole time."

"So what next?"

"CCTV from King's Cross for all the platforms she might have arrived at."

"Could she have got there in time if she'd used a taxi?"

"Yes. Provided there were no humongous hold ups on the M25 or M4. Or at Stevenage come to that, the A1 can get very backed up there in the morning rush hour."

"So that's the next line of enquiry?"

"It is. And I think we're going to need more bods on it. There are loads of taxi and private hire companies in Peterborough. And it's airport transfers that most of the private hire lot do."

Upwood promised to see what he could arrange.

Chapter 77

After the meeting, Mo telephoned Gavin at PeeBo. Much to their surprise he said he didn't think his uncle would have a problem with their examining the car. He'd check and call them back. Less than ten minutes later he called to confirm that the car could be taken in and gave them the necessary information. Mo immediately made arrangements for its collection.

Upwood had rustled up a couple of uniforms to help Margaret with the tracking of Veronica from Peterborough to Heathrow. They could phone the taxi and private car hire firms leaving her, with her better chance of recognising their target, still watching CCTV.

Mo and Debra decided that it would be useful to find out what else Veronica had been up to while she was in Peterborough. If they could establish that she'd bought a new coat, for example, it would help Margaret in her search.

They knew that she'd taken delivery of the car mid-morning so concentrated their search for later in the day. Queensgate was the most likely place for her to shop, with a good-sized John Lewis and a number of chain stores. If she was looking to change her outfit she probably wouldn't be worried by the lack of a high end outlet. In fact all they needed to do was watch footfall in Westgate and see if she left the hotel and then came back with shopping bags.

Half an hour or so after taking delivery of the car she left through the front door of the hotel, crossed the street and entered Westgate Arcade. That would take her straight into Queensgate. She appeared to be wearing the clothes that Pete had described: the black coat with fur collar and big fur hat. It occurred to Debra as she watched her that the collar on the coat might be detachable, a useful feature if she were travelling between cold and warmer climates. It could well be the coat she'd worn over the trousers when picked up on CCTV at Heathrow.

They watched hours of footage, focusing on that part of the street closest to the entrance to the Bull. The shops in the centre closed at six on a Saturday evening, so they were confident that she'd be out no later than that. But no one appeared dressed as she had been when she went in.

They went back through the footage again, looking for any woman vaguely matching her appearance in terms of height and build who was also carrying one or more large carrier bags. Nothing. They decided to go out for a quick pub lunch.

They both settled for soft drinks and a sandwich.

"Where the hell is she, Mo?"

"She could have gone down to the bus station at the other end of Queensgate and caught a bus."

"Where would she go? And why?"

"Don't know. Any better ideas?"

"Well she might just as well have gone a bit further and gone over to the railway station again."

"Then I've got the same questions. Where did she go, and why?"

They chewed on their sandwiches. Cheese and tomato for Debra. Beef and horseradish for Mo. They could have swapped over and not known the difference.

"Is there another entrance to the Bull. Like the Great Northern? Car park at the back maybe?"

"Only one way to find out."

They telephoned. There was. Veronica could have come out of Queensgate on Long Causeway, turned left, gone over the crossroad and up Broadway. She could get into the hotel via one of the side streets.

They started all over again checking footage for Long Causeway and the crossroad. After more than two hours they thought they had her. This time she was wearing a hooded jacket much as Margaret had described earlier. She was holding a carrier bag big enough to hold the coat and hat she had previously worn. They relayed the information to Margaret.

The uniforms had checked all the taxi and private hire companies in the immediate area of Peterborough and none had apparently taken a single woman to Heathrow carrying only cabin bags leaving between eight and eleven on the Monday morning.

Margaret eventually got lucky. Confident that Veronica was wearing a hooded jacket, she had found one of her potential targets from Peterborough station getting off a fast train in King's Cross. She'd have to go to Heathrow the next day to see if she could find her in the Departure Hall. Debra was going with her – it had been decided that the check-in staff handling the Aeromexico flights should be interviewed to see if they could recognise her.

Upwood went home a bit earlier than usual. He was pleased that they now had Maskell-Grant locked up but he felt they were making heavy weather of the Mallon case. He was brooding over this issue, glass of Scotch in hand, when his phone went. It was Emily.

"Evening, James. Have you seen the evening paper?"

"No, I didn't bother to get one tonight."

"There's going to be a bloodbath. Peter Shelford read the report in Monday's paper about someone being arrested on suspicion of Waldorf's death and had another massive stroke. Fatal."

"Oh shit."

"It gets worse. His daughter-in-law is saying that he was furious that there was no mention of anyone suspected of Fred's death, that we weren't taking the case seriously enough."

"Oh Christ. But you know that's not true."

"I do. But it won't stop the media having a field day. Come and see me tomorrow – seven am. We need to get on top of this."

Upwood didn't think there was any chance of getting on top of it – they were way behind this curve.

Chapter 78

Upwood rose early feeling thoroughly jet-lagged. The six o'clock news started on the car radio as he set off for town. It was the lead story. He hadn't bothered switching the television on before he left. He knew Emily would have all the papers in her office.

She did. Carefully arranged so that in each case the headline showed. On two there were photos of a tearful Molly Shelford. *They killed my father-in-law* was one of the more restrained headlines.

"How did this happen, James?" There was no greeting and her face was grim.

"I'd like to know which bastard leaked the story. If we'd been able to release a statement to the press when we had charged Maskell-Grant with all the offences this would never have happened. And you know why we couldn't charge him with those straight away. Because the bloody CPS wanted more time to consider what was best." He ground to a halt. "By the way, it's a small detail, but we did check out his claim of having bought the laptop case at a charity shop. They had no recollection of ever having had one like it and did not recognise him. And he did not appear on CCTV outside the shop any day that week.

"I'm going to try to find out where the leak came from."

"Good luck with that. Frankly, hanging, drawing and quartering the person responsible is not my priority."

"But it should be. People have to learn to understand the consequences of sounding off like this."

"I said it's not a priority. It's important, but not the most important matter. Putting the lid on these lurid suggestions is the priority. When is the press release going out about Maskell-Grant?"

"This morning at the press conference was the plan. At eleven. We only got the go ahead from the CPS last night."

"And what have they decided?"

"Dangerous driving. Murder."

"What took them so long?"

"God knows. If you look at everything he did you couldn't possibly imagine that he hadn't meant to kill Shelford. Has Sir George been on to you yet?"

"The dear man has taken himself off to Antigua for a few days. Wanted to use up some accumulated leave before he retires at the end of the month. Bless." When Emily was in the mood, she could do sarcasm like no other.

"The media will love that too. So is Clarke holding the fort?"

"Yes. God help us. He'll have to run the press conference, of course. And I'll be there, too. I'm seeing him at nine. I want you back here with a suitable response to this incident before then. If we don't present him with a fait accompli there's no telling what sort of a fuck up he'll make."

There was nothing Upwood could usefully add to that observation. He left to get on with it.

This press conference was even worse than the last. All the national press and main TV stations were there. And there were some reporters from France and the Low Countries. Sir George could count himself lucky to be out of it.

The top table looked lighter without him, though. He did cut a fine figure in his uniform with all his medal ribbons flashing. Clarke just didn't have the same bearing. Not only that, he found it hard enough to control an internal meeting never mind the bloodbath that this briefing turned out to be. He read the statement prepared for him but had to stop frequently because the reporters were making so much noise, demanding that he answer their questions. Jan Murray, the Press Officer, stood several times insisting that they let him finish delivering his statement before they put their questions. Unfortunately this only served to disempower him, consequently they carried on. Only when he stood up and banged a gavel loudly on the table, causing a water bottle to fall off, did the reporters quieten somewhat.

"Ladies and Gentlemen. I propose to read the statement again in full."

Clarke managed to read the statement in one go, including the final paragraph which dealt with Peter Shelford's death. Condolences were offered to his family and friends. It ended with an appeal to the media to show respect to the family and to avoid adding further to their grief by publishing misleading, inaccurate and inflammatory material. Uproar broke out. Clarke and his team left.

Upwood was deeply depressed when he got home that night. He'd spent most of the day dealing with paperwork on a number of other serious cases of which he was nominally in charge. It didn't seem to make any difference how much time he put in on it, the paper mountain seemed to grow. Added to that, he'd had no feedback from any source in relation to possible progress on the Mallon case. Even Katie was out when he phoned and he was too disheartened even to leave a message. When he found that the only thing in his freezer that might conceivably be cooked for supper was pizza that had been there too long, he nearly threw it across the kitchen like a Frisbee. It had that unmistakeable white edge to the base, which meant it would be as tough as old boots. He did the only sensible thing he could do. He opened the last good bottle of wine he had – an excellent Barolo.

Absolutely the final straw was watching the press review on television later that night. One headline said it all: *Careless Talk Costs Lives.* Another paper showed a picture snatched by a paparazzo of Bland sunning himself on the patio beside the private plunge-pool of his beachfront cottage, cocktail in hand. The headline was *It's a Bland life*.

Chapter 79

Upwood had asked that all those who had worked on the Maskell-Grant case attend the following morning's briefing. The meeting room was packed.

"Good morning everyone. Thank you for coming in so early. Firstly, I want to thank you all for your efforts to track down the person who was responsible for three deaths."

"Four, Sir", came an unidentifiable voice from the back.

"No, three. As most of you know we are confident that Dr Mallon was killed by someone else."

"Peter Shelford", came the voice again.

"Stand up. Whoever said Peter Shelford, stand up."

A uniformed constable did.

"We cannot attribute Peter Shelford's death to Mr Maskell-Grant. His actions may or may not have been contributing factors. We are not medical specialists.

"Neither can we attribute responsibility to whoever it was who allowed a misleading report to be published in Tuesday's paper. Neither, however, can we rule it out. It causes me considerable grief even to think that one of my team might have been the source.

"I am inviting whoever was responsible to come and see me to discuss it. Allowing that story to be picked up was an appalling lapse of judgement and reflects badly on all of us.

"Did you see the headline in one of today's papers? *Careless Talk Costs Lives.* Some of the papers are suggesting that Mrs Shelford sues us. I'm hoping one of the red tops offers her an exclusive for a quick pay cheque instead. But be in no doubt, an awful lot of mud is going to stick to us for a very long time.

"Now, let's get on."

"I'll start, Sir. I've got some good news to report." Morton was the only one there who looked remotely cheerful. However, since he looked a lot fresher than he had done for some time, it might simply mean that Minda hadn't kept him awake all night.

"Good. We could do with some."

"We got the forensic report back on the PeeBo hire car. The tyres are the same type as those on the vehicle that visited the gravel pit where Mallon's car was found and one has a nick in the tread that featured in the cast made by Penny's team. We've also got a partial latent that matches a print found in Mallon's car, and a bit of fingernail with bright red Chanel polish on it. We've sent that off for DNA analysis. I think we're close to proving Veronica was responsible for her husband's death."

"Very encouraging. How long before we get the DNA results?"

"We've asked them to fast-track it. But then we almost always do that, so it's a bit like crying 'wolf' as far as the lab's concerned. If we're very lucky we might get it back by the end of the week."

"Good. Let's hope so. Now how are we doing on tracking Veronica's movements?"

Margaret answered. "Mo and Debra established that she had bought new clothes in Peterborough, specifically a hooded jacket. We managed to track her from Peterborough Station to King's Cross and then again at Heathrow. Debra and I interviewed the Aeromexico check-in staff. We found the agent who checked Encarna in. She says she's not sure but she thinks she recognises the woman in the photo we showed her as being the passenger."

"I didn't know we had a photo."

"There was one in the evening paper just before Christmas. At some fund-raising do for Kmag. She's not certain, though, which is not surprising given the number of people she must see every day."

"Nonetheless, it builds up a picture. If we get a DNA result, we should be home and dry."

The meeting broke up after just a short while and everyone dispersed.

Debra and Upwood had an appointment to keep that neither was looking forward to: Tom's funeral. It had been arranged by a nephew, to be held at the Cambridge Crematorium near Bar Hill, about as depressing a place as Upwood could think of. The grounds were expertly laid out and well-tended and the building itself was not unattractive from the outside, if you could take your eyes off the chimney clearly visible behind the tower on the roof. When they arrived, they found only a handful of other people there. Tom had made it clear, in the note he left acknowledging his intention to take his own life, that he wanted a short service and only immediate family there. Even so, Upwood had decided that it would be inexcusable if the force were not represented and Debra agreed, not just because she had worked most closely with him in recent months but because she felt guilty about him for all kinds of reasons.

While they were waiting for the service to begin, Upwood whispered to her: "How's the cat?"

"He's fine. Young and affectionate. He's good company."

"Good, I'm glad."

"I call him Tom Tom." Words failed Upwood.

The service was held in the smaller of the two chapels but the congregation had looked isolated. It was conducted by an Anglican minister who clearly had not known Tom. The eulogy, such as it was, was given by the nephew. Upwood gained the distinct impression that he hadn't known his uncle very well either.

He shouldn't really have been surprised that one of the hymns was the one which had been haunting him recently, sung to Parry's *Repton*. It was a popular choice at funerals. The final verse was the one which resonated with him:

Breathe through the heats of our desire
Thy coolness and Thy balm;
Let sense be dumb, let flesh retire;

Speak through the earthquake, wind, and fire,
O still, small voice of calm.

They left after paying their respects to the nephew. Whether any kind of wake was planned they didn't know; there had been no announcement during the service and there was none on the Order of Service. They were glad to be away.

Upwood spent another frustrating afternoon wading through reports and other paperwork, before turning to his email. He nearly missed it. When he opened the message from the head of the lab he was surprised to see that it started with an apology. He read on. It seems the report on the examination of the gun found in the gravel pit was incomplete. The final paragraph had somehow been omitted. While no latents of any kind had been found on the Glock itself, there were latent prints on two cartridges remaining in the magazine. They were a match for that found in the PeeBo car and the Mallon car. Upwood heaved a massive sigh of relief. This case now looked even more solid than Maskell-Grant's.

When he got home the first thing he did was phone Katie. He might be tempting providence, but he wanted to fix lunch with her for Sunday to celebrate.

Chapter 80

As soon as he arrived at the station he headed over to Morton's desk. He was there already, red-eyed again after another no doubt badly interrupted night. Upwood told him about the news and asked him to take someone out to Knapton and bring Veronica in for questioning. If she did not come voluntarily they were to arrest her.

Morton took Margaret with him. Apart from the interviews at Heathrow she seemed to have done little else but study screens for days on end. She seemed excited at the prospect that they might be closing the case so quickly after the charging of Maskell-Grant. Her excitement turned to anxiety as they realised that Veronica was not at home. They tried both front and back doors, and called both landline and mobile. Given that it was still not eight o'clock, they were anxious. They were standing there trying to decide what to do when a next-door neighbour came out. "Are you looking for Mrs Mallon?"

"We are, madam." Morton showed his warrant card.

"Ah, she said you might come round again. She's had to go back to Mexico. Her mother has just died. I'm looking after the dog."

"Did she leave a contact number?"

"No. Sorry."

They thanked her and got back in the car. "Hell and damnation." Morton was furious. They'd asked her not to leave the country and she had ignored them. He drove back to town in a thoroughly bad mood, unusual for him. Margaret kept quiet.

Morton went straightaway to see Upwood. "The bitch has flown back to Mexico. Her mother died, apparently." He sank into the chair in front of the desk and stretched out his legs.

"Oh shit. If we have a resort to the extradition treaty we're in for a seriously bad time. It will take for ever."

"We could ask her to come back."

Upwood laughed. "You seriously think she'd come?"

"She'll have to at some stage otherwise she won't be able to wind up his estate."

"I hope to God she didn't give her solicitor power of attorney before she went."

Morton looked deeply shocked. "Hell's teeth. We'd be screwed."

"Get us some coffee, would you Morton? We need to think this through."

Morton went out, leaving Upwood to brood on the age-old problem of one step forward, two steps back.

A few minutes later Morton came back and handed Upwood his coffee. "When is Mallon's inquest? Have we got a date yet?"

"Don't know. I can soon find out. What are you thinking?"

"That we spin her some yarn about it being a legal requirement that she attend."

"She still might not come."

"But so far as she knows, she's not even on our radar for his murder. In that case refusing to come would be suspicious."

"Would we get away with it?"

"We won't know if we don't try. Let's send a text to her mobile."

Upwood got his phone out. "Maybe my rank will carry a bit more weight. *Condolences on the loss of your mother. Sorry, but urgent you return UK before your husband's inquest which is to be held on Tuesday 7th March. Please confirm you will meet me at Cambridge Parkside Police Station on Monday 6th March at 10.00 am. Regards DCI James Upwood.* Does that strike the right note do you think?"

"Well it's worth a go, Sir. What will you do if she refuses or doesn't answer?"

"Worry about it when it happens." He looked at his phone again as a message pinged in for him. It was Katie apologising that she couldn't make lunch on Sunday after all and would call him later. It never rained but it poured.

And needless to say, no one had yet admitted disclosing information about Maskell-Grant's arrest. If they hadn't done by now, it was unlikely they would ever find out. If the source of the leak was a conversation between colleagues in a bar or café he was sure that none of the parties would confess. They'd stick together.

That evening Margaret and Mo got together for a meal, going back to the Italian where they'd enjoyed their first outing. Mo was secretly thrilled that she had again gone to some trouble to make herself look attractive. While she was a very good-looking woman there was also something a little tom-boyish about her appearance at work.

"So how was your day, Mags?"

"Frustrating. Did you not hear what happened?"

"Not really. Just that they came back without her."

"She'd gone back. Mama had died it seems."

"The boss isn't going to be happy about that."

"He's not, from what Morton said. But should we even be talking about it? I know we are being discreet…"

"You're probably right. Anyway, when we're off duty we shouldn't talk shop. Shall we try to make that one of our rules? It would be good for both of us."

She smiled and sipped her wine.

"So are you going to have Spag Ag again?"

"What?"

"I can't pronounce it. That garlic spaghetti you had last time."

"I might do. Do you mind?"

"No. I'll just keep my distance."

She looked at him. And this time there was a look of gratitude in her eyes. "You are good to me, Mo. I'm not used to having someone I can really talk to. My self-esteem took such a battering."

Mo was trying hard to steer the conversation out of dangerous waters. "You always seem very confident."

"I'm OK at work. Otherwise it's a front. I still get panic attacks from time to time. So just when I feel I'm getting on top of my self-esteem, it gets knocked back."

Mo reached out and put his hand over hers and squeezed gently. "You've got me to lend you a bit of support, Mags, OK? Not that you ought to need it. You're beautiful, talented and warm. You should think highly of yourself. I certainly think highly of you and I'm sure everyone who works with you does." He had intended this to sound fairly formal. He'd succeeded.

"Thank you. It's a long time since anyone has given me that kind of pep talk."

"I mean it."

The waiter came. Since they hadn't even glanced at the menu, they ordered exactly as they had done before – Spaghetti Aglio Olio for her and Pizza Quattro Stagione for him. This time when it came, Mo asked for spicy oil to trail around the edge of his pizza. Margaret's spaghetti needed a bit of competition.

Later as he took his leave, Mo kissed her lightly on the cheek. He left, with two parts cheer to one part frustration. He did care for her. His frustration was not selfish, well not entirely, it was more that she had endured such a dreadful assault and been so damaged by it. It wasn't surprising that she felt nervous when she was alone with any man.

Upwood's own frustrations continued. Katie had called to say that she had been asked to stand in for a colleague at a conference in Edinburgh on Monday and she needed to travel up the day before to rehearse the PowerPoint presentation that he had prepared but could not now deliver. Giving someone else's presentation was, in her experience, not an easy task to accomplish. Upwood, who had more than once been in a similar position, had some sympathy with that view. It didn't stop him feeling as though he had been stood up, though.

Chapter 81

When Upwood arrived at the station on Monday morning he had no idea whether Veronica would appear or not. He was afraid she wouldn't. He was wrong.

When told of her arrival he asked that she be taken to one of the interview rooms. He wasted no time in taking Morton along with him.

"Mrs Mallon, Good Morning. Firstly let me apologise. I am sorry to say that your husband's inquest is not being held tomorrow. I asked DI Harrison here if he knew when it was to be. He thought I was asking him an entirely different question." Morton nodded. They had agreed this as an opening gambit because as they were about to interview her under caution they did not want to have some clever lawyer stirring up a stink about having her come back under false pretences. "However we do want to interview you. We are arresting you on suspicion of the murder of your husband, Jeremy Mallon."

She shot out of her seat. "You can't possibly be serious."

"I am entirely serious. DI Harrison will take you to the Custody Desk to get various formalities completed. Then he will bring you back here."

Morton practically had to drag her to the Custody Desk and another officer stepped forward to take her other arm.

Sometime later she was brought back to the interview room. She was chaperoned by one of the officers to wait for her solicitor. She slumped down onto her chair. The colour was high in her cheeks and her dark eyes flashed. Her chaperone almost fancied that she had tossed her head, so fiery was her look.

A couple of hours later her solicitor, David Cotter, arrived. A tall, heavily over-weight man with brown hair silvering at the sides, he looked like someone who enjoyed a good lunch too often. In this respect he appeared rather old-fashioned, an impression reinforced by a dark three piece suit, the like of which neither Upwood nor Morton had seen in years. His voice was predictably public school. Upwood handed him a brief statement so that he understood the nature of the charge and had a general idea of what lines of questioning were to be pursued. He read it, commenting only that it was clear. He was given time alone with Veronica.

When the interview began, Upwood identified himself and Morton and asked Veronica to confirm her name. Her solicitor did likewise and the other formalities were concluded.

"Mrs Mallon, we propose to interview you under caution. Are you familiar with the phrase? I am now advising you that you do not have to say anything. But it may harm your defence if you do not mention, when questioned, something which you later rely on in court. Anything you do say may be given in evidence. Do you understand, Mrs Mallon?"

"No I don't understand. This is madness."

"I say to you again: You do not have to say anything. But it may harm your defence if you do not mention, when questioned, something which you later rely on in court. Anything you do say may be given in evidence. Please confirm that you understand."

She nodded.

"We need to hear your answer, for the tape."

Her answer was given reluctantly. "Yes."

"Mrs Mallon, please tell me your mother's name."

She shot him a venomous look. "Maria Rodrígues."

"That's not her full name is it? What is her apellido paterno?"

"Pérez." She was seething, so much so that Morton would later swear he felt the vibrations through the table at which they sat.

"Precisely. So her full name, as is legally required on all formal documents, is actually Maria Pérez Rodrígues, isn't that so?"

She nodded. "Please answer for the recording."

"Yes."

"Can you explain how it is that your dangerously ill mother hired a car in Peterborough recently?"

"No."

"What is your sister's name? Her full name, with both apellido paterno and apellido materno."

"Encarnación Padilla Pérez."

"Can you explain how she came to be flying between Mexico and England recently at a time when your mother was so gravely ill?"

She was practically spitting her answers out now as it became clear to her that her subterfuge was in meltdown. "No."

"You have considerable experience with handguns, do you not?"

"Not since I was at university."

"How do you explain the presence of your fingerprint on one of the cartridges left in the magazine after your husband was shot?"

"Someone must be framing me. It's all lies."

"How did you manage to smuggle the Glock into the UK?"

"I didn't."

"Why did you not allow the car hire company to retain a copy of your mother's passport and driving licence?"

She refused to answer.

"Why did you change into new clothes from John Lewis before returning to your hotel?"

She turned to her solicitor, who raised his eyebrow. Upwood was beginning to think the lawyer was happy to see her hang herself, metaphorically. He had been making frantic notes as the interview progressed even though he would have a full copy of it later. He had kept quiet so far because there were no grounds on which to intervene in any way that might help his client, unless it were to advise her not to answer. And he knew as well as Upwood did that her failure to answer important questions would encourage jurors to draw conclusions which were unlikely to be favourable to her.

"Can you explain how your fingerprints came to be in a car hired in Peterborough recently?"

No answer.

"Do you always wear Chanel nail polish?"

At this point a loud wail came from her and she dissolved into tears.

"Chief Inspector, I think an interval would be a good idea."

"By all means, Mr Cotter. Interview suspended at thirteen thirteen. Please let the officer on the door know when you are ready to resume."

Upwood and Morton withdrew. Upwood grinned at Morton as they walked along the corridor. "Who'd have thought the question about nail polish would be the one to get to her?"

"That's a very un PC question, Sir." But his grin was almost as wide as that of his boss.

It was more than an hour before they were given the message that Veronica was ready to resume the interview. Her solicitor said that she was prepared to admit to the murder of her husband and would co-operate fully. Upwood could not recall any case in which an admission of murder had been offered by their suspect in such a short space of time. After weeks of punishing work it was a good feeling. Word soon got round that he was picking up the tab in the Star and Garter that evening. It was a full house.

Chapter 82

Upwood and Katie were finally able to get together the following Saturday. Mid-March could often be bitterly cold, but that day the sky was blue and the temperature hovered around twelve degrees. They decided to head over to the coast: Upwood for one was keen to get some fresh air into his lungs and stretch his legs a bit.

They ended up in Blakeney on the north Norfolk shore, walking for several miles along the coastal path. By the time they had made their way back into the village they had worked up a good appetite for lunch.

Katie had seen the reports of the charging of Veronica. On his behalf she was annoyed that the nationals seemed less interested in the case now that Jeremy Mallon's killer had been found. It seems they far preferred to run stories about perceived police incompetence than their success.

"Does it ever get you down?"

"Sometimes. We just have to put up with it. It's an occupational hazard."

"It's not fair, though, is it?"

He laughed but it sounded cynical. "Life isn't fair. You know that as well as anyone."

She fell quiet again. It was on their trip to Southwold some years before, the year in which her partner had been murdered, that she had told Upwood so much about Mark.

"Tell me about Anne."

"Don't ask, Katie."

"But if I don't know, it will always be the elephant in the room." He could see her problem, but was still profoundly unhappy at telling her.

"Darling Katie. You'll wish you hadn't asked. Trust me."

"No. It's time you trusted me, James. If our relationship is going to become any more serious, I have to know."

He took a long draught of beer and gazed out of the pub window. The silence between them was palpable.

"She was the most lovely young woman. Attractive, vibrant, funny. Our marriage was a gift. Her pregnancy –"

"You didn't tell me you had a child." Now she was beginning to feel anxious.

"I don't."

"But..."

"I can only tell you this my way. It's too painful otherwise." She bit her lip and nodded.

"Her pregnancy was a breeze. She loved it. The birth however was very difficult. She was overdue and I think the hospital should have induced her sooner. She had a really bad time and lost a lot of blood.

"She was in hospital for nearly two weeks. It was obvious even before she came out that something was wrong. Not with our daughter. She was fine. But with Anne. She was having terrible mood swings, more than postnatal depression.

"After she came home it became worse. On the second night she was hallucinating so badly I had to call 999.

"They took the baby into hospital with her but she was in no state to look after her or feed her. She was diagnosed with postpartum psychosis.

"They discharged her after three weeks and gave her anti-psychotics and other drugs. They helped a bit but she wouldn't always take them.

"She started self-harming. Anne was sectioned for three months. Her sister looked after our child; it was well beyond my competence. When she was released she began self-harming again. Then our daughter died. She was seven months old." He looked at Katie. Tears were running down her cheeks. "I did warn you, my darling.

"The inquest returned a verdict of natural causes – cot death if you will.

"Three weeks later Anne committed suicide."

"Did you ever won –"

"Don't go there. Don't even think of going there." It was the first time she'd ever heard him angry and realised that her question had been unforgiveable.

"Oh God, James. I am so sorry." Katie rummaged in her bag but found only an empty tissue packet. James passed her his unused handkerchief. She sobbed for longer than James could bear.

"There is nothing to apologise for. It's a story that would upset any normal person."

He stayed quiet for a couple of minutes. The fact that he remained so calm helped her regain control. She realised he had been preparing for this conversation for some time, had probably been rehearsing it.

"Have you ever wanted children, Katie?"

She looked at him curiously. "Why d'you ask?"

"Because I couldn't bear the idea of asking any woman to take that risk."

He let the implications of this sink in.

"You do know that I love you, don't you? Deeply, madly, passionately. How could you not know? I know that you care for me. But I am terrified that you don't care as much. And now is not the time to ask. I am sorry I told you about Anne. But I can understand your wanting to know. I just hope that it doesn't become an even bigger elephant in the room.

"I had nightmares for years afterwards, even after I moved to Cambridge and bought a new house. It rarely happens now. In fact these last few weeks when we've been seeing more of each other it hasn't happened at all. I've got over it, Katie. I remember the good times we had before she became ill, as you do the good times you had with Mark. We have to learn to make the best we can of the present and the future. Please don't let this become a burden for you."

He sat back in the wooden chair, exhausted and suddenly conscious of how uncomfortable it was. He was however glad to see that the couple who had glanced at them when Katie began crying had resumed their conversation and no longer seemed interested.

Katie was shaken to the core. She had had no idea what to expect, but it was not this. Upwood had not told her that he believed Anne had been responsible for their daughter's death. The problem was, Katie now recognised that it might be a possibility.

They drove back to Cambridge, speaking little on the journey. He drove into the garage at her apartment block, parked and turned off the engine. He turned to look at her.

"I'm not going to ask you up, James. I shan't be good company. I need a bit of time on my own tonight."

He nodded. He had known that would be her response. He kissed her gently and briefly on the lips. "I'll give you a call tomorrow, then. Night."

She got out of the car and closed the door quietly and disappeared into the gloomy forest of pillars that supported the apartments above.

Upwood drove out to his cottage in the village west of the city. He heard a message ping on his phone and hoped it wasn't work. He looked at it as soon as he'd parked. It was Katie. She asked him not to call her for a few days. She needed a bit of space.

He went to bed that night more depressed than he had been in months. He was terrified he was going to lose her. He tossed and turned for hours. Once he got up and went downstairs and poured himself a large whisky. It didn't help. He eventually drifted off on the sofa with Parry's *Repton* playing over and over in his mind.

Chapter 83

Emily had been on leave the week in which Veronica Mallon confessed. Upwood was waiting for her when she arrived on the Monday of her return. She looked refreshed and seemed to be in a much better frame of mind. She greeted him warmly, as though all memory of their argument had been banished. For this he was deeply thankful.

"Come in. Tell me all about it."

He grinned. "I'm glad to say we cleared that case up very quickly in the end. If we'd charged Maskell-Grant but hadn't solved the Mallon case, the press would have been all over us. And those conspiracy theorists who call themselves the Friends of King's Mere Wind Farm would have had a field day."

"It was his wife?"

"Yes. She's a lot younger. He had told us that they met at the Rio Summit in 1992. She was doing a Masters in environmental science at a university in Los Angeles."

"Why there? I thought she was Mexican?"

"She is. But her parents moved there when she was eight. They only moved back to Mexico when her father retired. Anyway, even though he was nineteen years older – a big difference given the ages they were then – they apparently fell passionately in love. She followed him to England after she'd got her degree and they got married. And passion fuelled the marriage by all accounts."

"How d'you mean?"

"They were very much in love but could have violent rows, although she says they stopped short of physical violence. They were both fanatical environmentalists, both convinced about climate change, but disagreed about what causes it. They also had diametrically opposing views on wind farms."

"She was a member of Kmag?"

"Yes. But her husband supported the development."

"And is that what made her kill him?"

"No, it was more personal. He'd had prostate cancer a couple of years ago and surgery left him impotent. All the signs are that she has a very healthy sexual appetite. If you remember, his senior partner told us that she had flirted with another guest at their party some ten years ago and we know that she was having an affair with Ken Lloyd at the Riding Stables. He denied it originally, but now confirms it. Veronica told him she wanted to marry him but that Jeremy would not give her a divorce: they're both Catholic. I think Lloyd's glad, frankly. I think he was as much scared by her as infatuated by her."

"Why do you think that?"

"Apparently, he made mention of the praying mantis in his most recent interview."

She chuckled briefly. "Is that spelt with an 'a' or an 'e'?"

"Take your pick!" He carried on. "He's very fortunate to have such a forgiving wife – she says that if she can't make love to him anymore she can't blame him if he finds sex elsewhere. And, to be honest, we all agree with her that Ken probably does love his wife very much.

"But it's not just that issue. Veronica said that she was becoming increasingly concerned about Jeremy's mood swings. His senior partner thought he was addicted to prescription drugs. She says he also drank heavily in the evenings and was afraid that his outbursts would lead to violence."

"So we have a husband who seems to have an addictive personality, behavioural problems and is impotent. And who might contest a petition for divorce. He doesn't sound a very agreeable bedfellow I'll give her that. But why now?"

"The other murders gave her cover. She clearly thought she'd concealed her tracks very skilfully."

"But she would have been found out in the end, surely?"

"Not necessarily. If Maskell-Grant hadn't had a cast iron alibi for Mallon's death, we would probably have charged him with that too. We've solid evidence for the other crimes, and having two murderers on the scene is not common. She was just unlucky."

"So how did she do it?"

"Borrowed her sister's passport to travel. Smuggled a Glock 17 handgun in her hold luggage. She's skilled enough to have broken it down into all its component parts – all thirty odd – to make discovery less likely. Once she landed at Heathrow she used disguises when there were cameras around. And she borrowed her mother's passport, driving licence and credit card to hire a car and make other purchases."

"And she looked like both of them enough to get away with it?"

"Yes, clearly. The picture of her mother is remarkably similar given the age difference. Her sister is a dead ringer. Very attractive women, all of them."

"And the evidence is solid?"

"Yes. Latent on one of the cartridges still in the magazine. She'd thrown the gun into the gravel pit near where she'd shot him. We're confident we'll get a positive DNA result on a sample from the hire car we've sent off. We've matched a damaged tyre on that to a cast made at the scene."

"Presumably if she does plead guilty she'll base her defence on his abusive behaviour."

"She can try but I don't think she's got a prayer. I've no doubt she'll put on a performance in court good enough for an Oscar. If she'd shot him on the spur of the moment, maybe. But this degree of premeditation? She's going away for a very long time."

He rose to leave her office when she signalled that he should stay. He sat down again.

"We have a couple of problems."

"With either of the cases?"

"No. Entirely different."

He fumed quietly. Get on with it woman. I don't need winding up.

"Have you seen any of the blogs following the *It's a Bland life* article?

"No, why should I?"

"It's not a bad idea to know what people are saying about us, James."

"But blog normally means garbage."

"Not the point."

"So what is?"

"The thread got a little tangled after that article. But someone in the press office has just picked up a reference to you saying that after the death of your wife and child you shouldn't have been allowed to stay on the force."

"Christ Almighty."

"Quite. We can only hope that it sinks without trace, but I thought I should warn you." He nodded.

"Now. DS Debra Graf. How well do you know her?"

"Not well. I've spent a little bit of time with her since Tom Turner killed his mother and then himself. She feels guilty that she didn't spot possible symptoms of his cancer sooner. I've told her she shouldn't. She's not got medical training for heaven's sake. She does feel guilty that she didn't follow up more quickly after she learnt that he'd had a biopsy, and that I can understand. She's good at what she does. Why?"

"Did you know she played bridge?"

He thought about it for a minute and then remembered the brief conversation he'd had with Morton about the mug. *"Old bridge players never die, they just lose their finesse."*

"What?" It was Emily's turn to be confused.

"It's a mug she has on her desk. She told me she played competitively."

"Ah. Did she tell you who her bridge partner is?"

"No. Why should she?"

"Our esteemed Assistant Chief Constable."

"John Clarke. Oh shit." He looked at her, trying to read her expression. She stared back, fiddling with the pen on her desk.

"He's got a mug on his desk, too. *Old bridge players never die, they just go for a strong take-out.*"

"What the hell's that supposed to mean?"

"No idea." She continued to stare at him.

"Are you saying they are partners in other ways?"

"My informant tells me it is highly likely. She plays with the same club. She's seen them together, going in and out of each other's rooms on tournament weekends. And it wouldn't be the first time he's played away. To coin a phrase."

"Oh, Christ Almighty."

"Quite. So you'll have a word with her, will you?"

"Bloody hell, Emily. Why me?"

"Because you're her senior officer."

"But why can't you have the conversation with Clarke?"

"Because he's my senior officer."

"Oh bollocks, Emily. That's not fair. You're as close to him in rank as I am to Debra. And anyway, what the hell am I supposed to say to her?"

"You might tactfully suggest that sleeping with a senior officer is not a good career move."

"And who is going to have that conversation with him? I'm not prepared to talk to Debra unless you give me an assurance that someone will deal with Clarke."

"I can't do that."

"You'll have to. If I've got to tell Debra her career is on the line but nothing will happen to him, I am going to be seriously pissed off."

Emily continued to stare at him. He knew she agreed with him. He also knew, or assumed he did, that there was no one leaning on her. She would hardly have told the Chief Constable given that he was retiring in little more than a week. On the other hand, why shouldn't she? "Why don't you get Bland to speak to him?"

"For one thing, he would refuse. And even if he did, I doubt Clarke would take a blind bit of notice."

"Even if Bland said he would report it to his successor?"

"Clarke might be his successor."

"Christ, no. You can't be serious. The man's a complete tosser."

"He's an effective ACC."

"But the roles are quite different. He's got no leadership qualities. Even Jan Murray showed more authority in that last press briefing he held. Half my lot would trust their own judgement rather than follow him out of a burning building." Upwood ground to a halt.

She let him calm down for a moment. "No one's going to speak to Clarke, James. I am instructing you to speak to Debra and make sure she puts a stop to it."

"I'll think about it." He stormed out of her office.

Chapter 84

The week was busy, not perhaps as frenetic as while the investigations were under way, but they were all anxious to begin the process of documenting the cases against Maskell-Grant and Veronica Mallon as quickly as they could. They all knew, Upwood more than most, that the odds were there'd be another major case before too long. In that event it would be easy to let slip the preparation that the CPS would require before either suspect could be brought to court.

Upwood was looking forward to having the following weekend free and had hoped to hear from Katie by then. He knew her well enough not to call her. In many ways they were very alike. Each was fiercely independent. Each had been scarred by the loss of a partner (and in his case, his child). Both had successful careers and were used to taking responsibility for others. He would let her take her time.

Dawn broke just after six o'clock on Saturday and although there was a slight tinge of pink in the sky, Upwood knew that the forecast was good. He made himself a light breakfast and a strong cup of coffee and headed off towards the Norfolk coast. By the time he reached Cley the first of the season's sea frets had blown in, reducing visibility substantially. The visitor centre wouldn't be open for another hour and he now regretted not having brought a flask of coffee with him. He resigned himself to a chilly wait in the car park, hoping that the mist might disperse before the centre opened. As he began to thumb idly through his notebook to remind himself of what he had seen over the years, his phone pinged, signalling an incoming message. It was from Katie. *Sorry I've not called. Am in Buenos Aires. Partner there ill – am having to cover. Be in touch when I get back. Not sure when that will be.*

Pleased though he was that the suspects had been charged with all the wind farm cases he became more and more depressed sitting in the car park. They had no idea who Bland's successor might be and Upwood was seriously worried that Clarke might be in the frame for it. As far as Upwood was concerned he was no more than a pen-pushing wanker. And the idea that he might be having an affair with a much junior officer, one of his, was a real anxiety. He still had no idea whether he should speak to Debra if no-one was going to tackle Clarke, much less what he should say to her if he did.

Then there was the major reorganisation that was rumoured to be in the pipeline. Would that be change for the better or not? Only time would tell.

Finally, his thoughts turned to Katie. What should he read into the fact that she had not said how long she'd be away? He brooded on the thought for some time and could come to no conclusion.

Then he wondered whether she was anxious about the news coverage of the recent cases, much of which was uncomplimentary about him. Perhaps she didn't like being associated with someone whose reputation had been shredded so often.

Perhaps she had seen the blogs.

And then the most terrifying thought of all occurred to him – that she might think he'd been responsible for their child's death. Or Anne's. Or both. The idea hit him like a sledge-hammer.

He howled. In rage. In despair. In fear.

Rage, that wankers like Clarke had the power to destroy a junior officer's career.

Despair at the thought Clarke might replace Bland.

Finally fear, a truly visceral fear, that Katie might never trust him enough to believe that he had not killed Anne. Fear that those in Gloucestershire who believed that he had killed her might never let the matter rest.

And then he wept, as he had never been able to do for Anne. The knowledge filled him with self-loathing.

Notes and acknowledgements

Writing this second book in the DCI Upwood series has been even more fun that the first, not least because I had so much encouragement from those who read *When Good Men Die.*

This time my thanks go first to Tracy Jardine who helped me solve a plot issue that held up my writing for too long.

Ben Gunn was noble in wading through the whole book and saved me from a number of police procedural howlers. This is not to say the book is without procedural flaws. Sometimes I have simplified issues in order to improve the flow of the story.

I thank Dora Baker, whose choice of hymns for the splendid memorial service for her husband David inspired the title.

Susana Sanchez Amor very kindly set out Spanish name protocols.

Dexter Petley again provided invaluable editorial feedback. He has the capacity to encourage me to deal more competently with some of the technical aspects of writing. Some of his comments about two of the characters in this book spurred me to greater creativity, and as a consequence I found myself developing entirely new storylines. Some of these will undoubtedly feed into the third book in the series.

All the characters are fictional. I try to keep my facts accurate, although I have taken considerable liberties with the geography of the area north of Cambridge and, like most authors, I sometimes exercise a little literary licence. But there will be errors and I'm happy to take responsibility for them.

Please leave a review on Amazon – all feedback is welcome and instructive.
If you haven't read the first book, *When Good Men Die*, please do.

Rosemary Rowntree
September 2017

About the author

Rosemary Rowntree's career began in HR and she held directorships in a number of well-known British companies before setting up a new business with a former colleague. The company has gone from strength to strength and specialises in international HR consulting and business services. While Managing Director she also acquired skills in finance and IT on which she drew in her first novel.

With her husband she has lived in Cambridgeshire for many years. She retired in 2004 and now divides her time between England and Spain.

79649345R00209

Made in the USA
Columbia, SC
06 November 2017